BROKEN CROWN

SABRINA LOZIER

Copyright © 2022 by Sabrina Lozier

Map by Abigail Hair

All rights reserved.

No part of this book may be reproduced in any form or by any electronic or mechanical means, including information storage and retrieval systems, without written permission from the author, except for the use of brief quotations in a book review.

For my husband who has never ceased to believe in me.

ERINYA
CONVENT OF THE SAINTS
SKARSDEN BAY
OHAN TERRIT
THE CITADEL
THE RAVAGED WOOD
TH
THE NORTH PLAINS
LAUGHING DOG INN
SOUTHERN MARSHES
ASIF'S VILLAG
ARMY CAMP
GREA
CART

TARAN SEA
BOREADS GLACIER
FENRIC'S KEEP
THE DEADWOOD
WHITESAW MT RANGE
ROSE RIVER
GRASSLANDS
ENCHANTED WOOD
HARROW FOREST
VER
ESIA

BROKEN CROWN

1

JILL

Jack and Jill went up the hill
To fetch a pail of water;
Jack fell down and broke his crown,
And Jill came tumbling after.

The first time Jill saw a paladin in her father's court, she was seven years old. She and her brother stood in awe as the young warrior marched forward. An emerald cloak rippled behind her, fastened by a golden clasp bearing the king's insignia. At her side were sheathed butterfly swords. And when she knelt before the king to receive her honors, a ghost of her smile landed on Jill, an unspoken bond forming between them.

The next day, Jill picked up a blade for the first time. And she hadn't put it down since.

A decade passed, and not a day went by without Jill recalling that moment. Second only to the king, the paladins were the fiercest warriors in all Erinya. And one day, she knew it would be her kneeling before her father, accepting the paladinship and swearing undying loyalty to the throne.

But first, she had a boarman to defeat.

She ducked the spiked mace, letting momentum be his enemy. Her opponent huffed in frustration. He was heavyset and dark skinned, and small tusks protruded from his mouth. He rushed forward, swinging again, this time at her knees. She jumped at the last moment, struck by how close he'd come to smashing her kneecaps.

The boarman was strong and two heads taller than her. But he was slow. While he swung his mace, she brought her butterfly swords together, locking them in a single quick motion before blocking his strike. The twin blades were dangerous on their own and even deadlier together.

Adrenaline will be your foe if you let it control you. The words of Master Ravala echoed in her head as she slid her blades forward along the shaft of the man's weapon, connecting with his knuckles. His grip loosened in surprise, and with a few quick steps, she spun, separating her swords before crossing them under his chin.

Jill heaved a breath as polite applause resounded from onlookers in the training grounds. She sheathed her swords and turned, giving a small bow as her opponent shuffled away, grumbling at his loss. Another hopeful paladin, he'd traveled from the Southern Marshes to compete in the Paladin Tournament. It was the most important and prestigious in all Erinya, occurring once every five years. There was no position more coveted than paladin, and no competition more deadly. She knew he wouldn't last long tomorrow.

"Well done, Your Highness." Master Ravala's deep voice echoed through the grounds. "That is your tenth victory this week."

The tattoos on his face swirled and twisted, the ink carving a path across his skin, dancing with powerful magic. Jill often had to remind herself not to stare at the inkwell man, who'd been covered in the markings since birth. She never ceased to be amazed by them though.

"Thank you, Master," said Jill, bowing. Her stomach twisted. "Do you think I stand a chance?" She glanced at the other sparring competitors. So many had come this year, and yet only one could win.

Master Ravala fixed her with his stony gaze. He wasn't a tall man, but he held himself in a manner that intimidated all who met him. It'd served him well in the past decade as he'd risen through the ranks, eventually becoming the general of her father's armies.

"I think you already know the answer to that." He gave a rare smile, and Jill couldn't suppress the excitement that raced through her veins. *One more day.* One more day, and then she would be free.

Free from the burden of being a princess. Free to come and go as she pleased. Free to marry whomever she wished.

Jill *had* to win.

A slow clap echoed through the grounds. Jill turned to the newcomer, whose familiar black hair fell in front of a devilish face.

"Jack!" She rushed forward, wrapping her twin in a hug before pulling away to look at him. He was lean and pale, and shadows hung under his eyes. "Where have you been? You look awful!"

He shrugged. "I still look better than you. Have you been sleeping out here?"

"At least I'm practicing instead of sneaking around with the maids."

Jack shrugged, unaffected by her gibe. "Some of us have interests outside of this arena."

Jill's jaw flexed in a forced smile. Whether Jack understood the meaning of discipline or not, she wouldn't let idleness become her enemy. Unlike him, she couldn't afford to lose tomorrow.

"Does flirting count as an interest?"

Jack smiled, an eyebrow quirking. "Not my fault if people actually like me." He winked, a practiced move.

"You haven't visited the grounds in weeks."

"I can still beat you," he said.

Jill smiled. "Prove it."

Jack's gaze narrowed. "Fine. Master Ravala, do you have a decent set of daggers?"

"I do, Your Highness, but I must warn you, the princess hasn't lost a single duel this week."

"Then I'll just have to end her streak."

A servant rushed over, bringing him two daggers that were sharpened on one side and serrated on the other, Jack's weapon of choice. Where Jill's strengths lay with her butterfly swords, Jack excelled with small weaponry. In fact, Jill was surprised to see him without his usual set strapped across his chest. He usually wore them wherever he went.

He made his way across the arena before stepping into the starting position and spinning his daggers eagerly. It was an impressive trick, but Jill knew he was really getting a feel for the blades, making sure the weight was the same for both.

The training grounds sat in a large rotunda, open to the sky. Columns surrounded the space, topped with statues of the Saints. There were others practicing, but the presence of the royal siblings drew the attention of passersby, visitors eager for a preview of their skills.

Master Ravala's stern gaze rested on Jill. She rolled her shoulders and stepped into starting position opposite Jack. They both wielded a blade in each hand.

Jack's smile curled, a wicked gleam in his eye. She inhaled, picturing his attack in her head. *Never underestimate your enemy.* It was the very first thing she'd learned, and it had saved her life on more than one occasion.

"To arms," said Ravala, and the pair stepped forward, crossing their fists over their chests with a slight bow. "To fight is to hold hands with Death."

"To fight is to hold hands with Death," they echoed, the air thickening around them.

"Begin."

Quick as lightning, Jack dove forward, sliding on the ground before popping up in front of Jill. She backstepped, bringing her blades up just as he slammed a dagger at her. She caught the hook of his blade, sensed his feint, and blocked his other dagger. She knew her brother's technique. He always tried to get in close. But she wouldn't allow it.

"You've improved." Jack smiled.

"That's because I practice."

"And yet you're still struggling." He smirked, toying with her. He dropped and swung a leg out to trip her.

She collapsed to the ground as he stood over her and drove a dagger at her head. Rolling, she leapt to her feet, swearing under her breath. He spun to face her, but she was prepared. Going on the offensive, she slashed at him. Her blades collided with his. The sound of clanging steel rang through the air, echoing in the rotunda.

Sweat dripped down Jack's brow, but Jill pressed forward without mercy. "You're out of shape, Jack."

His expression darkened. His defense was good, but nobody won by defense only. Sooner or later, he would slip. Still, she refused to relent, pushing him back, driving him closer to the arena line. If he stepped over, the fight was hers.

Then she saw it: an opening. His attention snagged on something behind her. She lunged, smacking his hand with the flat of her blade. He dropped one dagger, retreating as she swung her blade at his neck and forced him to kneel before her.

She flashed a smug grin.

"I still have this dagger," he said.

"But look where you're standing." She nodded to his foot, the tip of his boot jutting outside the boundary line.

"Your Highness?" a timid voice cut in.

Jill turned, feeling a surge of irritation that her victory had been cut short. "Yes?"

She recognized her maid, a small girl around her own age. The girl swallowed, eyes shifting between Jill and Jack. "I'm sorry." She dipped into a curtsy. "Madame Sorelle asked me to let you know the tailor is ready for your fitting."

Jill gritted her teeth and nodded. "I'll be there in a moment."

"Yes, Your Highness," she said, giving another curtsy before scurrying off.

"New maid?" Jack asked, his eyes following the girl as she hurried away. "Why is she so scared of you?"

Jill pressed her blades together, locking them before sheathing them as a single blade at her waist. "That girl is scared of her own shadow."

"What's her name?"

Jill glared at her brother. "Don't even think about it. She's the best maid I've had in a while. I won't let you break another girl's heart." Jack had taken an interest in her last maid too, until she'd fallen ill and left her position. Jack had seemed almost as devastated by the maid's absence as Jill had been.

"You always think the worst of me," Jack said, walking over to return the daggers.

"Well done, Your Highness," Ravala said. "Your father will be pleased to hear of your progress."

Jill grimaced. She doubted it. Even though she spent hours training each day, her father had never once complimented her skill or her drive. He had other plans for her, and they didn't involve fighting.

"Thank you, Master," she said, bowing.

She turned to Jack. His brow was furrowed as he stared off into the distance, his body present but his mind faraway. She'd seen that look more and more recently. Perhaps he was thinking about their father as well.

"Walk with me to my fitting?" she asked.

He nodded, and together they walked the long marble halls that led to Jill's quarters. Dread pulled in the pit of her stomach as she thought again of the tournament.

Her royal position was no guarantee. She would have to fight along with all the rest, would have to earn her position and place if she was ever to be respected as a warrior. If she was ever to escape her arranged marriage.

"Have you spoken with Father yet?" Jill asked, pushing thoughts of the tournament away.

Jack's face darkened. "No, not yet."

"Well, you should do it soon, perhaps when he's in a good mood."

"So, never?"

Despite themselves, they both smiled, bound together by the sharp fear of their father's temper. It was no secret that Old King Cole was ruthless, his mood a constant storm on the horizon.

"Still, it's worth asking. You'll be king soon; it wouldn't hurt for you to explain the diplomacy of a trip to the Distant Lands. Maybe you'll find something that could aid us in the war." The reasoning sounded feeble even to her ears.

Jack gave a weak smile, and Jill was struck by how strange it was that he should have secrets of his own. In the last year, something had changed between them. They weren't nearly as close as they'd always been. When had they become so distant?

They arrived at her quarters. The double doors were engraved with scenes of the Battle of Shadows, the designs weaving together in intricate patterns that reminded her of Master Ravala's tattoos.

"Think about it, Jack. Promise me you'll ask as soon as possible." She turned to her brother. He'd always been taller than her, but in the past year she'd grown. Now he stood only a few inches taller, his green eyes locking with hers.

"I will. Now you'd better go before Madame Sorelle hunts you down." He laughed.

Jill's stomach flipped. Madame Sorelle was nearly as fearsome as her father. But where he was a raging fire, she was an icy river, swift and deadly if you dared cross her.

Jill entered her quarters and found the tailor, a feline man with pointed ears and the eyes of a cat, with Madame Sorelle towering over him. She raised an eyebrow, no doubt taking in Jill's ragged appearance.

"I know." She sighed. She knew just what the woman would say. "I'll clean up before I let the tailor get anywhere near me."

Madame Sorelle gave a tip of her head, revealing short horns that curved in an upward spiral. "Good. And be quick about it."

Jill nodded and entered her washroom. She peeled off her armor before splashing her face with water piped in from the stores.

She sensed it before she saw it, the *thing* hanging in the corner like a dead man on a noose. She allowed herself a glance, taking in the intricate beading and long gold train.

Her mother's wedding gown.

The scarlet ball gown dripped to the floor like blood, a daily reminder from her father of her approaching nuptials. Her insides churned. The very idea of marrying a stranger from Welynn was enough to send her into a panic.

She looked back at her face in the mirror, droplets sliding down her flushed cheeks and into the washbowl. She took a steadying breath. Tomorrow everything would change. Tomorrow she would win the paladinship, and then she'd be in charge of her own life, once and for all.

2

———————

MILLIE

Little Miss Muffet
Sat on a tuffet,
Eating her curds and whey;
Along came a spider,
Who sat down beside her,
And frightened Miss Muffet away.

Millie hugged the rail as she hurried down the spiral staircase, taking the steps two at time. The torches along the wall did little to ease the bitter cold of the prison. She shivered, picking up the pace. She had to hurry if she wanted to see Doon before the princess finished her dress fitting.

The princess. Millie's stomach churned at the thought of returning to her mistress. It wasn't that she disliked working for her, only that Her Highness expected everyone around her to have the same relentless drive she did, and when you failed to meet her standards, she thought you weak. But then, most people already thought Millie weak.

Millie reached the bottom of the stone staircase, where blue-fire torches flickered from their braces on the wall. She pulled her shawl tighter around her shoulders as a draft blew down the mildewy halls of cold stone. She took a deep breath and started forward; she knew the way by now. The scent of refuse reached her nose, and she gagged, sadness gripping her for all the prisoners who lived in this pit.

Millie held her breath as she passed a set of guards, head bowed. Because she was a maid, the guards let her pass without question, knowing that few would willingly traverse these desolate halls. After she was safely past the guards, she wound her way through the prison cells, ignoring the jeering from crazed prisoners, the way they grabbed her dress or begged her to find the keys. She shuddered as their clammy hands reached for her, but she forced herself to keep moving. She didn't have time for them today, nor any day for that matter.

She stopped at the top of another staircase and grabbed a torch before descending, the stones slick beneath her feet. At the bottom, she paused, taking another deep breath. This was the darkest part of the prison, Murderer's Row.

Without a single torch, the prisoners here sat in complete darkness day and night. Some said it was a fate worse than death, and truly, few lived long after being sentenced to Murderer's Row. It was the main reason the king did not execute murderers; his sense of justice was twisted.

Millie stopped in front of the first—and only—occupied cell, her body shaking with cold and fear.

"Doon?" she whispered.

Like a wraith materializing, his face came into view, gaunt in the blue torchlight. "Millie?" His hollow voice sent a wave of anger through her. His dark skin had paled, and his eyes were yellowed and bloodshot. He was a mere shadow of the big brother she'd always known.

Millie rushed forward, wrapping her fingers around his through the bars. They were stiff with cold, and she forced herself to keep from crying at his touch.

"I missed you. I'm so sorry I couldn't come sooner. The princess, she keeps me so busy." She rushed to get the words out, knowing their time was short. Someone would soon notice her absence and come looking for her, and she shuddered to think what might happen if they found her here.

He pulled away. "You shouldn't have come, Millie," he whispered.

"I had to see you. This was the only chance I'll have for a while, especially if I am to . . ." She paused, noticing the grimace of pain that crossed his face, the sweat on his brow, the garish circles beneath his eyes. "Doon, what's wrong?" she asked, her voice grave.

She watched him swallow slowly before a fit of coughing racked his body, a thunderous sound that echoed through the hall. Fear gripped her throat, a cold hand choking her as she watched her brother stumble and fall, splatters of blood around his mouth.

"Doon!" she cried, kneeling in front of him.

At last, the coughing stopped, and he heaved a crackling breath. "Millie, you know I love you, right?" he said, eyes glistening.

Millie's jaw clenched. "Doon, what's wrong? Please just tell me." Tears trickled down her cheeks. Curse her soft heart, she always cried. She wished he didn't have to see her like this. He was the one suffering, not her. Still, there was deep pain in watching someone you loved suffer.

"I have a slight fever is all," he said, his features twisting in pain as he clutched at his stomach.

Millie inched away from the bars, staring at him. His black hair was plastered to his forehead with grease, and his body shook with cold.

"What kind of fever?" she asked. In her head, she made a list of all the possible tinctures and herbs she might sneak down to him.

"Never mind that," he said, forcing a weak smile. "I want to hear about you."

Millie stared into his brown eyes. Once the color of golden rye, they'd dulled to the color of dirt. Oh, how she longed to open this cell door and hug the brother who had spent his whole life protecting her. She wished she could turn back time, go back to before Doon had been arrested and dragged down to this dungeon. Maybe she'd protect him for once.

"There isn't much to say, I'm afraid. All I worry about is you." She gave him a soft smile.

Another tear slipped down her cheek, and she had the strangest sense that this would be the last time she saw him. Her heart ached at the thought, and she shoved it away. She would see him again. He would be just fine.

"How is . . ." He paused, searching for the right words. "Your condition?"

Her heart clenched. It was Millie's turn to look away. She tried not to think about "her condition" — if it could even be called that. Every day she gained more and more control over it, though it wasn't easy. And it was getting harder and harder to keep a secret.

"I'm getting stronger," she said at last. "I'm . . . I'm going to use it. In the tournament tomorrow."

Doon was silent. Up until that point, Millie had not told him she'd planned to compete. She herself had not even been sure until a few days ago. But once she'd decided, there was no going back. If she could become the king's paladin, she could investigate Doon's case once more. She could prove his innocence and set him free.

"Millie, it's too dangerous."

"And what other choice do I have? I won't simply sit here and let you die in this prison cell!"

Doon gave a ragged breath, staring at the ground. Water dripped from the ceiling, and the torch flickered beside them, the fire eating away at the wood.

"Millie, I think it's time you moved on, lived your life. You shouldn't be bound to this dungeon as well."

Millie's heart felt like it had been dunked in cold water. "What? I don't understand. Doon, if I can win—"

"It won't matter if you win." His searing gaze bored into her, brighter than ever. *Too bright*, she realized. His eyes were only that bright when—

"It's not just a fever, is it?" The words were hollow as she spoke. "You've caught the Night Flu, haven't you?"

His face twitched as he stared at her, and she realized now why this meeting felt so different. He hadn't teased her like he usually did. He hadn't cracked his jokes about the prison guards. He hadn't made plans for a future outside of Erinya.

They said the Night Flu was the result of living in the dark and damp of the prison for so long. With fever, shakes, and stomach pain, it was a slow and painful death. And there was no cure.

"I'm sorry," he said, his voice breaking.

And in that moment, Millie felt undone. This couldn't be happening. Her brother had always been the strong one. He would fight this. He would survive. She *needed* him to survive.

"You should go," he said, his voice lacking its usual warmth.

"I don't want to—"

"Please, Millie," he said. His voice shook as he gripped the bars until his knuckles turned white, his eyes dim.

"Doon," she pleaded, tears stinging her eyes now.

"Go!" he growled.

Before he could say any more, Millie turned and ran up the stairs as fast as she could, tears blinding her vision. When she reached the top of the stairs, she stopped, waiting, hoping he would call her back. Instead, she heard him crying. In all her life, she'd never heard such an awful sound.

· · ·

MILLIE WAS SO DISTRACTED that she didn't see the young man until she collided with him head-on, tripping over her feet. Strong hands caught her before she fell to the ground and made a fool of herself. She looked up at the man who'd caught her, and her stomach somersaulted.

With a jolt, she was on her feet, dipping into a low curtsy, face burning. "Your Highness, I'm so sorry. I didn't see you there."

It was Prince Jack. She had nearly run right over the prince of Erinya. Her cheeks flushed as she risked a glance up at him, his stunned face taking her by surprise.

"Your Highness?" she asked. "Are you all right?"

He shook his head, a nervous smile crossing his face. "Yes, I'm, um, I'm all right. Are you okay?"

She nodded quickly. "I'm fine."

For a moment, they both stood there, Millie's heart pounding fiercely in the awkward silence.

"I should—"

"You're my sister's maid, right?" the prince asked, interrupting her.

Millie nodded, not sure what else to say. Having lived in the Citadel for most of her life, she'd seen the prince often, but usually from a distance. Until a few months ago, that was, when she'd become the princess's new maid. But she'd heard the rumors about Prince Jack and Princess Jill's former maid, about the stolen glances and secret kisses. And then her maid had fallen ill and left her post, though many suspected she'd been sent away to keep from distracting the prince—or perhaps worse.

"What's your name?"

She swallowed, looking at the marble floors. "Millie."

"Millie," he said, testing the name out. Then he smiled, a twinkle in his eye as he looked at her. "I like it. It suits you."

"Thank you, Your Highness," she said, keeping her gaze locked on the ground, staring at the gold laced in the cracks of the marble.

"My name's Jack," he said before giving a nervous laugh. "But I'm sure you knew that, obviously, with me being the prince and all. I just meant—" He paused, swallowing. "I'm sorry. I just meant you can call me Jack. You don't need to call me Your Highness." He smiled again, waiting for her to respond.

But Millie found her tongue stuck as she glanced at the prince. She'd heard him speak many times, his words smooth and sweet as honey. But now he stumbled over them like a colt learning to stand, and she couldn't help but wonder why.

After several seconds, she realized he was still waiting for her to say something, and she licked her lips. "I'm not sure that would be appropriate . . . Your Highness." Her palms started to sweat as she looked around the halls for anyone who might come to interrupt their conversation by pulling one of them away.

But there was no one in this part of the Citadel this time of day. It was why she'd chosen this time to visit Doon. Inwardly, she cursed herself. She didn't have time for this. The princess would need her soon, and she rarely tolerated tardiness of any kind.

"If you'll excuse—"

"Did you come from the prison?" he asked, interrupting her again. His attention focused on the door at her back.

Her heart raced. Technically, she wasn't supposed to enter the prison. There were maids assigned to prison duty, and she wasn't one of them. However, the guards rarely paid close enough attention to discern which maids came and went. It was the only reason she was able to visit her brother at all.

"I was, um, just delivering a meal to a prisoner." The lie felt foreign on her tongue, and she was certain any minute the prince would see right through her. Maybe he'd drag her back down there to throw her into a cell himself.

The prince's brow furrowed. "The maid to the princess is delivering a meal to prisoners? You shouldn't have to do that. I'll speak with my sister at once—"

"No, it's okay!" she said before she realized she'd just interrupted the prince. She bowed her head. "I'm sorry. I was covering for a friend. She's ill, and I said I would take the meal for her."

Silence pounded between them as she sensed the prince absorbing her words before he smiled. "That's very kind of you."

"Well, it's my duty, Your Highness."

"Still, I'm sure you had better things to do. I know my sister can be a bit demanding." He cracked a smile, and Millie smiled back despite her nerves.

"Her Highness is merely dedicated to everything she puts her mind to." It was all she could think to say. It wasn't far off from the truth, however. For better or worse, the princess was one of the most disciplined people she'd ever met.

The prince chuckled. "Are you always so gracious?" He cocked his head, eyeing her with curiosity.

Her face heated as they locked eyes. Millie got the distinct impression she should look away, yet she found she couldn't. His dark eyes studied her with interest. He was as handsome as everyone said, but unlike the princess's former maid, Millie had no desire to draw the prince's attention.

"She isn't so bad. She's been good to me." The princess may have been intense, but she'd never been cruel. Millie knew other servants weren't so lucky.

Prince Jack nodded, his eyes distant for a moment before looking back at her. "Well, that's good. I was worried earlier when I saw you. My sister is not particularly . . . kind sometimes."

Millie swallowed as the sound of Fifth Bell echoed throughout the halls. "Speaking of, I must go. I can't be late." Before he could say another word, she dipped into a quick curtsy and hurried off, eager to be free of his presence.

That was too close. She rounded a corner before allowing herself a breath of relief, her blood still racing. Why did she feel so nervous all of a sudden? Because she'd nearly been caught by the prince? Or was it because the prince himself had made her nervous?

She shook her head, thinking of her brother. She couldn't afford to be distracted by that strange interaction with the prince. Her stomach pitched when she thought of Doon, stuck in his cell, sick and dying while she chatted with the prince.

Doon. Her brother. Her only family member. She could *not* lose him.

After taking a deep breath, she walked back to the princess's quarters, her decision made even as fear gripped her. Tomorrow she would enter the tournament and win. And then she would free her brother.

3

JACK

Jack stared out the large window overlooking the slate-gray sea. Waves crashed upon the sand, foam lingering long after the tide pulled the water back into its black depths. For a moment, Jack allowed himself the briefest fantasy of boarding one of his father's ships and taking the helm, the salt air lapping at his face, the wind at his back. And, of course, he wouldn't object to the occasional mermaid or two. His lips quirked at the thought.

Ever since he was a boy, he had loved the sea and everything it stood for: freedom, adventure, a chance to see the world. It was all he'd ever wanted. A chance to visit the Distant Lands. A chance to see what the world had to offer.

Jack sighed, turning away from the window. Unlike his sister's, Jack's quarters were a mess. Discarded clothes lay piled in the corner. Empty mugs rested on every surface. He'd left various daggers scattered around the room, having forgotten to take them back to the armory.

He ran a hand through his hair while sinking into a leather chair, panic gnawing at his insides. He felt time pass like a rushing wind around him, and it made him restless. He wanted out of the Citadel, away from it all. He wanted more of it, more time. He couldn't stand the thought of living out his days trapped on a throne, bearing the weight of the crown.

He wanted to leave Erinya.

What a pity your father would never let you go.

Jack bristled at the Voice in his head, clenching his teeth. He knew it wanted him to respond, wanted to taunt him. He could feel it lingering in the back of his head, grinning as it toyed with him. He should have been used to it by now, this *thing*. But after nearly a year, he'd hardly come close.

Jack rose from the chair, too anxious to sit any longer, and picked up one of his throwing knives.

He and the Voice had reached a mutual tolerance of each other, but even when the Voice was silent, Jack could feel it like an ominous shadow in the corner of the room, a hunter stalking its prey.

Jack flipped the cold knife in his hand, comforted by the weight of it, before flinging it across the room. It struck a portrait of his father in the center of his head.

You don't know that, Jack responded inwardly.

He'd discovered early on that he didn't have to speak aloud to communicate. Often he didn't need to speak at all. Though he didn't understand it, the Voice had become a part of him, ingrained in every word and fleeting thought, binding itself so tightly to him that it was hard to tell where he ended and the Voice began. That knowledge alone scared him more than anything.

Why don't you ask him then? It was a rhetorical question and perhaps the reason Jack felt so irritated now. They both knew his father wouldn't let him go.

It's not that simple. Jack picked up another throwing knife, spinning it in his hand.

It never is with you humans, the Voice chuckled darkly.

Fear curled in the pit of his stomach. After a year, he'd come no closer to understanding what lived inside him or what it wanted, only that it was waiting for something, and Jack could only imagine what that might be.

Jack looked out the window again, watching sailors on the docks as they loaded cargo onto the hulking sea vessels. The Citadel had been built on a high cliff at the edge of the Eastern Sea, overlooking Skarsden Bay. Jack had spent his entire life watching ship after ship leave his shores to trade and explore the Distant Lands.

Frustration boiled over, and he turned, throwing the second knife at his father's portrait. It knocked the first knife down, and Jack allowed himself a dark grin.

If only he'd been able to show his skills when he'd fought against his sister. But instead that girl had distracted him.

Millie.

That maid was very pretty, the Voice purred, interrupting his thoughts once again.

Jack tensed, images of his sister's maid flitting through his head so fast that he knew it must've been the Voice's manipulation. He saw curly black hair pulled into a thick braid and warm brown skin bronzed in the sunlight. His heart skipped, and he cursed it.

She was pretty, obviously. But there was something else about her, something almost magnetic. He was usually so smooth with his words, charming girls easily. But when he'd spoken with her, she'd bewitched him somehow.

What makes her different from the other girls, do you suppose?

The question made Jack uneasy, mostly because he didn't know the answer.

Don't you dare get her involved. She's innocent.

I wouldn't dream of it, Your Highness.

He felt the Voice smile, using his title to patronize Jack like a child. Anger burned through his blood, flooding his chest. If he did not rid himself of the Voice soon, it would drive him mad.

Jack rubbed the cut on his palm, thinking over the past few days with dread. His trip to the Deadwood had been a complete waste of time. Once again, he'd found himself no closer to a solution of ridding himself of the Voice.

He was beginning to fear he would never be free.

You didn't really think it would be that easy, did you? Getting rid of me. As if you'd have the power to do so.

What do you want with me?

It was a futile question, and one he'd already asked too many times. Never did the Voice deign to respond.

I see great things for you, my prince, the Voice said, sensing Jack's frustration. ***You need only ask for my help.***

Never.

A loud knock startled Jack from his thoughts. Clenching his fists, he walked to the door, preparing to tell whoever it was to get lost. He didn't have the patience to interact with anyone else today. In these moments, he nearly regretted dismissing his manservant, but he couldn't risk anyone else becoming suspicious of the creature lurking in his head.

He whipped the door open, and a dismissal was moments from his lips when he froze. His father's grim figure stood before him, a suspicious glare already bearing down on him. Jack swallowed and gave a quick bow, his pulse quickening.

"Father, good evening." Sweat beaded on the back of his neck. His fingers twitched as he moved to the side, allowing his father to step inside. He hated that his father always made him react like this.

"I heard you lost a duel. To your sister, of all people."

Right to the point, I see. The Voice chuckled.

Shut it, he hissed back.

King Cole ignored Jack, instead walking back to his window overlooking the sea. With hands clasped firmly behind his back, he didn't even attempt to look Jack in the eye.

Jack balled his fists again. *Look at me, you bastard.*

His father eyed him sideways, waiting for an explanation.

"I did, but—"

"The Paladin Tournament is tomorrow, and you are wasting your time indulging your sister's fantasies?" His voice was even and low, but Jack knew it for what it really was: A warning. The calm before the storm.

"Well, she —"

"How come it's been days since you've visited the training grounds? Do you want to disappoint me?" He paused, but Jack knew better than to speak. "You take a trip to Saints know where, fooling around with Saints know who? You will never become paladin if you continue acting like a child."

His words lashed at Jack's chest like a dragonwhip. He thought after all this time they would sting less. His father turned at last to look at him, eyes searching him like they would a stranger. Although Jack had surpassed his father in height, the king had a way of looking down on him that made him feel small.

"Father, if you would just let me explain—"

"I grow tired of your *explanations*, Jack." The king turned to look out the window again, his black eyes never settling on one thing. Although he stood perfectly still, Jack sensed his father's restlessness. It echoed in the tension wrapped around them, in the way his brow furrowed and his knuckles tightened. Either his displeasure with Jack's performance was more intense than Jack had originally thought, or there was something else troubling his father.

It's not like he would ever tell you.

Jack ignored the Voice and sighed, his own restlessness magnified by his father's sudden appearance. "Father, is there some reason that Jill shouldn't win tomorrow?"

His father's jaw tightened, and he knew he'd asked a dangerous question.

"I have humored your sister for many years now, and I'm beginning to think it was a mistake."

Jack looked at his father, unable to hide his confusion.

"She is a good fighter, though I want to deny it," the king explained. "But what use does a wife have for those skills? Instead of focusing on poetry and music, she's focused on nothing but her blades from the moment she first held a sword." He gave Jack another sideways glance. "I had hoped her dedication would rub off on you, but that does not seem to be the case."

Jack's stomach churned at his father's words. What was he saying?

"Father, I don't think you understand how valuable Jill could be as one of your warriors. Perhaps she could even be a general some-day." Jack couldn't keep the excitement from his voice as he pictured it.

His father turned to him, irritation flashing across his features. "Your sister is an asset, nothing more. Her purpose is to marry a prince or a lord and establish an alliance. After that, the most she'll be good for is birthing heirs."

After all these years, it shouldn't have surprised him, his father's dismissive treatment of Jill, yet Jack couldn't meet his gaze. He thought back to a year ago, his stomach twisting as he remembered what his father had made him do. He knew the cruelty his father was capable of.

What a fool.

For once, Jack agreed with the Voice, and he forced himself to bite his tongue.

Why shouldn't he hear what you have to say? You will be king one day. Isn't it time you stood up to your own father?

You're right.

He thought of what Jill had begged him earlier. His resolve hardening, he stood straighter and met his father's gaze head-on. The Voice was right: he would be king someday. It was time he started acting like it.

And here I thought you didn't want to be king? Jack imagined the Voice grinning. It did that sometimes, meddling with his mind, planting thoughts and pictures in his head until Jack began to believe them.

I'll deal with you later.

Power is precious, my prince. And you have more than you know.

Warmth swelled in Jack's chest. Excitement pulsed through his veins. Perhaps it was the Voice.

"Father."

The king raised an eyebrow, looking mildly amused. Jack knew that look. It was the one he wore right before he played the final winning move in rosepin.

Still, Jack plunged forward, gripped by newfound confidence. "I want to take a trip."

His father stared. "A trip? You just returned from one."

His heart thudded painfully in his chest. "I mean, I want to take a trip to the Distant Lands, across the Eastern Sea. I want to sail the sea, visit different kingdoms and countries, see the falls at the edge of the world. It's all I've ever wanted." Fear and adrenaline pounded through his veins as he watched his father, waiting for an answer.

"No."

Jack stared, heart sinking. "Why not?"

His father turned back to the window, impassive. "You are a prince, not some penniless explorer. I know what would happen. You'd meet some girl, or a few, pass your days in taverns, drink and gamble and sire illegitimate children. Or worse, you'd fall in love and give up everything for some poor pretty maiden."

Thick silence wrapped around them as Jack stood there, stunned. He wasn't sure if he should feel angry, disappointed, or offended.

I told you he'd never let you go.

"Of course . . ." His father gave a rare smile. "If you were a paladin as well as the prince, you would be free to travel where you wish. A few of the older paladins have made journeys to the Distant Lands before, serving as ambassadors. A paladin with such a skill set would be *very* desirable."

The king turned back to him, the words unspoken but the meaning clear.

"I'm afraid I have another meeting I must be off to. The Ohans seem to have more complaints about the Sisters every day. I shall see you tomorrow when you win the tournament."

King Cole turned before walking across the room and opening the door. "I look forward to your victory tomorrow." The way he said the words—soft, as if they were a promise, as if he'd already seen the future—twisted Jack's stomach into knots.

The door shut, and the king was gone. Jack found himself breathing a sigh of relief.

Jack cut a glance at the sun. It was dipping behind the sea, sending shards of light across the ocean into his room. He wanted to see the sun set on the waves every day of his life. He wanted to feel the spray of salt water against his skin. He wanted to be lulled to sleep by the rocking of the ship every night. He wanted this.

What will you do, my prince?

I'm going to win the tournament.

4

___

DAVID

Humpty Dumpty sat on a wall,
Humpty Dumpty had a great fall;
All the king's horses and all the king's men
Couldn't put Humpty together again.

The scent of sulfur permeated the air. Gray rain drizzled down David's back while squelching mud sucked at his feet. For the hundredth time, David cursed whoever had come up with the idea to search for a route through the Southern Marshes. He'd been trekking through these parts for nearly a month now, searching for a way across the border and into Carthesia.

So far, they'd found nothing.

The marshes were miserable to begin with. There was the occasional sinkhole that swallowed men whole, drowning them in muck. And then there were the Komodos, giant fire-breathing lizards that would lie in wait deep in the mud and arise to blow fire on their prey before devouring it. Of course, fire and swamp gas made for a grisly end long before you were eaten.

The rain picked up strength, the drops pelting his skin with such ferocity that he feared his skin might crack again. At least he'd been reassigned from the raids. He'd lost pieces of himself every time he'd accompanied his squad across the border.

But now he was here, searching for a way to sneak an entire army into enemy territory. He sighed. Why him? Why this? But he just shook his head. There was little use in asking why. His scarred face was a testament to the fact that life wasn't fair.

David fingered the bowstring across his chest as he surveyed the swamp, a niggling feeling scratching at the back of his mind. Something wasn't right. He and his squad had been traveling for miles and had yet to see another creature of any kind. It was far too quiet.

"Humpty!" a deep voice behind him called, and David turned, rolling his eyes.

"It's Humphreys, Grimzy. Honestly, it's like you're not even trying."

The mountain man smiled, toying with him. "And it's *Paladin* Grimzy."

David turned to the paladin, looking at him head-on. At nearly ten feet tall, Grimzy towered over him. His bronze biceps were larger around than David's thighs and covered in red and black ink. Grimzy was one of the Whitesaw mountain men, son of the chief of the Whitesaw tribes. It was said their voices were so like the mountains' that they could coax tunnels and caves to appear from the earth.

David had yet to see Grimzy do anything even remotely close to that. Mostly, he lorded his position over David, messing with him any chance he got. David still didn't understand how the man had managed to become a paladin, let alone what he was doing out here in the marshes with the infantry.

"Well, *Paladin* Grimzy, does anything feel off to you?"

Grimzy stopped, rain running down his bare muscles. The

Whitesaw man insisted on wearing nothing but a traditional loin-cloth, rain, sun, or snow—and in this case, even in the marshes.

Still, the mountain man was useful. David watched as Grimzy closed his eyes, listening to the swamp.

On an ordinary day, crows would've been cawing from their roosts in the marsh grasses or picking away at any rotten carcasses that hadn't been claimed by the mud. But today they were silent.

Behind them, Luca, another of David's squad members, stopped too. Luca was from the Feline Clan, pointed ears and slitted eyes giving him away as not fully human. But it was his animal instincts that had kept them all alive during their many missions through the marshes.

"Smell anything?" David asked.

Luca curled his nose. "Besides swamp gas, no. But that's a problem too. Usually there's more out here."

The three stood in silence while their comrades did their best to catch up.

New recruits. They were always given the worst assignments, like trudging through the rotten mud. Consequently, they were also usually the ones to walk straight into a sinkhole or meet a Komodo head-on and get burned to a crisp before they even knew what had happened. David had seen it on more than one occasion.

"Hurry up," David called to the stragglers. There were ten of them total, and for the other seven, this was only their second mission out there. They moved so slowly that David knew they'd have to turn back soon if they wanted to make it back to the compound before dark. You did not want to be out here in the dark.

"Hey, I'm leading this mission, Humpty," Grimzy said, glaring down at him.

David sighed, not bothering to correct him. "Fine. What do we do then?"

Grimzy frowned, considering. For all the jabs between the two of them, David had been under Grimzy for nearly a year now, and despite the fact that he chose to wear a loincloth in the marshes, David knew Grimzy was sharper than most gave him credit for.

Beside them, Luca tensed, his spine curling in anticipation. David's shoulders tightened, and he reached for his bow.

A deafening shriek sliced through the air like the sound of a thousand wailing wraiths. David turned back to his squad just in time to see a creature emerge from nowhere, shadows twisting to form a grotesque monster unlike anything he'd ever seen.

In the space of a heartbeat, the creature surged forward, a tangle of spindly legs and teeth, grabbed one of the men, and bit his head off.

David gaped, heart in his throat, as he watched the monster chew, blood dripping from razor-sharp teeth, claws still wrapped around the lifeless man's body.

Who was that? David scanned his men, pulling off his bow and nocking an arrow. He watched the recruits scatter, tripping and falling over themselves in the mud, hurrying to get away from the monster.

Quicker than a lightning strike, the monster dropped its previous kill and grabbed two more men with clawed hands, this time squeezing their torsos as they screamed.

"Help!" one of the men screamed.

What is his name again? Jasper! He was a seventeen-year-old kid who'd been conscripted into the king's army.

David plowed forward, slowed by the mud pulling at his feet.

The sounds of snapping spines and squishing entrails stopped him in his tracks. The creature turned toward him. Its face was only a gaping hole filled with teeth. Fear paralyzed him as he looked at the creature. The screams of his men sounded distant. Sulfur filled his lungs, but it was a welcome relief compared to the scent of blood that now tinged the air.

"Fall back!" Grimzy roared above the chaos. *Leave it to him to remain so calm.* "Do not engage! Fall back!"

The remaining squad members did their best to obey, running

from the monster as fast as they could. But this time the monster did not seem interested in them. Its gaze, if it could be called that, still lingered on David.

David gritted his teeth, drawing his bow. He'd always been an excellent shot. He pulled back the bowstring, breathed, and released, the arrow aimed straight at the monster's face.

It zipped through the air, his aim true.

And then, as quickly as the monster had appeared, it vanished into a pool of inky shadow. The arrow flew and then fell, burrowing itself deep in the mud somewhere. David grimaced. He wouldn't see that arrow again.

He pulled another from his quiver, waiting as silence descended on the marshes once more. His hands shook, and he bit his tongue, focusing on the pain as he scanned the area.

But it was gone.

He lowered his bow slowly while walking over to the men who remained. *Three men dead in mere seconds.* Bile rose in his throat as he took in the sight of the mangled bodies. An arm lay separated from its body next to a headless corpse already sinking in the mud.

He looked around at the men left. Hawkins, another kid who'd joined the army only a few months ago, stared at one of the bodies. Jasper. Or he thought it was Jasper at least. Between the muck and blood, it was difficult to say.

Gregory was vomiting on hands and knees while Elric and Mavi sat in the mud, blood splashed across their faces. Even Luca looked vaguely ill, and he was rarely rattled by anything.

The only one who remained calm was Grimzy, towering over them.

"What was that thing?" David asked, his voice shaking. He gripped his bow tighter to steady his hands. He'd been a hunter for half his life, and he knew you never put your weapon away before you knew your prey was actually dead.

Grimzy's expression darkened. "I'm not sure. But we must get back to the compound and inform the commander. If there are more creatures like that out here, we may have to abandon finding a route through here."

David looked down at the mess of body parts, stomach churning. "What do we do with them?"

Grimzy glanced at the bodies, then looked around at the remaining survivors. "We leave them."

"You'd just leave them here without a proper burial?" Luca asked. Although his speech was smooth, David could sense the anger behind the words. A proper burial was important to most of the animal clans, but particularly to the Feline Clan, who often built large ornate tombs.

"We have no choice. These men will barely be able to get themselves back, let alone carry the body parts of their comrades. And if there's another one of those things out there, we'll have to abandon them anyway."

David watched the staredown between Luca and Grimzy. As much as he hated to admit it, the paladin was right. They couldn't afford to waste any time getting back.

"If we leave them here, they will be picked apart by animals," Luca said, his ear flitting in irritation.

"They knew the risk coming out here. We need to leave, now." Grimzy turned on the recruits. "Stand up, fall into first formation, and keep your weapons drawn and eyes alert. Signal if you see movement of any kind."

For a moment, the men stared at him blankly.

"Now!" Grimzy growled.

In less than ten seconds, they were moving again. David stayed to the rear, eyes never resting. His eyes landed on the men they were leaving behind, and a pang of sorrow and regret flooded through him. Once, he would've insisted they carry the men back too. Once, he would've argued with his commanding officer until he was reprimanded. But he'd been a soldier long enough now that he knew it didn't matter. War took its share of every man's soul.

The trek back to the compound was slow and tedious, fear

walking beside them with every step. Night fringed the edges of the sky by the time they were a half mile away, and black smoke curled into the sky. Cries and shouting rang through the air, and David heard the sounds of battle.

David and Grimzy exchanged a glance.

Ahead, a lieutenant ran toward them, panic evident on his pale face.

At last, the man crumpled in front of them, blood streaking down his face. "Paladin Grimzy, the compound is under attack!"

"Under attack by whom?"

The lieutenant shook his head, fear wresting logic from his face. "Monsters. We're under attack by monsters."

5

———

MILLIE

illie's hands shook as she helped the princess into her leather armor. It was light and flexible, and she knew the princess preferred it to the bulky armor that some of the competitors wore.

Millie swallowed. She had no armor. No weapon. Only her strange ability. Would it be enough to keep her alive, let alone allow her to win the competition?

There was a reason the Paladin Tournament was the deadliest competition in Erinya. Unlike an ordinary tournament, which involved duels and traditional fights, the Paladin Tournament was more than just a fight. It was also a race. Nearby, an arena had been erected and filled with dangerous obstacles and vicious creatures, and each competitor would fight their way toward the finish line. But in the end, the most dangerous part of the tournament wasn't the challenges or the wild animals; it was the other competitors.

Once Millie finished tightening the straps of Jill's armor, she watched as the princess examined it closely, adjusting where needed. The princess rarely spoke to Millie beyond her orders and requests, preferring silence to mindless babble. Millie had been serving the princess for months now, yet she could recall only a handful of conversations that hadn't revolved around tasks for Millie to complete.

Millie's heart raced as she looked to the ground, hands growing clammy. She cleared her throat, mustering her feeble courage. "Your Highness?"

At first, she thought the princess might ignore her, but after a few seconds, her mistress turned to look at her like she'd forgotten she was there. Her brow furrowed. "Yes?"

Millie swallowed. "Will you be needing anything else?"

The princess's gaze swept across the tent like she was searching for some way she might put her maid to work. At last, she said, "No. I think I'll be fine."

Millie dipped into a low curtsy, holding it. "Then, if you please, I was wondering if maybe, perhaps . . ." She tripped over the words, nerves tangling her tongue. "I was wondering if I might have the rest of the day off?"

Silence wrapped around the pair as the princess considered her with wary eyes. Millie hoped and prayed that the princess would relent. This was her only shot to enter the tournament, and she couldn't do that if she was stuck sharpening weapons and polishing shoes.

Doon needed her.

"I suppose that would be all right. Are you hoping to watch the tournament?"

Millie suddenly second-guessed herself. Lying did not come naturally to her, but she feared what the princess might do if she learned that Millie planned to enter the competition.

"Yes, Your Highness," she said at last, guilt lancing through her chest.

"I'll allow it, so long as you root for me." The princess gave a rare smile, and Millie was struck by her beauty.

Millie nodded, giving another quick curtsy.

"You may go. But I will need your help after the tournament."

"Of course, Your Highness."

Before she could say anything more—or change her mind—Millie scurried from the tent. Outside, a city of tents had been built, each one belonging to some noble family, clan, or tribe. Children raced between the tents with ribbons tied around their wrists to indicate who they were rooting for. Smiths had set up makeshift forges, the sounds of hammers on iron ringing throughout. Merchants and traders had come too; a gathering like this was sure to put coins in their pockets.

Millie kept her head down and raced through the tents. A crimson tent stood taller than the rest, a flag flapping in the breeze that was always present. It was there that she could enter the tournament, there where she could change her life forever.

She slowed, legs numb with fear. The Paladin Tournament—unlike other tournaments—allowed anyone to participate, so long as they were fourteen years of age. You didn't have to be of noble birth to compete, and though it was rare to have commoners compete, it wasn't unheard of.

The fact remained, however, that a commoner had never won.

Millie stopped, staring at the crimson tent where competitors had lined up. Lumbering mountain men towered over everyone, and wolfmen and felines alike brandished their weapons. Even a few boreads from the North had come, their frosted skin so pale they appeared almost blue.

She took a step back. She could still turn around, change her mind. After all, no one expected her to compete. She would likely just get herself killed anyway, even with her power.

But Doon's face flashed through her mind, his dark skin unnaturally pale, his yellow eyes gripped by pain. He would die down there, alone, in the dark, and she would be the only one to mourn him. Anyone else would remember him only as a murderer.

Strangely, it was that fact that propelled her forward, each step heavy, like fighting against a fierce gale. She could not let her brother die abandoned in shame. She alone knew he was innocent, and she alone could save him.

Before she could doubt herself, she joined the line, eliciting curious looks from the other bystanders. She wrung her hands as the line moved faster than she'd expected.

Soon she was at the front, sweaty hands gripping her smock, the cotton fabric wrinkling. She looked up into the suspicious gaze of Kylian Doyle, the king's adviser. Doyle's hair was tied at his nape, his clothing impeccably pressed and clean. A relatively young man, he was fully human, his skin a warm brown, lighter than Millie's.

"Are you here on the princess's behalf?" he asked, raising an eyebrow.

Millie found her tongue stuck in her mouth, drier than sand. She shook her head. "I'm here to enter."

Ever the diplomat, Doyle only barely registered surprise before he smiled. "Are you sure that's the wisest decision?"

Behind her, an inkwell woman grunted in irritation.

"It doesn't matter. I can enter, can't I?" She gripped her smock again to keep her hands from shaking. She wasn't sure what she'd expected. Skepticism, sure, but Doyle looked at her with such pity that she began to doubt herself.

"You can, yes, but . . ." He looked her up and down, his smile tightening. "This tournament is not for the faint of heart."

Tears stung the corners of her eyes, threatening to spill over. Her face heated, and she was keenly aware of the line growing longer behind her, of the irritated sighs, skeptical looks, and not-so-subtle whispers. She wanted to disappear, to crawl into a hole and hide forever. More and more people were turning to look at her, the meek little maid who was going to get herself killed.

I'm sorry, Doon.

"What's going on here?" a familiar voice interrupted.

Millie turned, her stomach leaping to her throat at the sight of Prince Jack, who looked regal and dashing in a forest-green uniform with daggers strapped to his chest. Confusion pulled at his features as he looked from her to Doyle and back.

"Millie, what are you doing here? Did my sister send you on another useless errand?" At the use of her first name, Millie flushed even more, if that was possible. It was this sort of interaction that kept the gossips and eavesdroppers in business.

"She's here to enter herself," Doyle said flatly. It was well-known among the staff that there was no love between Doyle and the prince. For whatever reason, the two butted heads as if they were blood brothers.

While Doyle's face was practiced composure, Prince Jack's was blatant shock.

"Really?" He looked at her, the question sincere. Millie's heart skipped in a way that had nothing to do with the tournament. Still tongue-tied, she nodded, her attention drawn to the ground.

By now, more people were staring at them. She could only imagine what they must have thought, the foolish maid and the sly prince.

She waited for a reprimand, for the prince to tell her she was silly, that she couldn't compete, or that she'd only get hurt. Instead, he stepped forward, his face collected as he spoke to Doyle. "Let her compete. There are no rules stating that she can't."

Doyle's smile faded. "Your Highness—"

"Let her compete."

The two stared at each other while Millie's blood pounded a galloping beat through her veins. Some part of her had hoped she would be turned away, that she could give some reason why she hadn't tried to help her brother. But it seemed that would not happen, and she didn't know how to feel about it.

Guilt coursed through her once more. Of course she wanted to help her brother. And if this was what she must do, then she would do it.

"Very well then," Doyle said at last, looking toward her. "Name please?"

"It's Millie. Millie Muffet." She glanced at Jack, who rolled his eyes and shot her a crooked grin.

Doyle wrote her name down, then pointedly looked behind her. "Next."

Millie nodded and turned to go, curious eyes still looking at her. She felt like a mouse being hunted by a cat.

Soft footsteps sounded behind her. "Wait, Millie!"

The prince. Her stomach lurched again, and she turned, dipping into an automatic curtsy. "Your Highness?" As usual, her gaze was lowered.

"It's Jack, remember?" He smiled, crossing his arms.

She nodded, though she had no intentions of addressing him as anything other than his proper title.

"You don't have to look down, you know."

She looked up at him slowly, and their eyes locked.

"Can I help you with something?" Once again, she was trapped by the prince's presence and feeling rather breathless.

"I just . . . Are you going to be all right? In the tournament, I mean. It's incredibly dangerous." The look of genuine concern on his face surprised her. Why would he be concerned about his sister's maid?

"I'll be all right," she said.

"What can you do?"

"Do?" *Don't make me answer that question.*

"How do you plan to fight? With what weapon?"

Millie had no answer. She didn't dare tell him the truth. But it was obvious she had no weapon, no armor. Like Jill, most of the competitors here had been training their entire lives for this competition.

"Well, it's, um . . . a secret." It was a poor excuse, but what else could she say? "But I'll be all right."

The prince stared at her, and she cringed under his gaze. Could he see right through her? Would he haul her back and demand that she remove herself from the competition?

"All right. I trust you. Just . . . be careful out there. There's a reason so many people start this competition and so few finish it." He paused, his confident face hesitant for a split second. "I would just hate to learn that you didn't make it. I don't know if I could forgive myself if something happened to you."

All the tension in Millie's chest warmed at his words. She couldn't recall anyone looking out for her like that before—aside from Doon, of course.

She smiled at him. "I will. Thank you." She turned to go, inhaling deeply.

"Wait," he called.

She stopped, looking back at him.

"Why are you doing this? Why are you risking your life for some tournament?"

She considered that for a moment. Of course, she couldn't tell him the real reason, but she had to tell him something. "If changing your destiny meant risking your life, would you still do it?"

Before he had time to answer, she scurried off. And as she wound her way through the maze of tents, she realized she hadn't lied to the prince at all.

6

JACK

***T*hat girl is hiding something.**
Jack watched Millie slip through the crowd, her black braid swinging at her back before she disappeared altogether. The Voice was right; there was more to Millie Muffet than met the eye. The way her expressions were guarded, the way her eyes always kept watch, the way she shied away from any questions.

That girl is going to get herself killed. Jack's fists clenched.

You may be right, my prince, and yet . . . The Voice paused, and Jack could almost see the wheels turning.

Yet?

Yet I doubt she would've entered had there not been a reason.

Jack started forward, following the maid. Her dark eyes flashed through his mind, and he pictured the way her lips twitched into a soft smile, the confused look that she got whenever he spoke to her. His chest warmed, a strange tingling starting at the tips of his fingers.

He walked faster through the crowd, his eyes scanning the labyrinth of tents that had been assembled outside the Citadel for the tournament. This year there was more excitement than ever because both he and his sister were competing for the first time. Many were eager to see who would become the next paladin.

The toll of the midday bell sounded, and a hush fell over everyone. Jack's chest tightened, and he stopped walking. It was time.

He thought of his father's promise, or the closest thing to a promise his father had ever given him. They would discuss the Distant Lands after he won. But first he had to win.

Do you still believe he'd really let you go?

I have no choice but to hope he will.

Hope. The Voice laughed, a grating sound. ***That is the problem with you, Jack. You always believe you have no choices. You've built a prison of your own design. I could give you the freedom you've always craved, if only you would trust me.***

Images materialized within his mind: sailing ships cutting through turquoise waters, new lands filled with treasure and mystery, sunsets and forests and stolen kisses.

Stop.

The images faded, and a dull ache settled at the back of his head. He didn't have time for daydreams. If he wanted to be free of his father's grip, he had to win the tournament.

As you wish, my prince, but one day soon, you will come to me, begging for help. Pray that I am merciful in that moment.

Jack swallowed. He didn't know what that meant, but there was no time to dwell. After another quick scan of the crowds for Millie, he jogged through the masses to the arena.

Even from a mile away, it was a sight to behold. The Order of the Saints had come a week ago to begin work on the arena. The challenges changed every tournament, but one thing always stayed the same: the Hedge.

No one knew when it had first appeared. As far as anyone knew, it had always been there. The Hedge stretched a hundred feet high and ran in a complete circle with a diameter of five miles. One entrance faced the east, and the other faced the west. To be named paladin, one had to be the first to cross the finish line at the western entrance.

Thousands of people stood by the eastern entrance, from the highest nobles to the lowliest of commoners. At the front of it all stood his father on a wooden stage, and beside him stood Kylian Doyle. Heat flared in Jack's veins at the sight of Doyle. After all this time, he still couldn't put his finger on what bothered him about the adviser.

Jack tipped his head and walked to the competitors' area, where nearly a hundred entrants stood, each one of them decked in weapons of every kind: wolfmen with daggers and knives, mountain men with clubs and slingshots, felines with crossbows, boreads with sabers of ice that didn't melt. And among them stood a girl with no armor, no weapon, looking like a child beside every other warrior.

Millie.

He was there in an instant, his blood pounding with a fervor he didn't understand. She hadn't been lying; she really planned to compete. What the *Saints* was she thinking? Why had he vouched for her? She was going to die, and it would be all his fault.

"Welcome to the Paladin Tournament!" The king's voice boomed across the clearing.

A storm of cheers erupted, thunderous in its scope. Jack sidled up beside Millie; the girl's attention was focused on the king. She'd changed in the short time they'd been apart and was now sporting a sky-blue tunic over leggings and brown leather boots.

"Millie," he whispered.

The maid jumped, her eyes wide as she looked up at him. With the sunlight glaring down on them, he noticed the freckles splashed across her nose.

"Your Highness." She bowed her head and started to curtsy, but he gave a sharp shake of his head.

She straightened, though her eyes still looked to the ground. He found himself wishing she would just look at him.

"To be honest, I'd hoped you were joking about competing, or at least that you'd give it a second thought. You didn't really answer my question earlier, you know."

She bit her lip. "I'm not sure why someone like you would want to know." Her eyes focused on the king, who was giving some speech about honor.

He gave her a half smile. "I like to know things. But I can't seem to figure you out."

She looked up at him, eyebrows pulling together in confusion. "I'm not sure why you'd want to figure me out. I'm not a riddle."

He looked down at her and found himself at a surprising loss for words yet again.

The Voice chuckled. ***I've rarely seen you speechless, my prince.***

Shut it.

"No, you are not a riddle," he conceded, feeling strangely guilty. "I'm sorry. It's just—"

"And now, if the competitors will step forward to the starting line," Kylian Doyle said, tossing a glare at Jack, "the Matron of the Saints will explain this year's competition."

Bodies shifted and moved forward as one, competitors marching to the starting line at the Hedge. Jack moved with them, a cold hand of fear suddenly gripping his core.

Only the competitors were allowed inside the Hedge. After the competitors entered, onlookers traveled safely around to the other side to eagerly await the victor. Because of this, no one knew exactly what happened inside the arena, only that many went in and few came out.

On the stage, an older woman walked forward, holding a cane even though she moved with an unnatural grace. The Matron of the Saints. She was the keeper of the Saints' secrets and head of the

Sisters, who pledged their lives and services to the Saints. Little was known about them, though the theories were plentiful.

A hush fell over the competitors, everyone in thrall. Her eyes scanned them as if she were searching for the next paladin herself.

"To become paladin is not for the weak of heart." Her voice was an icy wind that sent shivers down his spine. "Inside the Hedge you will find many things: temptations, fears, monsters, riddles. It will require strength, bravery, cunning, and, above all, determination."

The old woman looked over the crowd again until her gaze landed on someone toward the front. Jill, he realized. The Matron's gaze had landed on Jill.

"Upon entering, three paths will greet you. The center path will lead you straight to the finish line, but not without many hardships. To the right and the left you will find easier paths, but longer ones. And should you desire to forge your own path, be warned that hungry creatures wait for those who stray too far."

Around him, people shifted uneasily, and again Jack glanced at Millie, whose eyes were wide. Just what was her plan to make it through alive?

He gritted his teeth. He would make sure she made it through safely.

And if you must make a choice between protecting the girl or winning, what will you choose?

Jack didn't answer. He didn't even know this girl. Perhaps she was perfectly capable of taking care of herself. His mind turned back to the question she'd asked him earlier.

If changing your destiny meant risking your life, would you still do it?

His father's voice called him back to the present. "Only one can become paladin." His father's gaze found him in the crowd, his stormy eyes burning. "For many of you, these will be your last moments. If anyone would withdraw, they may do so now."

Exchanged glances and steady breathing filled the silence. Jack heard Millie suck in a sharp breath and hoped that she would change her mind, that she would leave and forget about the tournament altogether. Instead, she stared forward into the darkness of the Hedge.

"Very well then," the king said, his expression grim. "Death before disgrace!"

The competitors shouted back the royal family's motto. "Death before disgrace!"

"Let the tournament begin!"

In the space of a single breath, chaos erupted. A hundred bodies stormed forward, each with their own agenda, each vying for paladin. Swords were drawn. Bows snapped. There were shouts from the competitors, and the crowd roared behind them. The air filled with chants and laughter and the clashing of steel.

In mere seconds, Jack lost sight of both Millie and Jill. He heard the twang of an arrow being released and barely dodged it in time. He turned to see an inkwell woman, her shaved head covered in squirming tattoos, a crossbow in hand.

Jack drew a throwing knife from his waist and flung it toward her. The woman cried out as it sank into the flesh of her leg. He didn't wait to see what happened to her after that.

Around him, several already lay slain on the ground, their blood soaking into the earth. He looked ahead into the Hedge, where figures raced down the different paths. Few, he noticed, took the path straight through.

He'd learned from previous competitors that there were two main strategies employed in the tournament. Some chose to fight as many as possible at the beginning of the race, opting to wipe out their competition. Others did their best to avoid the fight altogether, concerned with putting as much distance as possible between themselves and those who would pick others off at the beginning.

Jack bolted into the Hedge. Inside, darkness reigned. Towering trees stretched high, snatches of light falling through. As the Matron had said, three paths greeted him, though swarming shadows kept him from seeing what lay ahead. Sweat dripped down his forehead as he considered the paths.

Which path would Millie have chosen?

A familiar scream answered that question for him. Before he could give it a second thought, he ran down the path to the left, blood pounding through his veins. *Please let her be okay.*

He saw her pinned to the ground by a wolfman, whose pointed teeth dripped saliva on her face as she struggled against him.

Jack's vision blurred in anger as he reached for another knife, prepared to end the wolfman's life if it came to it. But in the half second it took him to draw his knife, Millie vanished.

Jack stopped, as did the wolfman, confusion stilling the man. And then, from a distance, they saw it: a mass of black . . . things, moving as one. They crawled up the wolfman's arms and legs. Jack watched as he stood, twitching and convulsing, swatting at the black that had started to cover him.

Jack drew closer, fear and intrigue twisting inside him.

Now* that *is interesting.

Another step forward, and the wolfman cried out, snarling in fear and anger. And then Jack could see what covered the man from head to toe. A shiver raced down his spine.

Spiders.

Jack's feet stayed rooted to the spot as he watched another spider, bigger than all the rest, climb up to the wolfman's neck. The wolfman flailed an arm about, a panicked look in his eyes, his instincts and training leaving him unprepared to deal with a thousand tiny enemies.

The large spider reared up and drove its fangs deep into the wolfman's neck. The wolfman froze, his eyes going blank before they rolled back into his head. He fell limp, and his body hit the ground with a soft thud.

Silence.

Jack watched the mass of spiders, gripping his knives so tightly his knuckles whitened, though he doubted they would do him any good against such an enemy.

And then the spiders moved as one into a great pile, coalescing and twisting until a familiar figure stood before him: Millie Muffet.

For a moment, the two of them stood there, watching each other, waiting.

Magic. It was the only possible explanation.

"How?" Jack breathed the question.

This should be very interesting indeed. I knew she was hiding something. The Voice sounded almost giddy, and Jack sensed it watching Millie with an interest that only made Jack more uneasy.

Millie shook her head. "I don't know."

Jack looked around, making sure they were alone, before he stepped closer, replacing the knife at his waist. She stiffened as he drew near, and Jack wondered if that was normal for her. Was she always afraid to have people close to her?

"You don't need to be afraid." He raised his hands like he was calming a spooked horse. "I won't tell anyone."

She stared at him a moment before relaxing. "Thank you, Your Highness."

He smirked. "Jack, just Jack."

At that, her lips twitched, and Jack hoped she'd smile. But perhaps now was not the time.

He glanced around. The tournament was still going, and they did not have time to stand around discussing . . . whatever Millie had done. They had to keep moving if they were going to make it out alive.

"Let's move," he said, turning toward the path ahead of them. "But, Millie?"

"Yes?"

"Once this is all over, you owe me an explanation."

For once, she met his eyes. Their brown color was deepened by the dark forest. She nodded, her jaw set.

They took off down the path, Jack drawing his blades once more.

With a quick glance back, he saw the wolfman still lying there, his breathing shallow.

I sense, my prince, that this girl may be the key to everything you've ever wanted.

Jack's stomach flipped. He glanced at Millie as they ran. For her sake, he hoped that wasn't true.

7

JILL

Jill dove headfirst into the fray, cutting down anyone who stood in her way. She would waste no time in pointless battles. She'd waste no time avoiding the challenges for an easier path.

The sounds of clanging steel and zipping arrows filled her ears as she ran into the Hedge. She'd been preparing for this moment her entire life. She would not fail now.

Despite the chaos behind her, an unnatural silence enveloped the arena. The shadows loomed like sentinels, watching her every move. Immediately, she was greeted by the three paths the Matron had spoken of.

Heart pounding, she plunged down the straight path, swords drawn. Every instinct urged her to run, but she couldn't risk being careless. The challenges were there for a reason, to test strength and mettle and cunning. She would never last as paladin if she ran straight into a trap.

It did not take long for the scenery around her to change. The towering oaks were replaced with flowering fruit trees, shrubs, and bushes with bella mushrooms as tall as Jill's knees, glowing blue and green and violet. A soft breeze caressed her face, carrying with it the most glorious scents, of fragrant flowers, yes, but of other things Jill was certain did not grow in the ground: warm hay, spiced tea with honey petals, a newly forged blade, blue-fire torches, ocean spray.

She stopped walking, her resolve melting. She wanted to stand there forever, breathing in the scent of every fond memory she had. She wanted to lie down and rest. Her body ached already, sore from every fight she'd ever been in, every injury she'd ever sustained. She could curl up against a tree and rest, just for a moment. There would still be time to finish the tournament. Her skills far exceeded those of everyone else competing. She could afford to take a break.

She took a step forward, her muscles relaxing, her grip loosening. A warning sparked at the back of her mind, but she ignored it as she took another step forward into the most beautiful garden she'd ever seen. Flowers of every color dripped petals like jewels. Weeping willow branches danced in the breeze, blossoms fluttering through the air like tiny faeries.

One of her swords fell to the ground with a soft thud, and her knees followed. She knelt there, warmth flowing through her, eyelids heavy. She could lie down and sleep, forget about the tournament, forget about her father, forget about everything. It would be easier that way.

"Jill, get up."

Her eyes shot open. Ice flowed through her veins. She knew that voice, but it wasn't possible. He was dead.

Frantically, she stood, grabbing the sword that had fallen as every hair on her skin stood at attention. Her eyes searched for the source of that voice, the voice of the boy she'd loved.

But there was no one there.

Because he's dead.

Suddenly, the flowers around her smelled too sweet, and the air felt too warm. The path in front of her had narrowed, sloping down and down and down. She followed it, forgoing her slow pace.

Memories washed over her like she'd been doused with cold

water. His smile. His laugh. His calloused hands. Her breaths came shorter now as she started to run. Flower petals swarmed her, spinning around her, tugging at her.

She swallowed. She had been prepared for so many obstacles, so many fights. But how did one fight flowers? She pushed forward, letting her glance swing side to side, her eyes always keeping careful watch for any enemies.

"Jillianna," a voice hissed, and she spun, eyes darting everywhere.

Nobody called her by her full name except her father.

What is going on?

"Princess," a slithering voice said behind her, and she spun, the breath in her chest catching. A bloodred serpent was coiled around the branch of a tree, golden eyes piercing her with the wisdom of an ancient being. Its forked tongue shot in and out of its maw, a knowing smile landing on her.

The Whispering Serpents. Clever and tricky, they were the objects of children's stories, warnings about deals that could not be trusted, words that could not be believed. Jill remembered the poem her nanny had sung when she was a child.

Beware the serpents,
Who tell half-truths.
Beware the serpents,
Who bring good news.
Beware the serpents,
Hissing "friend."
Beware the serpents,
'Til the end.

Jill swallowed. "What do you want?"

The serpent shifted closer. "Only to warn you."

Jill knew she should walk away, knew the serpent couldn't be trusted, yet her feet stood fast, and she was unable to pull her gaze from those gleaming eyes filled with knowledge.

"Warn me of what?"

The serpent smiled wider, revealing pointed fangs glistening with pink venom. One bite was enough to kill a grown man in a matter of minutes.

"Darkness approaches. War. Bloodshed. And choices. Choices *you* must make."

She considered the serpent for a bit. This was a test, she was certain. The serpents' whisperings were always full of mysterious prophecies you thought meant one thing but that meant another.

Beware the serpents.

"You don't scare me, snake." She turned to leave. She'd already wasted enough time in this garden as it was. She couldn't afford to listen to the fruitless babbling of a trickster.

"I care not for your fear. I care not about you. I care only to see how this will end."

She turned back to face the serpent. "This tournament will end with me as paladin. I will make sure of it."

The snake gave a hissing laugh, the sound like knives scraping on glass. "You think this tournament is the end? How foolish you are. Why, this is just the beginning."

"I'm done here." She would not turn back, no matter what he said. She would keep on walking. Already, the end of the garden was in sight. She was nearly through.

"Princess. Traitor. Usurper. Queen. These are most precarious things."

She stopped, fear lancing through her. *Traitor? Usurper?* She whipped her head back around, but the serpent was gone. Around her, the garden stilled, the breeze dissipating. Unease plagued her as she forced her feet forward.

She inhaled slowly, filling her belly first and then her chest, holding it until she could do so no longer, then breathing out as slow as she was able.

It was lying. The Whispering Serpents always lie.

But she supposed that wasn't true. The serpents told half-truths, not outright lies. So, what was that nonsense about her being a traitor? A usurper? Queen? She wasn't meant to be queen.

The sound of a knife slicing through the air brought all her thoughts to a halt as she spun and blocked a blade. A cloaked attacker moved in, slashing and stabbing at her. The figure stood about Jill's height with their hood pulled low. The figure moved faster than she'd seen anyone move before, and Jill struggled to keep up. It was a feeling she wasn't used to.

At this rate, she would tire and make a mistake, and then her chances of becoming paladin were over. With renewed vigor, she hacked at her attacker's legs, pushing them back and back. The figure danced away from her blades easily but stepped back nonetheless.

Sweat dripped down the back of Jill's neck, but now she had the advantage. Her attacker wielded only a knife while she had both of her swords. She swung, going on the offensive. Still, the figure dodged her blows easily. And then, as she prepared to deal a deadly blow, the figure vanished, melting into shadow.

Blood pounded furiously through her veins as her eyes scanned everything around her. *Where did they go?*

Her question was answered by the sharpened edge of a cold blade at her neck. She gasped.

How?

"I have my ways," the voice behind her said, reading her mind. The voice was higher, female, and distantly familiar. "I'm impressed. No one has made it past the garden yet."

Jill's mind reeled. The knife bit into her neck so that she could barely swallow without risking being cut. She sorted through her options. She could smash the back of her head against the woman's nose, but she risked the woman slicing her neck open. She could attempt to pry the blade from her hand, but that was sloppy at best, and again she risked the woman simply slitting her throat.

Her head pounded in time with her heart. Her last option was somehow the most frightening. She could try and talk to the woman. But talking was Jack's strength, not hers. Somehow, she always managed to make people hate her when she opened her mouth.

But what other choice did she have?

"What do you want?" she asked, her voice strained to keep the knife from cutting her.

"My task is to see that only worthy candidates make it through."

So, she was part of the tournament then, not another competitor. The question was, would she kill her?

"I take it I failed then?" Jill kept her guard up; this was not the end of their fight. She refused to believe she'd failed.

She could feel the woman breathe deeply behind her, taking her time. "Not yet," she said at last.

Jill's patience was wearing thin. It seemed time was her greatest enemy in this competition, and everyone she'd encountered seemed intent on wasting it for her.

"Just tell me what I have to do," she growled.

The woman sighed. "It's true what they say, you know. Youth is wasted on the young. You lot are always in such a hurry."

Jill rolled her eyes. She was done. Inhaling through her nose, she jabbed the woman with her elbow as hard as possible while lifting her heel to scrape down the woman's shin before stomping on the instep of her foot. Jill heard the crunch of bones as the woman cried out in pained surprise.

She used the moment to her advantage, clawing at the woman's hand and wresting the knife from her grip before wheeling around to face her, the woman's blade pointed at her now.

The woman wore a green cloak. Her blond hair was cropped at her chin, and her green eyes flashed. Recognition rolled through Jill, followed by a sense of awe.

"Paladin Willa?"

The paladin was a decade older from the last time Jill had seen her, but Jill would never forget the young woman who'd knelt before her father, the woman who'd given her a knowing smile, challenging Jill to become paladin too.

She nodded, a sad smile pulling at the corners of her lips. "Princess."

Jill's eyes narrowed. "What must I do to be a 'worthy' candidate?"

"You already are, Your Highness."

"So, then I can go?" Why did it feel like a trap? And why was she looking at her with pity in her eyes?

"You can. Or you can turn back now and forget about becoming paladin."

"And why would I do that?"

Paladin Willa's face darkened. "The weight of paladin is heavy. It is not for those seeking to escape their destiny."

Annoyance surged through Jill. This woman knew nothing about her. "You don't understand. If I don't become paladin, I will be married off. I *have* to win." Desperation clawed up her throat, panic swelling in her lungs. She couldn't think about these things now, but it was true. She *had* to win. There were no other choices.

The paladin nodded, her eyes understanding but still vaguely sad. "Go then. And hurry. Something strange rides the air. Treachery."

Princess. Traitor. Usurper. Queen.

The words came unbidden to her mind, and her hands started to shake.

"Thank you, Paladin Willa." She gave the woman the customary bow to honor her, then tossed her knife off into the bushes before running down the path.

"Don't thank me yet," Paladin Willa whispered.

Jill glanced back, but the woman had already disappeared.

8

DAVID

The monsters swarmed the camp. They were twisting, garish shadows with claws. Soldiers fled in every direction, unprepared for an attack of this nature. Some attempted to fight. Most charged the creatures head-on only to fall victim to the monsters' terrible teeth.

David's blood boiled as he looked to Grimzy. Chaos had descended, and it would take a skilled leader to regain control. David could see the wheels turning in the paladin's head as he sized everything up.

The compound was two miles end to end and comprised of sturdy wooden huts that sat on stilts a few feet off the ground. Four quadrants were intersected by two perpendicular roads. A large courtyard in the center of the compound served as the training grounds.

"Your orders, sir?" David asked.

Grimzy's jaw flexed. "Gregory and Hawkins, circle around and order all soldiers to retreat to the outskirts of the northwest quadrant. Elric and Mavi, make your way to the explosives barracks and gather everything you can. David, Luca, and I will draw them to the southeast quadrant. Meet us there."

"Yes, sir." With a quick salute, the men were off, disappearing into the rabble.

Heart thudding, David plunged into the compound alongside Grimzy and Luca. Screams echoed, and the scent of blood and smoke hung thick in the air. Bodies lay scattered all around, missing arms and legs and heads.

David drew his bow and nocked an arrow. Up ahead, a monster rampaged, moving with blinding speed. It was the same as the one they'd seen earlier, and two more joined it. In front of David, Grimzy picked up a fallen soldier's mace, deadly spikes protruding from the end.

Grimzy charged, wielding the spike with frightening force, smashing it deep into the monster's neck. The creature screamed, shadows rather than blood bursting from the wound Grimzy had inflicted. Nearby, the other monsters turned, drawn by the ear-splitting screech of their kin.

"David, now!" Grimzy boomed.

David let loose three arrows at once, each landing in the wound Grimzy had created. The monster screamed again, louder this time, leaving David's ears ringing.

"Fall back!" Grimzy shouted, his voice sounding distant.

They fled the training grounds, making their way to the southeast quadrant, where the explosives barracks were. As they ran, soldiers fled to the outskirts, headed for the opposite end of the compound.

Behind them, the monsters gained speed, their ravenous snarling growing louder. Luca did his best to evade the monsters, jumping from hut to hut with grace only the Feline Clan could claim. The whistle of Luca's throwing stars zipped through the air, though few seemed to penetrate the monsters' thick skin.

Ahead, David saw Elric and Mavi dumping black powder from a barrel into a pit. David's stomach curdled. For this to work, someone would have to make sure the monsters stayed in position while another shot a flaming arrow from afar.

Beside him, Luca seemed to understand, nodding at him. David swallowed. He was the only one skilled enough for such a long shot.

Grimzy stopped running and turned to face the creatures head-on. Holding the mace high, he charged again, bringing the mace down on the same monster he'd attacked earlier. Smoke billowed around them as the creatures swarmed, but Grimzy was a furious blur, moving with an unnatural speed for someone of his size.

David ran to the outpost at the far corner of the camp and climbed the ladder into the basket, the sentry who'd been stationed there long gone. Anger squirmed in his chest. If the sentry had done his job, he could have rung the bell as soon as he'd seen the creature off in the distance.

Unless the creatures appeared from thin air. It was an unsettling thought, but he recalled how the last creature had come from nowhere and vanished in the same way.

A blue-fire torch burned in a bronze brazier beside him. David pulled several arrows from his quiver and dipped them into the pitch kept in all the outposts. Down below, Luca and Grimzy danced around the creatures, drawing them closer to the pile of explosive powder.

David steeled himself. He had to fire the arrows quickly, otherwise he'd burn himself, and once he fired that first shot there would be no going back.

One of the monsters drew closer to the pile as Luca leapt away.

"Now!" Grimzy's voice carried over the cacophony that roared around them.

A second later, David flicked the arrowhead into the brazier and released the arrow, aiming straight for the black powder.

The explosion rocked the earth beneath him, and the blast sent him flying off the outpost. Fire flared, the monsters screamed, and David's back shattered as he hit the ground.

Pain rolled through him like thunder and lightning, fierce and violent and blinding. He could feel his back broken in multiple places as he inhaled the scent of burning flesh. Muffled cries reached his ears, but he couldn't stand, couldn't move. Every breath stabbed his lungs, and he wondered if this would be the end, if he would finally leave this cursed life behind.

There was no way Luca and Grimzy could have survived the blast unless they'd gotten away in time. Perhaps they had. Above him, the trees swayed in the breeze, indifferent to the suffering around them.

"David!" The voice was distant, and his ears rang so badly he could scarcely identify who was calling to him.

A figure towered over him, kneeling beside him. So, Grimzy had survived then. David saw no sign of Luca, and his stomach churned.

Grimzy reached down to lift him up, but David shook his head, too breathless to speak. Before he could stop him, though, Grimzy had pulled him up, pausing as he stared at the shards of David's back that fell from his shirt onto the ground.

David's shirt was shredded and burnt, and he ripped it off. He no longer cared. He knew what the mountain man was looking at: the gaping black hole in his back, David's glass-like skin broken like a piece of pottery.

David struggled to draw breath, to explain. In the end, all he could manage was, "Put them back."

The paladin stared at him a moment, dark eyes questioning before he picked up one of the shattered pieces and, like a puzzle, began putting him back together again.

It was an agonizingly slow process. He could feel the pieces suture themselves back together, transforming from brittle glass to flesh-and-blood skin, leaving ropey scars in their wake. His entire body was covered in scars, every one an instance when his skin had broken. After all this time, he still didn't understand how it was possible.

David bit his tongue as Grimzy placed the last piece, a burning sensation rippling across his back as the skin regrew itself. David inhaled deeply. His breath was still ragged, but at last he felt clear enough to speak.

"Thank you," he said, his voice hoarse from the smoke.

The compound burned around them. The monsters had vanished once again, leaving destruction in their wake. Smoldering ruins stood where the southeast quadrant had once been, soot staining everything.

"You have some explaining to do, Humpty." The paladin grabbed his shoulder. Pain lanced through him, but he gritted his teeth. He was nothing if not used to the pain.

"Luca?" David asked.

Grimzy shook his head, and David nodded. He'd known the risk, and he'd fought anyway. Still, David's heart plunged with guilt, heavy as a stone in water. He and Luca had served side by side for years now, and Luca had been the closest thing David had to a friend.

"Paladin Grimzy." The cold voice cut through the heat surrounding them, and they turned to see the commander standing before them.

One of the Ohans, he bore the signature scales of the Reptile Clan around his eyes and cheekbones. The Ohans were one of the most powerful families in Erinya, and the commander was no exception. His slitted eyes stared down at them, his green scales covered in ash and soot. Immediately, David dropped into a kneeling position with his fist across his heart, but Paladin Grimzy merely nodded his head. As paladin, he was of higher rank than the commander, a fact that annoyed the commander to no end.

"I trust you have an explanation as to why you blew up half of my compound?" He raised an eyebrow, or rather the section of his face that would have been an eyebrow if he'd had any hair.

"I trust you have an explanation as to why *your* compound was in such disarray when we arrived? If we'd come any later, you might all have died." Grimzy's voice rumbled in warning, and David looked up at the two to find them glaring at each other.

The commander's eyes flashed, but he gave a tight smile. "I had it well-handled."

"It certainly looked like it," said Grimzy, his voice a note of warning.

For a moment, the two continued to stare at each other, the commander looking much less daunting next to the Whitesaw man.

"I trust you have news to report from your scouting mission?"

Grimzy smiled. "We saw one of those monsters in the swamps as well. We aren't certain where they came from or what their goal is."

"Their goal is to kill, Paladin." The commander's tone was icy. "I would think you of all people would have noticed that."

David's knee started to ache as the two men went back and forth, his back still burning. He took a labored breath.

"This incident will set the operation back by months, months we can't afford. Do you want us to lose this war?" the commander hissed.

"You seem to care an awful lot about this operation, Commander, and very little about the lives lost today."

The commander looked back at David, eyes narrowing. Quickly, David dipped his head.

"Aren't you the hunter?"

"Yes, Commander."

"Rise."

David stood and saluted the commander, keeping his eyes focused on a tree in the distance, just as he'd been trained.

They have us whipped like dogs. He could hear Luca's voice in his head, could see that devilish smile sliding across his face, and David's chest tightened with unexpected grief.

The commander observed him, looking at him as if he weren't a person but an animal up for auction, sizing up its size and strength.

"You two will hunt these creatures down. I don't want word of this incident getting out. Who knows where Carthesian spies may be lurking? If they learn the compound was attacked, they will seize the opportunity to push through the border once and for all." He spoke matter-of-factly, as if the only thing that mattered was this operation, not the innocent lives these monsters might take.

"We should send word to the king," said Grimzy.

The commander stiffened, his distaste for the king scrawled blatantly across his face. "Old King Cole is busy with the Paladin Tournament. We need not bother him with trivial matters such as these."

"Trivial? Those monsters killed a hundred men!" The words were out before David could stop his tongue.

The commander turned on him. Tilting his head, the man smiled. David sucked in a breath as the commander moved closer, inches from his face. David waited for him to strike.

Instead, he whispered, "I've heard about you, Hunter. I've heard about the prey you sought. I would think twice before speaking out of turn again." With that, the commander stepped back, his gaze flitting between the two of them. "Gather your things and hunt these creatures down. You leave at dawn."

9

***

MILLIE

Millie had lost count of how many opponents they'd taken down. As the Matron had promised, the path they'd chosen held little resistance; it was the other competitors they fought hardest against.

She shook with exhaustion as they ran, an inkwell man behind them firing arrow after arrow at their backs. They zigzagged through the undergrowth, and every now and then Jack turned to deflect an arrow or two. Sooner or later, the man would run out of arrows, and then they would confront him.

Millie's lungs burned, and her legs ached. She was not a warrior like Jack. She had not trained at all. Her daily tasks did not force her to exert herself like she was now, and it showed, her pace much slower than the prince's.

An arrow lodged into a tree by her head, the bark shredded by the pointed tip. She'd been foolish to think she could compete among such trained warriors, even with her power. If not for Jack's help, she would probably be dead now.

"Millie, do you think you can transform again?"

She simply nodded, too tired to speak. In truth, though, she wasn't sure if she could. It took a massive amount of energy, and after nearly a year, she still didn't completely understand her power.

She stopped running and closed her eyes, concentrating on the beat of her heart. It was much too fast; this would never work. She tried harder, imagining her body separating itself, imagining her body collapsing.

The world plunged into darkness for a second before she was blinded by a million lights. Her body dissolved into a thousand pieces of shadow skittering around the ground. She rushed forward toward the inkwell man, and his eyes went wide. He cried out in alarm, smacking at her spiders, but there were too many, and they were too small for the action to be useful.

It was a strange thing, to have her body, her senses, her awareness separated into a thousand different spiders. If she was not careful, she was sure the sensation would drive her mad.

The man spun, continuing to smack at her until she heard a loud thump, and the man went rigid, collapsing onto the ground. Jack stood over him, the butt of his dagger spattered with blood.

Millie focused all her energy inward, calling the spiders back. When she opened her eyes again, she was in her own body. She stood over the man, hands shaking.

"You didn't—" She stopped, her stomach lurching.

"No, he's just unconscious."

She took a ragged breath and looked up at the prince. "Thank you," she managed to say.

"Do you need to rest?" he asked.

More than anything, she wanted to do just that. But she knew they couldn't afford to. They'd spent enough time fighting off other competitors. If they didn't keep moving, they were sure to lose.

She shook her head. As they moved, her mind reeled.

What would they do when they reached the end of this? Would the prince leave her behind and try to win the tournament himself? Would she do that to him?

Her thoughts turned to Doon, alone in that dark prison cell, his body racked with fever seizures until his mind was gone and his heart gave out. She clenched her fists. Doon was her only family member. He wouldn't hesitate to do whatever necessary if their roles were reversed. If it were her instead of him suffering in the suffocating darkness, he would do anything.

She was grateful for Prince Jack's help, but she knew when the moment came, she would win, even if that meant betraying the newfound trust.

They walked side by side in silence, but she could tell the prince was on alert, eyes scanning and ears listening to their surroundings. He'd grown up hunting and fighting. No doubt it was second nature for him to listen and observe, to be prepared for anything. Once again, she felt foolish to have thought she could survive this tournament without him.

"How long have you had your power?" he asked, breaking the silence.

Her heart skipped. How could he ask such a question so casually, as if he were asking how her day had been or where she was from?

"About a year or so."

She shuddered as she recalled the day her power had first manifested. Her blood pounded faster at the thought of that day.

The prince glanced at her, brow furrowed. "A year?"

She nodded. "Yes, why?"

He stiffened. "No reason." He gripped his daggers tighter, knuckles going white. "We're nearly to the end, I think. But aside from the other competitors, I haven't seen a single obstacle."

"Isn't that a good thing?"

"No. It either means we missed something or the Sisters have something nasty in store. Or perhaps . . ." He cocked his head as if listening to something only he could hear.

Millie took another step, and her stomach dropped, her foot falling over an unseen edge. One moment she stood on solid ground, and the next she was met with a cliff face, sheer and deadly.

Jack reached out and grabbed her arm, pulling her back with such force they collapsed to the ground. Fear stabbed at her heart as she sat up and looked at the edge she'd nearly walked right off.

"What? How?" Her body shook. The ground lay hundreds of feet below, a dizzying drop. A ravine stretched between them and the cliff on the other side, a ten-foot gap that separated them from their destination.

The prince's face darkened. "That was close."

Millie looked up at him, inches between them, and her face heated as she realized his hand still gripped her arm. She eased away, rising to her feet, doing her best to ignore her pounding heart. She'd come so close to losing her life.

"What do we do now?" She peered over the edge and instantly regretted it, her head spinning.

The gap was too wide to jump, and there were no ropes or bridges nearby. It was also too deep to scale or climb, and they didn't have the time to waste.

She eyed Jack as he looked around, searching for anything that might aid them. Above, the sun was beginning to dip in the sky, the shadows around them elongating.

One of the hardest parts of the entire competition, Millie realized, was never knowing where you stood. You could press forward and face every obstacle, every opponent, but still cross the finish line second or third or last. You wouldn't know whether you'd won until you reached the end.

Millie's palms started to sweat, and she glanced at Jack again. He seemed lost in his thoughts, and she could tell he was as stumped as she was. Then her eyes caught a flicker of movement hanging over the ravine. Tree branches from the opposite side touched the tree branches from their side of the ravine.

An idea buzzed at the back of her mind. She opened her mouth to speak, then stopped. They could not climb across the branches; they were too thin and flimsy. They would barely hold her, let alone the prince, who was nearly twice her size.

Unless . . .

Guilt clawed at her as she looked back at the prince. If this worked, it would mean leaving him behind, but she wouldn't have made it this far if not for him.

The prince doesn't matter. All that matters is Doon.

Still, it seemed a poor way to repay him. Before she could lose her nerve, she ran to the base of the tree that hung over the ravine.

"Did you find something?" he asked.

"I'm sorry," she said.

Before she could explain, she plunged into darkness once more, her mind scattering into a thousand spiders. She sent them up the tree as fast as possible, ignoring Jack's shouts behind her. She couldn't bear to imagine his face as her spiders skittered up the base of the tree, using the branches as a bridge to cross the ravine.

A thousand hearts pounded in sync as she reached the other side. Her body reformed, her consciousness melding itself back together. When at last her body returned to its usual form, she shivered, a strange fuzzy feeling washing over her. It was getting harder and harder to use her power, and her body could feel it.

"Millie!" Jack called. She looked back at him, her heart twisting as his face drooped and he realized that she had no plans to help him across too.

"I'm so, so sorry." Before he could respond, she took off down the path, tears burning the rims of her eyes.

She'd betrayed him. She'd left him behind. After everything he'd done to help her, she'd just left him there. As long as she lived, she wouldn't forget that look on his face.

Then she thought of her brother's face, pale and sickly. She gritted her teeth. If this was the price she must pay to free him, then so be it. She ran faster, tears streaming down her cheeks. She brushed them away as the path opened in front of her.

The Hedge loomed ahead, along with the finish line. A crowd of people waited to see who the next paladin would be. Her body ached all over, and her stomach churned, but she forced herself to speed up.

A blurred figure caught her attention, a flash of auburn hair and shining blades.

The princess. She was nearing the finish line, her jaw set and gaze burning, focused only on one thing.

It occurred to Millie that since the princess was ahead of her, she hadn't seen her. She likely had no idea Millie was even competing.

Blood roared through her veins as she realized how much closer Jill was to the finish line. The princess would win, and Millie would lose. Doon would die.

No.

One more time.

It was getting easier, dissolving into bits of shadow. This time, the spiders that formed were fewer but larger. And faster.

She jolted forward, leaping farther and faster. Still, the princess didn't see her. She was nearing the finish line now, and Millie was so close.

One of her spiders launched forward, landing on the princess's back, and she turned, slashing with her swords. But, like everyone else, she was not prepared for an opponent like Millie.

Jill's eyes widened as she took in the mass of giant spiders swarming her, and Millie could sense Jill's fear. Still, she pressed forward, guilt tugging at her even as she sent her spiders up the princess's body.

The princess screamed, releasing a piercing, terrified wail that twisted Millie's gut. She swatted at the spiders, tripping backward and falling to the ground.

Pain zipped through Millie's many bodies as the princess landed on several of her spiders, her weight crushing them. Millie knew instantly they were dead, but she couldn't focus on that as the princess writhed beneath her, shrieking.

She saw tears streaming down the princess's face and stilled. One moment her essence was scattered, and the next she stood over her mistress, guilt swarming inside her. Somehow, in less than an hour, she'd betrayed both royal twins.

Recognition flared across the princess's face, followed by confusion and then boiling anger as she rose to her feet and began searching for her swords, which had been dropped in the commotion.

But Millie could not beat the princess in a fight with weapons, so she ran. Behind her, Jill shouted, screaming curses Millie doubted Madame Sorelle would approve of.

Up ahead, the finish line was near. She was almost there.

A sword landed in the ground next to her. A desperate attempt from the princess, it hadn't even come close to hitting her.

A rock popped up beneath her foot, and she tumbled to the ground, the rocky soil biting into her hands. Her heart pitched until she looked down. Her hands were across the finish line.

She heaved a sigh of relief before looking up at the stunned spectators, each one wearing a more outrageous look of surprise than the last.

A familiar figure stepped forward. Kylian Doyle. He eyed her with an interest that had been absent earlier that day. Behind her, the princess marched forward. She yanked Millie to her feet and shoved her.

"You *cheater*!" The venom in her voice was alarming.

Millie trembled, her knees buckling beneath her, but the princess stepped forward, grabbing the front of her tunic and pulling her close. "What the bloody *Saints* was that?"

"I . . . I . . ." Millie fumbled for words.

"Unhand her, Jillianna. You're embarrassing yourself," the king's stormy voice bellowed. The princess glared at her one last time before shoving her away again. Millie's legs barely held her up. She glanced at the spectators nearby and realized they must have seen what she'd done.

Ice trickled down her spine. What would they do to her? Would they lock her up like Doon? Would they execute her?

"Tell me your name, girl," King Cole said.

Millie looked up at him, and his gaze was a mixture of disbelief and suspicion.

"It's Millie. Millie Muffet."

The king nodded and turned to the crowd. "May I present to you this year's paladin, Millie Muffet."

10

JILL

Jill's chest was a vacuum, hollow and aching as she stared at her reflection in the mirror. Her skin felt the memory of hundreds of tiny legs skittering across it, and she trembled. A sob wrenched from her chest, and she covered her mouth, fighting back tears.

She had faced the garden and the Whispering Serpent. She had faced Paladin Willa and her warnings. But when confronted by her own maid, she had failed.

A scream ripped from her throat as she grabbed her hairbrush and smashed the mirror in front of her. Flecks of glass sprayed in her face, cutting her cheeks, but she hardly felt them.

That had been it. Her one and only chance to be free of her father's hold on her, to be free of her forced engagement, was gone. The next Paladin Tournament would not be for another five years.

"You always were one for dramatics."

Jill swiped her tears away and turned to see Madame Sorelle standing in the doorway of her washroom. Madame Sorelle's eyes were the color of midnight.

Jill inhaled, recalling Madame Sorelle's teachings. Where Master

Ravala had taught her discipline of body, Madame Sorelle had taught her discipline of mind. And smashing one's mirror was hardly the sign of a disciplined mind.

"Life isn't fair, girl. Now bring me a chair."

Jill opened her mouth and then closed it, her resolve crumbling. If anyone else had spoken to royalty the way Madame Sorelle just had, it would've ended in a whipping. As it was, few people scared Jill more than her old tutor.

Huffing loudly, Jill grabbed a chair from her foyer and dragged it into the washroom, resisting the urge to grumble. She knew the madame would only roll her eyes and perhaps even swat her hand like she'd done when Jill was a child.

"Sit," the woman ordered.

Jill obeyed, though not without sighing loudly. It was easier to pretend she was mad, easier than admitting what she really felt. She glanced at the wedding dress hanging in the corner. It was strange how something so beautiful could elicit such fear.

She pinched her eyes shut, forcing back the nausea that threatened to overwhelm her. She couldn't marry a stranger, not when she still loved—

She shoved the memory away. She would *not* think of him. What she'd seen in the Hedge had been some twisted magic playing tricks on her mind. He was dead, and there was no bringing the dead back to life.

Madame Sorelle picked up the hairbrush and shook out the shards of glass before setting herself on Jill's hair, pulling out pins and ties, brushing out dirt and tangles.

Silence wrapped around the pair as Jill looked at herself in the broken mirror. Her face was multiplied in the shattered glass, less a reflection of her appearance than the state of her heart. Madame Sorelle dipped the hairbrush into the bowl of water sitting on the counter before brushing through her locks again.

It would ordinarily have been Millie doing her hair now. But Millie was occupied with her latest promotion. Jill's hands curled in her lap, fingernails digging into her palms. Her chest pinched, fury pooling like blood within her.

Little Millie Muffet had taken everything from her. Her paladin-ship. Her freedom. Her destiny. Because of Millie, she would marry a stranger. Because of Millie, she would never escape her father's grasp.

"I remember the first time I did your mother's hair." Madame Sorelle's voice was soft, the tendrils of memory sweeping into her.

Jill's attention sharpened, and she straightened. It was rare that anyone spoke of her mother, and Jill could not resist the longing that rose in her at every snippet of memory anyone could give her, forever craving stories of the mother she no longer had.

"That girl never could sit still." Madame Sorelle smiled, a unique occurrence for the stern woman. "She loved her hair done up, but she hated sitting through the process. She had the most beautiful raven hair, like Jack's."

Jill's heart dropped. She knew Jack looked like their mother. Still, every time someone remarked how little Jill looked like the queen, she couldn't help the sorrow that bloomed in her chest.

"But you have her spirit, her drive." Madame Sorelle paused, the hairbrush halfway through Jill's hair. Jill looked up at her, and their eyes locked in the splintered mirror. "She rarely took no for an answer."

Jill's breath hitched, her soul swooping. *What is she saying?*

The woman's dark eyes landed back on Jill's hair, now smooth and free of tangles. "You have beautiful hair too. If you let it grow out, you'll have many options for hairstyles at your wedding," she said, running her fingers through Jill's long hair. It was nearly to her waist now.

Jill's heart pounded. "I'm not sure. Perhaps shorter hair would display a veil better."

Madame Sorelle smiled wickedly. "I think you may be right."

Jill grabbed the scissors from her desk. "Cut it."

11

JACK

*J*ack had never felt the Voice so amused. The Voice continued to chuckle darkly long after Millie had abandoned him, leaving Jack to find his own way through the Hedge.

And to think you were worried about her.

Jack's fists clenched, anger burrowing in his chest like a bothersome tick. He didn't want to be angry with Millie. After all, only one of them could win anyway. But still, she'd just left him there to find his own way across that chasm.

I'm sure she had her reasons.

Yet he couldn't deny the way it had stung as he'd watched her transform and cross without him. He wondered if she'd won. He still wondered why she'd competed.

It would be wise to keep an eye on that girl.

You don't think I know that?

I think you are more concerned about her than about the power she wields.

Jack nearly snarled aloud. *And why shouldn't I be?*

I think you are taken in more by her pretty face than

her power. But you should know, my prince, that power is dangerous in the hands of those too weak to wield it.

Jack didn't know what to say to that, and his stomach twisted uneasily. Millie didn't seem weak to him; she'd held her own more than once inside the Hedge. Perhaps she was a bit timid, but not weak.

The Voice was silent after that, but Jack still felt its presence, like he always did. It took Jack another hour or so to find a way over the chasm and then cross the finish line. When he finished, however, it was clear by the look on his father's face that someone else had already won.

To anyone else, his expression might've seemed passive, neither happy nor sad about whoever the victor was. But as Jack stepped out of the Hedge, their eyes locked, and his stomach plummeted. Rage burned in his father's eyes. The king would not lose his temper in front of the crowd, but Jack was certain to hear about it later.

A fist gripped his heart. Since he'd lost, there was no way his father would ever let him journey to the Distant Lands. His one opportunity for adventure, to see the world beyond his own small kingdom, was gone.

And yet, for all his disappointment, he found he couldn't be upset with Millie. If anything, she'd spared him from making the same decision in the end. He wasn't sure he could have abandoned her. Or if he had, he'd never have been able to live with himself.

The crowd was thinning. The commoners were heading back to the town for their own festival while the nobles made their way to the Citadel for the Paladin's Ball. It would be a week of parties and feasts, hunts and games. Jack would be forced to smile through it all, to pretend losing the paladinship meant nothing, to endure the whispers and gossip wondering just what had happened within the Hedge.

"I suppose that girl was special after all."

Jack gritted his teeth. He knew that pompous voice. He turned to see Kylian Doyle standing behind him, examining him thoughtfully.

"Did you know what she could do?" he asked, his blue eyes piercing Jack.

"No, I didn't." Jack started to walk away. It was bad enough he'd lost the tournament. He didn't need to add a conversation with Doyle to make it worse.

"She won, you know."

Jack froze, a smile tugging at his mouth. Millie had won. A strange mixture of sadness and warmth twisted in his belly.

"Good for her. I was worried."

"Yes, I thought she was going to get herself killed. Instead, she took down your sister, stealing the victory out from under her." Before he could explain further, Doyle turned and walked away, a ridiculous smirk on his smug face.

Jack's stomach dropped. *Millie beat Jill?* She'd be furious. And Millie would bear the brunt of it. He swallowed. He had to find Millie, and he had to find his sister, talk some sense into her before she did something rash. She'd never handled losing well.

Your sister's pride will be the death of her.

The Voice seemed to relish the thought. For reasons Jack couldn't figure out, the Voice disliked his sister, and hostility swirled through Jack each time he spoke with Jill. Even now, he could feel a surge of vehemence pulse through his mind.

Jack turned to go, to find Millie and warn her, to tell her to stay as far away from his sister as possible. He broke into a jog, following the crowd across the plains at the base of the Citadel.

"Jack."

He stopped, turning to meet his father's stormy gaze, his face a placid lake with a raging undercurrent. Jack swallowed.

Suddenly, he was ten years old again, standing in his father's pristine quarters. He'd done something wrong, and his father was livid. The king yelled at Jack, gripping his shoulders and shaking him so hard that his head hurt for a week after. Hot tears streamed down Jack's cheeks. He should've known better than to cry, though, as all it did was earn him a smack across the face.

"Father," Jack said, nodding. He couldn't look into those eyes.

"I will speak to you later. After the ball. I would love to hear your story about your time in the maze." The king's eyes bored through him, and all Jack could do was nod for fear his voice might abandon him.

Will you be sorry when he's gone?

Jack started. For once, he'd been so absorbed with fear he'd nearly forgotten about the Voice.

I don't know what you mean. It was a lie, and the Voice knew it. They both did.

My father was hard on me too. The Voice sounded almost wistful. It was a tone Jack had never heard it take before. ***I was never enough for him, no matter what I did.***

Jack knew he shouldn't ask, but he couldn't stop himself.

What did you do?

The Voice's melancholy shifted to glee. ***I killed him.***

A HALF HOUR LATER, Jack paced in front of Millie's door on shaking legs. He knew it was Millie's door because it was where they'd planned to put this year's paladin. Yet despite knowing where she was and knowing he was the prince, he found himself struggling to gather the courage to knock.

His stomach churned, fear and dread knotting his stomach. It was simply what the Voice had told him earlier, nothing more.

He stopped pacing and approached the door, lifting a hand to knock. His breath caught in his chest.

What exactly was he going to say? She'd left him to fend for himself in the middle of a deadly competition. She was the reason his father was going to rail at him later that evening, suffering his abusive words.

So why did he want to talk to her? To see her? He should've been furious with her, yet all he'd wondered from the moment she'd told him she planned to compete was why she'd entered.

Just then, the door opened.

A surprised face greeted him. Then she lowered her head respectfully, dipping into a graceful curtsy.

For a moment, he was just as stunned as she was, and then he realized his fist was still up in the air, poised to knock at nothing. He quickly dropped it and cleared his throat.

"I'm sorry, I was just—I came—" *Saints!* Why were his palms so sweaty? "I just came to say congratulations." He gave her an awkward smile, cursing his bumbling tongue. He'd always prided himself on being good with people, good with words, and yet this girl —this maid—seemed to erase every word from his head the moment her eyes met his.

"Thank you," she said, her voice soft. Her eyes looked to the ground.

"I, um . . . just wanted to tell you . . ." He stopped, breathing in. "I wanted to tell you that you don't have to feel guilty. For leaving me. Even if it did take a ridiculously long time to find a way across that chasm." He smiled at his own joke, but Millie's eyes only widened.

"I'm so sorry!"

"No! Don't be! It was a joke. I'm sorry!"

You have a way with words, my prince.

"Shut it," Jack mumbled.

"What?"

"No, not you! I meant, I'm glad you're okay."

Millie's brow furrowed; she was clearly confused. Jack swallowed, his heart hammering. *Bloody Saints!* What was the matter with him? It was like he'd never spoken a proper sentence in his life.

"I'm sorry, I'm a little tired," Jack said, sighing. It was true. His body ached, and his head had begun to pound a steady rhythm behind his eyes. "I just wanted to make sure you were okay. After you left, I was worried. And then I heard . . . I heard you took down my sister."

Millie's skin paled as she gave the slightest nod. "Is she . . . all right?"

Jack shook his head. "I don't know. But I know one thing: she wanted this more than anything. She won't be happy she lost. And I'm afraid—" He stopped himself. He couldn't bring himself to tell her what he was thinking, that he was afraid his sister would torture the poor paladin maid. "I'm afraid it will take her some time to adjust."

"I'm sure," she said, picking at her fingernails. "Your Highness?"

"It's Jack."

She swallowed, unable to meet his eyes again. "Will you tell her I'm sorry? That I . . . I didn't want to do it."

He nodded, doing his best to give her a reassuring smile. "I will."

"It's just, your sister is many things, but I haven't found 'forgiving' to be one of them. And—" She stopped herself, realizing what she'd just said.

Jack couldn't resist. He laughed. "Well, I'll start by not telling her you said that." He smiled at her, but she still looked panicked. "I'll speak with her. You won. She lost. There's nothing more to it than that." But even as he said it, Jack knew it wasn't quite that simple.

Millie nodded but said no more. Jack wanted to stay and speak with her longer, to ask her more questions, but he could see his presence was no longer wanted, if it ever had been. Still, turning to leave proved to be harder than he'd imagined.

Don't get too attached.

Jack grimaced. "I'll see you at the ball?" he asked.

She looked down at her clothing, her face flushing, perhaps just now realizing she would be attending as something other than a maid this time around. "I guess you will," she said, her voice small.

Jack flushed despite himself as he realized that the two outfits he'd seen her in were likely all she owned. She'd never needed a beautiful dress for a ball as a maid. It was only the noblewomen who wore new gowns to every event they attended.

Jack would be sure to send some gowns to her room. It was only fitting that she be dressed to match her new role. He smiled at her. "Good. It was nice seeing you again, _Paladin_ Millie."

12

DAVID

David and Paladin Grimzy left at dawn while the soldiers did their best to clean and rebuild the compound. David had lived there a year, yet it had never once felt like home. The endless rain and muddy swamps made sure of that. He wouldn't miss it in the slightest.

David shifted the bow on his back. Horses had been provided to them, but they were small packhorses, suited for carrying supplies more than people. But David cared little. It would be easier to track these monsters on foot anyway.

Unless these creatures vanish into thin air.

Which it appeared they did. They also had to confirm whether one of these creatures could even be killed. Where had they come from? He was sure a monster like this would have been mentioned in his circles before.

David had been a hunter before he'd been recruited to the king's army, had trained under the famous feline hunter Siad-Asad, but he'd never heard of creatures like the ones they'd seen yesterday.

"Tell me something, Grimzy," David said, breaking the silence. "Why are you here?"

The paladin glanced down at him, his hulking bronze muscles glistening in the early-morning light. Behind them, their packhorses followed at a trudging pace.

"Commander's orders, Humpty."

David rolled his eyes at the mountain man's nickname for him. "You're one of the king's paladins. You don't have to take any orders you don't want to. Why take this one?"

Grimzy glanced at him, his dark eyes piercing David with magnetic force. "Why are you made of glass?"

David's adrenaline spiked like he'd come across a wounded animal. In all the chaos of the day before, he'd nearly forgotten about his back shattering, about the Whitesaw man piecing him back together like a broken piece of pottery.

Visions flashed across his mind as he recalled that day. Snow had pelted him as the wind had wailed a pitiful song, the tips of his fingers turning black and blue.

He shivered at the memory. He'd never been so cold in his life. He'd nearly died that day, following a trail of ghosts into a blizzard. In the end, the thing that had saved his life had been the very thing that had cursed him.

"It's a long story." David grimaced, staring out at the landscape before them. Endless gray hills greeted them, covered in sandy yellow brush.

"We have nothing but time," Grimzy said.

A week passed before they caught a trail. The creatures had proved just as elusive as David had feared. And worse, reports had emerged that the monsters had started entering small towns and villages on the fringes of the larger cities.

With every town they entered, the news grew worse: missing persons, attacks, entire towns disappearing in a single night. They heard of search party after search party lost as people sought their missing loved ones.

"We should've sent word to the king." Grimzy was in an unusually foul mood as they left a small fishing village. The stench of rotten fish clung to them long after they'd left. Beside them, the Rose River rushed by, so named for the red rock that ran underneath, giving the water its pink hue.

"What would the king do?" David felt his own bitterness rise in him. As much as he would've liked the help, he knew the king wouldn't bother to send anyone.

"He could send the legionnaires."

David looked up at Grimzy, raising an eyebrow. The legionnaires were the second-most elite warriors in Erinya, comprised of noblemen trained from their teenage years until they were twenty-five. They were talented, but because only noblemen could become legionnaires, they rarely saw any real action in battle. Best to leave that sort of fighting to people who were disposable.

If there was anything David and Grimzy agreed on, it was their mutual disdain for the king's legionnaires. They may have been talented, but their egos left little room in their heads for any brains.

"I hate to tell you this, Grimzy, but *you* are who the king would send. There's no one else."

That wasn't entirely true though. There were plenty of noble warriors to compete in the Paladin Tournament, yet never enough to fill soldiers' ranks. It was the reason the age of conscription lowered every year while the nobles feasted and merely played at being heroes.

In that respect, he admired Grimzy. The Whitesaw man was the chief's son, nearly a prince in his own right, and he had only ever done his best to serve the people of Erinya. It was why he chose to serve at the compound instead of choosing a more luxurious assignment somewhere else.

"He could've sent Paladin Willa or Paladin Salazar. Surely they'd know what to do," said Grimzy, his eyes scanning the river.

"Are you admitting you don't know what to do?"

Grimzy's gaze shifted back to him. "Are you claiming you do?"

David snapped his mouth shut, fingering the drawstring of his bow. He'd restrung it the night before, the cord nice and taut. There was a certain comfort in the weight of the bow at his back, one that gave him permission to let his mind wonder what his life would look like if he hadn't been conscripted into the army, to wonder if he ever could have been just a hunter instead.

Grimzy was right though. It would be arrogant to assume they knew what they were dealing with. Those sorts of assumptions got people killed.

"Have you ever heard of monsters like these? I know your tribe tells stories of several creatures lost to the New World's memory."

Grimzy looked thoughtful for a moment. Above them, churning thunderclouds loomed in the distance, pulsing with shadows and rain. They would need to find somewhere to rest for the night soon, or they would be stuck out in the storm.

"Perhaps a few creatures, but none that fit the description perfectly. Though—" He stopped, tilting his head, and David knew he was listening to the earth around them.

"Yes?" David's heart leapt, and he instinctively reached for his bow, prepared for any threat.

"Something about those creatures isn't natural."

David rolled his eyes. "Of course not."

"No, I mean, I could not feel those creatures' lifeblood."

David stopped walking. There were many things he didn't understand about the mountain man's gifts, but he knew about lifeblood, the energy that lived in every person and beast alike.

"Is that possible?"

Grimzy shook his head. "It shouldn't be. There is lifeblood in everything—the earth, the water, the air. The mountain men can sense this lifeblood. But those creatures . . . They had none."

"What does that mean?" David asked, swallowing. An icy finger pricked the back of his neck.

"I don't know."

. . .

A SQUAT VILLAGE LAY AHEAD, filled with square-shaped huts in the style of the Feline Clan. Grass thatch covered the huts, and red and purple hieroglyphs were painted on the sides, each symbol representing a family member and the prophecy given to them at their birth in the Naming Ceremony.

Luca had once told David all about it. It was one of the most sacred traditions that belonged to his people.

David felt the blow like a punch to the gut as he remembered his friend was gone, blown up in an explosion he had caused.

Smoke curled from the holes in the tops of the huts, but silence filled the air. Storm clouds swirled above them, filled with rain. The distant boom of thunder cut through the empty town.

Harrow Forest stood at the edge of the village, dense and dark, its timbers blowing in the stormy breeze. Although David thrived in the woods, Harrow Forest had always made him nervous, as if something sinister watched from the shadows. Even now, as crows flew overhead, singing their mournful cries, he could feel his skin crawl.

An uneasy feeling slid through David's chest. It did not look like the other abandoned villages they had seen, chaos and destruction giving them the story of what had happened. Instead, the people of this village seemed to have vanished into thin air.

Just like the creatures.

"Where is everyone?" Grimzy rumbled, his voice as low as the distant thunder.

David ground his teeth and walked to the first hut. After knocking on the wooden door hanging from leather hinges, he waited.

Behind him, Grimzy walked down to another hut, pounding on the door there too. They waited for several minutes, but inside there was silence. Sweat started to trickle down the back of David's neck as he looked around. There could've only been twenty little houses; surely someone would be home. He searched for a house with smoke rising from it and started out to it.

Once again, he knocked on the door and waited for an answer. "Is anyone in there?" he said. "I'm here to help. Anyone?"

Once again, he was met with silence.

"Perhaps people left," Grimzy suggested.

"Why would there be smoke coming from their chimneys? They wouldn't leave the fires going."

They tried knocking on three more houses. By the time they got to the fifth house, David pounded on the door so hard a piece of his finger snapped off and went flying into the grass.

David sighed, turning to face the giant man. It occurred to him then that perhaps there were people in the village, but the presence of a giant like Grimzy was keeping them from answering the door. David was just about to suggest he go wait outside the village when he saw a rustle from the corner of his eyes.

The mountain man started to turn, but David held up a hand, and Grimzy froze.

As quietly as he could, David stepped forward. Across the street sat a pile of hay, flies buzzing around the heap. He was certain he'd seen it move as if something—or someone—was inside it.

He tiptoed forward. When he was only a few feet away, he launched forward, diving into the hay and throwing it around to disperse it as fast as he could. A strangled scream echoed before someone clamped down on his forearm, biting as hard as they could. That was a mistake.

Another scream sounded as a young feline boy spit out chunks of glass skin covered in blood. The boy couldn't have been more than ten, but the second he laid eyes on Grimzy, he turned to run, blood dripping down his chin.

"Hey, wait!" David shouted, running after him. The boy zipped between two small huts, jumped over a fence, and took off toward the river. Fortunately, David wasn't far behind.

"Stop!" he shouted again. He reached out toward the boy and wrapped his arms around his waist, the child kicking and squirming as he lifted him off his feet.

"I'm not . . . gonna . . . hurt you!" David grunted, carrying the child back into the village.

"Let go of me, you molded sop! I'll slice your neck open, you coward!" the boy screamed, rage burning through his slitted eyes.

The kid was strong despite his small size, and David struggled to hold him. Ahead, Grimzy stood there, a thick eyebrow raised in interest.

"Some help here?" David asked as the kid elbowed him in the side.

"I think you have things under control," said the paladin, smirking at him.

"You're useless."

Once David reached the bale of hay, he dumped the kid on the ground. The kid tried to bound up again, but David grabbed his shoulders and pushed him to the ground. "Sit."

The kid snarled at him but stayed put, staring up at them, a defiant look in his gleaming eyes. His brown skin was covered in filth from head to toe. His long hair was stringy with grease, and his pointed black ears flattened in defiance.

"Are you going to kill me?" he asked.

"No," said David, "but I'll whoop you if you try to run again."

"You can't whoop me."

David squatted to the ground, looking the kid in his slitted green eyes. "Try me."

The boy considered him, and for a second David thought the kid might try to run again, but he stayed there, blood drying to his chin.

"What's wrong with your arm?" the boy asked, curiosity winning out.

In all the chaos, David had nearly forgotten he'd been injured. He glanced down at his forearm, shattered by teeth marks with cracks spreading outward. He scanned the hay and began picking up the cracked pieces. "I'll show you."

The kid watched as he held the pieces with one hand and began putting them back into place, but the pieces were small, and there were sure to be holes. Every time he reattached a piece, it felt like a beesting, but he was so used to this by now that he hardly noticed the pain.

At last, as many pieces as he could find were fitted back into his arm, and a web of scar tissue now twisted around the area. As far as David knew, it would remain that way until he died.

"What's your name?" David asked the kid.

The kid looked up at him, curiosity mingling with suspicion. "Who are you?"

David sighed. "My name is David. I'm here to help. Where is everyone?"

For the first time since they'd met the kid, his eyes went soft. "They're gone."

"What do you mean? Did they leave? Were they taken?"

The boy stared at the ground, looking like he might cry before saying, "The hunting party left to find my sister and a few others. But they didn't come back. After the third hunting party didn't come back, everyone left."

David looked over at Grimzy, concern touching his stone-faced features. It was a story that was growing more and more common.

"Where did they go?" Grimzy asked.

The feline boy looked up at the mountain man, confusion pulling at his brows. "They went to the Lost Tribe, of course."

Grimzy and David exchanged a glance. David didn't know what the Lost Tribe was, and it was clear the paladin didn't know either.

"Where's your family? Why didn't you go with them?"

The boy's face hardened. "It's just me and Lyra. I couldn't leave without finding her."

"I see." David nodded. He knew what it was to be without family. "What's your name?"

The boy hesitated, looking between the pair. "Asif," he answered at last, still eyeing David.

"How long have you been waiting here, Asif?"

Asif squirmed under his gaze. "A fortnight."

A fortnight. Two weeks. The first attack on the compound had only been a week ago, yet this boy had been waiting here two long weeks. Alone. But as David looked at Asif, he saw the rebellious set to the boy's jaw that explained perfectly why he had survived on his own so long.

"Come, let's get you something to eat, and you can tell us what happened."

13

MILLIE

illie would have to send the dresses back. It was too much. Even now, as she stared at the silk and jewels and colored bodices, her face flushed, and her chest squeezed in a way that made it hard to breathe. How many times had she helped the princess into gowns just like these? How many times had Millie done her hair and applied her makeup for balls and festivals? She knew how to do this.

But the difference was that Jill was a princess and Millie was not. She was a maid, a servant.

A paladin.

Millie felt like she'd be sick. What had she done? She wasn't a fighter, and she certainly wasn't a noblewoman. But in less than an hour, she would be expected at the Paladin's Ball, and if she didn't change into something soon, she'd be dragged out in what she wore now: a dirty tunic covered in blood and mud.

For the millionth time, she wished Doon were there. He always knew what to do in these situations. But he was trapped in a cell half a mile below the palace, and she was the only one who could get him out.

Just put on a dress, Millie. She heard the words in his voice and nodded her head as if he were there to see her.

They had arrived nearly fifteen minutes ago now, a dozen ball gowns, each more beautiful than the last. One gown dripped with rubies and lace. Another black dress was layered in gold brocade, the sweetheart neckline dipping far lower than Millie would ever be comfortable with.

A midnight-blue gown lay beneath all the others, catching her eye. She would have missed it if not for the fact that the other dresses seemed too outrageous for her. She tugged on the dress, freeing it from the pile, and held it up, inhaling sharply.

Doon's voice spoke to her again. *That's the one.*

MILLIE'S HEART thudded a panicked rhythm. If she'd thought she felt sick before, it was nothing compared to how she felt now. The ballroom doors loomed in front of her, as welcoming as a mausoleum. She gripped the front of her dress, wiping the sweat from her hands.

One more step, Millie. Do it for Doon.

An announcer stood at the doors, decked in Erinyan colors of green and gold. Millie took a shaky step forward, doing her best to breathe evenly. In many ways, entering the tournament had been far less terrifying. At least no one had known who she was when she'd entered. But now everyone would be looking at her, at the maid who fancied herself a paladin, at the girl with strange powers.

"Wow."

Millie pinched her eyes shut. She knew that voice, had heard it more in the last two days than ever before. She glanced back. Prince Jack stood there staring at her.

Heat rose to her cheeks as she glanced down at the dress she wore. It was the simplest one the prince had sent her, yet it felt more right than anything she'd ever worn, the dark blue silk hugging the few curves she had.

"You look stunning."

Millie's heart skipped in a way that had nothing to do with the night ahead of her. She swallowed, her mouth suddenly dry. "Um, thank you. You too. I mean—" The words tumbled out, and her face burned brighter.

For the first time, she noticed just how handsome the prince really was. His dark green suit highlighted his tan skin and dark black hair, and the amused glint in his eyes warmed something in her belly.

"Thank you," he said, his lips quirking. "May I escort you in?"

Millie stood there, eyes wide and mind blank. The prince? Escort her in? Several more seconds passed as she stared at him.

"Unless you don't want me to?" Jack stepped back, a flush rising to his cheeks.

"No, I was just surprised, that's all. Are you sure you don't want to—" She stopped herself. How could she finish that sentence? "Won't people think—" *Saints, why can't I talk?*

He smiled, stepping beside her and looping his arm through hers. "Let me tell you a secret, Millie," he said, leaning down to whisper in her ear. "People will always talk, no matter what we do, so we may as well do what we want."

A shiver raced down her spine, her blood thrumming beneath her skin as she looked up at him, those dark eyes bright with curiosity.

The doors opened before them, and she gasped.

Millie had been in the grand ballroom many times, usually scrubbing floors or dusting off the pillars on tall rickety ladders, but this was altogether new and wonderful.

A hundred chandeliers hung from above, dripping with crystals that caught the light and sent it swirling around the room. Gold sconces holding Neverfade candles hung from every wall. Pillars around the great room depicted the twelve Saints, each carved from a different stone, their hands lifted high to support the ceiling. Evander the Just was carved from pure gold, a tear sliding down one cheek and an eye patch covering the opposite eye. Zillah the Vengeful was carved from sapphire, a scarf wrapped around her mouth. On and on they went, each saint with their own stone, their own story. Millie remembered her mother telling stories about each of them and of the great battle they'd fought against the Black King.

But as wondrous as the ballroom was, the people were the grandest spectacle. A feline couple danced around the room with such haunting grace that it made everyone around them seem clumsy by comparison. A young boread boy with blue skin and ebony hair ran around the room, freezing people's drinks when they weren't looking. A representative of the wolfmen was in attendance as well, a blue-and-silver uniform marking him as one of Alpha Volkov's men.

"Shall we?" the prince asked, and Millie looked up at him, nodding.

Together they descended the marble stairs, and people stopped what they were doing to see the prince arm in arm with the newest paladin.

Millie's chest constricted, and she gripped Jack's arm tighter. Her steps faltered, and she slipped. Her body tipped forward, her knee nearly connecting with a marble step, but an arm around her waist caught her. Around her, people snickered and whispered. Her cheeks burned.

"Ignore them, Millie," Jack whispered as he pulled her upright.

In that moment, she'd never been more grateful for anyone as he walked with her down the last few stairs, flashing his charming smile at the crowd. When they reached the bottom, he grabbed a drink from a servant's tray and raised it high into the air.

"Welcome, everyone, to the Paladin's Ball! I trust you've heard all the gossip by now? Tell me, what is the most interesting thing you've learned so far about Millie Muffet?"

An uncomfortable silence settled over the room as people cast wary glances at one another. Millie eyed the prince.

What on earth is he doing?

"Perhaps you've heard the rumor that Millie and I are engaged? Or you've heard that she has used a love potion that keeps me under her spell? Or maybe you've heard she wields some dark power we've never seen before?"

Millie's heart pounded, her breathing getting shallower. *Why is he saying these things?*

The prince flashed a cunning smile. "I heard an interesting rumor about myself recently, that my beautiful hair is, in fact, a wig made of horsehair." The prince smiled and tugged on his hair, pulling at it with comical strength.

He stopped, smiling at a nearby boarman. "Would you care to see if that's true?" Jack bent his head toward the pudgy boarman, and the man's brow furrowed in confusion as he reached out to pull on Jack's hair. After a few tugs, the man stopped, glaring at the prince.

"Thank you," Jack said, unperturbed by the boarman's indifference. He turned back to the crowd. "You see, no wig."

With that, the crowd broke into laughter as everyone relaxed.

"The truth is, Millie Muffet is a name I'm sure you've never heard before today. But I can assure you, it is not one you will soon forget. Within the Hedge, Millie fought with bravery unlike that of anyone I've ever fought beside."

Jack glanced at her, and Millie sensed that he truly believed every word he said.

"So, you may go ahead and spread your rumors and your gossip, but you can be certain of only one thing: the words you use to describe her will never do her justice. There is far more to her than you could ever know."

Millie's chest swelled, her eyes pricking with tears.

He raised his glass higher. "To Paladin Millie!"

"To Paladin Millie!" the room echoed, cheers and claps resounding through the ballroom. Millie released a breath, giving a timid smile to the crowd.

One by one, people turned back to their conversations, their dances, and their food until no eyes remained on her. Jack set his glass on a passing servant's tray before he grabbed her arm and led her to the center of the ballroom, pulling her into a dance. Millie shuffled awkwardly as Jack pulled her along, his feet light and his body close.

"Thank you," she said.

"Of course." He smiled down at her.

"They'll still gossip, you know," she said.

He released her waist and spun her, her dress flaring out before he caught her again, her heart in her throat.

"They will always gossip. You must learn to listen to yourself and not what others say about you."

Millie's heart twisted. The prince made it look so easy, his words smooth and his smile genuine. It was no wonder so many people felt at ease with him. Even now, she felt herself relaxing into his embrace as he spun her around on the dance floor.

The ballroom doors opened again, revealing the last person Millie wanted to see.

Princess Jill stood at the top of the steps wrapped in a dark green dress that highlighted her every curve. She usually preferred her long auburn hair curled into a bun, but her hair had been cropped to her shoulders, and a single braid wrapped around her head like a crown. Her eyes looked red.

Millie's stomach dropped. Who had helped the princess get ready? And why had she cut her hair?

At the top of the stairs, the princess waited for all eyes to turn to her, her face as hard and sharp as glass. When at last it seemed all eyes rested on her, she smiled, but Millie could tell even from far away that it didn't reach her eyes.

She glanced up at Jack, who'd stopped dancing to look at his sister. He stiffened.

"Will you excuse me, Millie?"

Before she could reply, he was gone, making his way toward his sister. Once Jill reached the bottom of the stairs, Jack grabbed her arm and whisked her off to a corner.

Not wanting to look like she was spying, she turned her back on the twins, watching the nobles milling about the ballroom.

Technically, she'd been to a ball before, but as a servant, not a guest—and certainly not as the guest of honor. Nervous, she folded her hands in front of her. Part of her longed to join in on the conversations around her, but mostly she was content to stand in the corner. She had received enough attention to last a lifetime.

"Paladin Millie," said a deep voice, and she turned.

Quickly, she bowed her head and curtsied. "Your Majesty." She risked a glance up at the king, who eyed her with curiosity.

"My son seems to be quite taken with you."

Millie wasn't sure what she had expected from the king, but that hadn't been it. "Your son is very kind and chivalrous."

The king grunted as if unconvinced. "Perhaps." His eyes navigated to his children, who stood in a corner, clearly arguing. Millie swallowed, hoping the king would walk away. Instead, he turned back to her, his eyes narrowing.

"I wonder if you could answer a question for me, Paladin Millie," he said, his voice cold as steel.

"Of course, Your Majesty." Blood pounded through her veins frantically as she considered what he might ask her. If he asked about her powers, would she tell him?

"You bested my daughter, a feat not easily done. And somehow you escaped my son as well. How did you manage that?" He stared at her before taking a long swig of his drink.

Millie's mouth went dry. Had he not seen what she'd done to the princess? Was it possible her secret remained safe? Or perhaps he wanted to hear the words from her.

"Well, I—"

Suddenly, the king's face purpled, and he coughed, a violent shudder rolling through his body.

"Your Majesty, are you all right?"

A fit of violent coughing overtook the king. Blood splattered across his fist and onto the floor. Millie's eyes widened as he toppled forward, collapsing to the ground. She watched in horror as seizures racked his body. His eyes rolled into his head, blood drying on his chin.

Shouts echoed around the ballroom, and Millie knelt beside the king, cradling his head.

Bodies pressed against them, and she was vaguely aware of Jack and Jill coming to kneel beside her. At last, the king stopped seizing. And then he was still.

14

JILL

*J*ill was a whirlwind of emotions, but she dared not let it show.

Discipline your mind. The body will follow. Master Ravala's words came to her, a mantra to keep her calm. She ran a hand through her hair, once again surprised at how light her head felt since Madame Sorelle had cut it.

She glanced around her father's quarters, which were filled with nobles and dignitaries. Along with her and Jack, there was Kylian Doyle, the king's adviser; Dahab Asad, chief of the Feline Clan; Master Ravala; Ohan-Jin, head of the Ohan family; Paladin Salazar; and the newest paladin, her maid, Millie.

She clenched her fists, her nails biting into her palms as she stared at Millie, who looked small among her father's closest allies. *Millie.* The girl who'd helped her in and out of dresses and armor, who'd cleaned her wounds and braided her hair. The girl who had apparently been keeping all sorts of dark secrets. The girl who'd taken everything from her.

Eyes burning, she looked to her father, lying on his bed, a black coverlet over him as the physician examined him. Whispers slipped through the room as eyes slid sideways. Jill watched her father's adviser; his expression was as guarded and neutral as ever.

At last, the physician turned, his jaw flexing, and Jill knew the news couldn't be good. What she didn't know, however, was how she felt about it.

She recalled the last true conversation she'd had with her father, nearly three weeks ago now. He'd come to her quarters and informed her that it was time to put away her swords and focus on more important things than the Paladin Tournament.

"Like what?" Jill had asked.

"In two months, you will journey to Welynn, where you will marry Prince Gaelor. Your marriage will secure an alliance with their territory." Her father was so matter-of-fact. The conversation was already over, the bargain struck. Somehow, she'd known even before he'd said anything. She'd always known it would come to this sooner or later. But that didn't make it any easier.

"What? No. I didn't agree to this!" Fury pounded through her. How could she leave everything she loved behind and marry a stranger? How could she marry anybody other than *him*?

Her father's gaze darkened as he crossed the room to her, blood-shot eyes boring into hers. "You will marry him, or else."

Jill stiffened, fear lancing through her chest. "Or else what?" She'd wanted to throw the words in his face, but instead they'd come out as a whisper. After all this time, she still feared his temper, still feared the man who would not hesitate to hurt her.

"Or else I will make sure you're never able to wield a sword again." With that, he stormed from the room.

The next day, her mother's wedding gown had appeared in her room, a threat and reminder all in one.

"I'm afraid the king's been poisoned with hellbane."

The words ripped Jill back to the present, jarring her from her thoughts.

Around the room, whispers swirled and eyebrows rose. Hellbane was incredibly rare, an herb that could only be grown in the Distant

Lands. Slow and painful, it caused seizures and hallucinations until it killed you. And there was no known cure.

Jill glanced at Jack, and their eyes locked, his skin paling at the implications. Their father was dying. But not just that. Someone wanted him dead. Jill looked around the room. Any number of people may have wanted her father dead and gone, but few would have had the means to do it.

"How is this possible? Isn't the king's food and drink checked at every meal?" Ohan-Jin asked, stepping forward. He was head of the Reptile Clan, and his slitted eyes and scaly skin accentuated his glare. He glanced around the room as if the culprit might be among them.

A shiver ran down her spine. The Ohans were one of the most powerful families in Erinya. They controlled one of the last mines still filled with impendium, a resilient and pliable metal perfect for forging strong and light weapons. Her father had come to rely heavily on their weaponry in the war efforts against Carthesia.

The physician, an older gentleman, replied, "It seems the poison came into contact with his skin, and while the effects are slower acting, they're still deadly."

Jill's stomach churned. "What does that mean?" she asked. Everyone looked at her as if they'd nearly forgotten she was there, as if they'd forgotten who she was. Her temper flared, heat lashing at her cheeks.

The physician glanced at Kylian, sweat beading his brow. "It means the king's fate is sealed. He has two months. Maybe three."

Shock rolled through the room, but everyone remained quiet.

A million questions flooded Jill's mind. What would happen to her? Would she still be forced to marry? What would happen to Jack? She didn't think he was ready to be king. He was only seventeen.

"Are we certain there's no cure?" Jack asked, stepping to the foot of the king's bed.

"If there is, I don't know of it," the physician replied.

Everyone's eyes turned to Jack, the future king. Jack's eyes widened, his expression caught somewhere between fear and grief.

"If I may," came the slithering voice of Ohan-Jin as he walked to the head of the king's bed. His silk suit bore the Ohans' insignia: a snake wrapped around a pole, fangs bared. "As you all know, the king and I have been discussing trade dealings now for well over a decade, since before the war began."

An uneasiness settled over the room as people shifted.

"The king has remarked many times how deeply he cares for his son"—the reptilian man looked at Jack, giving him a hollow smile—"but time and again he has wondered if the boy has what it takes to be a king."

Anger flashed across Jack's face as he lunged forward, grabbing the front of the man's suit before shoving him up against the wall.

"How dare you?" Jack shouted, his gaze burning.

Jill's heart pounded as she looked between the two. A slow smile crept up the Ohan man's face. Kylian marched forward and pulled Jack off the man. Poison dripped from Jack's gaze. Jill had never seen her brother so angry before, had never known he was capable of such outbursts.

"Your Highness," Kylian hissed, but Jack only turned on their father's adviser.

"Stay out of this, Kylian," he growled.

Jill stepped forward, pulling her brother back to stand at her side. As uneasy as the Ohans made her, they couldn't afford to make enemies with them either. Reluctantly, Jack let himself be pulled away, his face still burning with black anger.

"As I suspected, you're young, foolhardy, and impulsive," Ohan-Jin said, smoothing out the wrinkles on his suit. "You've confirmed everything your father told me." The man turned back to the room. "Is this the kind of *boy* we want leading our kingdom?"

"Watch your tongue, Ohan," came Ravala's rumbling voice. "You speak too easily words that sound like treason."

"What are you suggesting?" said Kylian, leveling Ohan-Jin with a curious gaze.

"A regent. Until the prince is older." He glanced at Jack. "And wiser."

"And I suppose you think you should be the one to fill that position?" Jack spat out.

"I never said that." Ohan-Jin was calm and confident, neither denying nor admitting he'd been thinking anything along those lines. "I'm merely suggesting a way forward. You are, after all, still quite young to be king."

Jack's jaw clenched, but he remained silent.

Jill's thoughts roiled, discomfort squirming in her chest as she examined all their paths forward. She wasn't sure her brother was ready to be king, but she didn't like the idea of a regent either. A regent would follow through with her father's plans to secure an alliance through her marriage. A regent would mean Jack may never be old enough, or wise enough, to ascend the throne.

A cold hand gripped her wrist, and she jumped, whirling to face her father, lying in his bed. His eyes were wide, and his grip was surprisingly strong.

"Jillianna," he rasped.

Her blood thundered. She wanted to yank her hand back, but she forced herself to remain still, her mouth dry.

"Yes, Father?"

He heaved a strained breath, his face twisting in pain when at last he spoke again. "Save me," he said, then let loose a fit of coughs before looking back at her. "Save me, and I will make you paladin."

She froze, watching as his eyes rolled back and he collapsed into his pillow, asleep once more.

Thick silence wrapped around the group as Jill's mind whirred faster than ever.

Paladin. It was a second chance. Her father was offering her everything she'd ever wanted, if she only saved his life.

"What if we found a cure?" she asked.

"There isn't a cure," Ohan-Jin bit out. "You heard the physician."

Jill's chest tightened, and she glanced at Master Ravala, who gave a subtle nod. It was her turn to step forward.

"There's no *known* cure, but that doesn't mean there isn't one," she said, her blood racing. She could hardly believe her own mouth. She and her father had never been close. But if saving him meant becoming paladin . . .

"The king has only a few months. Where would you even start?" asked Kylian, brow arched.

Jill faltered. She had no idea where she'd start. She knew nothing about medicine, nothing about poisons and herbs and cures. But there had to be something.

She glanced at Jack, whose expression was torn. Perhaps he felt as she did, conflicted. She knew she wasn't the only one who'd been hurt by the king, yet here she was, attempting to save him.

"There may be someone who knows of a cure." The voice that spoke was small, almost childlike, and it sent a fresh wave of anger rolling through Jill as she, along with everyone else, turned to Millie.

Millie still wore the dress she'd worn at the ball, her long black hair cascading down her back, so different from the servant's braid she usually wore.

Jack's head perked as he looked at her. A surge of annoyance flickered through Jill at her brother's interest. It wasn't the first time Jack had taken an interest in one of her maids, and she feared it wouldn't be the last either. But still. Why did he have to be interested in *this* girl?

"Who?" asked Jack.

Millie's gaze flicked around the room, her hands visibly trembling. "I'm not certain it would be of any use." She looked back to Jack, who nodded for her to continue. "But there is a woman I've only heard rumors of. An old apothecary. She's supposed to be very good at her craft. She may have a cure or know of someone who does."

"An old apothecary?" mused Jack. "I didn't know there were any apothecaries left in Erinya. I thought most had fled over the border during the Crusades."

Jill shivered. The Crusades had taken place a decade before she and Jack had been born, but from everything she'd heard, they'd been brutal and bloody. A great drought had swept through the land. Rivers and wells dried up, crops and livestock perished within a matter of weeks, and then the sickness spread.

Jill had often heard fear brought out the worst in people, and never had that been truer than of the Crusades. When the land became diseased, the people looked for someone to blame, and the apothecaries, since they could do nothing to prevent it, were as good a target as any. Many took it upon themselves to rid the land of magic, of anyone connected to it by even the slimmest thread. The results were barbaric.

Any of those who weren't killed fled the kingdom, though some clearly remained, still in hiding to this day.

Jill glanced at Kylian, and his expression was one of interest for once.

"If the rumors I heard are true, she may be able to help. I know a few girls who've gone to her personally," said Millie.

"For what? Love potions and fertility charms?" Jill snapped, irritated. How had Millie found her way into this anyway? A day ago she'd been making Jill's bed, and now she had a say in the king's future.

Millie stiffened, hands balling into fists. An unexpected spark lit her gaze. "More like the Night Flu and Necora."

Jill went cold. Both the Night Flu and Necora were deadly if contracted. Few ever recovered from such ghastly diseases, and the ones who did usually wished they'd died.

"It could be worth looking into," said Master Ravala, glancing at Kylian. Jill bit the inside of her cheek. She may have been the princess, but Kylian Doyle was the one who made the decision in the end, not her.

"It certainly warrants investigation," Doyle said, though something still clearly troubled him.

"I'll go." Jill spoke before anyone could stop her, before anyone could speak ahead of her. She would find this cure, save her father, and become paladin like she'd always planned.

"Jill, are you certain that's wise?" Jack said, turning to her.

"You heard Father. If I save him, he will make me paladin." She gestured to her father and then looked around the room, ignoring Millie. "If there's a chance to save him, there isn't a moment to lose."

Jack's gaze bored into her.

"I must object," said Ohan-Jin. "The princess should stay here, where it's safe. Erinya is filled with many who would gladly take advantage of her."

Anger blinded her as she reached for the blade that wasn't there. Suddenly, her brother's actions made far more sense. She was halfway across the room when Master Ravala stepped between them.

Jill was tempted to shove him. She could already picture her attack on Ohan-Jin: a knee to the groin, and then when he lurched forward, she'd knee him in the head.

"Enough!" Kylian's voice was calm but held a weight she'd never heard before. She turned, teeth still grinding. "Your Highness, I think Ohan-Jin may be right. As the princess, you should stay here, though not because anyone doubts your abilities." He tossed a meaningful glance at the reptile man. "If the king has been poisoned, you and your brother may be targets as well."

"I can do this," she said, straightening. "I am the princess. You may be my father's adviser, but you aren't the only one with power. You cannot make me stay here. My father himself asked me to save him. Would you deny the king's dying wish?"

Kylian regarded her carefully as he rubbed the head of his cane thoughtfully. In her mind, it didn't matter what he decided. She would go with or without the adviser's permission. If she failed and the king died, her brother would be king, not some regent.

She looked at her brother. His face was torn. "Jack, please. Let me go. Let me do this."

"The decision isn't his to make," Ohan-Jin hissed.

"And it isn't yours either," she shot back.

Kylian stared at her. "Fine. You may go. But you'll take Paladin Millie with you."

"What?" Jill and Millie said in unison. Heat rolled through Jill's chest all over again. Under no circumstance would she allow *that maid* to come with her.

"Wait," said Jack, "Millie just became paladin. She needs to be trained before she can be assigned—"

"And the princess is just the one to see to that," said Kylian. "She nearly won the tournament herself, you know."

Eyes flitted between the two girls.

"I'll go too then," said Jack. "He's my father as well."

"With all due respect, Your Highness, that is rather unadvisable," said Kylian. "If something should happen to you, who will ascend the throne?"

"If we are targets, the safest place for us to be is somewhere no one would ever guess." Jack stared out the window as if he was listening to something no one else could hear. His eyes snapped back to Jill's. "Besides, if something happens to me, then Jill will be queen. She would make an excellent queen." He smiled at his sister.

But Jill felt nauseated. *Princess. Traitor. Usurper. Queen.* The words whispered through her mind.

"But I'll make sure that doesn't happen. Don't ever underestimate Jack and Jill."

15

———————

BO

Little Bo-Peep has lost her sheep,
And can't tell where to find them;
Leave them alone, and they'll come home,
Bringing their tails behind them.

lood dripped down Bo's arm, drying around her wrist. She took a deep breath, her vision beginning to blur. Soon she'd be lucky if she could stand at all. It was now or never.

She yanked on the fangs buried in her arm, red crouching at the corners of her vision. They were half a finger long, nearly touching the bone. She squirmed as she shifted, her fingers slick with blood and venom as they oozed down her arm. She bit down on a stick, fighting to keep from passing out.

She hated basilisks.

The small snakes had abnormally large fangs given their size and their venom could be deadly if left untreated. This one had been hiding in the trees when she'd disturbed it, and it had moved so fast she hadn't even seen it until it plunged its fangs deep into the flesh of her arm.

And then, like honeybees lose their stinger, the basilisk lost its fangs and slithered into the shadows as though nothing had happened.

And now here she sat, back pressed to the bark of a tall oak, pulling out the fangs before the venom made its way to her heart. Every movement, every twinge, stung and burned, but she couldn't afford to leave the fangs in there.

Sweat coated her forehead as she paused, taking a deep breath. Basilisk venom was painful, but it would only kill you if you didn't get the fangs out in time. Even so, Bo's body already ached like she was coming down with a fever.

She grabbed the fangs again, took a few shallow breaths, and yanked as hard as she could. The fangs loosened and slid out, covered in green-tinted blood.

The stick in her mouth snapped as she screamed and collapsed on the ground, tears running down her cheeks. For a moment, she lay there, looking up at the branches above her as they swayed in the breeze. She gulped, wondering if it would've been less painful if she'd chopped her arm off instead.

At last, she sat up, blood still leaking from the wound. She would need to clean it and bandage it at some point, but she didn't have time for that yet. She tore a strip of cloth from her tunic and then, with one end in her teeth, tied it around the puncture wounds to keep them from bleeding everywhere. Pain seared up her arm into her shoulder.

She climbed to shaky feet, cursing every last saint she could think of. Her head swam from the venom. She licked her chapped lips and swallowed; she'd need goat urine to counteract the venom. But until she could find a goat, she would continue on her way.

She glanced at the sun through the trees. She was losing daylight fast, which meant they would be active here soon, and she had to find them before then.

Closing her eyes, she listened to nothing but the sound of her own body, of the blood rushing beneath her skin. Slowly, the sound of her pounding heart faded away until she could feel the tenuous connection, the strings that tugged on her mind, guiding her to her flock.

She opened her eyes. They were close. She could sense them, feel them lingering at the corners of her consciousness.

She set out southward after grabbing her crutch to lean on for support. Her clubfoot could be a nuisance at times, but she rarely noticed it anymore. All her life it had been a challenge to overcome, but what challenged her more than her twisted foot was people who thought so little of her.

Sweat dripped down her back as she hiked through the forest, cutting through the foliage. One hand was on her stick, and the other was on the knife she always carried with her. She slowed to a stop and took a few more deep breaths. Perhaps she would need to rest a bit longer before she went after them. But she'd already lost so much time.

She'd heard the reports of terrible creatures attacking an army compound nearby. She knew it was them. They had to feed. But they'd always stayed away from the towns.

Then again, they'd never left her before either.

She remembered waking up to find them gone, but she had no memory of the day before they'd disappeared. And every time she thought back on it, all that remained was a haze.

She cursed, spitting on the ground. If only she could remember that bloody day! Perhaps then she would know why they had left, why they'd succumbed to their instincts instead of listening to her.

She continued moving as the day shifted into evening. Twilight slinked across the land until she walked in the dark. Bo didn't fear the dark though. Unlike other humans, she had heightened senses. In the dark, she could see for miles. She could hear the ants whispering among themselves. She could smell blood on the wind.

She paused, listening. The sound of her heavy breathing filled her ears, but it slowly died to a dull roar. The ants chittered, their tiny legs scraping along the ground. So small they were, yet their tenacity never ceased to amaze her. She wondered what people would be capable of if they lived like ants did.

The wind picked up, carrying the scent of burning campfires, dead bodies, and rotten bog. Her nose curled. She was close to the compound then. Close to her creatures.

A hundred feet later, she saw the end of the tree line and the raised huts that stuck up from the muddy ground like thorns poking through the undergrowth.

Leaning her crutch at the base of a nearby tree, she eased forward, hugging the shadows, heart pounding. Up close she could see the camp had been badly damaged. Bodies lay on the outskirts in a pile near a large bonfire. Half of the huts were crumbling and destroyed, covered in a layer of black char. Ash floated in the air, coating everything it touched.

Bo's stomach churned. *They* had done this.

This was the reason she lived tucked away in the depths of the forest, the reason she spent her days in hiding and her nights controlling where they went and what they fed on. This was the reason she dared not risk coming within fifty miles of any villages or towns.

As she stared ahead, all she felt was anger. Heat blossomed on the back of her neck, her chest roiling. She thought of her mother, a woman who should've protected her daughter, protected herself. Except she hadn't, and now Bo had to clean up her mother's mess.

She was just about to storm from her hiding place when a whisper of voices sliced through the dark night. She froze, inhaling a quiet breath as she listened.

"—received word just this morning that the king has fallen ill, Commander," said a gravelly voice.

"And the prince?" a cold voice asked. The commander, Bo assumed.

"He seeks a cure for his father. They believe sending him away is best for his safety."

A pause. "How interesting. And what of Ohan-Jin?"

"He has planted the idea of a regent among the nobles."

Bo's heart gathered speed. She should not have been hearing this.

"Excellent. I've spoken with Carthesia's representative. They will support our efforts. We need only present them with the prince's head."

"Shall I inform Jihoo?"

"Yes. Dispatch him immediately. And tell no one," said the commander.

A bead of sweat slid down the back of Bo's neck. Here she'd come to investigate the attack from the monsters, and now this? She needed to leave now, to forget this entire conversation.

But what about the prince?

She shook her head. Screw the prince. Screw the king. They didn't mean a thing to her. None of that mattered if she couldn't regain control of the monsters before they destroyed the entire kingdom.

Bo took a hesitant step back. The snap of a twig echoed through the trees, loud enough for a deaf man to hear. Her muscles froze.

She heard the crunch of footsteps a second later, and then a man stood a few feet away, reptilian eyes glaring down at her. His dark green coat told her this was the commander. Behind him stood a reptile man wearing the gray uniform of an Erinyan soldier.

For a breath, they stared at each other. And then the commander shot forward, wrapping a scaly hand around her neck. He lifted her off the ground, his sharpened claws digging into her skin.

"How much did you hear?" he said, his tone even.

She knew it didn't matter how much she'd heard. If he would kill the prince, he would kill her too. Instead, she lifted her good leg, kicking him in the chest with all her might.

His grip loosened, and she dropped to the ground, a shock of pain lancing up her leg. She turned, searching for her crutch. The commander recovered quickly and grabbed for her, taking her to the ground.

"It's no use fighting," he said, his slick voice sliding down her neck.

Bo bucked and flailed, letting every curse she knew fly from her mouth. Swearing had a way of making her feel stronger. She reached for her crutch with one arm while bringing her other elbow back toward the man's face.

He was prepared, though, his grip only tightening as he easily dodged the blow. And then another pair of hands grabbed her, dragging her up before shoving her to her knees.

The soldier stood behind her, one hand with a fistful of hair, the other holding a knife to her throat. Her chest heaved as she let more curses spill from her lips.

"I can see you're going to be a problem," the commander said, rising to his feet to look down on her. He glanced at his man. "Kill her."

The knife bit into her skin, and she screamed.

The ground beneath her gave way as shadows converged. A familiar ear-splitting screech sounded behind her, followed by a hot splash of liquid across the back of her neck.

The commander's eyes widened as he stepped back. Bo rose to her feet and grabbed her crutch, a pool of blood seeping into the ground at the foot of her monster.

It towered behind her, blood dripping from its razor teeth, swaths of darkness whirling around it like smoke as it whispered in and out of form.

It was waiting for her.

"Go!" she shrieked at the monster. Immediately, it obeyed. Shadows twisted as it turned and took off into the forest like a spooked deer.

"You."

She spun back to face the commander. His expression was not one of fear but of interest. She tumbled backward, gripping her crutch like a weapon.

"Leave me," she said, "or I'll call it back."

In truth, she wasn't sure she could. It was a miracle the monster had responded to her at all. The connection between them was growing thinner and thinner the farther away they roamed from her.

"You can control it?"

"I can." *Sort of.* She didn't say that aloud though.

The commander smiled, an eerie look on his scaly face. "Very interesting."

Before she could react, he whipped out a weapon she'd never seen before, metal and wood banded together. And then it collided with the side of her head, and everything went black.

16

JACK

Jack was in the stables, though he couldn't remember how he'd gotten there. The king's finest horses were sheltered away from the common herds and given special treatment by the stable hands. He walked through the stalls, the sharp scent of manure reaching his nose.

He was looking for someone, but he couldn't remember who. His feet moved of their own accord, an invisible force tugging him forward. His heart pounded, and sweat blurred his eyes.

Something was wrong with him. His body ached, and his stomach sloshed like a wine bottle rolling on the deck of a sea-tossed ship.

Voices reached his ears, but they were muffled. One was a young man's, the other female. Some instinct told him to turn around, to walk away, that nothing good could come from knowing who they were.

Instead, he took a step forward.

. . .

JACK WOKE WITH A START, sweat beading down his back. He grasped at the wisps of dreams already receding to the shadowed corners of his mind.

It's nearly dawn, my prince. Did you sleep well?

What do you think?

The Voice smiled, and Jack's heart shuddered.

What was that? Did you show me that?

I did.

What is this? What does it mean?

In time, my prince. When you are ready to face your future. And your past.

Jack growled but didn't respond. He knew the Voice was toying with him like it always did, yet that did nothing to ease the dread swirling inside him. What did that dream mean? Why had it felt so real?

A knock sounded at the door, rousing him from his thoughts. The day before came rushing back to him. The tournament, the ball. *My father.*

And, above it all, the persisting image of Millie in that dress. Just the thought sent his pulse racing. He chided himself. Now was not the time to think about all of that.

His father was dying. Jill was furious for some Saints-forsaken reason, Millie was paladin, and together they were setting out to find a cure for his father.

There was another knock at the door, and Jack leapt out of bed before walking across the room. A year ago, after the Voice had first come to him, he'd dismissed his manservant, which meant he did everything himself now. But he was fine with that. He'd rather do things himself than worry about being caught talking to himself like a lunatic.

Jack opened the door, and his heart flipped.

"Millie, hi!" he said.

Millie wore the same outfit she'd competed in, and her hair was pulled back into a long black braid, dark ringlets attempting to escape.

"Um, Your Highness, hi." She looked to the ground, a flush rising to her cheeks.

Confused, he looked down at himself, only just realizing that he stood shirtless in front of her. He swallowed, suddenly nervous.

"Um, sorry, give me a moment." Before thinking it through, he slammed the door in her face, then spun around his quarters, searching frantically for a shirt.

Are you sure you don't want to invite her in?

Jack didn't respond, heat rising up his neck. Blast it! Why couldn't he find a shirt? He was a prince, for Saints' sake! He should've had a hundred shirts!

He ran to the opposite end of the room and threw on the shirt from the night before, then rushed back to the door. Millie's stunned face greeted him before she smirked.

He leaned against the doorframe, doing his best to hide the sheen of sweat that had formed in his rush to find something to wear.

"Hi," he said again.

Millie smiled. "Hi."

Jack swallowed, his tongue swollen and dry. "Is everything all right?" he asked. He had the distinct impression that something important was supposed to happen, yet all he could think about was the way that Millie's smile was like being shot through with a sunbeam.

"Well, I came to see if you were ready to leave, but it appears not." Millie bit her top lip, fighting back a laugh.

Jack's mind whirled for a second before things clicked into place. His father. The cure. The journey. His mood deflated. He'd promised to meet Millie and Jill at the stables. He must have overslept.

Despite everyone's warnings, Jack was insistent that he go on this journey with them. He didn't care if it left the throne vulnerable. If he was honest, he didn't care too much about finding a cure for his father. But he knew he couldn't let Millie go on a journey alone with his sister. And, if he was really honest, part of him wanted more time with Millie.

"Right," said Jack, nodding. "I'll be down in a minute."

Millie curtsied and turned away, and Jack wished he'd had the guts to tell her to stay.

Take care that you do not get distracted.

Why do you care if I'm distracted?

The Voice was silent, as if it was thinking how best to respond. Perhaps what the Voice didn't know was that Jack could sense its intentions as well as the Voice could sense Jack's. Something linked them together, but Jack had yet to figure out what. After his trip to the Deadwood had been a complete failure, he feared he'd never learn who this Voice was and where it'd come from. And what it wanted.

We are not so different, you know.

Somehow, I doubt that. Jack rummaged around his room, looking for a clean shirt.

You'll see it soon. You and I, we both want the same things.

Jack threw on clean clothes and began packing a bag. *Yeah? And what's that?*

Freedom, Jack. We both want freedom.

Twenty minutes later he was at the stables being greeted by Jill's and Kylian's disapproving frowns. Jill's eyes burned, and he sensed somehow that some of her anger lay with him, though he couldn't imagine why. Her shorter hair still took him by surprise. Her hair had always been so long. He couldn't think of a single haircut she'd ever had.

"Nice of you to show up," she ground out. Jill was always eager to be off early at the start of a journey. He had no doubt she would hold this over his head for the rest of the day.

"Nice of you to wait for me," he said, flashing a smile at his twin sister. He was determined not to let her sour mood rub off on him.

Jill opened her mouth and then shut it, rolling her eyes before marching off to grab her horse. A prickling feeling slid down his spine as he recalled his dream. Even now, as he struggled to piece the snatches of his dream back together, he sensed that he was missing something. Something important.

A thunderous neighing cut through his thoughts, and he looked up to see Millie on top of a dapple-gray mare, her eyes wide as the animal shifted beneath her.

Jack was there in a second, calming the horse with a few sugar cubes he'd swiped from the kitchens, patting the beast on its chest. The horse stilled, and Jack glanced up at Millie as her fingers twisted in the reins.

A thought occurred to him. "Have you ever ridden a horse before?"

She swallowed and nodded. "Yes, but I was never very good at it."

"Well, try to relax. They can sense when you're nervous. Luna will take good care of you."

Millie nodded, but Jack could tell she remained uncertain. He was just about to say something more when a curt voice interrupted.

"If you two are done, we need to be going."

Jack turned to see Jill walking alongside her own horse, a dark blue stallion named Adelram. With a quick movement, her foot was in the stirrup and she was on her horse.

A surge of annoyance shot through him as he went to grab his own horse, which had already been saddled by one of the stable hands. He didn't understand what had gotten into Jill recently. He knew she'd wanted to win the competition, but she seemed even angrier than usual. And now she wanted to save their father? He knew she wanted to be paladin, but at what cost?

His stomach clenched as guilt clawed at him. It wasn't that he wanted his father dead, but he thought of their last conversation, of his father's threats. With his father gone, Jack would be king, and he could do whatever he wanted.

Unless they place a regent on the throne.

That won't happen.

And who is going to make sure of that? With your father ill and the heir absent, anything could happen to your kingdom while you're away.

Jack didn't answer. He didn't want to think anything about it. The truth was, he knew that becoming king would mean a trip to the Distant Lands wouldn't happen for a long time, not until the dust had settled and his reign was secure. And by then he would be pressured into taking a queen and siring an heir.

He swallowed, glancing over at Millie, who was riding out of the stables and down the boulevard. With the sun rising behind her, light glinted off her hair. An incandescent halo floated around her brow like a crown before it vanished.

He blinked once. Twice. What had he just seen? Had that been a trick of the light? Or something more?

The Voice sneered, ***You really don't know anything, do you, boy?***

Jack mounted his horse, heart thumping painfully as he followed Millie and his sister.

Know what?

Just where do you think the girl got those powers?

17

DAVID

David stirred the boiling pot of stew, onions, and squash wafting in the little hut they'd raided. Asif had told them it belonged to the Samyr family, who'd left a week prior, after the first attack.

"Where did they go?" Grimzy asked as the feline boy scarfed down his stew.

David glanced up at the mountain man, who was far too big for the hut they were in. Even sitting, his head nearly reached the ceiling.

When at last Asif finished his bowl, he looked up, cat eyes flicking back and forth between the two of them. He swallowed, one of his ears twitching.

"I told you. They went to the Lost Tribe." Irritation fluttered across the boy's features as he stared at them, and David couldn't help noticing how his eyes strayed back to the pot.

David stretched out a hand for the bowl, and Asif gave it back eagerly, clearly hoping for a refill.

David paused, doing his best to hold the kid's attention. "You mentioned that earlier. What is the Lost Tribe?"

The kid's eyes left the bowl long enough to narrow in confusion. "What do you mean? I thought everyone knew about the Lost Tribe?"

David glanced at Grimzy, and it was clear he had no idea either. Apprehension swirled in the pit of his stomach. Erinya was filled with many tribes and clans and peoples. Few of them agreed on anything. A new tribe forming could mean the start of another civil war, and with Carthesia pushing farther into Erinya's borders, David could see the land splintering like his own skin.

"What is it?" David asked.

"For everyone who's lost something, or someone . . ." The kid paused, the weight of his words sinking like a boulder in a lake. "Most have lost their homes and land in the war. But now, with the creatures . . ." He didn't finish, nor did he need to.

A weight slammed into David's chest, choking the air from his lungs. They may have called it the Lost Tribe, but he knew what it really was: a refugee camp. It shouldn't have surprised him. There were more refugees every day, but he hated the thought that there were enough to form a new tribe.

David handed Asif another bowl of stew and watched as he slurped it down, taking in the boy's ragged appearance. With dirt smeared on his face and his cotton clothing torn, it was clear the boy had been on his own for a while. The boy had said it was just him and his sister.

Tamas. Orphans.

David recalled what Luca had told him about the Feline Clan's belief about orphans, that they were bad luck and that their parents had died because the children had summoned evil spirits to kill them. Because of this, orphans were not permitted in certain places, and anyone accused of helping an orphan was ostracized by the clan.

David's blood boiled as he looked at the boy, who'd been on his own long before anyone in the village had ever left. David knew the feeling of not being wanted, of being unloved. It was far more painful than any wound he'd ever suffered.

After the kid had eaten four bowls of stew, he curled up in the corner and fell asleep, his soft snores rumbling through his body like a purr.

The fire burned low in the center of the hut, casting ominous shadows around them. On the walls hung scrolls painted with symbols David barely recognized. While many of the animal clans had evolved over the years, the Feline Clan clung tightly to their old beliefs of spirits and Saints, regarding their patron, Saint Nadia, as one of the greatest beings in Erinya's history.

David sighed. "What do we do, Grimzy? We can't take this kid with us, and we can't leave him here."

Grimzy nodded, his bronze skin darker in the dimming light of the fire. "I don't know. But something is changing, even now. There is something shifting in the earth, the stars. I fear these creatures are simply the beginning."

David swallowed, heart thumping. "The beginning of what?"

Grimzy's gaze locked on his. "The rise of the new Saints."

"You can't make me!" the boy shouted as he pounded the back of Grimzy's shoulders. It was nearly dawn, and the birds were waking, calling out to one another as they made their way out of the little village.

Despite all their arguments, Asif had insisted he stay behind, leaving them no choice but to have Grimzy carry him over his shoulders like a rag doll.

"Let me go!" he cried again, arching his back. David knew the boy must have been nearly twelve or thirteen, but in Grimzy's broad arms he looked like a toddler. And his behavior wasn't helping.

"We can't, kid," David said. "It's not safe for any of us here."

"I. Don't. Care. I'm not leaving without my sister!" he said, his face red from straining to pry himself from Grimzy's grasp.

A shiver cut through David's heart. Surely this kid was old enough to know that if the search party hadn't returned with his sister by now, it likely never would. But as he stared at the kid struggling and straining, David couldn't bring himself to tell him that. Soon enough, he would figure it out on his own.

"I'm sorry, kid. I really am. But I'm not leaving without you. Now be quiet, or you'll lead the monsters right to us." David pulled his cloak a little tighter. The weather here was not rainy like it had been near the border, but a sharp breeze blew through the valley, as if even the wildwinds could not leave this place fast enough.

The kid fought for miles, but he was no match for the mountain man's strength. In fact, Grimzy didn't struggle with the task at all. Finally, after hours of kicking and squirming, Asif stilled, and David couldn't be certain the kid hadn't fallen asleep.

"You know, even if we find a safe place for the kid, he might just run back here," Grimzy said, breaking the silence that had fallen.

David soured. "I know. But we couldn't leave him there."

"Why not? He was doing fine on his own without us."

David turned to look up at the behemoth, incredulous. "The kid was starving and exhausted. Sooner or later, one of those things would have come for him too."

"What will we do with him then?" Grimzy asked, raising an eyebrow.

David sighed in response. He had no idea. He couldn't very well hunt down these creatures with a loudmouth kid who could barely swing a sword, much less actually fight. But he feared leaving him on his own. The boy was almost as stupid as David himself had been as a kid.

David stopped and turned, looking at Asif again. "Put him down."

Grimzy glared at him.

"Please, *Paladin* Grimzy."

The mountain man smirked and set the boy gently on the ground. Sure enough, he'd fallen asleep. David stared at him a moment as he slept. He looked almost peaceful. David opened his canteen and splashed water in the kid's face.

Immediately, Asif sat up, wild-eyed and wet, panting like a dog. When it was clear Asif understood where he was, he glared at David, a curse moments from his lips.

"You wanna save your sister, yes?" David asked before the feline boy could speak.

Asif's eyes focused on him as muddy water dripped down his scowling face, his pointed ears twitching. "Of course."

David tucked his canteen back into his belt and knelt on the ground, then grabbed a large stick and tossed it at the boy. "Then, for starters, never let your guard down." The stick thumped the kid on the head and fell back into the sand.

David grabbed another stick of equal weight and size and motioned for the kid to stand. For a moment, he thought the boy might simply run back the way they'd come. But there was something in the boy's green eyes, a fire and fury that burned bright with longing. David recognized that look. He knew what it felt like to want more than this world had to offer.

Asif grabbed the stick and rose to his feet.

"First, tell me one thing. Do you want to save your sister, or do you want to be a hero?"

The boy cast him a wary glance. "I just want to save my sister."

"Good. I don't have time for heroes."

They arrived at the Lost Tribe the next day. Makeshift tents were crowded together, and campfires burned low. Dust-covered people wandered through the narrow walkways between tents, aimless and apathetic as they carried pitiful bundles of firewood and large jugs of grimy water. Despite so many people living in close quarters, a silence had settled over the camp—a silence that made David's skin crawl. David ground his teeth together. A new sort of anger itched through his body, spreading like a rash.

"Is there a tavern nearby? I think I need a drink."

18

MILLIE

illie had lived her entire life in the Citadel, with its tiered city centers descending the mountain like a waterfall of domed roofs, white marble buildings, and pink-paved pathways. And at the top, overlooking the Ataran Sea, sat the king's palace, gleaming with green and gold spires.

It would take them nearly a day just to leave the Citadel, winding in a spiral down through the four tiers of the city. Which each new level they descended, the wind blew colder and the colors dulled. Instead of the bright and airy feeling at the heart of the Citadel, dilapidated gray buildings stared back at her.

As the sun slipped down in the west, the lanterns in the lower town were being lit, doors were being locked, and Millie felt the silence press on her like an iron weight.

Not for the first time, she wondered how Doon was doing. She remembered how pale he'd looked, how bloodshot his eyes had been. An icy fist squeezed around her heart. Her mother had died when she was ten, her father before she was born. Doon was all the family she had left.

She would not lose him too.

All she had to do was find a cure for the king and maybe her brother as well. She could only hope that helping the royal siblings and saving the king would be enough to reopen her brother's case and prove his innocence. But she feared the time it would take. She couldn't be sure how much time her brother had left. If he spent his last days alone in that prison cell, she would never forgive herself.

Wrapping the reins tighter around her hands, she urged her horse faster in an effort to catch up to Jill. Her stomach swooped as the horse obeyed and trotted forward, a sensation she still wasn't used to. Behind her, Jack plodded along on his horse, brow furrowed.

As her horse caught up to Jill's, her hands began to shake. Two months she'd served the princess, and Millie's nerves had yet to settle around her. Always she waited for the day that she would mess up and the princess would dismiss her. Or worse.

She swallowed hard, pulse racing as she looked over at Jill. "Your Highness?" Millie's voice shook.

Although she must have known that Millie's horse walked beside hers, Jill slid her eyes toward Millie without ever turning her head. "Yes?" she replied curtly.

Millie nearly lost her nerve but pulled the reins tighter until the leather dug into her skin, a reprieve from the tightening she felt in her throat.

"I just wanted to apologize for . . . the other day." It was a pathetic apology, and they both knew it. Millie knew that Jill wanted to be paladin more than anything, more than breath itself. And Millie had taken that from her. The guilt ate away at her like a flame to paper.

The clopping of horse hooves filled the air as Jill's gaze became fixed on the road ahead of them.

"You lied to me," she said, her voice as sharp as the blades she wielded. "You asked for the day off, but you failed to mention that it was so you could compete."

Millie bit her lip, a lump rising in the back of her throat. "Would you have let me go if you'd known?"

The princess was quiet for so long that Millie thought she wouldn't answer.

"No," she said at last, still refusing to look at her. "You're a maid, not a paladin. You're only going to get yourself killed." With that, she spurred her horse faster, leaving Millie behind.

Like a dam bursting, the tears started to fall. She barely choked back a sob as all her fears cascaded and tumbled into one another. Perhaps the worst part of it all was that Millie knew the princess was right. Given enough time, she was bound to get herself killed, power or not. She knew nothing about fighting. Despite the fact that her own brother had been a stable hand for years, she could barely mount a horse without help.

If she were braver, she would have turned around and made her way back to the only home she'd ever known. She'd been born a maid. Why should she be anything else?

A wildwind wound through the main road they were on, twisting in a vibrant hue of orange and red. Unlike an ordinary wind, the wildwinds blew wherever they pleased, leaving a trace of dust wherever they went. It zipped through the street, zigzagging like a spooked animal fleeing from a predator.

Chills ran up Millie's spine as she watched the wildwind spiral into a gray cottage and smash into a pile of golden dust, never to move again.

Jack sidled up beside her on his own steed. She realized that she'd brought the horse to a halt, puffy eyes focused on the place where the wildwind had died.

"We should keep moving," he whispered. "We don't want to be caught in the lower town after dark."

Dragging her gaze away, she kicked her horse like the princess had, doing her best to wipe the tears from her eyes without alerting Jack. It was humiliating how easily she was brought to tears, how every moment of her life seemed like one careful step after another. Always she waited for something to go wrong.

"How long have you worked in the palace?" Jack asked, bringing her back to the present.

She glanced over at him and found his dark eyes studying her. She looked back down at the mare she rode. "I've lived there my whole life. Started working when I was ten."

"Really? How come I've never seen you before?"

A sudden tightness gripped her chest. She'd seen Jack and Jill growing up, had watched as they and the other noble children played in the grand halls or hid in the king's vast library, but never had she been allowed to play with them. Because she was a maid. The princess had said so herself.

"You have, but I was one of many maids. Why would you remember me?"

She could feel him staring at her. "I'm not sure how I could forget you."

Her face burned. She'd have been lying if she said she wasn't flattered, but this hardly felt like the appropriate time to be talking about things like this. The king was on his deathbed, and so was her brother for that matter.

And then there was Jill.

"Your Highness?" she asked, unable to meet his gaze any longer.

"Please, Millie. Call me Jack."

"You're still my prince," she said, voice solemn.

"And as your prince, I command you to call me Jack."

Millie bit the inside of her cheek, eyes focusing on the back of Jill's head. No doubt she could hear every word of their conversation, and still she didn't bother to look back. Millie suspected the princess would have greatly preferred to see to this mission on her own, without the help of Jack or the deadweight that Millie was.

"Forgive me, Your Highness. It's just that we each have our place, and I think we'd do well to stay in them." Millie's blood thrummed beneath her skin. Perhaps she was overstepping, or perhaps the words were completely unnecessary. Still, she didn't trust the strange swooping of her stomach every time Jack was nearby, and she felt something needed to be said sooner rather than later.

"With you as paladin and me as future king, your place is with me."

Millie shook her head. "My place was as a maid. I overstepped when I dared compete." Before she could let him respond, she kicked her horse faster, zipping ahead of him the way Jill had done to her.

Maybe, if she'd known her place, she wouldn't have been here now.

Two days later, they plodded along a worn dirt path that ran beside the Rose River. Pink waters crashed against rocks, foaming and swirling before following the current out to sea. Tall willows blew in a gentle breeze, and if Mille hadn't known better, she would have thought it almost peaceful.

But Jill had hardly uttered a word that she didn't have to, Millie's legs ached from riding, and her worries only grew with every second that passed. Her thoughts turned back to Doon and the sickness that racked his body.

She'd heard many things about this apothecary, about her ability to cure illnesses and diseases. She must know of something that could cure Doon.

"Paladin Millie," came Jack's voice, a hint of playfulness in his tone. Millie's stomach churned as she glanced at Jill.

"Yes, Your Highness?"

He rolled his eyes and then smiled at her, a dimple tugging at his cheek. She smiled back despite herself.

"What would you say to a little wager?"

She frowned. Of all the things she'd expected him to say, a wager hadn't been one of them. "What kind of wager?"

He leaned over, dropping his voice to a whisper. "I bet I can toss ten acorns into my sister's hood without her noticing." He raised an eyebrow, daring her to oppose him.

"There's no way," she whispered back. "She'll know."

"Then you have nothing to lose."

Millie glanced between the royal twins, nerves singing. "What do I get if I win?"

Jack grinned, his dark eyes glimmering with mischief. "Why, you would get the joy of besting a prince in a wager, of course."

"And if I lose?"

"How about a kiss?"

Millie's eyes widened. "No!" she nearly shouted before realizing she'd responded a bit too quickly.

"I didn't realize kissing me would be such a horrible experience," he said, mocking offense.

She swallowed, heat rising at the back of her neck. "I mean, that just doesn't seem entirely fair."

"You're right. You should get a kiss if you win too." He winked, and her heart flipped despite itself.

"No kissing."

"You're no fun." He smirked, seeming pleased that he'd gotten under her skin. "All right, how about if I lose, I set up camp by myself tonight, and if you lose, you have to answer whatever question I ask."

Millie stared up at the prince. She knew she shouldn't agree, shouldn't even entertain the idea, and yet . . .

"Deal. But I still don't think you can do it."

Fast as a blink, Jack's hand twitched as he tossed something into the air. The acorn landed in the hood that hung at Jill's back.

Jack held up a single finger, clearly amused with himself. Millie shook her head, though she couldn't hide her amusement either.

Jack tossed another acorn. It landed with the faintest click inside Jill's hood. This time Jill stiffened, looking around.

When at last she relaxed, Jack tossed another. And another. On the eighth acorn, Jill spun back to look at them, eyes narrowed.

"What are you two doing?" she said.

"Nothing." Jack morphed his expression into such genuine confusion that for a second even Millie almost believed he was innocent.

The princess glared between the two of them as if trying to determine which of them she hated more. Millie figured she already knew the answer to that question.

At last, she faced forward, fuming. Jack turned to Millie, holding the last two acorns in his hand.

Millie shook her head.

Jack nodded back and then tossed the acorns at the same time. Both landed in Jill's hood. At that, Jill perked up and spun her horse around to face them.

"What—" She reached her hand into her hood, pulling out a fistful of acorns. Jill's face turned bright red as she threw the acorns at them. "Is this some kind of joke to you?"

"Well, it is a bit funny," said Jack, smiling at Millie.

Millie, however, did not find it nearly as humorous as she had a few seconds ago.

"I *knew* this was going to happen!" Jill fumed. "I just *knew* you were going to screw off like you always do."

"It was just a joke, Jilly. Calm down."

"Don't call me Jilly! You know I hate that nickname." Jill's voice rose, a crescendo of irritation. "We are on a mission to find the only thing that might be able to save our father, and all you care about is messing around and flirting with yet another one of my maids."

Millie felt like she'd been slapped in the face. She knew the princess didn't like her, maybe even hated her, but hearing her say it out loud hurt worse than she'd expected.

"She's not a maid anymore, Jill. She's a paladin." Jack's voice grew serious, the teasing gone from his voice.

Jill sneered at Millie, and Millie found she couldn't meet Jill's gaze. "This girl is a liability. I would've won that tournament, and she knows it. Don't you, *Paladin Millie?*"

Millie's throat tightened. She wanted to scream and cry and yell at the girl she'd served for the past two months. She wanted to tell her about her sick brother who'd been wrongfully accused of murder. She wanted to tell her about her dead mother and her life as a servant in the palace. She wanted to tell her that she understood what it was like to feel trapped in a life you had no control over, to feel like everyone else had the upper hand except you.

Instead, she slumped in the saddle, too afraid to say everything she wanted to.

"That's what I thought." Jill grabbed at her hood again, pulling out another acorn and staring at it before tossing it to the ground without a second thought. Millie got the distinct impression that Jill thought more of that acorn than she did of her.

19

JILL

Once Jill had made up her mind, she knew there was no turning back. She couldn't—no, she *wouldn't*—travel with Millie and her brother. Every longing glance and sideways smile made her ill. Jack had been so quick to accept Millie as paladin, as if she hadn't been a maid just a week ago. As if she hadn't taken everything from Jill.

They camped that night along the Rose River, and the crashing water did nothing to soothe her frayed nerves. The moon was high in the sky before Jill felt certain Millie and her brother were fast asleep. She packed her horse as silently as possible, her fingers stiff from the chill in the air as she tightened the saddle. She drew a shaky breath, considering once more if this was the wisest decision.

She shook her head. She knew it wasn't, but she no longer cared. The acorns had been the final straw. If Jack wouldn't take this mission seriously, then Jill would continue on her own.

She stuck her foot in the stirrup and swung her leg over the horse, then rode away from their camp. Behind her, she could hear Millie's delicate snores until they faded into nothing.

Jill almost felt sorry for Mille. The poor girl would likely die a tragic death without any sort of proper training, but that was her own fault. If her ability had been enough to win the tournament, then it would have to be enough to keep her alive.

Jill shivered as she recalled the feeling of being covered in spiders, of hundreds of legs skittering over her skin, of the panic she'd felt as she'd stumbled and rolled around in panic, fear suffocating her. She had never felt so weak before. So weak and so afraid.

Jill's hatred burned brighter. She didn't know what Millie was, but it wasn't natural. She understood why the apothecaries had been killed and chased out of Erinya. There was something dark and unnatural about the magic that belonged to Millie, and it disturbed her that the girl had been waiting on her all this time, hiding that kind of secret. If she'd known what Millie was, she'd have sent her away long ago.

The sun ascended slowly, as if Jill's own dark thoughts kept back the light. But eventually it rose, its warm rays cutting through the gossamer trees. The Ravaged Wood had long ago been hunted to the near extinction of its creatures. The warthogs no longer tussled in the undergrowth; their teeth were instead used for jewelry and face powders. The merry firebirds no longer crooned their jaunty tunes that warmed the forest. The beetles and brittlebacks no longer danced in the cool of the shady rocks.

It was altogether quiet. She supposed there was a reason it was called the Ravaged Wood.

And the quiet left her mind to wander into forbidden territory. The what-ifs pounded on the doors of her brain. The worries toppled into one another, a rising tide of frustration and fear building inside her.

What if we don't find a cure in time? What if the council calls for a regent? Are they right? Is Jack even ready to be king? Why am I risking everything to save my father?

She couldn't deny that it would be simpler to let him die, to fight for Jack to take the throne and convince him not to marry her off like their father had planned. But was she really so heartless as to let her father just die? Or was there more to it that she couldn't bring herself to admit?

Her entire relationship with her father had been characterized by one disappointed look after another. Her memories were riddled with disapproving lectures and harsh words, bitterness laced into every interaction they'd had. For once, she wished he'd see who she really was, what she was truly capable of, that she was more than a bargaining chip to be married off.

But he'd never see that if he died.

She tightened her grip on the reins and kicked, urging her horse into a canter. An hour later, Jill stepped out of the dark of the Ravaged Wood and onto the North Plains. It was a barren land where nothing but silt grass grew, and one of the ancient Rock Giants stood in the distance, a waterfall pouring from its open mouth and evaporating into mist before it ever hit the ground. The Rock Giants were scattered all over Erinya, giant stone statues said to come to life every hundred years. Jill wasn't sure she believed that but felt uneasy anyway as she passed it, the giant towering a hundred feet above her. The sooner she left the plains, the better she'd feel.

Dark fell as Jill found herself in the first village, a small town called Kylo. It was a measly farming town with a mix of humans, inkwells, and animal clans. As she roamed the streets, she saw boarmen and women, tusks jutting from their mouths, and a few inkwells, their tattoos depicting sad images of farming and death. Something pricked her chest as she observed the ramshackle huts barely standing, such a stark contrast to the Citadel's vast marble structures and gleaming domed rooftops.

Jill kept her head low as she wound her way through the dusty streets, walking her horse to give it a break until she found herself standing in front of the Laughing Dog Inn. While the rest of the village was shrouded in a quiet darkness, light poured from the establishment. She pushed open the creaking door, stepped inside, and was immediately greeted by the smell of grease and stale beer and the sharp scent of fernroot smoke, a pungent weed that dulled the senses when crushed and smoked.

In the corner, a feline man played a fiddle as a chorus of drunkards sang along to the endless ballad of "The Maiden's Feet," an old folk song about a prince discovering on his wedding night that his bride had the feet of a donkey. Each new verse slurred into the next as the rowdy group sang in the center of the inn, beer sloshing from their mugs as they described the maiden's body parts, proclaiming how beautiful she'd be if only for her feet.

Most of the tables were filled with farmers and fishermen, dusty and drunk on cheap mead to escape the toil of everyday life. Some played cards, and some simply sat in silence, as if wondering what the point of it all was.

Jill grimaced. She knew the feeling.

She made her way to the bar, where a balding inkwell man with sausage fingers was busy yelling at a young maid, who looked on the verge of tears. On the back of the man's neck was a tattoo of blood dripping into a puddle.

Jill cleared her throat.

The man turned, annoyed. "Yes?"

She held her head high and looked the man in the eyes; she'd found this tactic often unnerved men into doing just what she asked. "I need a room, a hot bath, and a meal delivered to that room."

The man gave her a once-over, his eyes narrowing on her fine traveling clothes. "We have no rooms and no hot water. Take a seat, and Ari here will get you a meal." He gestured to the maid he'd been yelling at. "Saints know it's the only thing she's good for."

The young girl bowed her head, dark hair covering her face, but Jill didn't miss the tear that slid down her cheek and landed on the floor.

A spark flared in Jill's chest as she looked back at the man, a smug grin spread across his bloated face. "Apologize to the girl," she said.

The man raised his eyebrows. "Excuse me?"

"I think you heard me, but in case you're deaf as well as dumb, I'll repeat myself just this once. Apologize. Now."

Blood flooded the man's cheeks. "Just who do you think you are? Telling me how to treat *my* maid." The man hacked, and a glob of spit landed on her cheek.

She stood there for a moment, stunned. And then anger burned through her veins like a torch dropped in a dry field. She wiped the spit from her cheek and threw a fist at the man's face. An ear-popping crunch rang out as her knuckles made contact with the man's nose, and blood began spurting like a fountain.

The man stumbled backward, momentarily dumbfounded as he pressed a hand to his face. "Bloody *witjka!*" he cried. *Demon witch.* He rushed forward, arms out, but she easily dodged and stuck out her foot. The man tumbled to the floor.

Everyone in the pub was looking at them now, perhaps wondering if they should intervene, and it occurred to her that she probably shouldn't draw too much attention to herself. *Too late for that now.*

The man rose to his feet and glared at her, blood dripping down his chin and onto his hairy chest. He raised a hand. Despite his strength, Jill caught it easily. She twisted his wrist until it popped, then dropped the man back onto his knees. She leaned forward, unable to quell the delight of triumph blazing through her. "I'm not going to ask again."

The door burst open behind her, and a rush of cool air blew across her back, followed by the sounds of boots and metal. She knew before she glanced back what she'd see: Erinyan soldiers, a fire-breathing lion emblazoned on the front of their uniforms.

"Let him go," one of them said, his voice much higher than she would have expected from a soldier.

"No," she said, indifferent. "Not until he does what I say."

The man looked up at her, a mix of rage and fear battling within him. Rage won. "Never," he said, his teeth coated red.

Without a second thought, Jill brought her fist down on him, her knuckles colliding with his nose again, sending a fresh wave of blood pouring down his face.

The soldiers behind her surged forward. Jill released the man from her grasp and spun, drawing both her swords in one fluid motion. A feline soldier came at her, his overly large sword heavy in his hands. Jill easily knocked the blade from his grip and kicked him in the chest, sending him toppling to the ground. She couldn't spare a thought for how young he looked, his acne-riddled face, or the fear so blatantly scrawled across it. But she took the details in, as she'd been trained to do her entire life.

She whirled on the second soldier, this one taller and stronger and wielding an axe instead of a sword. He swung at her, but she caught the head with one of her swords and shoved, throwing him off-balance. He'd underestimated her strength.

"Didn't expect I'd know what I'm doing, did you?" she taunted.

A flush rose up his cheeks as he swung again, wilder than before, emboldened despite his stumble. He would be harder to throw off this time. She brought her swords up in an X, once again catching the axe at its head. She tried to shove him back, but he was prepared, pushing back against her, nearly driving her to her knees.

Sweat beaded on her forehead as a flurry of movement drew her attention. *The third soldier.*

He came at her, swinging his sword. Her heart somersaulted as she realized she could not move without bringing the axe down on herself, and she was not strong enough to shove the second soldier away.

Tell them who you are.

She opened her mouth to speak, but a clash of metal rang in her ears. A fourth man, clad in black and covered in scars, knocked the sword from the third soldier's hands.

Her strength renewed, she dropped to the ground and swung her leg into the soldier's knees, toppling him in a graceless heap.

"Behind you!" the scarred man cried, and she spun in time to see the acne-covered kid. Having abandoned the too-heavy sword, he now held a wicked-looking knife curved like an eagle's claw. She thought it was a much wiser choice for him.

He slashed at her once. Twice. Each time she dodged, but he was driving closer, backing her into a corner. She knew what he was trying to do. But it wouldn't work.

He slashed at her again, but this time she was ready, catching the blade in its crook with her own and once again sending his weapon flying. The feline soldier stood still, cat eyes wide as the point of her blade touched below his chin, pressing into his soft flesh.

Saints, he's young. Hardly more than a boy. She was at least several years his senior. And yet here he was, conscripted into her father's army, destined to fight and die for a war he'd had no part in starting.

It was at that moment she noticed the silence pressing in as everyone in the room grew still, waiting to see what she would do. Her eyes passed from the boy to the bloody pub owner to the young maid huddled in the corner. Jill glanced at the other soldiers, jaws tight and nostrils flaring, until her gaze settled on the scarred man who'd stepped in to help her. There was something strange about him, his gaze both curious and wary and maybe even amused.

"All I wanted was an apology," she said, her voice tired. "And a hot bath." She looked back at the maid, whose brown eyes were wide as she stared at her. "You should go."

Without protest, the maid slipped out a back door, all too keen to obey. Jill turned her gaze back on the boy in front of her. He was shaking like willow grass in the wind. "You should go too. I doubt your commander would be happy to know you were in a position like this."

The boy nodded, and she lowered her blade, eyes never leaving the soldiers as they reluctantly gathered their things and left, shoulders slumped in defeat. Some part of her had imagined it would feel gratifying to see her own father's soldiers cower in defeat by her hand, but instead it left a bitter taste in her mouth. They were supposed to be fighters, warriors. Instead, they were cowards bearing her father's insignia.

She turned back to the owner. After fishing a few coins from her pockets, she threw them to the ground at his feet. "You may want to get that taken care of." She pointed to his nose and the blood already crusting to his face. "And find yourself a new maid."

She turned and walked out the door. She'd find somewhere else to rest for the night.

20

BO

Bo's head pounded, her hands were tied, and she was pissed. Without having to open her eyes, she knew she was on a horse, bound and headed for who knew where. Her entire body ached, and every bounce and jostle of the horse sent a fresh wave of anger rolling through her.

She squinted, doing her best to peek at her surroundings without alerting anyone she was awake. Her horse was tied to another, and a man rode beside her, armor glinting in the light. The gray scales on his face gave him a sickly demeanor, and his shifting eyes never rested on anything long.

Another rider trotted behind them. This man was fully human and missing an eye. He carried one of the strange weapons she'd seen the commander with. Though she had no idea what it was, she knew it was dangerous.

"How much longer?" grumbled the man behind them.

"A day. Maybe less," said the reptile man.

"What's so important about this girl anyway?" the grumbler asked.

"You're not being paid to ask questions."

The grumbler huffed but said nothing.

Bo inhaled slowly, doing her best to get her bearings. She was nowhere near where she'd been knocked unconscious. She tried to call the creatures, but she could sense they were too far away. She was on her own.

Being careful to move as slowly as possible, she wiggled her wrists, testing how tight her bonds were. Thankfully, they were loose. These morons must have supposed that since she was unconscious it didn't matter.

Their mistake.

It wasn't the first time she'd been kidnapped. Once, she'd been caught trying to steal food from a raiders' camp across the border. They'd tied her to a tree without bothering to check to see if she'd had any weapons on her. A nine-year-old girl probably hadn't seemed like a threat to them. She'd spent the entire evening being as annoying as possible, so when everyone fell asleep that night, she pulled out her knife, sliced the ropes, and took off.

She'd hoped that, by being annoying, they wouldn't bother to come looking for her, and they never did.

This, however, was different. She had information this time, the kind of information that could start wars in the wrong hands. Too bad she didn't care whatsoever. All she wanted was to find her monsters and retreat into the shadows of the forest.

As slowly as she was able, she eased one of her hands out of the rope that bound her wrists. She could deal with the other hand later. All that really mattered was getting enough distance between her and her captors before they realized what had happened.

Lucky for her, they hadn't bothered to bind her feet.

Reaching a hand up, she grabbed the horse's mane and sat up, whipping a leg around to straddle the steed before digging her heels into the beast's ribs. Immediately, the horse broke into a run. The rope tying the horses together snapped as she took off.

Bo had only ridden a few times before, and that was painfully obvious now. Without a saddle, she clung to the horse for dear life, willing it to go faster while praying she was strong enough to keep from flying off. Curses and shouts were lost in the wind behind her.

She leaned forward, fingers tangled in the horse's mane, the world a blur of color around her. She knew she needed to go somewhere, but she had no idea *where* she was. And the men behind her were getting closer.

Desperate, she yanked on the horse's mane as hard as she could, wheeling it around to face her pursuers. Fear threatened to overwhelm her as she charged forward, hoping to take them by surprise and then escape.

Surprise registered on the men's faces. They were getting closer. Either they would have to let her pass, or they would collide. She willed them to let her through, to let her go.

When she'd nearly reached them, the grumbler panicked and moved aside. A rush of relief flooded through her before something slammed against her chest, sending her toppling off the back of the horse.

She hit the ground with a bone-shaking thud that knocked the air from her lungs. For a moment, she struggled to breathe, panic racing through her veins.

She had to get up, to run, to fight. She couldn't be taken. She would fight them until they killed her.

The reptile man stood over her on his horse, looming like an oppressive guard tower. Irritation pinched his features. His yellow eyes filled with loathing. She sensed the only reason he didn't kill her was because of his orders.

"That didn't end well, now did it?" he taunted her.

She rose to her elbows, prepared to pull him off his horse if need be.

A click stopped her, and she turned to see the other man with his strange weapon pointed at her head. She froze, uncertainty clawing at her insides.

"Do you know what this weapon does?" the reptile man asked, his voice smooth.

She gritted her teeth, her tongue swelling with blood inside her mouth. She must have bitten it at some point during her escape attempt. She shook her head reluctantly.

"I thought not. This weapon could revolutionize warfare. Too bad even the king doesn't know of its existence." He nodded to the grumbler.

He lifted the weapon, aiming at something off in the distance, and a loud bang rattled her ears. Half a second later, one of the trees sported a gaping hole, sap dripping from it like blood.

Her ears rang, head spinning. What had just happened?

"I have orders to bring you in alive. The commander thinks you might be useful yet," said the reptile man. "But if you try to run again, your head will look like that tree over there."

Bo swallowed back her rage. She didn't know who these men were or what they wanted with her. All she wanted was to keep the monsters from hurting more people. But she couldn't do that if she was held hostage by men with weapons like that.

Her chest heaved. Despite it all, she still wanted nothing more than to whack the man over his head with her crutch. Many times. Until his head hurt as badly as hers did. No, worse than hers did. She would make him pay.

"Tie her up. Tighter. And bind her feet as well. We won't make that same mistake again."

RAW FLESH CIRCLED Bo's wrists, the coarse rope digging deeper and deeper into her skin. The venom from the snake bite was wearing off, but it had left her feeling terrible. She'd nearly forgotten it in all the chaos.

As day yawned into night, the scenery around them changed. What had been fields and pastures turned to rocky plateaus and cavernous outcrops. Vaguely, she was aware of the light of a town of some sort off in the distance as they wound their way down a worn path. Rotten huts were cramped together with barely the flicker of candlelight coming from inside. Hunched figures kept to the shadows, heads and backs bowed low.

Bo's stomach churned. She didn't know where she was, but she didn't like the look of it. The unsettling quiet scratched at her insides, warning her that something was not right.

From her vantage point slung over the horse, she could tell a large mansion loomed up ahead. Black stone towered high, looking more like an ornate tomb than a household. As they drew closer, she began to understand just how massive and oppressive the mansion was. It was all hard lines and sharp corners. Monstrous statues sat on every turret, and their eyes seemed to follow them as they neared the grand door carved from bloodred wood.

Their horses stopped, and the rope at Bo's ankles was cut. Relief flooded through her, but before she could truly enjoy the freedom, she was grabbed roughly from behind. Pain lanced through her entire body. If she'd felt better, she would've cursed at the man. As it was, she felt weaker than ever.

That was okay though. As soon as she figured out just where she was, she would make a plan. And then she would escape this ominous hellhole.

Glancing around, she noticed armed men everywhere—some human, some inkwell, but mostly reptile men, each one carrying nasty-looking blades and daggers. All of the men were covered in an assortment of scars and burns, and some were missing various body parts.

Bo realized the men had obviously forgotten her crutch, which meant she would have to put weight on her foot and shuffle along slowly. A hand at her back shoved her through the doors and into a dark lobby. A wide staircase greeted them. Blue-fire torches flickered, lengthening the shadows and bathing everything in a strange blue light.

In the distance, she heard raucous laughter and swearing, and her stomach tightened into a ball of knots.

"Why am I here?" she asked the reptile man, her voice hoarse.

"You'll see," he answered smoothly.

She scowled at him. "I'm not moving another inch until you tell me where I am." Her voice felt weak, but she was determined. She would not walk into whatever this was without some knowledge.

The reptile man's eyes flicked to the grumbler. "Carry her."

At that, Bo's temper snapped. The man reached for her, but she was prepared and slammed the back of her head into his nose. She heard the crunch and felt the gush of blood on the back of her neck. Before the other man could grab her, she raced up the stairs, her hands still bound and her limp prominent.

It would be a miracle if she made it up the stairs before they caught her.

Just as she limped to the last step, a thick elbow looped around her neck, crushing her windpipe.

"You know, I'm getting really tired of this," said the reptile man as he dragged her back down the steps.

Bo fought and kicked, wriggling and bucking as wildly as she could. But with each movement, the man's grip around her neck tightened until her air was cut off completely.

Panic clawed her lungs.

"You will cooperate," the man whispered into her ear, "or I will personally carve your eyes from your skull. You understand?"

Bo didn't want to give the man the satisfaction of a response, but she needed air, so she nodded slightly. The man's grip loosened just enough for her to suck in a small breath.

"I hate you," she sputtered out.

"The feeling's mutual."

This time she didn't fight as she was shoved down the long hallways toward the sound of laughter. Her neck was already beginning to ache, and she was sure bruises would surface in a matter of minutes. She didn't care though. All she cared about was getting out of here.

She closed her eyes again, feeling for the monsters. The connection was weak, and she could tell they were nearly out of her reach, which would do her absolutely no good.

They turned a corner, and bright light nearly blinded her after the darkness of the halls. Heat enveloped her, and it took a moment for her to absorb her surroundings. She was in a large dining hall. A long firepit stretched down the center of the room. Tables sat on either side, filled with more grisly-looking armed men. At the head of the room, sitting on a raised dais, was another reptile man eyeing her with interest.

The room quieted as everyone turned to stare at her. A flicker of movement caught her eye, and she saw a young girl carrying a tray, passing around goblets and flagons of wine and mead.

Another shove at her back told her to keep moving until she stood at the front of the man in the chair. Up close she could see it was carved from bone. She was forced to her knees, and a knife at her back told her she was done if she tried anything again.

The man who'd escorted her in stepped up to the man in the chair. They whispered back and forth until the man in the bone chair quirked a scaly eyebrow. His yellow eyes narrowed on her.

"What's your name, girl?" he asked.

Bo didn't respond. She wouldn't. The knife at her back dug into her skin, and she hissed. "Bo," she said through gritted teeth.

"Bo," he said. "Well, welcome, Bo. My name is Ohan-Jin. Kiro here warned me that you might be a problem."

"Funny, he didn't warn me that you were ugly," she snapped back.

A slice of fire slashed down her back, and she doubled over in pain, tears springing to her eyes. She bit her tongue to keep from crying out. She would not let them see her weak.

"Come now, Bo. I'd hate to get off on the wrong foot. Though I do understand why that would be a problem for you," said Ohan-Jin. "You can be civil, can't you? Or are you one of those savage forest orphans they tell me about?"

Her gaze shot up to the man. He smiled down at her, revealing sharpened teeth.

"Ah, I see I've got your attention. A bit sensitive about that, are we?"

She didn't answer. Instead, she pictured all the different places she'd use her crutch to beat him if she could.

The man rose from his chair, standing tall as blood dripped down her back. For all her limited knowledge, she knew about the Ohans, about how powerful they were. They were not the sort of people you wanted as your enemy. It was now clear why.

Ohan-Jin took his time coming toward her. The crackling fire was the only sound that dared penetrate the silence of such a powerful man.

At last, he knelt in front of her, running a finger down her cheek. Instinctively, she tried to bite it.

He grabbed her chin, forcing her to look at him. His nails dug into her cheeks, and she had to fight the urge to spit in his face even now.

"You will behave," he said, his voice almost soft, "or you will pay the price. I imagine you can still do what you do without fingers. Or hands. Or perhaps even a nose."

At that, she stilled.

"Good girl," he purred.

Bile rose to the back of her throat as she glared at him. She wouldn't beat him with her crutch. She'd file it into a stake and stab him through the heart. More than once.

He stood, letting go of her face. "Take her down to the cellar. A few days down there ought to adjust her attitude."

She was yanked to her feet again but stopped, glaring back at Ohan-Jin. "What do you want with me?" she demanded.

She didn't expect an answer.

Instead, he looked at her. "Oh, I don't want a thing with you. But I think your monsters could be very useful."

21

JACK

Jack was in the stables again, roaming the stalls. Soft neighs reached his ears, the only sound in the silent night. Outside, darkness hung like a black curtain. A moonless night. Erinyans believed evil lurked on nights such as these, when the whispering wind sliced into skin and hungry spirits searched for souls to devour.

A few rows down, he saw a figure organizing saddles and bridles. It was one of the stable hands, staying later than usual. The hair on the back of Jack's neck rose. Something wasn't right. Other than a guard stationed out front, nobody should have been there. Come to think of it, where was the guard?

Jack started forward, his boots thunking on the stone floor, hay scattering in his wake. He would investigate; he would find out just who this stable hand was and why he was here. Perhaps he was a thief posing as hand.

Another voice cut in, feminine and familiar. Jack ducked into a stall, heart racing. Why was his heart racing? He was the prince. He could go wherever he wanted whenever he wanted. He had no need to fear a common stable hand.

The couple retreated, their voices growing quieter and quieter until it was clear they were gone. Jack knew he should follow them, but he stood there, paralyzed. Why couldn't he move? Why did his body feel so foreign to him?

Do you remember yet?

Jack swallowed. *Do I remember what?*

The Voice grinned, glee shooting through Jack's own body. **Soon. Soon.**

JACK WOKE WITH A START, his body tight with fear. Around him, the silence of the forest was nearly suffocating, and he thought of his dream. There was something he was missing.

He glanced over at Millie, her chest rising and falling. With the moonlight hitting her face, she could have been one of the beautiful river spirits that roamed these parts of the Ravaged Wood, or used to. He'd never seen one.

A loud snap echoed through the trees, and his hand went straight to the daggers strapped across his chest. He glanced around, chest constricting.

Jill was gone.

She should have been keeping watch; instead, she was nowhere. He glanced at the horses. Hers was gone.

She left you.

What? No. She wouldn't. His mind began to race. Why would she leave him and Millie behind? He knew she'd been angry after the acorns, knew she'd been upset ever since she'd lost the tournament, but she wouldn't leave him, would she?

It was only a matter of time. Everyone leaves, Jack.

Not everyone.

Really? What about the last girl you thought you were in love with?

Something like lightning struck his heart. A wound he'd thought had healed felt raw again. It'd been a long time since he'd thought of Anna.

But he barely had time to think as the quiet whistle of something sounded through the trees. Half a second later, Jack was on his feet, and an arrow was buried in the ground where his head had just been. Adrenaline raced through his veins. Another arrow zipped through the trees, and he barely dodged it in time.

"Millie!" he hissed, nudging her with his foot.

She sat up, bleary-eyed. A third arrow fired, and Jack launched forward, tackling Millie to the ground. It barely missed them.

His heart raced as he stared down at her. Her eyes were wide with fear.

"Stay low," he whispered. "Transform if you can."

She nodded as he stood, and more arrows whistled overhead.

"Show yourselves, cowards!" Jack yelled into the darkness.

Another arrow shot out of the darkness, straight for Jack's heart. Without hesitation, he flicked his arm up, barely blocking the arrow with his metal brace. He let out a growl of pain as the arrow nicked his arm, blood already beginning to drip. A second slower and the arrow would have lodged itself in his ribs.

He gritted his teeth. "Is this the best you can do?" he taunted. "I see why you hide in the shadows!"

Jack glanced at Millie, who was still lying on the ground, paralyzed by fear. He didn't want to be rude, but he needed her help.

"Anytime now," he said as another arrow headed their way, this time catching in his shoulder.

Pain exploded down his arm, his flesh burning.

"*Millie.*"

"I'm trying!" she said, sweat beading on her brow.

Was this really how he was going to die? Killed by faceless attackers in the middle of the night like a common thug?

If only your sister were here.

Jack couldn't help but agree. She was supposed to be keeping watch, warning them if any threats arose. Instead, she'd abandoned them. Now they would die, and it would be all Jill's fault.

"Millie!" he said, anger surging into his voice this time. He knew it wasn't fair, that it wasn't her fault Jill had deserted them.

"I can't!"

"You have to!"

"I can't!" Tears were running down her face now.

Another arrow shot toward them, aimed straight at Millie's heart. Jack's heart stopped, his body frozen with fear. He needed to move, but he couldn't. Millie was going to die.

The world around them stilled as a brilliant light lit up the forest. The arrow, Jack realized. It was the arrow. An inch from Millie's chest, the arrow glowed and splintered into a thousand tiny pieces.

And then the light vanished, leaving them in the pitch dark.

"Millie!" Jack screamed, running to her and pulling her into his chest. She trembled in his arms, her head pressed against his racing heart.

A thud echoed in the trees, like a body hitting the ground. Jack's stomach somersaulted as he pushed Millie behind him.

A second later, they were surrounded by six figures cloaked in silver as bright as the moon, hoods and masks covering their faces. One of the figures stepped forward, holding the limp body of a reptilian man in their arms, a quiver strapped his waist.

The figure dropped the man, whose scaly skin glinted in the moonlight. The man gave a grunt but lay still.

Blood seeped through Jack's fingers as he stared at the figure in front of him, his shoulder throbbing. He didn't know who these people were, but he knew they wouldn't last another fight, especially if Millie couldn't transform.

The figure pulled back the hood and yanked down the mask, and Jack's breath caught. She was the most beautiful feline girl he'd ever seen. Green cat eyes watched him intensely, black hair cascaded down her shoulders, and orange markings lined her face.

"Who are you?" Jack asked, keeping his voice steady. "What do you want?"

At first the girl didn't answer him, tilting her head to the side in curiosity. Then her gaze flicked behind him. "Millie Muffet."

Jack grabbed Millie's arm protectively. "What do you want with her?"

The feline girl looked back at him, her green eyes burning with quiet fury. "I wasn't talking to you."

Jack's jaw flexed. "Do you know who I am?" he said before he thought better of it.

"I know who you are, Your Highness, and we're not here for you. We're here for your paladin."

"Jack," Millie said, her voice quiet, "don't worry about me." Millie stepped out from behind him, holding her head high. "Yes?"

The feline girl glared at Jack again before turning back to Millie, softening a little at the sight of her. "Miss Muffet, we were sent to find you as soon as you left the Citadel. There is someone who wants to speak with you."

Jack glanced at Millie, an uneasy feeling settling in his stomach. ***They know what she is.***

"Who wants to speak with me? Why?" Millie asked, her voice calmer than he'd ever heard it.

"That is not for me to say," said the feline girl. "But I can give you the answers you've been seeking."

Jack saw Millie stiffen, her thoughts clearly racing. He wanted to scream at her not to trust them, not to believe anything they said. Something didn't feel right about this.

"What kind of answers?"

The girl smiled. "We know the power you possess, the wrestling within you. We know the burden of a power like yours, the fear of the unknown that gnaws at your soul. You are not alone in the world, Millie Muffet."

22

DAVID

*D*avid had never seen anyone fight like that, with such effortless grace that it was more like dancing than swinging weapons of war. And he'd never seen such a fine young woman in these parts of the kingdom. The travelers who passed through a village like this one were often starving or searching for a new place to call home. He knew immediately the girl was hiding something.

His eyes followed her as she turned to leave. She sheathed the butterfly swords at her waist, never dropping her guard. His own hand gripped his blade as he eyed the bloody innkeeper, who was still snarling at the door. The man picked up the coins that had been tossed at his feet before shuffling back to the kitchen, refusing to look at anyone.

David sheathed his blade and followed the young woman outside. He'd come for a drink, but perhaps he could leave with something else.

It took a moment for his eyes to adjust to the sudden darkness of the street after the warmth and light of the inn. He looked around for the girl, his mind turning the pieces over. Something didn't add up.

On his first hunting trip as a boy, he and his father had encountered a lone wolf. David still recalled the fear he'd felt as the beast snarled at him from a distance, saliva dripping from its maw. His father told him to leave the creature be, that a lone wolf would bear its teeth and its hair would rise, but only because it was afraid. Without the protection of its pack, it would be on the defensive, hiding behind its fear.

He heard voices from around the corner and followed them, careful not to make a sound. From the shadows, he watched as the girl spoke with the young maid she'd helped, heard the subtle clink of coins passed from one hand to another. The maid gave a quick bow before she turned and ran into the arms of a young man he hadn't noticed until then. The couple slipped into the darkness together as the girl watched them go, her expression looking as mournful as the lone wolf he'd seen all those years ago.

David considered turning around and going back into the pub and finishing his drink. He didn't know a thing about this girl, just that she was a fighter, a survivor. That alone pulled him from his hiding spot.

He cleared his throat, trying not to startle her. "I'm surprised someone like you would help a common kitchen maid."

The girl spun, hands on her weapons. "Who are you?"

He held up his hands in surrender. "A friend, I hope. I'm not here to fight you. Somehow, I think that's a fight I'd lose."

The girl stepped from the shadows and into the light emanating from the inn. His breath caught, and he glanced at the ground, keenly aware of his own scarred face.

"Few are able to beat me," she said. Her tone was a statement written in stone. There was something about her, a confidence that the people in these parts lacked. Her posture, her fighting, her clothing—all of it gave her away like tracks leading to prey.

David chuckled to himself. "You're not from around here, are you?"

For a second, it seemed like she might not answer, but then she drew one of her blades, looking at it carefully. "No, I'm not," she said. "I don't think you are either."

With the gentleness of a mother holding her child, she carefully wiped down her blades and checked for any chips or cracks. It was something even the best swordsmen forgot to do after a fight.

"I'm not from these parts, no, but I'm definitely not from the Citadel."

Her eyes flashed as their gazes locked, a predator eyeing its prey. "I don't know who you are, and I really don't care, but I think you should go." The tilt in her voice hummed with warning like a cornered animal.

He knew he should turn and leave, but he thought of the monsters roaming the countryside, of Asif's sister, of the people of Erinya being forced to live in fear. Somehow, he knew this girl could help him. But would she?

"Perhaps, but I'm curious. What exactly is a young noblewoman doing traveling on her own?"

"I don't need your help or protection if that's what you're asking," she answered in a cold voice, raising her sword slightly as if to prove her point.

David pursed his lips. "Don't worry, I can see that." He paused, an idea playing at the back of his mind. There was no way. It couldn't be. "Just wondering what the princess of Erinya is doing so far from the palace by herself."

In a second, she had him backed against the wall, her sword pressed tightly to the porcelain skin of his neck. Fire burned in her eyes as she looked up at him. It was clear that this girl, whoever she was, was not to be underestimated.

"Who *are* you?" she asked, her voice a deadly whisper. "How do you know who I am?"

David's heart slammed into his rib cage. It had been a guess, nothing more. He hadn't actually expected to be right. Despite himself, a laugh escaped his throat, and he smirked. "Well, I didn't know for sure until just now. Tell me, does your temper always get the better of you?"

An iron fist slammed into his side, and his skin cracked from the blow. He stood there for a second, speechless, the air swept from his chest, pain splintering down his side. He gritted his teeth. Since nothing had broken, the skin would heal in a few minutes. But the scar would stay. The scar would always stay.

"My temper keeps me alive," she said, her flat eyes boring into him, and he knew she was telling the truth. At last, she huffed, giving him a good shove before turning away. "I don't have time for this."

His muscles tensed. The princess of Erinya stood in front of him, and she was just as arrogant as he'd always been led to believe.

"Time for what?" he asked. He still didn't understand why she was here.

"It's none of your business."

"It is if you don't want me to tell those men who you are and where you're going." He knew it was low to threaten her, maybe even treasonous, but that was what she got for giving him more scars.

She froze, giving him a glare sharper than her weapons. "Excuse me?"

"I think you heard me." David's blood rushed like a raging river. He recalled what Grimzy had told him just days ago. These monsters were just the beginning. Something was wrong in Erinya. And it couldn't be coincidence that the princess was here now.

At last, she turned and sighed. "What do you want? Name your price, and I'll see to it that you get it. But please don't tell anyone I was here."

David was silent. What *did* he want? Money? Land? A chance to be something other than a soldier?

A way to break the curse, he thought bitterly.

"I want to know what you're doing here," he said at last. "Last time I checked, princesses aren't really supposed to be traveling all alone."

The princess stared at him, her eyes narrowed to slits. Finally, she stuck her hand into her horse's saddlebag and pulled out a purse of coins before tossing it at him. He caught it with one hand, but his eyes never left hers.

"I can't say. But I trust that's enough to earn your silence."

He scoffed. "I don't want your money," he said, tossing the purse back to her. Slime coated his insides at the mere thought of taking the king's money.

She caught it, surprised. "Everyone wants money," she said, tossing the purse back to him.

"All the money in the world couldn't fix my problems," he said grimly.

She rolled her eyes. "I haven't found that to be the case."

"Spoken like the daughter of a bankrupt king!" He laughed humorlessly. If he'd had any lingering doubts that she was a princess before, he certainly didn't have any now.

Her fists curled at her sides, the only sign that he was getting under her skin. "Who are you, and what do you want?"

David crossed his arms and leaned back against the wall behind him, examining her. Her black riding coat and breeches were in stark contrast to the freckles splashed across her nose. Of course, he'd heard of Princess Jillianna's beauty, and she certainly was beautiful. A blind man could've seen that. But he knew the king's cruelty. Would she be the same?

"I doubt you're truly as interested as you claim to be, but if you must know, my name is David. Just another nameless soldier in your father's useless army. As for what I want, that's actually quite simple."

"Things are rarely as simple as we'd like them to be. If you're looking for something other than money, I'm sorry to say you'll be disappointed." The look of disgust she shot him made her meaning clear.

David rolled his eyes, annoyance flaring. He was already second-guessing himself. If this was how she was going to treat him, then perhaps he had no business with her at all.

"You're hardly my type, Princess, and I assure you, nothing quite so distasteful as *that*. I'm not like some of your father's other soldiers, though I'll admit I'm a rarity." He paused, gathering his courage. "No. What I need, Your Highness . . ." He gave her a meaningful look. "Is your help."

For a moment, the princess looked as though she couldn't decide between being offended or intrigued. In the end, it seemed her curiosity won out.

"What do you need *my* help with?"

He gave a grim smile. "I need help hunting monsters."

23

MILLIE

Millie's heart raced as she stared at the feline girl in front of her. This girl knew what she was, why she had this power. She hadn't realized how desperately the questions had gnawed at her until that moment. She wanted to know who she was.

She took a step forward. "Show me."

"Come with us, and we'll tell you everything you want to know," the girl said, examining Millie with watchful eyes.

She nodded, taking a step forward. A hand grabbed her arm, pulling her back. She swung around to Jack. His shoulders were hunched like a spooked cat.

"What are you doing?" she asked, an uncomfortable heat spreading through her arm. His fingers pinched her arm before loosening, but he didn't let go.

"You're going to follow them? Just like that? We don't know anything about them." His eyes shifted, his unease settling against her skin like a spider's web. He let go of her arm and gripped his shoulder. An arrow was lodged there.

"You're injured!"

Blood dripped down his arm as sweat beaded on his forehead. "I'm fine."

"No, you're not." She turned back to the girl. "Can you help us?"

"We don't need their help," Jack hissed.

She swallowed. She knew she shouldn't be so trusting. "Do you always look for an enemy?"

"Do you always look for a friend?"

"Ymira, help him," came the girl's voice.

To their left, another girl pulled her hood down. Millie's eyes widened. She'd seen many inkwells over the years, but she'd never seen one with such a prominent tattoo. In the center of her forehead, a black flame burned, flickering ever so slightly.

Ymira stepped forward, rolling up her sleeves to reveal two silver cuffs around her wrists, pulsing with light. The girl closed her eyes and grasped the arrow in Jack's shoulder. It was gradual at first, the light rising from her cuffs and wrapping around the arrow. And then, like the arrow that had nearly struck Millie, it dissolved into light.

The light swirled around Jack's shoulder, pulling at his skin and knitting it back together, until it vanished, and they sat in the dark marveling at the smooth skin left behind.

Millie's hands shook as she locked eyes with Jack, his gaze confirming her own suspicions. Magic.

She glanced at Ymira, whose milky skin was in such stark contrast to the blazing tattoo on her forehead. "Thank you."

The girl smiled. It was a smile nearly as radiant as the light she possessed. "*Khat*," she said, an inkwell word meaning "it is a pleasure to help."

A tug in her chest pulled Millie back to the feline girl, who had yet to give her name.

"Aaira," the feline girl said, as if reading her thoughts. "My name is Aaira. The moon is fading fast, so we must be going."

War raged in her chest as she looked up at the prince, whose dark eyes glowered in the dim light. A breeze swept around Millie, and she thought of the first morning she'd discovered her power, how she'd awoken to find her consciousness scattered in the minds of thousands of tiny spiders. In her panic, she'd sent them all running in different directions. It had taken half a day to reform, and when she finally did, she'd been so exhausted she'd slept for days after that.

A year later, she'd come no closer to finding any answers, only more questions.

But now things were different. Now she'd bound herself to the crown, had sworn to serve until she died. Millie's heart sank at this realization. Without Jack's permission, she wasn't free to follow them. For the first time, she felt the weight of what it meant to be paladin.

"And if I don't come?" Her skin prickled under the strangers' gazes, spider legs skittering across her skin.

"That's for you to decide."

The prince's jaw flexed. Despite the fact they'd just healed him— or maybe because of that fact—she could tell he didn't trust them. She saw a door closing in her mind, the answers to her questions being sealed away like a body in a crypt.

"You should come with us, Miss Muffet. The fate of Erinya may depend on what she tells you," said the feline girl. "But she won't wait for you."

"Who won't?" Jack asked, his stance guarded.

"That isn't for me to say." The girl's face flickered as she looked at her comrades. "Trust me or don't. We won't wait forever."

Jack rolled his eyes. "How very cryptic of you." He looked back at her, a hand absently rubbing his shoulder. "We don't have time for this. We need to find my sister and keep moving." He started packing their things, shoving them into his horse's saddlebags.

Millie nodded, her throat closing up. She didn't trust herself to speak. A weight sat heavy on her chest, pressing her lungs. All her life she'd been at the mercy of others, at their beck and call. She'd never known what it felt like to want something herself, want something *for* herself.

Until now.

"Your Highness," she said, palms sweating, "I think we should go with them."

Jack turned, his eyes narrowing first on her and then on the strangers. "I don't trust them."

"They just saved your life!" she whispered furiously before biting her tongue. "Please, they might be able to help us. They might be able to help your father." She knew the chances were slim. But she'd never asked for anything before.

"Fine." He didn't look happy, and Millie couldn't help but feel guilty. "We'll hear what they have to say. And then we keep going."

Millie turned back to the girl and nodded. Aaira simply raised her hood and turned, the other cloaked strangers following after her. Millie was glad she'd been so tired that she hadn't unpacked her things the night before. She went over and grabbed her horse by the reins before following the trail of silver cloaks, which moved like specks of starlight in the forest.

"I hope this is worth it," said Jack, his voice tight.

For the first time, she noticed the bags under his eyes, the way his body seemed taut with anticipation, as if he couldn't relax. She thought back on their time together, how one moment he would be smiling and laughing, and the next he'd turn pale and paranoid, as if the chilling presence of a wraith whispered through him.

Despite that, however, she was grateful for his continued support. He'd scarcely mentioned her betrayal during the tournament, he'd defended her at the ball, and he'd stood beside her against his own sister. There weren't words that could do justice to the gratitude she felt.

"Thank you," she whispered as they walked alongside each other.

Jack gazed down at her, a small smile pulling at his lips. "You know, you never did award me for winning that bet we made."

"That's because you didn't technically win, remember? Your sister caught you on that last acorn."

"Technicalities," he said, waving a hand. "Besides, you owe me one." He nodded to the cloaked figures in front of them, and her stomach churned. Guilt washed over her again as she realized he was walking away from his sister and his father so that she could get answers.

"Fine," she relented, suddenly nervous. According to their deal, she owed him an answer to whatever question he asked. She supposed it was fitting given that she herself wanted answers too.

"You never told me, why did you enter the tournament?"

She pinched her lips, looking at the ground. At last, she sighed. "It's a long story." It was the question she'd dreaded most.

"We have all the time in the world," he said with a slight smile.

She considered him for a moment, eyeing the strangers ahead of them. "I never asked for this power, never asked for any of this, and sometimes I stop and think, 'Why me?' " She kept her voice low, her eyes slowly reaching his. "My brother was arrested a year ago for a crime he didn't commit."

Jack raised an eyebrow. "What kind of crime?"

Millie swallowed hard; the words were stuck in her throat. "They say he killed a boy. A stable hand. But I know he didn't. Doon wouldn't hurt a dragonfly, let alone kill someone."

Jack stared at her evenly. "And you thought by becoming paladin you could . . . ?"

"I thought I could reopen the case. Find the real killer. Set my brother free."

Saying the words aloud was both a sigh of relief and the fear of standing at the edge of a precipice. One step in the wrong direction, and that would be the end. To openly admit her plan made it sound pathetically plain, even to her own ears, yet letting go of the secret eased some of the weight in her chest.

"I had no idea," he said, his voice softer than she'd ever heard it.

"How could you?"

"Still, I understand what it's like to care for your sibling, to want to protect them, no matter what. There isn't anything I wouldn't do for my sister, even if she is a little uptight." He smiled, but it didn't reach his eyes.

"I'm sorry we're not following your sister." In truth, she was a bit relieved they weren't following her, but she still felt guilty for it.

"It's all right. We'll find her. She wouldn't dare stray from the mission."

24

JILL

'm surprised someone like you would help a common kitchen maid.

The words settled on Jill's skin like a flea-ridden horse blanket as she thought of Millie. She was keenly aware of the irony of the statement, and she hated the bitterness that was building like water trapped by a dam. Sooner or later, she would burst, and she wasn't entirely sure what would happen when she did.

"Hunting monsters?" she asked, staring at the scarred man who'd helped her. David. With the half-light of the moon, she could hardly see the scars, except for the long thick one that ran around his eye and down his cheek. She wondered how exactly one got a scar like that and lived to tell the tale. Then again, if he was a monster hunter . . .

He raised an eyebrow. "You haven't heard?" he asked, all manner of teasing gone.

She gave a slight shake of her head. She hated not knowing things, especially where monsters were concerned.

"What kind of monsters?" she asked, running through the possibilities in her head. There were the stone beasts to the north, who hibernated for centuries at a time and caused massive devastation to forests and villages when they awoke. There were the jakahls, worm-like creatures that lived deep underground, blind and deaf but able to smell blood from five miles away. Or, perhaps the most fearsome of all, there were the wraiths, who sucked the life from everything they touched. *Oh, Saints. Please don't let it be wraiths.*

David shook his head. "We don't know. I've never seen or heard of anything like them."

"You've seen them then?"

His jaw flexed, and he looked at her, eyes piercing hers with an intensity brought on only by fear. "Yes." He didn't elaborate, but Jill sensed whatever he'd seen had left him shaken.

"And why do you need my help?" She couldn't deny the strange tug in her gut as she thought of monsters terrorizing the kingdom, but she also knew that her father grew weaker every day. If she didn't find a cure for him soon, she feared she would not have a father to return to.

Would that really be so bad?

The thought crossed her mind before she could stop it. It was true she and her father had never been close, especially since he'd informed her that she was to be married off, but did that really mean he deserved to die? Not to mention, if he died, she could never prove to him that she was more than what he thought her capable of. No, she couldn't let him die, no matter what she might feel.

"You're a good fighter," David said, cutting into her thoughts. She looked up at him. "One of the best I've seen, if I'm honest." It sounded like it pained him to admit it, and she flushed.

"And what if I say no?" she said, still thinking of her father.

His stony gaze bore down on her. "This is your kingdom, is it not? Your people are bleeding and dying and leaving everything behind in the hope of finding safety. And you'd just turn your back on them?"

His playful smirk was gone. In its place was disgust, and she hated how it felt to have someone look at her like that. She looked down at her dusty boots.

"Are you just like your father?"

"I'm nothing like him," she snapped back before thinking. But the words tasted like a lie on her tongue. Was she really any better than her father if she wouldn't help her people? If all she cared about was finding a cure, and finding it to elevate her own status no less? She hated the wrongness of it all. She looked back at this stranger, unnerved by how easily he'd cut her to the core.

"Okay then," he said. "Prove it."

JILL'S PLANS were in shambles. She'd abandoned Millie and her brother. She'd abandoned her search for a cure for her father. Now she was following this scar-covered stranger to some unknown location to hunt down monsters she'd never heard of before. She was beginning to wonder if she'd made the right decision following him. For all she knew, he could've been leading her to a trap. His concern, however, seemed genuine, and his fear when he'd spoken of the monsters was evident.

No, she hadn't abandoned her search. This was merely a detour. The physician himself had said her father had a month or two. She would take care of these monsters and find a cure, and then her father would be forced to recognize how much more valuable she could be as a warrior and make her paladin instead of Millie. The thought alone sent her pulse racing with delight.

It was nearly midnight by the time they reached their destination, a makeshift camp an hour's ride from the dusty little village. The moon hung in the sky like a glowing scythe, bathing everything in front of her in eerie light.

A labyrinth of tightly packed, tattered tents rose before her, thousands of them. Her breath caught. Dirty people shuffled about, their gazes fixed on the muddy ground. Pitiful fires burned here and there, roasting meager meals of broth and small game. It was larger than any village she'd yet come across. Around the perimeter, a weak attempt at a wall had been half constructed and then clearly abandoned.

She looked at David, whose face was grim as he took it all in. "What is this place?" she asked.

His jaw clenched. "Of course you don't know."

"What is that supposed to mean?" she asked.

He sighed, shaking his head. "What do you think it is?"

She bit the inside of her cheek, glaring at him. "Well, it looks like a camp."

"Exactly." He kicked at his horse to get in front of her.

Frustrated, she trotted after him. "But why? Why are all these people here?"

David looked at her, his scars pale in the moonlight but haunting all the same. "You really don't know, do you?"

Her chest tightened as she shook her head. She hated not knowing something, and it was the second time that evening she'd been forced to admit that.

"These people are here because of your father. Your father has taxed them so heavily to fund his war that they've lost everything: their land, their livelihoods, their homes . . ." He paused. "Their families." He shook his head. "Now, with these monsters terrorizing the countryside, it seems the safest place to be is here."

He went silent, glaring at the horizon. Jill's skin crawled, and she was distinctly aware of the clothing she wore, how fine it was. Though it had been made from the softest material available in Erinya, it scratched at her skin, begging her to peel it off.

"I had no idea." She slowed her horse, a heaviness weighing down her shoulders. She wanted it all to be a lie, some elaborate charade. But she couldn't deny what she saw with her own two eyes. Her father had done this to their people, people he'd taken an oath to protect at all costs. Between the war and these mysterious monsters on the loose, it was clear he'd fallen terribly short of that vow.

"How could you? You've spent your entire life in a palace."

Jill wanted to retort, to tell him that she had her own troubles, but her tongue caught, stuck in her throat.

Why? The question whirled around in her head. Why had her

father let this happen? Why were they locked in this war? Why had it come to this?

She hated that one question simply led to another, with no answers to be found.

"Come," David said, his voice softening. "I'll see if I can find you a decent meal and a place to sleep."

They dismounted and tied their horses to the hitching post outside of the camp, then walked the rest of the way on foot.

They entered the camp through the main road, which was wider than any of the other paths that wound through the camp. A makeshift market had been erected, but it was quiet now. Jill's eyes roved, and she was surprised to find sentries posted everywhere, many of whom were women or older children. *Too young to join the army but old enough to protect the camp*, she realized.

Once again, she was keenly aware of her fine clothes, which drew people's attention. But her entire life she'd been told to hold her head high, so she did. She focused on the back of David's head. She would not be so easily cowed by these people.

She was reminded of a time when she was little, when she had longed to play with the servants' kids in a game they'd invented. It involved kicking a ball and trying to get it into the opposite team's base, a circle carved in the dirt with a stick.

She'd watched for an hour from the shadows before she worked up the courage to ask to play with them. When she stepped forward, though, all the children stopped playing their game, shying away from her. When she asked to play with them, they simply stared at her, too scared to say no. But Jill knew what they wanted to say.

She cried all the way to her bedroom, so distraught she crashed right into her father. Instead of getting angry with her, he knelt and asked her what the matter was. She explained through her tears, and her father's expression hardened.

"They will hate you for who you are. But you can never let them see that they get to you," he'd told her.

She clung to those words now.

They wound their way through the tents, and Jill soon found herself relying solely on David's knowledge of where they were. They rounded another corner and saw a young feline boy sitting in front of a small fire next to the largest man Jill had ever seen.

No, not a man. A Whitesaw mountain man. With a start, she realized she recognized the man in front of her.

"Paladin Grimzy?"

Her own surprise was mirrored as the mountain man turned to look at her. "Princ—"

"Just Jill," she said quickly, cutting him off before anyone else could hear.

Paladin Grimzy glanced between her and David, suspicion and confusion morphing together on his face. "Must have been some drink," he said, raising an eyebrow.

David's jaw clenched. "It's a long story. But she's here to help."

"Well, it's nice to know someone's doing something," said a curt voice. Jill glanced over at the boy. He was younger than she'd first realized, tall and gangly and covered head to toe in dirt. His face was made older looking by the expression of hatred he wore.

"And you are?" she asked, narrowing her eyes.

The kid glanced at her, looking her up and down. "I could ask the same of you. You don't look like you belong here."

David walked over and smacked him upside the head. "This is Asif. He's still a little ungrateful that we saved his life."

"You kidnapped me."

"We brought you to safety."

"Against my will!"

David rolled his eyes, and Jill found herself amused. This kid knew how to annoy David, and she couldn't help but admire him a bit, even if he was being a little prick.

She turned back to Paladin Grimzy, who was still staring at her, waiting for an explanation. "What *are* you doing here, Pri—Jill?" he corrected, though it clearly made him uncomfortable.

She looked over at David. "He said something about needing my help with monsters."

It was Paladin Grimzy's turn to look at David. "You think it's wise to allow . . . someone such as herself to embark on such a dangerous mission?"

David pursed his lips. Indignation flared up inside Jill like a spark to oil.

"I wouldn't have said that if I were you," David said, stepping back.

Jill glared at the mountain man. "For once, I agree with him. Trust me, *Paladin,* you want my help."

Although Jill knew Paladin Grimzy, she didn't know him well. She'd been younger when he'd won the tournament, and he had since taken up different assignments across the kingdom. While everyone who served the crown knew who she was, she'd taken it upon herself to learn about each and every paladin who had won in the past twenty-five years, which was the only reason she remembered him at all.

David nodded. "I've seen what happens to the people she goes up against. We want her on our side."

A strange pride swelled inside her. For all his biting words and his low opinion of the crown, he'd still complimented the part of her she liked best.

David nudged the kid next to the fire. "Come on, let's go find some food."

"I'm not hungry."

"You're always hungry. Come on." He grabbed the kid's collar and hauled him to his feet, and they wandered off between the rows of tents.

Fatigue overtook Jill, and she found herself wanting nothing more than to fall asleep and never wake up. But there was far too much to do for that. She sighed and sat down next to the mountain man, watching the flames as they consumed the wood, always hungry and never satisfied. They reminded her of her father.

She still felt uncertain about helping David, but he was right. If she didn't help her own people, then who would? It left her feeling more wary about her father than ever before.

"So, why are you here, Your Highness?" came Grimzy's low voice.

She looked over at the hulking man, and his eyes were watching her like a predator watches its prey. She swallowed. "I already told you. I'm here to help."

"I'm not asking why you came with David to the Lost Tribe. What were you doing so far from the palace to begin with?"

Fear twisted her insides. She couldn't tell him the truth—that her father had been poisoned and it was being kept quiet for the protection of the throne—nor could she tell him that she'd been traveling with Millie and the prince until a day and a half ago when she'd abandoned them to seek out a cure on her own.

"I would think," Grimzy continued, "that the princess would stay close to the palace after the Paladin's Tournament. Surely there's much feasting going on in celebration of the king's newest paladin . . . unless the waters are not quite as still underneath as they seem on the surface."

In the firelight, his eyes glowed. And though she could lie to him, she knew it wasn't worth the effort. "What do you want?" she asked, unable to hide the bitter tone in her voice.

The paladin chuckled, and Jill swore the earth moved beneath them. "Only to warn you, dear princess. My people have always had a connection with the land. We feel the earth shift, the water cut through the valleys, the trees whisper secrets, the mountains grumble." He paused, fixing her with a look that made her heart race. "But something is changing, Your Highness. The land grows quiet, and darkness looms on the horizon. These monsters may only be the beginning. Every day I hear whispers of rebellion, of the growing strength of Carthesia's armies. I do not know what has happened to the king, Your Highness, but now more than ever, Erinya needs a ruler to lead us out of the impending darkness, or I fear we may all be consumed."

25

BO

Bo was used to being alone. She'd been alone most of her life, living as one of those "savage forest orphans," as Ohan-Jin had said. But after three days alone in a dark cell, she was certain she'd never see the light of day again.

The venom from the snake bite had moved through the rest of her body until every part of her ached and burned. If she'd had the strength, she would have used every last swear word she knew, and she knew many. In several different languages.

As it was, though, all she could do was lie on the cold stone floor and wish that death would find her.

She wondered what death would be like. Would she see her mother again? Did she even want to? After all, it was because of her mother that she'd wound up in this situation to begin with.

She could still picture her mother's mess of braids pulled high onto her head, her brown skin glowing in the firelight as she told stories from her home in Jahdala, so different from anything Bo had ever known Erinya to be. Jahdala sounded bright, with brown canyons spanning the land and turquoise rivers rushing through them, with villages built high in the trees, where fruit she'd never heard of hung outside the windows to be plucked anytime anyone was hungry. How her mother had wound up in Erinya, she didn't know.

One day she would find a ship and go. She would see her mother's homeland. But first she had to escape.

Creaking metal pulled her from her thoughts. She listened as light footsteps padded down the stairs. Several times someone had come to give her water, but no food. It seemed they wanted to bring her to the brink before they tried to use her.

A pale face appeared at the bars of her cell. It was the girl she'd seen the other night, passing out drinks to the men. Was she a servant of the Ohans then?

"Bo?" the girl asked, her quiet voice somehow still loud in the cramped space.

"What do you want?" Bo asked, vehement. She knew her voice sounded harsh, that this girl wasn't the reason she was down here. Still, it felt good to take her frustration out on someone.

The girl swallowed before looking back at the stairwell she'd come down. "I've come to clean your wounds."

Bo scoffed. "Well, unless you can pull the venom from my veins, you needn't bother. I'm dead here soon anyway." Something hollow struck her throat. She'd spent so much of her life alone that there would be no one to miss her when she was gone. Somehow, that was harder than facing death.

The door to her cell swung open, and the girl stepped in. Bo sat up, her head pounding, and scooted back against the wall.

"Stay away from me," she said. She was vaguely aware of how she must've looked, ragged and dirty and covered in blood, like a mangy mutt that roamed back alleys searching for scraps. She didn't care though. In fact, she hoped the girl wouldn't come any closer.

"I'm here to help," the girl said, pity in her eyes.

Despite her exhaustion, Bo's temper flared. She didn't need this girl's pity. "I don't want your help. I don't want anything from your *master*. Let him kill me."

At that, the girl's gaze hardened. "Ohan-Jin is not my master." Her voice was firm as she knelt in front of Bo. "Let me look at your wounds."

Bo glared at the girl. "Why are you here then? Why are you helping me?"

The girl sighed. "It's complicated."

Bo continued to stare at her. She was a wispy thing, and dark hair framed her pale face. Blue ink danced around her neck, but in the half-light, Bo couldn't make out what it was.

"My name is Zyla. I serve in the Ohans' mansion, but they are not my masters." Leaning forward, she rolled up the sleeve of her dress, revealing a brand in the crook of her elbow. It was a bird in flight, wings outstretched so wide Bo thought it might begin flying in front of her own eyes.

Bo looked back up at the girl, something kindling in her stomach. "What is that supposed to be?"

The girl rolled down her sleeve. "The mark of the Saints."

"The what?"

"Do you always ask so many questions?"

"Do you always act so mysterious with complete strangers?" Bo countered. She didn't want to trust this girl. Trust was by far the most fragile thing to give to someone. It could be so easily broken.

"You know the Saints of Erinya, don't you?"

Bo swallowed, feeling rather stupid. She knew a little bit about them, about their magic and the battles they'd fought, but they were legends, bedtime stories. The only magic left in Erinya now was the tiny spells the few apothecaries still living used.

Her gut twisted. And her monsters.

"A little," she answered at last.

"We are the Order of the Saints."

Bo watched the girl carefully. She wasn't sure what the Order of the Saints was, but she sensed that letting this girl help her would drag her into things she had no desire to get involved in.

Zyla moved closer, pulling a bag off her shoulders and beginning to dig through it. "My sister is more of a healer than I am, but she's taught me a lot. I want to look at your back first to make sure it hasn't gotten infected."

Bo knew it was infected. It burned where she'd been cut, and it had only gotten worse. The first night she'd been in here, she'd torn part of her breeches to try and stop the bleeding, but without any help, the task had been difficult. At last, she'd given up.

"Turn around," the girl ordered.

Bo glared at her. "It's no use."

"Don't say that. Let me just see."

The girl reached for her, and Bo smacked her hand away.

The girl sighed. "Listen, I understand you don't trust me. But if you don't let me help you, you're going to die."

"I'm okay with that."

"Are you really?" The girl raised an eyebrow. "Because you seem like a survivor to me, and survivors don't give up so easily."

Bo crumpled, a tuneless chord ringing through her chest. Zyla was right. Bo couldn't escape in her current state, and if she didn't escape, who knew what the monsters would do. The fact was, she couldn't give up.

"Fine."

OVER THE NEXT FEW DAYS, Zyla tended to her wounds, which were many. She cleaned the cut on her back before stitching it up properly. She gave her the antidote for the basilisk venom and tended the other various cuts and bruises that she'd sustained during the journey.

Bo was begrudgingly grateful to the inkwell girl, and it was a feeling she did not like. Feeling grateful meant she would owe her something later on, and she hated to owe anyone anything.

"I'm supposed to inform you that Ohan-Jin would like to see you this evening," Zyla said as she smeared some sort of cream onto Bo's back.

Her fists clenched. "Why?"

"I'm not sure. A test, perhaps?"

"What does he want?" Bo asked. Over the last few days, and despite the fact that Bo had threatened Zyla while she'd stitched her back, a tentative trust had built between them.

The girl remained silent. Up close, Bo could see the tattoo across Zyla's neck, two dark lines that wrapped all the way around. Bo knew that the inkwells' tattoos predicted the lives they would lead, the events they would experience. She wondered what Zyla's tattoos could mean.

"How much do you know about the Ohans?" the girl asked at last.

"Only a little. That they're powerful, mostly." As little knowledge as she had about most things because of her upbringing, she'd heard of the Ohan family. Everyone she'd encountered feared them. They were known for their strength, brutality, and total control.

Zyla nodded. "Perhaps one of the most powerful families in Erinya, besides the king himself."

"And what does that have to do with the Order?" Bo asked. Over the last few days, she'd learned little about the Order of the Saints, Zyla's tight-lipped behavior keeping her in suspense.

"Theibes, where we are now, is one of the last mining towns in Erinya, largely because the Ohan family has mined the others to the brink." The girl began redressing the cut on Bo's back, her fingers careful and deft.

"What are they mining for?"

Zyla finished dressing the cut on her back, and Bo turned around to face her. In the half-light, the girl's face seemed paler than usual, her blond hair pulled back in a tight braid.

"They're mining impendium, one of the rarest elements in the five kingdoms. It's extremely strong and flexible, perfect for forging weapons with. They've been supplying the king's army for nearly a decade, since the war first began." The girl began packing her things into the leather satchel she carried, which was filled to the brink with medicines, bandages, tinctures, and herbs. She'd proven incredible healing skill. Bo wondered how her sister could possibly be any better.

"So, why are you here? If you're with the Order?"

Zyla gave a weak smile. "Well, the Order has an agreement with the Ohan family. Since this village is run by them, anyone who lives here must work for them in the mines. Men, women, children, all of them are forced to work, even when it's dangerous. Even if they're ill or injured." She paused, jaw clenching and tears tugging at her eyes before she swallowed. "The Order is the exception. Unlike the rest of the villagers, we do not have to work in the mines. Instead, several of us rotate shifts, personally serving within the Ohan household."

They sat in silence, the knowledge weighing on Bo's chest, heavy and suffocating.

Bo furrowed her brow. "That sounds awful. Why don't they just leave?" She didn't understand why anyone would choose to stay in a place where they were little more than slaves.

Zyla shook her head. "Things are rarely that simple. You see, the Ohans consider themselves the generous proprietors of the village, and anyone living here must buy all they need from them, meaning every last villager is in debt to the Ohans. And leaving before your debt is paid off is a death sentence. But, of course, they will never pay off their debts. The Ohans make sure of that. Most people are born and buried here without ever leaving, usually killed in mining accidents."

Bo felt unexpected anger flare in her chest. "Does the king know?" Bo had never been one to put her faith in the king, yet it seemed criminal that the king's people should be forced to work themselves to death to supply weapons for the king's war.

Zyla sighed. "He knows. He's visited the village many times but does nothing. He says that, as king, he cannot limit the economy by limiting the nobles, that it would do the villagers more harm to take away their only source of income," she explained. "But the truth is he's afraid of the Ohans. He knows how powerful they are. Angering them could incite a civil war among the nobles, and the people who would suffer most are the average citizens, or so he claims."

Something curdled in Bo's stomach. Fear. Disgust. Hatred. Anger. All of it simmered in her chest like a pot about to boil over. She knew the Ohans wanted to use her, to use her monsters for who knew what. Perhaps they would force her to threaten the people who lived here or take other people captive. Or perhaps they had even more sinister motives in mind.

She couldn't let that happen. She wouldn't. Unlike the other people who lived here, she would not allow herself to remain trapped forever.

She had to escape. And she had to do it soon.

2 6

———

JACK

$\mathcal{J}$ack didn't trust the strangers one bit. He didn't know what they wanted with Millie, but their secrecy set him on edge. They followed them for nearly a day with little indication of where they were going. They were headed north—that much he knew—the opposite direction of where they should've been going.

The Voice had been strangely quiet as well, another indication that something was not quite right. Normally, Jack would've felt relieved that it was silent, but instead it only served to make him more nervous. It was clear the Voice was hiding something. Something big.

The group traveled back roads, sticking to the shadows with a care that told him they were used to traveling in secret. Just one more reason not to trust them.

As the day shifted into evening, their progress slowed. The feline girl, Aaira, clearly the leader of this little troop, called for everyone to stop before turning to Jack and Millie.

"We must sneak you in under the cover of night. They cannot know you're here," she said gravely.

"Who can't?" Millie asked, dismounting her horse.

Aaira's cat eyes flicked between the two of them. "Now that we are closer, I can tell you more. Do you know where we are, Your Highness?" She had a unique way of saying his title that made it sound like an insult.

Jack swallowed. As the prince, he'd traveled all over Erinya for various diplomatic trips, but geography had never been his strength.

Reluctantly, he shook his head.

"We're nearing the city of Theibes, Ohan territory."

Jack's eyebrows shot up. He thought back on Ohan-Jin's suggestion of a regent, of the trepidation felt by everyone in his presence. The Ohans were the only noble family his father had ever feared. And rightly so.

"Why are we here?" Jack asked, his fists clenching.

"Because this is where the Convent of the Saints is, and that's where we're going," Aaira said.

Jack and Millie exchanged a glance. He wasn't sure what he'd expected, but the devotees of the Saints wasn't it.

"I don't understand," said Millie. "What does the convent have to do with me?"

The feline girl looked frustrated. "All will be explained, but you must trust us. Nearby, there is a tunnel that leads underground, straight to the convent's cellar. From there, the Matron will speak with you, Millie."

"And what about me?" Jack asked, irritation flickering through him.

Aaira glared at him. "What about you?"

"I'm going with her."

"The Matron has not asked to speak to you."

"I'm the prince."

"The Matron doesn't care who you are. If she doesn't want to speak with you, she won't." The girl smiled, green eyes glowing in the moonlight.

A hand touched his shoulder. "It will be all right, Your Highness," came Millie's soft voice. "I promise I won't let anything happen to me."

He looked over at Millie, and a reassuring smile lit her face. His stomach somersaulted. He knew she could take care of herself, that her powers were more than enough to protect her. It was that he didn't want to see her go.

He turned back to the feline girl. "Let me escort her through the tunnels. Then she can speak with the Matron on her own."

The girl's eyes narrowed, but she nodded.

A few people would stay behind with the horses, and Aaira, Ymira, and a young man named Orion would accompany them through the tunnels.

The moon slanted down through the trees as they approached a large boulder with a thin crevice cutting down the center. Ymira walked forward, pressing along the crevice. For a moment, nothing happened.

A slow grumbling like the sound of a landslide penetrated the air, followed by silence as a thin doorway opened between the rock. The group slipped through quickly and quietly, and Jack took one last look at the moon before following, his heart thumping erratically.

Be careful, my prince. You will find no friends among these people.

And with that, the entrance to the tunnel sealed, leaving the group in the dark.

The path sloped down, and the only light that illuminated the tunnels came from Ymira's golden bracelets, which cast strange shadows on the cobweb-covered walls. The tunnels were manmade, dug from the earth, perhaps by a mountain man or by the miners that Jack knew the Ohans employed. But then, if the Ohans had made these tunnels, he doubted the convent would be using them now.

Nearly two hours into their labyrinthian trek, they began making their way upward. With each step, Jack's muscles twitched more. What if they were walking right into a trap?

Millie's face was set as she walked beside him, intent on their destination. It was a look he recognized from his own sister. There would be no turning back; her mind was made. Still, Jack wanted nothing more than to grab her hand and drag her back the way they'd come.

At last, they reached a rickety wooden ladder stretching up into looming darkness.

"Millie first. We'll be right behind you. Don't stop. Don't look down. Once you reach the top, knock three times, and Orion will follow," Aaira explained.

Millie nodded and stepped forward, hands shaking. She ascended the ladder, disappearing into the darkness. Jack's blood pounded a frantic rhythm beneath his skin. What was taking so long? Had they really traveled so far beneath the ground?

The ladder wobbled, and Millie screamed.

"Millie!" Jack stepped forward, ice splitting his insides.

"I'm all right," she called down in a shaky voice. "I'm fine."

Jack forced himself to still even as his mind couldn't stop picturing her falling to her death.

Three knocks cut through the silence, and Jack breathed. He turned on Aaira. "Me next."

She looked like she wanted to fight him, and something told him she might have had he been anyone else. Instead, she nodded.

Jack climbed the ladder as fast as he could. He was no fan of heights, but he was nowhere near as afraid of them as Jill was. At last, he reached the top, where a trapdoor opened above him. He crawled through and stood in a dusty cellar.

Millie stood there, staring at him.

"Are you all right?" he asked, rushing toward her and grabbing her shoulders, inspecting her.

She nodded. "I'm fine. Really, Your Highness."

"Jack."

She looked at him, smiling weakly. "Prince Jack."

He swallowed, suddenly aware of how close they were, her chest just inches from his own, her breath warming his neck. Heat circled in his belly.

"Your Highness," a curt voice cut in, and Jack turned to see an old woman standing in the cellar, having appeared out of nowhere.

With a start, he realized he recognized the old lady. She had been at the Paladin Tournament. This was the woman he'd heard so much about.

"You forgot to knock," she said.

Jack's teeth clenched, but he leaned forward and rapped his knuckles three times against the trapdoor, and the sound echoed down the cavern.

The Matron watched him with the intensity of a hawk. Her gray hair was swept into a low bun that pulled at her temples, stretching the brown skin of her face taut like a drum. She reminded Jack of the head cook in the palace; although the cook was a large gazelle woman, the two shared the same severe look, a look that saw Jack as a troublemaker rather than a prince.

The rest of the group ascended the ladder until they all stood in the cellar. The tightness in Jack's chest built with every second that passed. It was a mistake to come here, he decided.

At last, the Matron turned her gaze on Millie. "You are the girl who won the tournament."

Millie nodded, her eyes cast downward. It seemed she still had not come to terms with her new standing. Or perhaps that was simply the Matron's effect.

"Come with me. We have much to discuss." The Matron looked back at Jack and then at the others. "Take him to one of the rooms on the second floor, one without a window. We cannot let the Ohans know we have the prince in custody."

"Wait, custody?" Jack asked. "You never told me that Millie and I had to split up. Where she goes, I go."

"Yet she is the one who won the tournament, and you are not."

The words were so unexpected that Jack's mind froze. The tiniest hint of a smile curled at the edge of the old woman's lips.

"Come with us, Your Highness." It was Ymira, her voice soft and gentle, and for a moment he felt himself relax. Before he could resist, he was being led away, watching as Millie followed the Matron somewhere he could not follow.

You should not have left the girl alone. They may turn her against you. Jack sensed the Voice's displeasure, its presence like icicles pricking the back of Jack's neck.

The girl's name is Millie, and why would they turn her against me? What do they want?

They want to see Erinya destroyed.

DAVID

avid ran a finger down the white scar on his arm, the first one he'd ever gotten after he was cursed. Over the years, his skin had broken and fractured and splintered too many times to count or keep track of, but this scar, a jagged slash along his forearm, hadn't faded as the other scars had come to.

He gritted his teeth and rolled down his sleeves. He didn't have time to sit around moping about his ruined skin. He had bigger problems, like how he was going to find these monsters and keep the princess's identity a secret.

His stomach clenched. *The princess.* She was here in this run-down pit of a camp. He still didn't understand why she was so far from the palace or why she had actually agreed to accompany him in the first place. It had been a calculated risk, threatening her and bringing her here, one that could end with his execution for black-mailing someone in the royal family.

Briefly, he wondered if he could die by hanging or if his neck would simply break and he'd be forced to live out his days without his body. As far as he knew, he would live as long as he could be put back together. And he could always be put back together.

He rose from the tattered cot he sat on, slung his quiver on, and counted his remaining arrows. In the army, he'd had nearly unlimited arrows, but here he was forced to collect and reuse the ones he shot, and any he couldn't find were lost until he made or purchased more.

The entrance to the tent fluttered open, and the princess entered, dressed and armed, her jaw set.

"Good, you're awake," she said.

"Good morning to you too," he grumbled. They had been here all of one night, and already she seemed anxious to be free of this place.

"Good morning," she gritted out, clearly annoyed. "So, when are we leaving?"

He frowned. "Leaving?"

"Yes, leaving. Are we hunting these creatures or not?" Her tone edged a note higher, her annoyance evident. He was beginning to wonder if he truly wanted her help or not.

"Well, first we have to talk to people."

"Talk to people?" Her face twisted, and he wasn't sure if she was disgusted or confused.

"Yes. I imagine as the princess you're good at talking to people."

She looked almost offended. "I've spent more time in the training arena than the ballroom."

David shut his mouth. He didn't know what he'd expected. All his life he'd imagined princesses cared only about gowns and suitors and palace gossip. Looking at Jill, though, that expectation seemed rather silly now. She was built like a warrior, her muscles lean and strong, not soft and dainty. And he'd seen her fight. He knew her claims must've been true. Still, he couldn't figure her out.

"Well, while you were sleeping last night, more refugees arrived. We need to speak with them. We need to learn as much about these monsters as we can. If we go running off on a wild-goose chase, we're likely to get ourselves killed."

Her back straightened as if she hadn't considered that point. At last, she nodded. "Fine. We'll talk to people." She turned to go.

David nodded, grabbing his bow off his cot before pausing. "And another thing," he said, stopping her in her tracks. "You may want to keep your identity hidden. If these people find out who you are, they won't talk."

Shock rippled across her face before it returned to its steely expression, and she nodded. "Understood."

An hour later, they walked through the narrow paths that wound through the camp. Paladin Grimzy towered behind them, his steps soft despite his size. In front of him walked Jill, her hands never straying from her weapons. David observed her. It seemed her gaze never rested on anything long, and her back curved like she was ready for an attack to come at any moment. None of it added up.

"You never did tell me why you're traveling on your own," David said, keeping his voice low.

Her spine stiffened as she glanced back at him, ribbons of hair curling around her face. "It's complicated," she said, turning her face away.

There was a heaviness in her voice that told him what she'd said was true. Their path turned as they reached a wider dirt road. Fires burned low, smoke perfuming the air. Children ran up and down the path, screaming and giggling, blissfully unaware of the danger that lurked all around them.

"Everything's complicated," he said, pulling up beside her.

She clenched her sword tighter, eyes drawn downward. "I doubt you'd understand."

His gut twisted like he'd been hit, though he didn't know why. Frustration pulled at his neck. "Because I'm just some common peasant?"

Her eyes flashed at him before she looked ahead of them, throwing her shoulders back. "No."

"Then why?"

"Aren't we here to interrogate other people?"

"If you think this is going to be an interrogation, then I can promise already that you're going to fail."

"What else would you do?" she asked, her voice rising.

He grabbed her arm and pulled her to a stop. "Listen," he said, dropping his voice low, "I understand who you are, but if we want to learn anything here, we need to do things my way. We *common peasants* get spooked easily when the king's men interrogate us. Saints only know what they'd do if they learned who you are."

Jill glared at him, and suddenly he realized how close together they stood. He swallowed and let go of her arm, his palms sweating.

"Fine," she gritted out at last. "We do things your way. But don't ever touch me again."

Heat flamed in his chest. "With pleasure."

Although David had only been in the camp for a matter of days, he already knew his way around. He'd spent half his life learning to get the lay of the land quickly, and now was no exception. They walked around, asking if anyone had seen the creatures or knew anyone who'd seen them.

The first hour they spoke to nearly a hundred people, each with less information than the last. No two stories seemed the same. A few people said they'd seen things; others had only heard the first inklings of rumors.

By midday they'd wound through half the camp, and David felt his nerves beginning to fray. The more people they spoke to, the more they risked accidentally spreading rumors that would send them off on a trip to nowhere.

Now they walked toward the center of the camp. A large common area had been set up with a market. Spices and roasted fowl blew through the air.

The cut of frantic words broke through the noise of the stalls. "—spotted in Harrow Forest. Three of them."

"Three? How did he even make it out alive?"

David slowed his pace just slightly, identifying the voices as coming from a feline couple up ahead, hoods drawn over their heads despite the glaring heat beating down on them. The feline woman pulled her cloak tighter.

"Jill," he whispered.

Her ears perked as she looked at him. "What?"

It appeared Jill was not the only one who'd heard him though. His gaze locked with the felines'—one male, one female—their expressions dark.

He swallowed. The Feline Clan was not, by nature, open with strangers, even where monsters were concerned. This would be difficult. He tried to remember what Asif had revealed about his people, but being an outcast himself, he had been given no divine insight.

Before Jill could barge onward, he stepped forward, examining the wares in their stall. It was clear wherever they'd come from, they'd left in a hurry. Random bits of clay jewelry and polished arrowheads were scattered across a rickety table. He kept his head low, feeling their gazes on him even as he thumbed a golden trinket, the flaking paint revealing it as nothing more than a carved wooden *jingah*, a charm they believed kept away evil spirits.

His fingers lingered longer than he intended. Luca had worn something similar, an ivory *jingah* in the crescent shape of a quarter moon with a blue feather hanging from the bottom.

He could sense Jill behind him, sense her eyes roaming over the stall. He glanced up at the couple, and their eyes watched him with measured care.

"How much?" he asked, picking up the peeling *jingah*. He knew it was worth no more than a few coppers, barely enough to buy a loaf of bread.

They spoke rapidly in Arajin, the feline tongue, the vowels sliding together in a lyrical way. David knew only a handful of words, but not nearly enough to understand, let alone speak to them.

The woman looked at him, dark braided hair wrapped in a crown around her head, calico markings adorning her bronze skin. "Twenty sterlings."

David struggled to keep his eyes from bulging out of his skull.

They must have been desperate if they truly thought someone would pay that much. But then, that was the game.

He shook his head. "Two sterlings."

The couple looked scandalized. "Twenty," the women affirmed, revealing sharpened teeth.

"You're lucky he's even offering two," Jill chimed in.

David's heart sank.

The woman's face twisted as she began snarling at Jill in rapid Arajin, her tone rising in pitch and volume until at last she spat out, "*Ella-horja!*"

Silence swallowed their corner of the market as eyes shifted to see what the sudden uproar was all about.

David's heart hammered. He knew that phrase, and it was not a kind one. And it seemed even Jill was aware of that. Her face flushed, whether from anger or embarrassment, he couldn't tell.

And then she stepped forward, her knuckles white on her sword. "What did you call me?" she hissed at the woman.

Instead of answering, the woman spat in her face.

For the space of a heartbeat, everything around them stilled. And then Jill wiped the spit away.

"You are going to regret that."

"I will never be sorry for treating a human *horja* the way they deserve." The woman's accent was filled with bitter loathing, her gaze burning with a cold hatred.

"Jill," David whispered, "let's go." He reached out to grab her arm, only to remember what she'd told him earlier. He would respect her wishes. For now. But if she caused a scene, he'd be forced to drag her away or leave her to fend for herself.

He wasn't sure which frightened him more.

Jill met the woman's gaze with her own fierce look until at last she turned, walking off, callous toward the eyes that followed her.

David felt like a hare caught in a trap. On one hand, he needed the information these people could provide, but to let Jill storm off seemed coldhearted.

Frustration boiled over in his chest as he gave the couple a quick nod before following the princess. The thought struck him as ironic. Here he was, chasing after the princess in disguise while monsters terrorized the kingdom.

There should be more people tracking these creatures down. He was just one man—a broken, scarred man who would spend the rest of his life serving the crown until he was broken so badly that he couldn't be put back together again.

He balled his fists as he broke into a run.

"Jill," he said, coming up behind her. "Please stop."

"Why should I?" she asked, picking up her pace. Her tone was so angry he feared she might draw her weapons at any moment.

"Listen, will you please just stop and look at me?"

She spun on him. "Why? So you can lecture me? So you can tell me all the things I did wrong back there? I knew coming here was a mistake!" Her tone bit through the air like a winter chill.

"Jill, please don't listen to them. They're just scared. Cornered animals always growl, even when they have nowhere else to go."

She looked up at him, green eyes shot with gold, staring at him. For a split second, he thought she might cry. But her face hardened to stone once more.

"Have we learned anything useful about the monsters?" she asked.

David shook his head. They needed more. *He* needed more. They couldn't risk tracking these creatures down without more to go on. There were still too many unknowns.

A ringing bell cracked through the camp, and they turned, following the sound. Around them, others looked to the sound as well, and everyone moved to the west of the camp to see what the commotion was about.

They ran to the outskirts, and David saw Jill stop short. He stopped behind her and followed her gaze.

The breath caught in his throat.

Hundreds of people dressed in dirty, bloodied rags inched toward the camp. Some carried bags of provisions, some carried small chil-dren, and others carried nothing at all. As a mass, they lumbered on, heads bowed low.

David recognized the look in their eyes. He'd seen it many times when soldiers had returned from failed missions. It was a look of despair, of hopelessness. A look of defeat.

MILLIE

illie's legs were beginning to wobble beneath her. Between the horseback riding and the hundreds of stairs she'd now climbed, she was wondering if she'd even make it to where the Matron was taking her.

The Matron. She wasn't sure how she felt about the old woman yet, but she had to admire her strength as she climbed the stairs with unwavering speed, cane and all.

At last, they reached a small landing. An old wooden door with iron scrollwork around the edges stood before them.

The Matron pulled a key from her pocket and slipped it into the lock before turning it and pushing open the door. A round room opened before them. A fire crackled in the hearth off to the right, and to the left loomed a large ornate window overlooking the town. An immaculate bed sat in one corner, and a sofa stood in the center with a small table and a pot of tea, steam twisting from the spout. Other than that, there were no signs that anyone lived here.

"Tea?" the Matron asked.

Millie felt suddenly parched, but her training as a palace maid told her she should decline. "No, thank you."

The old woman raised an eyebrow but said nothing, and for the first time it struck Millie how alone she was. First, her brother had been arrested. Then Jill had abandoned them. Now even Jack had been led somewhere else.

"I heard what happened at the tournament."

Fear stabbed at her core. "What?" It took every effort to keep her voice from squeaking.

"Don't look at me like that, child. I'm not as old as I look. I had spies everywhere in that tournament."

Millie was paralyzed. She should've run. That was what Jack would've told her to do. She should've fought. That was what Jill would've done.

But she was not Jack or Jill. She was just Millie.

"Paladin? Are you all right?" the Matron asked.

That caught her attention. Millie was the paladin. Paladin Millie. The title still felt foreign and unfamiliar.

"Why am I here?" It was a silly question. She already knew the answer: she was here because she had magic. And it appeared she wasn't the only one.

The old woman stared at her. Her age was hard to place. Fine lines crinkled around her eyes and mouth, yet there was a strange youthfulness about her. She'd proved that by climbing the endless stairs.

"Tell me, Miss Muffet, what do you know about the Saints?"

The question caught her off guard. She knew the stories about a wicked king and the Saints that had risen up to stop him. She remembered her brother telling her the stories as a child in the servants' quarters. They'd huddled around the fireplace, she and the other children, to listen as he spun stories out of thin air. They'd wrapped around her, those words, whispering into the darkest corners of her mind, telling her there was truth in the words he spoke.

But when she'd asked her brother if the stories were true, he'd always said the same thing. "Stories are just stories. But the good ones always have an ounce of truth."

She never knew what that meant.

"The twelve Saints had great power — power Erinya had never seen before." Millie's heart thudded a frantic rhythm. "They fought against the Black King, who used dark magic to enslave the land. And after the Saints passed, their magic did as well."

The Matron nodded. "You are almost correct."

"Almost?"

The woman sighed. "The Saints did indeed rise up with a magic that had never been seen before, and with their power they banished the Black King to the Shadowlands, the realm between life and death. But the Saints feared the Black King may try to return, so they gave their magic to their heirs, magic that would awaken only when Erinya was in grave danger."

Millie swallowed, the room tilting beneath her feet. "I don't understand." It was a lie though. She understood perfectly, and yet her mind refused to believe it.

The Matron nodded. "War is looming, Miss Muffet. Darkness spreads through the land. The Black King awakens. I believe the Saints' heirs are the only ones who can stop him."

Millie's mouth was dry, her stomach churning. "What does that have to do with me?" Inwardly, she prayed. She prayed she was wrong. She prayed that this was all some terrible nightmare from which she would soon awaken.

"You, Millie Muffet, are one of the Saints' heirs. You hold the key to banishing the darkness once and for all."

29

JILL

Jill's chest ached like she'd spent three days in the training arena without rest. A train of people stumbled forward, and their carts bumped over the land, carrying meager supplies. Some were humans, some were inkwells, and others were from the animal clans. They were all dirty and tired.

She knew she should do something, but what did one person do for so many people?

Beside her, David made the first move forward. Asif materialized at his side, and they ran toward the first group of travelers at the front of the long train.

She couldn't hear what they said but watched David take a small child from an older inkwell man and Asif help support the man to the edge of the camp.

At last, David set the child, a boy who couldn't have been more than two, on the ground and helped the man sit down beside him. Tear tracks raced down the child's grimy face.

"We need supplies, blankets, tents, food, anything that can be spared," David said, addressing the group that had gathered to watch the newcomers.

A young woman stepped forward, an eye patch over her left eye. Horns like Madame Sorelle's curled up from her head. "We barely have enough for ourselves, let alone hundreds more!"

"We have no more room!" someone else shouted.

"Why doesn't the king send aid?" another person asked.

Voices rose, and arguments broke out. Every person had a different idea for the refugees. Some thought they should leave, and others felt it was their duty to help. No one could agree.

"What happened?" Jill asked, her voice carrying over the din.

At that, people stilled, every person wondering how so many people had found themselves with nowhere else to go.

David's face darkened, giving his scars an ominous look. "They were attacked. First by a raiding party of Carthesians, and then by the monsters on their journey here."

Gasps echoed through the crowd, panic spreading like wildfire. Words of monsters and Carthesians were uttered like curses.

Anger washed over Jill, rage pounding through her veins. Monsters? And now Carthesians? Why weren't there soldiers to protect these people? Why hadn't her father been made aware of the state of the kingdom? How many had to die before somebody changed something?

What have you *done to change anything?*

The thought struck her like a blow to the gut, vaporizing her breath.

Before she understood what she was doing, she marched forward, stepping onto a stool left around a burned-out campfire. She turned to face the growing crowd.

"I need someone to gather as many bandages and medical supplies as can be spared and find anyone who may have healing experience." She glanced at the woman who'd first spoken. "Will you do that?"

The woman leveled her with a gaze so bitter it nearly knocked Jill off the stool. "Any experienced healer would have been sent off to the king's armies."

Jill's heart twisted. Of course. It made sense that her father would have wanted as many trained healers in his army as possible. Still, she could not fight back the flush that rose to her cheeks.

She swallowed. "Find anybody you can. Perhaps midwives or apprentices."

In the crowd, a few people nodded, but the woman continued to stare at her, and she was reminded of the look the feline woman had given her.

They will hate you for who are. They were her father's words told to her when she was younger.

"Why should we listen to you? You come into *our* camp dressed like a noble and start ordering us around, and you expect us to be grateful?" she sneered.

An awkward silence washed over the crowd. As the princess, Jill had spent an entire lifetime in the spotlight. She was used to eyes watching her carefully, waiting for her to slip up. She'd always held her head high, ignoring the people who would dare look down on her.

This felt different, not because these people were petty and selfish like the other people she'd spent her life with, but because they weren't.

These people, who struggled daily to survive, whose livelihoods had been stolen from them, whose children had been carried off by her father to fight in a decade-long war, saw her only as another noble exerting her will over them.

Light steps sounded behind her. "These people need our help." David's voice was soft, yet it carried over the crowd. "We should do what we can. Will you help?"

The gazelle woman looked at Jill and then back at David. "I will." She turned away, rounding up a few others nearby to help her, and they set off, determined.

Jill's face grew hotter. Never in her life had she felt so exposed.

David started requesting help from others, and every last person agreed to help him in any way they could.

Jill stepped down from the stool. A new feeling swirled in the pit of her stomach. She glanced at Asif, but he would not meet her eyes. She wanted to leave, to run as far away from this camp as she could get. She wasn't needed here.

Her mind recalled the conversation she'd had with her father just a few weeks ago. She wasn't needed there either. He'd said as much when he'd agreed to marry her off to one of the Welynn princes.

"You shouldn't listen to that woman," David said, startling her. "She's just scared. Fear makes people do things they wouldn't otherwise."

Jill looked over at the man who'd brought her here, the man who saw something in her that no one else apparently did. For a second, she wondered if the scar over his eye affected his vision. "You said that earlier."

"Because it's true."

Jill huffed. "I don't know what use I am here. It seems everyone wants me to leave." She hadn't expected the sting the admission would inflict.

David looked at her, his expression searching. "Come, you need to get out of your head." He started walking toward the newcomers without waiting to see if she would follow.

For a moment, she stood there. She didn't want to follow. To follow would mean bearing witness to the wrong done to these people. To follow would mean she could not unsee what these people had endured. She wanted to run, to flee this camp and continue her search for a cure for her father. Then her father could send someone else to help. Someone better.

She stepped forward.

Hours passed as she and David spoke to each and every person who had come. Everyone had lost something, and some had lost everything. Jill watched as David transformed before her very eyes; instead of the stoic soldier and keen hunter, he became a comforter and friend. He helped set up tents, gather blankets and clothing, build fires, and find food.

As the day dragged on, more people came to him, asking how they could help. Even Paladin Grimzy looked to him. David's confidence never wavered. He delegated tasks like a born general, and he helped like the lowliest servant.

By comparison, Jill felt riddled with guilt. She did whatever David asked, but she still could not look people in the eye. Shame clung to her like a damp cold, always lingering and never allowing one to get comfortable.

As the sun set over the camp, she and David were assembling one of the last tents for a young couple and their baby.

David pounded stakes into the ground alongside the man, sweat dripping from his brow. Jill stood awkwardly next to the young inkwell girl, who was barely older than she was.

The baby screamed, and Jill jumped, looking over at the chubby wailing creature as the mother bounced and shushed him.

Jill's heart pattered frantically. She had little experience with children, let alone babies. But the mother looked on the verge of tears as she started singing to the child.

To her surprise, Jill knew the song.

The woman's voice was soft and feathery as she sang.

Little bird, little bird,

Why do you sing?

Little bird, little bird,

Why do you fly?

Little bird, little bird,

Do you know? Do you know?

You are richer than a king.

THE YOUNG WOMAN looked at her, and Jill realized she had sung along. But the baby was also silent, watching her with big brown eyes.

"You have a lovely voice," the woman said, smiling at her.

Jill let out a breathy laugh. "Thank you. So do you."

They stood there for a moment, staring at each other. The woman was rather plain looking, brown hair tied back in a braid, but there was something sweet about her that Jill couldn't place.

"What is your name?"

The woman looked at her husband and then back to Jill. "Aeyla. My husband is Baedor, and this is Fyre," she said, looking down at the baby. He cooed in response, looking up at his mother and giving her a big toothless grin.

For the first time in days, Jill felt lighter as she watched the simple bond the two shared. Her mother had died when she was a baby, so she could only imagine shared moments like these. Suddenly, her chest ached.

"Do you and your husband want children someday?"

Jill's heart somersaulted, her eyes snapping to Aeyla's. "I—we aren't—he's not—" Jill's face burned as she glanced over at David. "We're not together."

The woman's eyes widened. "Forgive me, I assumed. You two seem so close."

Jill couldn't find the words, her heart racing as she suddenly pictured herself and David. She shook her head. "He's just a friend," she said at last. She wasn't entirely sure if that was true, but she wasn't sure what else to call someone who was blackmailing her into helping him hunt down monsters. "Friend" seemed much simpler.

David and Baedor walked over to them, and Jill released a breath.

"That should hold for tonight. In the morning I will see if there is something bigger for your family," David explained.

"You have done so much for our family already. This is more than we could have ever imagined," Aeyla said, tears gathering at the corners of her eyes.

"We are forever indebted to you," Baedor said, his voice deep.

"There is no need. As a soldier, I am bound to help my people." David nodded, giving them a gentle smile.

My people.

Jill looked over at David. His scar was pale in the waning light. He was not an ugly man, even with his scars, but she'd never thought of him as particularly handsome either. She thought of what the woman had asked her about David, and she blushed, looking at the ground.

"We should be going," David said. "Good night."

The couple echoed their good nights, and the baby chimed in with his own blabbering. Jill smiled despite herself, bending over to look him in the eyes.

"Good night, Fyre. Be good to your mama."

The baby responded by grabbing her hair and yanking as hard as he could before letting out a squeal of laughter. Aeyla pried his fingers out of her hair, and Jill gave another good night before turning back to walk with David.

"You are good with the people."

She rolled her eyes. "Right, and I'm also skilled at the tightrope."

He chuckled. "Honestly, it wouldn't surprise me if you were."

"Well, I can assure you, I am not."

The silence thickened around them as they walked side by side. Grimzy had taken Asif and a few others to set animal traps around the perimeter of the camp and scout out any decent hunting areas. With the addition of more hungry bellies came the need for more food.

"I wouldn't really have told anyone who you are." The statement was so random that it took Jill a second to figure out what he meant.

"What?" she asked.

"I wouldn't have told anybody you're the princess. Back at the inn. I just needed help, and you seemed like the best option."

She swallowed, not sure how she felt about being an option. She was pretty sure she'd been his only option. "You could've convinced me."

"Well, I admit, I was desperate." His face darkened, and her thoughts returned to why she'd come here in the first place: the monsters.

That turned her mind to another thought. "The Carthesians should not be this far inland. I don't even understand how that's possible." It puzzled her more than she cared to admit. She had enough problems on her mind without the added worry of potential invaders.

"I don't know either." He looked nearly as disturbed as she felt, his shoulders tightening. He shook his head. "Thank you for your help today."

She shrugged. "I didn't do anything. You were the one who rallied everyone, the one people listened to." She glanced up at him in the dark, waiting for him to deny it.

"They sense you are different. For now, it might be a weakness, but perhaps someday it will be a strength."

30

BO

Over the course of the past few days, Bo had determined that few people came to the dungeon where she was kept. There were four other cells, but none of them were occupied. Food was brought twice a day, she assumed in the morning and the evening, but without a window she couldn't be entirely sure. Zyla came in between the two meals to continue treating her wounds.

The long stretch between the last meal and the next must have been night. At least she hoped so.

The door at the top of the staircase creaked open, a random serving girl come to bring her the evening meal.

The servant was different every time. Perhaps because the Ohans did not want anyone to learn who she was, or perhaps because then there would be little risk of a servant helping her escape. Either way, it didn't matter; she would have to do this on her own.

The serving girl stopped outside her cell, sliding the tray through the slot at the bottom of the door. The Ohans were careful. There were never any eating utensils, and she was fed only a piece of dried meat and a hunk of stale bread along with a jar of water.

This was also the only time of day when they changed the chamber pot Bo used to relieve herself.

And for that they had to open the cell door.

"Place the pot by the door and then step back against the wall," the girl said, her voice monotone. It was the same every day.

Bo sighed. She picked up the container and placed it dutifully in front of the door, then backed up. The girl pulled out a single key and placed it in the lock.

The rusted hinges protested as the door whined open. But before the girl could even bend over, Bo launched herself forward, picking up the pot and splashing it on the girl before it dropped to the ground, shattering.

For a moment, the girl stood there, drenched and stunned. But Bo was prepared and snatched a piece of the broken jar off the floor before yanking the girl and whirling her around until the shard was pressed tightly against her throat.

"I'm really sorry," Bo said. And she was. The girl was likely just as much a victim as she was.

The girl squirmed, and Bo pressed the shard tighter against her throat, drawing blood. "Please don't make me do this."

The girl stilled. "What do you want?"

"I want out."

The girl scoffed. "You won't make it. They'll kill you the second you step out this door."

Bo's heart raced. "They can try."

She glanced over at the blue-fire torch on the wall. Any moment now guards would be down here wondering what that crash was. She had to act. And fast.

"Give me your apron."

"What?"

"Your apron, now!"

The girl untied her apron, now covered in muck, and shoved it at her. Bo grabbed it and then shoved the girl into her former cell, slamming the door closed. The girl's face was the picture of vehemence.

"What's to keep me from screaming?" she asked.

Bo stared at her, guilt washing over her again. She should've offered to get this girl out too. But it was too late for that. "Nothing."

Bo grabbed the torch and touched it to the apron. It burst into flames, and she ran, fire biting at her fingertips, smoke billowing into the air.

The girl screamed.

Bo limped up the stairs, torch in hand, prepared for whatever lay ahead. The dungeon door slammed open, and the guard who stood there looked confused. Bo threw the flaming garment in the man's face before smashing the torch into his groin. Bo stepped back as the man doubled over, tripping and falling down the stairs.

Bo moved to the side, narrowly avoiding being taken down with the man. He landed at the bottom of the steps and she continued up the stairs as fast as she could before slamming the door shut behind her. She needed to find something to use as a crutch or she wouldn't make it far.

She breathed a ragged breath, glancing around. She stood in a long dark hallway, and to her surprise, it was blissfully empty. It wouldn't be for long though. She'd hoped to use the apron to start a fire somewhere else and draw people's attention away from the dungeon, but now it was stuck to the guard's face.

Gripping the torch, she ran along the hallway as fast as she was able to with her limp. She had no idea where she was going and could only pray that at some point she would find a door or a window.

Voices sounded down the hall ahead of her. She panicked, looking around for any escape. All she found was an ugly tapestry. She would be doing these people a favor. Without thinking, she lit the tapestry and darted down another corridor.

Shouts and smoke filled the hallway. She hobbled, wishing, not for the first time, that she had her crutch with her. Then, up ahead, she saw it.

A window.

She ran to it and pried at it with her fingers, but it was locked fast.

Wielding the torch like a club, she smashed the window and climbed through, shards cutting at her skin. She threw the torch back inside. The light would only make her a target in the dark.

Voices drew closer from within; she had seconds before they found her. She turned to run and froze. A man stood in front of her. A human, though, not an Ohan. He was clad in leather with buckles across his chest, and his mussed red hair glinted in the moonlight.

She swallowed, taking a step back, mind reeling. Now she was angry with herself for throwing the torch back in; it was the closest thing she'd had to a weapon.

But then the man stepped forward, pressing a finger to his lips. She wasn't sure if she obeyed him or if she was simply too afraid to resist, but she stayed silent as he raised a hand and closed his eyes.

She turned to look at the window. One second it stood broken, and the next it seemed perfectly intact. She blinked.

And then guards were there on the other side of the window, staring out at her, confusion pulling at their features.

"Could've sworn I saw her climb through," one of them mumbled.

"Let's keep moving. Ohan-Jin will have our heads if we don't find her."

Then they moved on.

Bo shivered despite the warm night. *What just happened?*

She looked back at the man. "What? How?"

The man raised an eyebrow. "Do you want to ask questions, or do you want to escape?"

Bo nodded and took off running, an eerie feeling climbing up the back of her neck. She didn't know who that man was or why he'd helped her, but she felt certain of one thing: he was like her.

Ahead stood an old stone building stretching high into the sky. Voices shouted all around her. If she could make it into that building, then perhaps she could hide.

For once, she wished for the monsters. They would have made easy work of her pursuers.

Her pace slowed, pain shooting up her leg. She had never pushed it this hard before, and she would pay for it later. She was paying for it now.

The closer she got to the building, though, the slower she went. A tingling grew at the back of her head, the darkness wrapping its greedy arms around her.

She wasn't sure how she knew, but something evil lay ahead.

Her breath was coming in gasps now, her leg and lungs burning. She pushed her way through the foliage surrounding the building and hunched down in the bushes, her back pressed up against the stone.

Her mind felt like fog, clouded and muggy. She shivered, sweat trailing down her spine. She sucked in a rattling breath.

A creak broke through the silence, and her head whipped toward the sound. A figure stepped out of the building, still and quiet.

And then he spoke.

Bo's heart hiccupped until she realized he wasn't speaking to her, but to himself. His voice was low as he mumbled to himself. Every now and then she caught words.

Afraid.

My father.

Dying.

The tingling at the base of her neck grew, buzzing louder and louder. Fear washed over her as the figure stopped speaking and turned, looking in her direction.

Bo was frozen. She could not think. She could not breathe. She could not force herself to move.

Shouting split the silence, and the figure disappeared back through the door. Voices were headed her way, and she knew she should rise, should sneak away and keep moving. Still, she was paralyzed.

She could only hide so long before they found her, and she could only run so long before she was caught.

It was now or never.

She stood and ran to the door the figure had disappeared through, shouts rising behind her. She yanked on the doorknob, desperation making her hands slick with sweat. She pounded, throwing herself against the door. But it wouldn't budge.

Fear eclipsed reason as she turned, her legs shaking from adrenaline. Three armed men raced toward her, weapons drawn. One of the men raised his bow, an arrow pointed straight at her.

"Don't kill her!" one of them yelled.

But it was too late. The twang of the bow echoed through the air, and the arrow raced toward her. Time slowed around her. It was the longest breath she'd ever drawn. And the shortest.

Pain exploded in her shoulder, and she screamed, dropping to her knees. Every breath sent a fresh wave of agony rolling through her.

"Take her to Ohan-Jin. He'll want to make sure she's punished."

Bo heard the words faintly, but pain consumed her. Rough hands dragged her to her feet. And for the second time in a matter of days, darkness overwhelmed her senses.

31

———

JACK

Jack's heart raced, and he pressed his back to the door as he listened to the girl pounding and pulling at the lock. His head buzzed, a headache forming at the base of his neck. Adrenaline pounded through his bloodstream. He knew he should just open the door, help her, but fear had already sunk its greedy claws deep into his chest.

A scream sounded outside, followed by a sickening thunk. And then silence.

Jack's legs wobbled beneath him. He should have let her in. She could be dead.

She isn't dead.

That did little to reassure him. Why hadn't he let her in? Why, even now, was his heart pounding like he was the one those guards were after?

That girl, she's different.

Jack had already guessed as much. He'd sensed her long before he saw her hiding in the bushes, his ears ringing.

Who is she?

The Voice was silent, but Jack could feel it stewing, thinking. For the first time, he wondered if the Voice was able to conceal its thoughts from him, even though he did not have that luxury.

I do not know. But she is incredibly valuable. I can sense her lifeblood even now.

Jack stiffened. After all this time, he had not realized that the Voice could sense the lifeblood of others. It made him wonder what else the Voice knew, what other secrets it was hiding.

You should return to your quarters. If they find you here, they may not be so free with you in the future.

Jack gritted his teeth, but he knew the Voice was right. After Millie had been escorted away, he'd been led to a small room with nothing but a cot and a lantern. He'd sat there for hours, waiting for someone to come to him, until finally he'd opened his door and slipped down the hall to get some fresh air.

He forced himself to walk back through the long stone corridors, his pulse skittish as he pictured the girl being taken. He should have helped her, should have done something! Instead, he'd panicked.

There was nothing you could have done. Those men would have killed you.

Probably. He knew the Voice was right. Still, he couldn't shake the feeling that he was responsible for her capture. Or worse.

Your heart is soft, my prince. You cannot lead Erinya well with it.

Jack stopped walking. The words were an echo of something his father had once told him long ago, long before the Voice had come to live in his head. The king had always seen Jack as too soft. Once, when he was a child, he'd found a small kitten that had been abandoned by its mother. Jack had taken it to his room, doing everything he could to nurse it back to health.

If only he'd known his father was visiting him that afternoon, he could have hidden the poor thing. Instead, his nine-year-old self had shown the kitten to his father. The king took the animal like it was diseased. He still remembered how dark his father's expression became; instead of being delighted by his son's rescue, he was furious.

"You know it cannot live without its mother. You have not saved it, only prolonged its death."

Jack's face fell. "But we have to help it. We have to—"

Jack still remembered the soft crack that echoed through his room. It was so quiet and yet so impossibly loud.

The kitten was still in his father's hands. "Your heart is soft, Jack. You must learn to do what needs to be done." He'd handed the limp creature to Jack and stormed from the room as tears fell down Jack's face.

Even now, the memory left him sick to his stomach. But the worst part of the entire incident was that he knew his father was right. It would have been far worse to let the kitten die slowly.

You should keep moving.

Jack didn't argue, shuffling down the hall. Ahead, a door opened, and a young man walked out. Orion, Jack recalled. His age was difficult to determine. He was shorter and stockier than Jack, yet he moved through the hall like he was made of feathers.

A tattoo flashed across Orion's fingers, a vine twisting up his wrist and bicep. Jack's breath caught as he thought of a similar tattoo—the tattoo belonging to the first girl he'd ever given his heart to, the girl who'd left him without a word of goodbye. His chest suddenly ached like someone had pounded a nail into his rib cage.

Orion turned, waiting for someone. Millie walked out of the door behind him, and her eyes instantly latched on to Jack's. His stomach flipped, and the painful memories vanished as he looked at her.

Millie gave him a weak smile, her eyelashes fluttering. Instantly, he was at her side.

"What happened? What did that woman want to speak to you about?" Jack asked.

"*That woman* is the Matron of the Order of the Saints," growled Orion.

"And I'm a prince," Jack snapped. "Don't you have anything better to do than correct people?"

"Actually, I do. But unfortunately, I have to babysit you two."

Wonderful.

Jack rolled his eyes, determined to ignore the inkwell man. "What did she want to talk to you about?" he asked, turning back to Millie.

Millie glanced at the ground, not meeting his gaze. "It's complicated."

Jack eyed Orion, sensing that his presence was keeping Millie from speaking. "Do you mind giving us just a few moments?"

The young man pursed his lips. Jack wondered if Aaira had gotten to him or if everyone here just hated him.

"Please?" Millie asked sweetly, giving Orion a smile. It was not seductive like so many of the smiles Jack had seen tossed his direction. Being the prince, it had been an almost daily occurrence. And while his sister never failed to tease him, he didn't enjoy it nearly as much as she might have thought.

A pang of jealousy knotted his stomach as he watched Orion's gaze flick between the two of them. His vine tattoos swayed on his skin.

"Fine. Two minutes. Then I'm to escort you to your quarters, Miss Muffet." He stomped down the hall, just out of earshot, making it clear that it was all the privacy they would receive.

"What happened? Are you okay?" The words rushed out of him as he took in Millie's appearance. Her skin looked pale, and he wasn't sure if it was the lighting or if something had happened.

"I'm okay, really."

"What did the Matron want to tell you?"

Millie sighed. "She told me where my powers came from, why I have magic." Her words were soft, like "magic" was a curse word she wasn't supposed to use. He couldn't blame her. Magic hadn't been seen in decades.

"And?"

She looked up at him, her expression guarded. There was more she wasn't telling him; he was certain of it. For the first time, it occurred to him that maybe she didn't want to tell him.

She bit her bottom lip. "They want me to stay here, to train me to use my gift."

Jack felt like he'd been struck in the gut. The air whooshed from his lungs. "What?" It was all he could say, all he could manage.

Very interesting.

Jack didn't want to respond to the Voice, didn't want to give it the satisfaction. But he could sense that, just like Millie, there was something it was holding back.

What?

She still has not told you where she got her powers.

You know, don't you?

I have my suspicions.

Jack was torn. He didn't want to force her hand, to tell her that her duty as paladin came before anything else, that it always would. But he knew he couldn't stay here, especially if the people hunting him were so close by. But if he was honest with himself, it was more than simply wanting her to fulfill her duty. He wanted her to be with him. But how could he ask her to leave?

It is quite the predicament.

Shut up.

Millie wouldn't meet his gaze. "They want me to stay. But I'm not sure . . ."

"I'm still not sure about this place. What exactly did they tell you?"

She licked her lips, still refusing to look at him. "I . . . I can't say."

His temper suddenly flared. "What? Why not?"

She stepped back, startled, fear scrawled across her features. She shook her head. "The Matron, she told me—Jack, I'm sorry. She asked me not to say anything. Not until we know more."

They don't trust you.

Jack's throat felt raw, and heat spread through his chest. He wanted to punch something. He wanted to fight. "If you stay here, you'll never see your brother again."

The words were out of his mouth before he could think them through. Millie took another step back, looking like she'd been struck. Tears welled in the corners of her eyes.

"What?" she mouthed. She took a step back.

In that moment, Jack wished she would have yelled at him, thrown something, hit him—anything other than look at him with betrayal. Stabbing guilt seized him, and he wanted to take it all back.

"Millie, wait, please. I-I didn't mean that! I'm sorry!" His voice was panicked. "Please, I—"

"Time's up," Orion cut in. If it was possible, his face looked even more sour than when he'd first seen Jack. He must have overheard them.

"No, wait, please. Just a few more minutes!"

"I think you should go, Jack." Millie had recovered, but still her voice was not hard. Jill would have punched him if she were here. He would've preferred Jill's wrath to the indifference Millie now looked at him with.

"Millie, please, I didn't mean it." His voice cracked, and it occurred to him that he was begging. He'd never begged for anything in his life.

"You should return to your quarters," came Orion's brusque voice.

Millie turned, following Orion up the hall until she disappeared around a corner. Jack stood there alone.

You're not alone. Not with me here.

"I never asked you to live inside my head!" Jack hissed aloud. He was certain the Voice was toying with him, messing with his emotions. The Voice had told him to say those things.

You and I both know that isn't true.

"Why are you here? What do you want with me?" He didn't care if talking to himself made him look crazy. He didn't care if anyone heard him.

The Voice gave a dark chuckle. ***One day, my prince, you will need me, and I will need you. Erinya is on the brink of a great war, one that will see you fall or rise. Together, though, we will rise.***

32

DAVID

David woke before the sun despite his exhaustion. Above him, the darkness had waned, leaving the gray light that came before dawn. For a whole week now, he and Jill had dedicated themselves to helping the newest refugees and learning all they could about the monsters. He wasn't sure who was antsier about tracking down the creatures, Jill or Asif. As best they could determine, it seemed the creatures were hiding out in the haunted Deadwood. Still, David was certain that the best course of action was to learn all they could before they went tromping off through the forest.

The silence suddenly struck him. Asif was supposed to be in the bedroll beside him, but it was empty.

His breath hitched as he sat up, reaching for his sword on instinct, and froze. It was gone. He released a torrent of swear words as he gathered his gear, fuming. *Damn kid.* What had he done?

"Asif!" he hissed into the quiet. "Asif!" he tried again, louder this time.

Panic gripped him as he walked over to Grimzy, who slept upright, his back against a tree. His snores shook the ground, breaking the serene quiet.

"Grimzy," he whispered, nudging him with his boot.

"*Paladin* Grimzy," he mumbled without opening his eyes, a smirk toying at his lips.

"Where's the kid?" he asked through gritted teeth.

The mountain man opened his eyes and glanced around, unconcerned. "Maybe he went to relieve himself. How should I know?"

"The kid took my sword," he said.

That caught Grimzy's attention, and his expression darkened.

The door to Jill's tent fluttered open. "What's going on?" she asked, looking between the two of them. She was already dressed and armed. She never ceased to be prepared.

"Asif's gone. He took my sword."

Her brows rose at the implication. "You don't think—"

"Yes." He knew it. Only yesterday Asif had begged David to begin the hunt for his sister. David had told him no, much to Asif's protests.

"Why?" Jill asked, looking almost as concerned as David felt. Over the past week, David had seen the way Jill cared for Asif, protected him, sparred with him. The two were outsiders to everyone but each other.

Grimzy rose, towering over the two of them. "His sister was taken by the creatures over a fortnight ago."

Jill looked pale. "He went after her."

David nodded, his jaw tight. He felt so stupid. He should never have taken his eyes off that kid. He'd been a quick study with the sword, and now he intended to put what little he'd learned to the test.

Jill's shoulders slumped, and it was clear she felt the weight of this as much as he did. "How many people have come back after being taken?"

He didn't want to answer, and he was certain she already knew what he would say. Their eyes locked as shame and guilt wrestled inside him. He should have told Asif the truth. He should have trained him better. He should have taken care of him.

Jill gripped the hilt of her left blade, a habit he'd begun to notice.

"We have to stop him. Whatever he plans to do, it won't end well. Have we learned anything new about the creatures?"

David tensed. In the past few days, he'd asked everyone he could what they knew about the monsters plaguing the land. There was more than one, it seemed, though just how many, no one could say for sure. By all accounts, it seemed they traveled in a pack, and piecing together what little information he had, they were heading north, toward the one forest David had never dared step foot in. He'd told Asif as much the night before.

"He's going to the Deadwood."

Jill's gaze was determined. "Then we leave now and pray we find him first."

THE DEADWOOD HAD ONCE BEEN HOME to the many apothecaries who'd lived in Erinya before the Crusades. Now nothing remained but ash and bone, as if every apothecary had used their dying breath to curse the ground beneath their feet.

A tangible weight hung in the air as they stepped into the woods, darkness covering them like a burial shroud. Little flags hung off branches. Broken and discarded weapons lay scattered everywhere. Trees still bore scorch marks from the Komodos, giant fire-breathing lizards the apothecaries had ridden like horses. It seemed like a massacre that had taken place mere days ago, not two decades earlier.

David glanced at Jill. One of her swords was poised and ready. It was easy to forget she was a princess in moments like these.

"Death lingers everywhere here," came Grimzy's deep voice.

"Thanks for the comforting words," David replied. Every word uttered felt wrong in this haunted place, as if speaking might awaken the dead. But that was impossible. The dead stayed dead. He should know.

Behind him, Grimzy stopped, and both David and Jill stared at the tribesman. His eyes were closed, brow furrowed in concentration.

"What are you—"

"Shh." Jill held up a hand, staring at Grimzy.

They watched for several minutes as his face twisted and contorted, morphing from pain to confusion to betrayal until, at last, he opened his eyes.

"What did you see?" Jill asked, her voice wavering.

Grimzy shook his head. "They never stood a chance. It was a slaughter. Here, the earth holds bones and memories so painful I can barely stand it."

Silence wrapped around them as the mountain man's words sank in. The apothecaries had fallen by their own people's hands, all because they were different. Because people listened to fear.

His pulse gathered speed. *Why, Asif? Why?* He wished he'd never agreed to help the commander. He wished he'd never met the kid. He wished he weren't as scared as he felt right now.

"Did you see anything that might help us find Asif or . . . or the monsters?" Jill asked, uncertain.

Grimzy shook his head. "I'm sorry, no. But I sense someone else has been here recently, and they awakened something. The earth, the water, the bones—they're restless."

David didn't know what that meant. Who would enter this Saints-forsaken place of their own free will? Why?

"We need to keep moving," Jill said, shaking her head. "Find Asif and get out of here."

David swallowed hard. "And what about the monsters?"

"I can't imagine even a monster wanting to live here," she said, glancing around.

David hated to agree with her, but he felt it too. He got the sense they were unwanted parasites crawling on a living creature. The sooner they left this place, the better.

They continued in silence, David getting a feel for the lay of the land. Not a bird crowed, and no crickets chirped. All was quiet. But his instincts were good. He sensed the broken branches and the shifted earth, smelled the heavy scent of death and blood. Something was indeed living in these woods, and it was on the hunt.

An unspoken tension seemed to settle on the three of them as they traveled deeper into the woods, and David couldn't help but be reminded of his hunt for the Silver Stags. It had felt like this—forbidden, treacherous—like every step he took was one in the wrong direction. But he'd been arrogant then, certain he alone could find the legendary herd that hadn't been seen in over a century, the one they said was protected by the Saints so that whoever killed the herd would bear a curse so terrible it would make death look like sweet release.

When he found the herd, he knew. He could feel their fear as he picked off each stag, one by one. And with each death, a piece of him broke inside, until everything about him became brittle, until he was made of glass.

He would rather have died than bear the curse he'd brought on himself. Pain followed him around with every waking moment. Death taunted him. Although he broke time and time again, it was never enough to release him from his agony. Whatever he was now, it was hardly human. One day he knew he'd shatter completely, but he didn't know if even then he would die, or if he'd be eternally preserved in torture.

Hours passed, but the light never changed. It was always dark in these woods, like Death himself prowled the grounds.

"David," Jill whispered, breaking the silence, "you saw these creatures, right?"

He swallowed. Nodded. It wasn't something he particularly wanted to remember.

"What exactly do they look like?" Her voice was sharp with fear, the first he'd heard from her. But then, his own heartbeat was racing too.

He paused, thinking of the best way to describe them. "They were fast and dark like shadow." He shuddered as he remembered the first attack in the marsh when he'd watched his comrades get torn apart. "But they're huge. And they had so many legs, almost like—"

"Spiders?" Jill stopped, her voice tight as she stared up ahead.

A chill ran down his spine as he followed her gaze.

Off in the distance, thick white webbing was wound in and around the trees, sticky netting clinging desperately to everything. As they ventured closer, they saw just how much there was. It was high in the trees, on the ground, everywhere. And in all the webs were bundles the size of people.

Fear blazed a hole in David's chest. Never in his life had he wanted to run from danger as much as he did now.

"Where are they?" Jill asked, her voice barely above a whisper.

It was a good question. David could almost always sense the presence of an animal nearby, as if his senses were heightened to detect any sign of life. But here it was still, like a smooth dark pond hiding whatever evil lurked beneath.

Grimzy's low voice broke the silence. "Some of these people are still alive."

David glanced at Jill, the surprise evident on her face. Terror pounded through his veins, but they nodded to each other, an acknowledgement of what they must do. They started forth, pulling their knives out and cutting through the bundles of webbing.

David went to the one closest to him, setting to work. The webbing was so thick he had to saw through it, all the while being careful to avoid cutting whoever was underneath.

He didn't see how anyone could survive in one of these cocoons. Surely they would suffocate or starve. He continued sawing away, praying to every Saint that whoever was in there was still alive.

At last, a small face appeared, eyelids half-closed and eyes rolled back in her head. Her black hair was tangled and matted and sticky with the tar-like webbing. But something about her face was familiar.

She looked like Asif.

David's breath caught in his chest as he sawed faster. *Please let her be alive.*

Sweat dripped down the back of his neck. His arm began to ache from his furious cutting. Then he heard the last thing he'd expected. The girl shuddered, taking a deep breath.

Relief flooded through him as he finished cutting through the webbing, and he caught the small child before she fell to the ground. Her eyelids fluttered shut as she curled against his chest.

She's alive.

In the middle of the dark forest, warmth like the sun rushed toward his heart in a way he'd never known before. *She's alive.*

He set the girl down before pulling off his cloak and laying it on top of her, daring to hope. If she was alive, then perhaps Asif was here too. The three of them worked fast, cutting through web after web. Some people were still breathing. Others were gray and lifeless.

With every person they freed, David could feel his fear melting away, clearing a space for hope, a feeling he usually denied himself.

An ear-splitting screech sliced through the air.

David covered his ears and spun. A dark shadow materialized in front of them, as if absorbing the shadows that surrounded it. He froze in horror as the shadows morphed together, converging to form a monster he had prayed to never see again. A misshapen torso resembling a man's sat at the front of a bulbous body, eight spiny legs protruding from its abdomen. The black creature stood taller than Grimzy, with no face except for a mouth filled with teeth sharp as daggers.

He watched as the creature stood there, looking straight at him despite having no eyes. It breathed heavily, bloody saliva dripping from its mouth.

He glanced at Jill, who stood horror-struck behind it. Even Grimzy looked like he couldn't believe his own eyes.

The creature lunged forward with blinding speed, it's humanlike arms extending out toward him. He drew an arrow from his quiver and launched it straight at the creature's torso. The arrow bounced off harmlessly as it barreled toward him.

Jill sprang into action, drawing her blades and charging forward, swinging at the creature's legs with an unstoppable fury. The creature screamed as her blades made contact and wheeled around to face her. The blades had hardly punctured the monster's armored legs.

Fear and anger battled across Jill's features as she swung at the creature's neck, but it reached up with its claws and caught the blade, yanking it out of her hands and tossing it aside.

David drew his bow again, aiming at the same spot Jill had targeted, hoping to draw the attention back to himself. Just then, Grimzy charged forward, tackling the monster head-on, swinging his massive fists at the creature's head. The monster's legs curled around the mountain man's body as they both crashed to the ground, filling the air with snarling and hissing.

Jill retrieved her blade, and she and David closed in. She hacked at the creature's legs while David waited for any clean shot he could get as Grimzy wrestled the creature.

A yell punctured the snarls as the monster sank its teeth into Grimzy's shoulder, and blood sprayed as he howled in pain.

David sucked in a breath. An inky black substance seeped into Grimzy's skin and began spreading through his veins. Jill hacked viciously at the creature's legs as Grimzy's strength failed, his movements becoming slow and heavy until his eyes drooped shut and he fell limp.

David's courage evaporated. If this thing could take Grimzy down, did they stand any chance at all?

The creature dropped the mountain man and spun on Jill again. She darted away just in time, rolling across the ground with blood splattered all over her. The creature lunged at her again and again, and each time she jabbed with her sword, poking at it but inflicting very little damage.

They wouldn't last much longer.

Unless . . .

The creature darted across the forest floor, careful to avoid any patch of light that dared break through the gloom of the forest. David's mind buzzed with thoughts: how these creatures only came out at night, how even in the darkness it avoided the scattered light, how the creature seemed to be made of shadow.

"Jill!" he shouted. "Keep it busy!"

She flashed him a glare, but she continued to dodge and slash at the creature.

David knelt on the ground and dumped the contents of his pack as he grabbed a large fallen tree branch from nearby. He tore a piece of his shirt before wrapping it around the end and dousing it in the bit of oil he always carried with him. Then he struck his flint.

The spark caught the oil and blazed into a brilliant bright flame, pushing away the fold of darkness in the forest.

He ran at the monster, swinging his new torch in desperation.

The creature reached for Jill, clawing at her shoulder before she could dodge. She cried out as blood seeped through her shredded skin.

David slashed at the monster's back legs with the torch. The creature turned to face him, snarling, blood—his friends' blood—splashed across its face.

Anger usurped the fear in him as he swung the torch at it. The monster reared back and screamed a painful, deafening scream that left him dizzy. Behind the monster, Jill rose, her arm covered in blood, her face pale. If she wouldn't give up, neither would he.

He swung the torch again, all the while jabbing at the monster's chest with his knife. His movements were wild, erratic. It took everything he had to stay standing.

One of the creature's legs swung forward, smashing into his wrist. He could feel it snap and watched as both his hand and the torch were sent flying. He fell backward into the dirt. The creature loomed over him, blood trickling from its teeth onto his face.

He scooted back as fast as he could on his broken wrist, pain lancing up his arm.

This was it. This was the moment he would finally die.

"Hey!" Jill called out.

The monster paused, its attention returning to her again. She stood there, covered in blood, wielding the fallen torch and her blade, now glowing red. She looked more fearsome than anyone he'd ever seen.

Angry, the creature wheeled around to her, but she was prepared. She dropped the torch and rolled forward under the creature's body. Then she drove her red-hot blade deep into the creature's soft underbelly.

The creature let loose a scream unlike anything they'd yet heard. Jill dove out of the way, landing near David. The creature spun and thrashed, screeching and hissing in pain. It tried to flee, but its legs collapsed beneath it. As the creature's body hit the ground, it vanished in an explosion of shadow and smoke.

Silence descended on the forest once more.

David's ears rang. He couldn't believe what he'd just witnessed.

They'd killed it. They had slayed the monster.

3 3

MILLIE

Jack's words twisted like a knife in Millie's chest. Days had passed since they'd last spoken, even though his room was just two doors down from hers.

He'd made no effort to speak with her, and she hadn't bothered to speak to him either, in part because she knew if she saw that crooked smile of his, all would be forgotten. And she didn't want to forget.

The truth was, she hadn't planned to stay, at least not for long. But the ultimatum he'd given her, the obvious threat against her brother, made her blood burn at the very thought.

If she were braver, she'd give him a piece of her mind. If she were braver, the very thought of seeing him wouldn't make her knees wobble and her heart skip. There were a lot of things she'd do if she were braver. But she wasn't.

Knuckles rapped at her door, and she crossed the room to open it.

"Miss Muffet!" It was Ymira, her flame tattoo blazing in the center of her forehead. Millie hated how her heart sagged in her chest.

"Please just call me Millie," she said.

The girl looked hesitant but nodded. Briefly, she was reminded of

Jack's own insistence that she call him by his first name. She hadn't understood it then, but perhaps now she did.

"The Matron has asked me to escort you to the dining hall."

Millie swallowed. For the last several days she'd had many meetings with the Matron, always in her own private quarters. But this was different. Since all her meals were delivered to her room, she had yet to actually see the dining hall.

Millie followed Ymira through the long dark corridors. Even in the daytime, the convent had a way of feeling like a cavern. Fires burned in sconces, doing their best to chase away the damp feel of the halls, but it was never enough.

"How have you been liking it here?" Ymira asked.

Millie startled and then, doing her best to plaster on a smile, said, "It's all right." It was the nicest thing she could say without lying.

Ymira laughed, a loud barking sound that echoed through the halls. Millie's eyes bugged; she was surprised that such a sound could come from such a beautiful girl.

"It's horrible here, isn't it?" The girl laughed with her whole body, refusing to hold back.

Millie gave a weak smile. "Well, it's definitely not the palace."

"I don't think this place has been updated since the Saints lived here!" She laughed again, this time giving a snort. Millie's eyes widened, and she couldn't resist laughing.

Ymira snorted again, making Millie laugh harder. It had been so long since she'd laughed, since before Doon had been arrested. Her brother had always been the funny one.

"Something funny?" a new voice asked.

The girls turned to the newcomer, a young gazelle man stepping out from behind them. His skin was breathtakingly dark, darker than Millie's, and he had a silver nose ring. Dreaded hair hung in a low bun at his neck, short horns curling at the crown of his head.

"Hasani!" Ymira dipped into a curtsy, a blush blooming along her cheeks. "We didn't see you there."

"People rarely do." He smiled at her before his gaze found Millie.

"You must be the paladin girl I keep hearing so much about. It's a pleasure to meet you." He grabbed her hand and bowed deeply, his lips brushing against her knuckles.

A shiver rushed up her spine, and she swallowed. "You can just call me Millie."

Hasani smiled, and her chest warmed. "Millie," he said, testing the name out. "I like it."

"Thank you."

He turned to Ymira. "We should hurry. The Matron is getting anxious."

Their expressions darkened, a silent exchange happening between them until Ymira nodded. Millie's blood began to race as she followed the two through the long corridors. She wished Jack were here. Jack had a way of making her feel at ease even when everything around her was uncertain.

At last, they rounded a corner. Large ornate doors greeted them, opened wide. They reminded her of the doors leading into the ballroom at the palace, and once again Millie wondered exactly what awaited her.

The three passed through the threshold into the dining hall. Her breath caught. It was not a spectacular space, certainly nothing like the palace, but it was still the most beautiful space she'd seen in the convent so far. Light flooded down from above in twelve distinct spotlights, each one landing on a statue. And not just any statues. They were the Saints. All twelve of them.

The doors scraped closed behind them, and a few girls barred the doors. It seemed no one would be going in or out anytime soon.

To one side of the hall were a handful of tables sitting empty. On the other side of the hall stood a handful of people, their eyes trained on Millie. Sitting on a chair at the head of the room was the Matron, looking as severe as ever.

Ymira and Hasani walked forward, and Millie followed, keeping her eyes on the ground. Once again, she wished Jack were here. He was the one who could talk to anyone, who cracked jokes and placed bets and looked at her like she was the most extraordinary thing he'd ever seen. She'd grown so used to his company that the past few days without him had left her with vertigo.

Her heart felt squeezed in a vise. She wanted to see him.

"Paladin Millie," boomed the Matron.

Millie's attention snapped forward. "Yes?"

"Thank you for joining us. As you can see, there are only a few people here because we needed to discuss the recent developments."

Recent developments. Right.

"Of course." She glanced at the people standing near the Matron. They were of all ages and races. Orion was there, as was Aaira, plus a few others she didn't recognize.

The Matron stood, leaning heavily on her cane. "I believe that Millie is, like some of you here, another one of the Saints' heirs."

Everyone nodded, but Millie's brain skidded to a halt. *Like some of you here.*

She wasn't alone. She wasn't even the first one to be discovered. It made sense, naturally. There were twelve Saints. Of course there would be more than one heir.

"How can you be certain?" Aaira asked.

The Matron's eyes found Millie's. "We must test her."

"Wait, what?" Millie asked.

"Don't worry," Ymira whispered. "We all had to do it."

Millie stared at her, suddenly recalling how she had healed Jack's shoulder in the forest with the light from her bracelets. Millie blinked.

"Orion, will you step forward and show Millie what you can do?"

Millie's attention snapped back to the front. Orion stepped forward.

"Orion, heir of Briar the Cunning," the Matron said.

Millie sucked in a breath as Orion held his arms out. For the first time, she noticed the vines that swirled around his forearms. He inhaled and then balled his hands into fists. The vines leapt off his skin, growing in number and size until they spun in the room like a brood of serpents. They multiplied, growing longer until the entire room was filled with vines.

They wound around the chairs and tables, the statues, the sconces, everything. A loose vine brushed against Millie's leg, and she shivered, realizing just how easily he could command them to wrap around her.

At last, Orion dropped his arms, tossing a smug grin her way.

"Well done," said the Matron.

Orion nodded, holding his arms out again. This time when he balled his hands, the vines dissolved in a burst of light. When the light faded, she saw that his tattoos had returned, the vines dancing along his forearms.

Millie's eyes found the statue of Briar. Of all the Saints, he was the one she knew the least about. It seemed that was about to change.

"Hasani?"

Beside her, the young man stepped forward, giving her a sideways glance and a wink. Millie's heart skipped, and she quickly looked at the stone floor.

"If I may," Hasani said, approaching the Matron.

"Of course."

The Matron held out her arm, and Hasani grabbed her wrist. She looked at Millie. "Hasani, heir of Inerys the Terrifying."

Fear clawed at Millie's throat, her eyes pinned to Hasani. He closed his eyes, and when they opened again, they were pitch-black. The whites, the irises—all of it was black.

She held her breath as what looked like ink spread from Hasani's hands into the Matron's veins. Her veins darkened, spreading from her wrist up her arm before reaching her neck and face. Her pallor changed. Her skin paled, and sweat beaded on her forehead. Her eyes turned yellow, and Millie thought she looked vaguely nauseated.

Hasani removed his hand from her wrist, and the Matron nodded to Ymira.

Ymira stepped forward, placing a hand on the Matron's wrist as Hasani had done. Light effused from her bracelets, wrapping around the Matron's arm. Millie watched as the old woman's color returned, the black in her veins dissolving as the light replaced it.

At last, the Matron inhaled deeply, smiling. Her face shone, bright and younger looking than it had been before. "Ymira, heir of Uri the Bright."

Ymira stepped back, beaming. Her own face glowed, and Millie didn't miss how the girl's eyes wandered over to Hasani.

Endless questions tugged at Millie's brain. Then a sudden thought struck her. She remembered her brother, wasting away in the king's dungeon, dying of Night Flu. She sucked in a breath. Could Ymira heal him?

"Paladin Millie, I understand you have quite the gift."

All eyes turned to her, some suspicious, some curious, all of them guarded.

Millie could only nod. She thought of entering the ballroom with Jack, of how many sets of eyes had been on her then. Somehow, though only a handful looked at her now, they were far more terrifying.

"Would you care to demonstrate?" asked the Matron.

Panic bubbled in her throat. She'd been improving, but it still took an unbelievable amount of concentration and focus, and that was without people staring at her.

But she had to try.

"It's a bit difficult to control at times."

The Matron nodded like she understood exactly what Millie was saying. "They have all stood where you stand now, afraid, confused, wondering why they were different. Do what you can."

Millie nodded again, closing her eyes. She could feel their gazes on her, wondering, waiting to see if she was anyone special. Her heart pounded faster, hands shaking at her sides. She needed to focus, yet all she could think about was that everyone was staring at her, staring at the maid turned paladin. Perhaps they would discover what she was: a coward.

You must learn to listen to yourself and not what others say about you. It was Jack's voice.

Jack, who always knew what to do.

She inhaled deeply, trying to slow her rapid pulse. It was a fuzzy feeling at first, lingering at the corners of her mind. Then she was doused in darkness, her mind splintering and fracturing. This was the hard part, the separation. Her being dissolved, and when she opened her eyes, she was aware of a thousand sets of eyes taking in more information than she'd ever thought possible.

The figures in the room towered over her. A few gasped, and one even shrieked. She sent her spiders forward as one, an army of spindly black legs.

There were more gasps as people stepped back.

She wasn't sure how long she could hold this form. She was already weakening. She would have to reform, or she would exhaust herself.

She inhaled again, calling her spiders back as her consciousness knit itself together again. She opened her eyes and was standing in the center of the room, staring at the Matron. Wide eyes watched her carefully.

The Matron smirked. "Welcome, Paladin Millie, heir of Zillah the Vengeful."

3 4

———

JILL

*J*ill's shoulder throbbed, fire blazing through her arm as blood oozed down it. She couldn't believe it. They'd done it. She had killed whatever that creature was. Now all she wanted to do was lie down and sleep forever, cursed forest be damned.

But there was more to be done. There was always more to be done.

She forced herself to her feet. She needed to check on David and Grimzy. *Saints.* She'd almost forgotten about Grimzy.

She turned to look at David, who was still lying on the ground, his face twisted in agony. Her mind flashed back to the moment she'd watched as his hand had been ripped from his body. She steeled herself as she made her way toward him.

She'd seen people lose limbs before during training. It wasn't pretty and often resulted in death if it wasn't taken care of immediately. She knelt beside him.

"Let me see your hand," she said, her voice hoarse.

David sat up and scooted away. "It's fine."

She rolled her eyes and reached for his arm before he could move away from her again. "Oh, for Saints' sake, now's not the time to be a hero. You lost a hand. Let me see."

She stared at his wrist, where his hand should've been. There should have been blood. Lots of blood. Instead, it looked like the stump of his arm ended in a hole, webbed cracks rising up his wrist, his skin hard and brittle as glass.

She looked up at him, taking in the scars on his face. They too were webbed, less like a healed wound and more like cracks. Her mind searched for an explanation.

David slowly pulled his arm away, never breaking eye contact, sadness haunting his expression. She watched him rise and walk across the clearing, picking something up off the ground. *His hand.* He held it up to his wrist, and the skin grew back together until they were connected once more. He flexed, rolling it around like someone who'd simply strained their wrist.

He walked back over, holding his hand out to her. She looked down at it. Where the cracks had been before was a series of twisted scars. She grabbed it and let him pull her up, noticing how his skin seemed soft again.

She stared at him, perplexed. "I don't understand," she whispered. Her chest hurt as she looked at him. She didn't know what had happened to him, but now she couldn't help noticing every scar that covered his body.

He sighed. "It's a curse."

"A curse?"

"Yes."

"What for? What kind of terrible magic could possibly cause such a thing?"

His jaw flexed, and he closed his eyes. "I hunted down the Silver Stags. This is the price I paid."

Jill stepped back in surprise. The Silver Stags were legendary, a story told by hunters to impress other hunters. They weren't supposed to be real.

Then again, Jill had seen some terrible things recently that had been all too real.

"Does it hurt?"

"Always."

They stood in silence, her heartbeat thundering like a distant storm. She wondered what would happen when lightning struck. Then Jill surprised herself by reaching a hand up to touch his face. He flinched but didn't move away as she trailed a finger over the scar around his temple. He closed his eyes, his body tense like a coiled snake.

Her breath caught as she examined each scar. Cracks and fractures trailed along his face, his jaw, down to his chest.

He grabbed her hand in his, stopping her. Heat rose to her cheeks.

"Please," he whispered, "I don't want your pity."

She yanked her hand back, any word she might've said caught in her throat.

A grunt cut through the silence, and they both jumped. On the ground, Grimzy stirred where he'd fallen. She took a deep breath to calm her nerves and looked back at David.

"We should free the rest of these people and get out of here. I don't want to face another one of those things," David said, and Jill nodded, heart still pounding away.

She bit the inside of her cheek. People did strange things in the heat of a moment, in the face of danger. Whatever strange feeling had overtaken her would pass. She couldn't afford any more distractions.

She made her way to Grimzy and knelt beside him. She examined his shoulder where the creature had bitten him. The inky black substance, whatever it had been, seemed to be oozing out and fading away, as if it were also made of shadow. She shuddered. Although they'd killed this one, they were no closer to determining what these creatures were or where they'd come from.

Grimzy's eyes fluttered open, his normally bronze face pale from blood loss. "Did I kill it?" he asked in a slurred voice.

Jill smiled despite herself. "I think it nearly killed you, I'm afraid."

Grimzy leaned forward to look at his shoulder. "That doesn't look good."

"I bet it feels even worse," she said, taking a closer look at it. The creature's teeth had torn at his skin, leaving it a bloody mess. Her own shoulder throbbed as she examined his, but there was no denying his was worse. "We need to stop the bleeding. Even you can only afford to lose so much blood."

Grimzy looked at her arm. "I could say the same for you, Princess."

"I'll be fine," she said, though she knew she needed to bandage her own arm soon, or it would be too late. "I hate to say this, but I think our best option may be to burn the skin to keep you from bleeding out."

He nodded. "Do what you must."

Jill swallowed. "It'll leave an ugly scar."

Grimzy gave a weak smile. "That's all right. Women love scars. Or so they tell me."

At the mention of scars, Jill's gaze drifted over to David, who was busy cutting away at the webs.

Grimzy grunted, and she looked back at him. He raised an eyebrow. "I can bleed out here if you've got something better to do."

Heat rose to her cheeks as she shook her head. "Sorry. Let's get to work."

Grimzy stared up at her, his eyes serious as she set to work. "Thank you, Your Highness. You have my undying loyalty. Your kindness will serve you well when you rule someday."

He closed his eyes, sinking into a deep sleep.

Jill stared at the hulking man. His breathing shook the ground. Her stomach sank.

Princess. Traitor. Usurper. Queen. The words flashed through her mind.

No. That wouldn't happen. She wasn't the heir. Jack was. He

would become king. He would take the throne.

A commotion cut through her thoughts, and she looked up to see Asif on the ground, looking up at David.

"What were you thinking?" asked David. "That was stupid!"

"I was being brave!" Asif said, rising to his feet.

"Yeah, well, bravery and stupidity often go hand in hand." He paused, sighing. "You could've been killed."

The kid fixed David with a ruthless glare. "But I wasn't!"

"You were wrapped in this creature's web! You're lucky you're still breathing."

Asif's jaw locked as he stared at the ground, silent. At last, he said, "I just had to know . . . if she was still alive." He swallowed hard, tears welling in his eyes. He wiped them away frantically, as if afraid of what David might think.

David shook his head and pointed to a small girl lying underneath his cloak. Jill's heart skipped. *Is it possible? Could she really have survived?*

Asif ran to the girl before pulling the cloak off her. This time tears did fall as he pulled her into his arms, holding her close. Jill's heart ached at the sight. How many people had lost loved ones to these creatures? How many would see them again? Did she really believe that she could help these people?

She finished tending to Grimzy's shoulder, and the mountain man barely stirred even as she burned the wound. Around her, people were slowly stirring, awakening from who knew how many days of being trapped inside those webs. Some never stirred at all, their forms ashen and unmoving.

It took several hours, but no other monsters showed up. One by one, they freed every last soul. Soon they finished, separating the living from the dead. Others appeared to be unaccounted for, but no one dared whisper what they all knew. In total, there were thirty-two living and a dozen dead. The monsters had made no distinction between man, woman, or child. There were humans, members of the animal clans, and even a mountain man. No one was safe.

Jill's blood boiled beneath her skin as she looked around at the survivors, who were gaunt, pale, and weak. Their eyes were sunken into their skulls, and their bones poked through their skin. On each of their faces was an expression so haunted Jill wondered if many would have preferred death.

She thought of her father, sick in his bed but safely tucked away in a castle, protected by guards and knights and paladins. She thought of the tournament, of the nobles battling and drinking and feasting as if just a few days' ride away there weren't a camp full of people who were starving and terrified for their lives. Her gut twisted. Who would help these people if her father wouldn't?

It was slow going, bringing the survivors back through the forest. They were weak, and many fainted. Everyone did what they could, but they were wounded and exhausted.

At last, Jill felt the warmth of sunshine cutting through the tree-tops, heard the sound of birds chirping, and felt a breath of fresh air kiss her face.

They stumbled out of the tree line, the camp in the distance. Jill turned to see David supporting an older woman. For the first time since she'd entered that haunted forest, she let herself breathe, smiling at him.

They made their way toward the camp, a dirty troop limping forward. She could only imagine what they must have looked like.

And then she heard the cries.

People rushed out of the camp. The survivors picked up speed, seeing faces they recognized, their strength renewed. The crowd met them, and Jill watched as people embraced, tears flowing freely. There were cheers of joy and howls of pain. She watched a young woman run forward, lifting a small child off the ground and holding him so tightly that Jill thought she might never let him go.

It was a joyous reunion, and Jill couldn't help the tears that welled up in her eyes at the sight of all these people returning home.

"Thank you," a gruff voice said behind her. She turned to see David standing there, watching the celebrations with a sad smile. "You saved these people."

Something like guilt snarled in her chest as she shook her head. "These people should never have had to face these monsters in the first place. Not alone at least."

Quiet wrapped around them as they watched people help the survivors back to the camp, everyone assisting in any way they could.

"Nonetheless," came David's soft voice, "I think you will find these people eternally grateful."

She looked up at him, her breath catching in her chest. She did not know what to make of this cursed stranger, snarky one moment and complimenting her the next. If things were different, maybe—

She stopped the thought.

Her father was dying. Monsters roamed the land. And the memories of the boy she'd once loved were still too close to the surface. To even think of such things was a betrayal of everything she stood for.

At that moment, Grimzy strode forward. He had lingered at the back, carrying and supporting the frailer of the survivors as best he could with his injured arm.

"There are still more out there, you know," he said in low voice.

Jill swallowed. "I know." She hated how confused she felt, how torn she was between returning to her quest to find a cure for her father and her desire and obligation to help her people.

There was still Jack, she supposed. He could continue while she helped track these monsters down. But she had no way of knowing if Jack and Millie were all right, and the way things had ended between them left her feeling more uncertain than ever. In truth, she'd avoided thinking about her brother as much as possible. Fear prickled in her chest at the mere thought of him.

She was certain there was more going on with him than she could see, and it scared her. If her father died, he would be the one to take the throne. He would be king of Erinya. So, why did that make her more afraid than ever?

35

BO

o didn't know if she was dead or alive. Murky shadows crowded the edges of her vision. Pain flickered throughout her body. She could hear voices, but the words meant nothing to her.

One of her monsters was dead. She could feel it.

Part of her was grateful. She wanted nothing to do with these creatures anymore, wanted no connection with them, no bond. But the loss was like a severed limb, invisible pain twisting in the hollow space her monster had left behind.

If any more creatures were killed, it would kill her too.

But she wasn't afraid. She welcomed the idea of death like a long-lost family member. At least in death she would be free. Free from pain, free from a lonely existence with only monsters for company, free from the fear of hurting others.

She was chained to a wall, her hands above her head. Her fingers had gone numb hours ago.

As she reflected on her pathetic life, she became more certain that everyone was out to get her. She should have let those bleeding monsters ravage the countryside. She should never have left her haven in the woods. She still didn't understand why they'd left her, but she no longer cared.

A familiar creaking echoed above her, followed by light footsteps. Bo could only imagine what was planned for her. She pinched her eyes shut, silently cursing the mother who'd given her this terrible power. Without it, she would be free. Without it, she would not be here.

A face appeared on the other side of the iron bars, glaring eyes beating down on her. It was the serving girl she'd doused and locked up in her escape attempt.

"I told you that you wouldn't make it," she said.

Bo lifted her chin in defiance. "You said they'd kill me. But they didn't."

She shook her head. "Believe me, you'll wish they had."

A guard appeared behind her, clad in red and black, the colors of the Ohan house. He shoved a key into the lock and stepped inside.

Bo's heart raced, palms sweating. The guard walked over and released her from her chains. Immediately, her arms dropped to her sides. Her shoulders ached, and blood flowed back into her hands so quickly that all she registered was an overwhelming tingling sensation.

The guard yanked her to her feet, sending shooting pains down her leg.

"Ow!" she cried loudly. She may not have been in any condition to fight back, but that didn't mean she was going to make this easy.

"Shut up," growled the guard.

"Make me," she snapped back.

She was met with a slap to the face. Tears sprang to her eyes, the sting of his hand leaving a welt.

Bo glanced at the serving girl, whose gaze hadn't left her.

"Take my advice. Stop saying stupid things, and maybe you won't get smacked around so much," she said, and Bo snarled at her. She jumped backward, her face souring. "I hope they kill you slowly."

Bo was half dragged, half shoved through the Ohans' labyrinthian mansion. Her body felt both unbearably heavy and light as a cloud. She was certain now that she'd been drugged. Would that make whatever came next easier or harder?

The guard escorting her walked her down a long hallway paved with black marble and lit by blue-fire torches. There were no windows, no other sources of light. They made another turn before she was ushered through a small wooden door.

Unlike the grand dining hall she'd been greeted by when she'd first arrived, this was a small bare study. A fire blazed in a hearth while a desk sat in the center of the room in front of a bookcase filled with books and trinkets. A skull rested on top of the bookcase, along with bottles full of liquid she could only guess the purpose of. She doubted that anything good could come of them.

A panel in the wall to her right shuddered, lifting away to reveal Ohan-Jin standing there, his scaled face glimmering in the firelight. He looked strangely calm as he entered the room, and the panel closed behind him so tightly it looked like part of the wall once more.

"Leave us," Ohan-Jin said to the guard without bothering to look at him. His eyes rested only on Bo.

Bo didn't look back as the guard left. Now she was alone with one of the most powerful men in the entire kingdom.

"Would you care to sit?" he asked, gesturing to a seat in front of the fireplace.

Bo gritted her teeth. "I want to leave."

Ohan-Jin looked her up and down before raising a brow. "Do you really? I doubt you'd make it out of the town before you collapsed. Tell me, what exactly did you hope to do? Did you really think escape was possible?"

Bo's confidence fled her. She wanted to bite out a harsh yes and curse at him in every language she knew. But fear gripped her throat like the cold hand of a corpse.

"Sit," he commanded.

Bo bit the inside of her cheek as she shuffled to the leather chair. She sat but refused to relax. After all, this wasn't a social meeting.

Ohan-Jin glided over to his bookcase, a clawed finger stroking the various books and potions assembled there. Her insides quivered as she grabbed at her grimy pants. She would not let him make her afraid.

"What are you going to do with me?"

The man paused, his hand lingering on a bottle the color of blood, before smiling to himself. "I admit, I like you, Bo. You remind me of myself."

"I'm nothing like you," she hissed.

"Aren't you?" He snatched the bottle off the shelf before turning to face her. "Willing to do whatever it takes to get what you want." He twirled the bottle between his fingers. "In your case, it's escape. Freedom. For me . . ." He paused, looking down at the potion. "It's power."

Bo's insides churned. Here was a man unafraid of anything, a powerful man seeking more power. Somehow, she knew it would never be enough for him.

"Why are you telling me this?" She fought to hide the trembling in her voice.

"A gesture of trust?"

"What makes you think I'd ever trust you?"

"Oh, I'm sure you wouldn't, but I must try all the same." He smiled, turning back to the bookcase and staring at the endless bottles. "Such a subtle art, poison. I don't think many truly appreciate it—that is, until they need to find a cure." He glanced back at her, smiling like he'd made a joke she couldn't hope to understand.

He grabbed the chair from behind the desk, dragged it over to the fireplace, and sat down in front of her, holding up the bottle for her to see. He sighed, staring at the potion, longing in his reptilian eyes.

She swallowed, scooting back in her chair ever so slightly.

"I know you far better than you think, Bolynn. And I believe we can help each other, if you're willing."

"Never!"

Ohan-Jin gave a breathy laugh devoid of any humor. "You don't even know what I'm going to say."

"I know enough."

"Do you? Because if you'll recall, I'm the one in charge here. I'm the only one who can grant you the freedom you desire."

Bo's jaw clenched, but she said nothing. Her skin tingled with apprehension. She knew he was lying. They would never let her go. Not while she controlled the monsters. Not while she could still be used as a weapon.

"I can see the gears turning," he said, as if reading her mind. "You don't think I'd let you walk free. But I would. I would do more than that. Because I know you can never be free as long as you're connected to those creatures."

Bo's heart shuddered. "What?"

"What if I told you I could take the creatures from you? Free you from the prison in your mind?"

She stilled, unwilling to breathe, unwilling to hope. It wasn't possible, was it? And even if it were, would she really let this power-hungry man use these creatures?

I could be free of them.

He was right. She was willing to do whatever it took to free herself.

"I'm listening."

Instead of responding, he grabbed her hand in his and pulled it toward him. Before she could yank it away, he poured a single drop onto the palm of her hand.

She flinched, pulling her hand away. "What—"

She was plunged into darkness.

A scene unfolded in front of her, shrouded in shadow. Bo's stomach dropped as her body moved of its own accord. She shook her head. "No. Please don't make me watch this!"

A voice sounded from above. "You must if you want to be free."

She shook her head, trying to resist her own body. "I changed my mind. Please, no!" Panic wrapped around her like a noose. But she was locked in the memory, locked in a cage her mother had built for her.

She stood in front of the home she and her mother had lived in, a run-down shack deep in the woods, far away from prying eyes. Her mother was one of the last great apothecaries, and secrecy was essential to survival.

Her feet moved forward. She opened the door and walked inside. The heat hit her instantly, a fire blazing four feet tall in the center of the hut.

"Ama!" she screamed. "What are you doing? This fire will burn down everything!"

"Trust me," her mother said, her silky voice tempting Bo to relax.

"Ama?" she asked. "What is going on?"

Her mother rose from the floor where she sat and walked over to her. Bo stepped back in horror. Instead of her mother's beautiful golden eyes, she was met with a gaze as black as death. Her eyes bore no pupils, no irises. Only darkness.

"Trust me," she said again.

Behind her, the fire burned higher and brighter, nearly licking the top of the hut.

"What—"

Her mother wrenched her forward, dragging her toward the flames. "Ama!" she screamed. "Please! Stop! What are you doing? What are you—"

Her mother pulled out a knife, swiping it across her hand. Pain seared her palm, blood seeping between her fingers. It landed in bubbling drops into the fire, hissing and burning until black smoke filled the hut, billowing like a dark thundercloud.

The color returned to her mother's eyes, and she blinked, momentarily stunned.

"Bo," she said at last, her voice suddenly tired. "I'm sorry. I don't know what happened. I was just making supper when—"

The house exploded.

Bo was yanked backward with overwhelming force and landed

on her back twenty feet away. Her lungs froze, unable to take in oxygen as her ears rang. She tried to turn and stand, searching the darkness for her mother.

Dark laughter echoed in the silence. Her blood froze as she tried to sit up.

What had once been her home was now only smoking rubble. Above it, a gleaming void hovered. It reminded her of a torn piece of paper, the edges flickering in the moonlight.

And then the creatures appeared. One by one, they filtered out of the hole until thirteen monsters stood in a circle around her.

Where was her mother? What had happened?

The tear above her demolished home flickered again as a shadowy figure stepped out. Its form wavered and rippled like a sail blowing in the breeze.

Free at last, a dark voice echoed through her skull.

Then the figure turned, looking down at Bo, who was still on the ground, frozen with fear. Suddenly, the figure hissed and howled in pain, stepping back and clutching at its head.

No! it screamed.

Around her, the creatures began skittering around like a herd of spooked sheep.

No! the figure screeched again before its form twisted in a snarl of shadows and shot up into the sky, vanishing as quickly as it had appeared.

Silence surrounded her, thick as water. Unlike the shadowy figure, the monsters stayed where they were, looking to her.

"Ama?" she called out, fearful of every sound she made. When she saw that the monsters remained where they were, she called louder.

"Ama!" She pulled herself to her knees, searching around until she saw a slumped body ten feet away, silent and still.

She crawled over to her mother, whose hair was a tangle of braids. Bo grabbed her mother's shoulders, turning her onto her back.

She screamed, toppling over backward as she stared down at her mother's melted face.

"Ama!"

The woman heaved a gasp. "Bo, I'm so sorry. You are—" She stopped, trying to swallow. "You're—" But the breath was yanked from her mother's chest, and then she was gone.

Bo opened her eyes, sitting back in Ohan-Jin's study, her entire body shaking. Tears streamed down her cheeks. She had vowed she would forget the events of that night. And now she had been forced to relive them.

"Very interesting," came Ohan-Jin's voice.

She looked up at him. "You're a monster."

"On the contrary, I believe it was your mother who was the monster, binding you to those creatures, freeing an ancient being who should never have been awoken."

She wanted to disagree, but she couldn't. How many times had she gone back over that night, searching for answers? But her mother had died before she could tell her why she'd done it or what she'd done.

"Forgive me, but I needed to understand. To confirm my theories."

"Your theories?"

"Yes. And you'll be happy to know that I have a plan. A plan that will free you from those dreadful beasts forever."

Bo's chest heaved. She no longer had the energy or the will to fight. She wanted to be as far from those creatures as she could.

"What do you want me to do?"

Ohan-Jin smiled. "So glad you've come to your senses. I need you to find a way into the Convent of the Saints. They think I don't know they've been stealing from me, but they're wrong. I see everything."

Bo thought of Zyla, of the secret order she'd told her about. "Fine. Then what?"

"And then I am going to make sure they never cross me again."

36

JACK

Jack paced the small room he'd been given by the Order. It had been this way for days. He knew he should find Millie, find a way to explain everything to her, but it was all so complicated.

They needed to leave this place and resume their quest. But after their disagreement, he didn't know how to make things better.

It wasn't the first time he'd had an argument with a girl, but it was the first time he'd ever cared enough to want to resolve things with one.

You linger, my prince.

Of course I do, Jack thought bitterly. Because even though everything in him wanted to leave, wanted to storm off, to fight, he couldn't. *I can't leave here without Millie, but I can't stay either. My father will be dead in a few weeks.*

If you let your father die, you will be king, you know.

The claim was so sudden that Jack stopped his pacing, his breath catching in his chest. His insides squirmed.

You know they want a regent on the throne, and I don't have the power to stop the council.

Yes, but they don't know about me. With me behind you, we can do anything.

Jack clutched the daggers strapped across his chest. *My throne.* It was not as though Jack had spent his life lusting after the crown. After all, he didn't need to. It was always meant to be his. But things had changed, and he hated how much he wanted it, how much he longed for the power and the freedom the throne would give him. He could end the war, end the fighting. He could see the world at last. He could be with Millie and free her brother.

Jack swallowed hard. Could he really do that though? Could he let his father die? Could he take the throne that was rightfully his?

Why shouldn't you?

Images flickered through Jack's head: Jack sitting on his father's throne. An obsidian crown resting upon his temples. Subjects bowing to him. At his right hand, his sister, fearless and brave and relentless. And on the throne beside him, Millie, queen of Erinya.

His heart thundered, a roaring tempest in his chest. It was perfect. And all that stood in his way was his own dying father. He wanted the crown. He wanted the throne that belonged to him.

A knock struck his door.

"Jack?" a soft voice mumbled.

Millie. Millie was at his door. Warmth flooded his chest. She'd finally come to see him. He hadn't realized how much he'd missed her until that moment, how he'd longed to apologize and take everything back.

He crossed the room and threw open the door, and her big brown eyes stared up at him. His eyes strayed to the curve of her lips, her neck, and he clenched his fists at his sides.

"Millie," he breathed, his blood pulsing.

"Are you all right? I thought I heard voices."

He froze, the warmth in his chest vanishing. Voices?

She is more attuned than you realize, the Voice chuckled.

A thought struck Jack as new visions entered his head, one

scenario after another showing him the danger his presence held for Millie, showing the danger *he* was to Millie. If she could hear the Voice, what would it do to her? Would the Voice use her against Jack? Would it hurt her? Could the Voice force Jack to hurt her?

He shook his head, the implications too frightening to dwell on. He couldn't let the Voice get to her, couldn't let anything happen to her. He swallowed hard. He refused to be the reason she got hurt.

"I'm fine," he spat out, flinching at the hostility in his own voice.

It's for her own good.

Hurt and confusion splayed across her face, and for a second he hated her vulnerability. Why couldn't she be more like Jill? Why couldn't she throw the same venom back in his face?

But that wasn't Millie. Millie was kind and warm and beautiful, and *Saints* he wanted to kiss her!

"Well, that's good," she said, staring down at her boots. "I just wanted to make sure because—" She stopped. "Listen, Jack, I've been thinking, and you're right. I made an oath when I became paladin. I will follow you wherever you go."

They stood there for a moment, eyes locked. He couldn't help but feel like he was waiting for something, some sign.

"Do you promise?"

"Yes." She nodded.

Before he could stop himself, he stepped forward, grabbed her neck, and pressed his lips against hers. Her body stiffened at first until she relaxed into him, her hands finding his waist. Sparks exploded behind his eyes, a vise tightening around his heart. He sank into her, longing tugged between them, a beating heart.

Jack had kissed many girls over the years, and he'd thought he knew all there was to know about women, all there was to know about love.

In that moment, he knew nothing. Love was too vast a thing, too heavy a burden.

He shoved her away, suddenly overcome with fear. The Voice would hurt her. *He* would hurt her.

I will follow you wherever you go.

He knew now for certain. He couldn't let that happen. He would keep her safe, no matter what. Even if that meant breaking her heart. Breaking his heart.

"I've been thinking too," he said, his stomach twisting into knots. "I think you should stay here."

Her face fell. "What?"

His face was a mask of steel. He would not let her see how every word he spoke killed him. "You should stay here. It's where you belong." The words were a flint, igniting something he could not stop.

She stepped back, anger coloring her features. "And where do you belong, Jack?" Her gaze cut him to his core.

"I am the future king of Erinya. I belong on the throne. Whatever this is cannot happen. We don't belong together." The words tasted like bile in his mouth, but a lifetime of lying to his father had prepared him for this moment well.

He expected tears. Anger. Protests. Instead, he was met with acceptance. He should've known better. Millie seemed able to pierce his armor without even trying.

Sad eyes found his, the only hint that what he'd told her bothered her. "I truly hope you find what you're looking for . . . Your Highness."

And for the very first time, he did not bother to correct her.

DAVID

David inhaled, drawing the bowstring back until it lined up with his ear. It was almost painful to shoot this slowly, but he needed to make sure he was demonstrating the technique properly. He released his breath and the string at the same time, sending the arrow flying. It stuck fast on the knot of a tree branch, precisely where he'd told everyone it would hit. Applause sounded around him, and his heart lurched uncomfortably. He wasn't used to so many eyes watching his every move.

He turned back to the crowd watching him, which was a strange mix of farmers and fishermen, more women than men, every one of whom had fled their homes after they'd been attacked by the monsters. Now they were here at the Lost Tribe, desperately trying to learn as much as they could about how to defend themselves.

A week had passed since he, Jill, and Grimzy had brought the survivors back, and in that time, he'd hardly spent more than a few minutes at a time with Jill. He and Grimzy had tried their best to organize a makeshift training camp to teach any able-bodied person how to fight so that hunting parties could hopefully be sent out. So far, however, few had a natural inclination with any kind of weapon, and David feared sending them out would be suicide.

To his surprise, Jill was a natural with the survivors, organizing sick bays for the injured, recruiting as many healers and apprentice healers as she could find to assist, and delegating tasks to anyone who offered to help. It was a strange change from the way she'd initially been treated when she'd first arrived. But he supposed slaying a monster and rescuing survivors would change just about anyone's opinion.

The shine of auburn hair caught his attention, and his eyes locked with Jill's as she stood among the observers. A tight smile flashed his way before her eyes flicked to the ground.

Something had changed between them in the last few days now that she knew about his curse.

He slid his bow over his shoulders, instructing a few of the trainees to begin sparring before he walked over to her.

"Come to teach us a thing or two?" he said, his voice higher than usual.

She bit her lip, and his heart sank.

"What's wrong?"

She glanced over at the group, who were barely managing to conduct sword drills. It would take a miracle to get them in working order.

"I'm leaving," she said, avoiding his eyes.

David found himself frozen. What a strange thing it was for a stranger to enter your life and change everything only for them to vanish forever. Except in this case, that stranger was the princess.

"I see," he said, keeping his voice even.

"I know there are more of those creatures out there. But now that we've taken down one, I'm sure you and Grimzy can handle the rest."

The words were a blow to the gut. How could she leave now? These people were barely clinging to hope, and the only reason they had any was because of her. If she left now, there was more than just the monsters to worry about. The people would lose the only person who'd bothered to care about them.

Heat rose to the back of his neck. "Why? Why now? What could be more pressing than all of this?" He gestured to the people around them, and a few turned to stare. But he didn't care.

Her tone dropped low. "My father . . ." She paused, unable to meet his eyes. "My father is dying. He was poisoned."

Shock pulsed through him. The king was dying? What did that mean for the people here, for all Erinya for that matter?

"I need to find a cure, and I have very little time left to do it."

"And what will you do if you find one?"

She gave him a confused look.

"Will you save him?"

"He's my father."

"That's not an answer."

She took a step back, a flush rising up her cheeks. "You don't understand. My father, if he lives, he can help! He can send soldiers to hunt these creatures down!" She grew quieter. "Look at these people." She pointed to the group. They were still working on basic forms, forms she'd undoubtedly learned as a child, forms that took years of practice and training to master. "If we send them back into those woods, we're as good as sending them to their deaths."

He knew she was right, but it didn't change the fact that the king had done nothing to help the people to begin with. Instead, he'd thrown his tournament while the rest of the kingdom feared for their lives.

"And what promise do I have that your father will do as you think? What if his life is spared and no aid comes?" He knew he should leave well enough alone, but anger kept his tongue moving. "And what about your brother, the famous Prince Jack?" he asked. "Is he doing anything to help us?"

She shook her head. "Stop. Don't bring my brother into this."

"And why not? Could he not be bothered to help his only sister save their father? Or does he—like everyone else—care so little about the king?"

"I said stop!" Jill's face flamed as she drew her sword with such speed that he barely saw the blade until it was pointed up at his heart.

For a while, they stood there, the silence thickening around them.

"We need your help, Jill," he said, his voice tired. "You give these people hope."

"I don't want them to put their hope in me!" she shouted, drawing eyes toward her. Her eyes burned bright. She lowered her voice so that only David could hear. "I'm not a savior. I'm not a hero. If I stay, I will only let these people down."

"If you leave, you *will* let them down." He couldn't bring himself to say the words he wanted: that he didn't want her to leave.

She took a deep breath and looked him in the eyes. "At least I won't be around to see it."

38

MILLIE

Millie sat on the bed in her little room. Her eyes burned, but she refused to cry. She refused to let anyone know how much Jack meant to her, how much he'd hurt her. She'd known how impossible it was; she'd known his reputation. Still, some small part of her had dared hope that Jack felt the same way she did.

The prince. Not Jack. She hated the fact that she'd ever started calling him that.

Her palms began to sweat. She had bigger problems. She was a Saint's heir, heir of Zillah the Vengeful. The very idea sent her mind reeling.

Of the twelve Saints, Zillah was the most fearsome. The legends of her ferocity were endless. One claimed that she'd fought an entire pack of wolves during an ice storm and won. Another legend said she'd been the one to slay the Black King in the end.

A shiver traced its way down Millie's spine. The Black King. A sense of uneasiness rose in the pit of her stomach at the thought, not because she was afraid, but because there was something about the evil monarch that struck her as vaguely familiar.

A knock came at the door, interrupting her thoughts. Hesitant, she rose from the bed and went to open it.

Ymira's bright face greeted her. Millie wondered if the light she wielded brightened people's spirits as well.

"Good morning!" She beamed. "Would you like to start your training?"

Millie glanced out the small window of her room. Sure enough, the sun's rays were stretching up over the horizon. Had she been up all night?

This is where I belong.

Here was her chance for answers, for training, for control over this dark power that had taken over her life. She straightened, looking Ymira in the eyes. "I'm ready."

As a point of fact, she was not ready.

She was tired. Although she'd spent a lifetime on her feet doing the bidding of others, nothing could have prepared her for the endless hours of training. More than once she found herself wondering what Jill would think of her. She pictured the princess rolling her eyes and calling her weak.

She would've been right.

That day she stood in the tiny training grounds beneath the convent. Because of the secrecy of their mission, it was critical that any training they did was kept from prying eyes. Stacks of crates stood in a corner of the room, filled with things Millie could only guess at. Blue-fire torches lit the space, drenching everything in an indigo tint. Dust kicked up from the dirt floor filled the air.

She stood opposite Ymira. Hasani watched them from the outskirts, his eyes never truly leaving Ymira. Millie had been at this forever now, trying to will her spiders to life. But it was exhausting.

"Again," barked Hasani.

"Give her a break," said Ymira gently.

"She needs to learn this."

"She will, but not if you keep yelling at her."

Millie's entire body ached. Magic, as it turned out, took its toll. In the past, she had relied on adrenaline to aid her transformation. Without that push, however, transforming at will was more taxing than she'd originally thought. She had succeeded in transforming only twice in the past few days, and each time had left her tired enough to sleep for a week. Unfortunately, there would be no sleeping anytime soon.

Millie rolled her shoulders back, a move she'd seen Jill do countless times. In many ways, she wished the princess were here. Though she would likely have been harder on her than Hasani, at least Jill was familiar with her powers and what Millie was capable of.

Only because you tormented her.

Guilt struck her suddenly, but she shook her head. She couldn't afford to be distracted. Not now. Not when all her efforts needed to be focused on trying to control her power.

"Millie, just breathe. It's harder when you force it," Ymira said.

Millie nodded, closing her eyes. She breathed deeply, reaching for the edges of her mind. So many times, she'd been close. It felt like she was trapped in a dark room, searching for both the key and the keyhole. How did anyone learn to master their magic?

"Good. Take another deep breath. Picture the spiders in your head."

Reluctantly, she did. Spiders filled her mind, and she swore she could feel their legs on her skin. Why her? Why this power?

"You can't be afraid of it," came Hasani's voice. "As long as you're afraid of it, your power will control you, not the other way around."

Millie laughed despite herself. "How am I not supposed to be afraid? I've been afraid my whole life!" The words were out of her mouth before she even realized what she'd said.

She opened her eyes. Both Ymira and Hasani were staring at her, their faces drawn. Silence filled the space between them until Hasani spoke at last.

"Don't think we're not as terrified as you are," he said. "We never asked for these powers either. My touch is poisonous." He paused. "And Ymira was not always around."

Millie looked at Hasani, at his eyes gleaming with pain. In that moment, she knew something terrible must have happened with a power like his. What would the power of poison do without a way to heal it?

It made her own magic seem mild in comparison.

She inhaled. "I'm ready to try again."

Ymira smiled, and Millie got the sense that she was a girl who always tended to look on the bright side. She supposed that was fitting.

She closed her eyes, wrangling the fear that threatened to overwhelm her. She pushed away all thoughts of Jack, of Jill, and of her brother.

The edges of her mind tingled, a blot of black ink spreading through her body. She pictured her spiders, resisting the urge to shy away from the skittering feeling that engulfed her. Instead, she forced her body to still, to embrace the sensation.

Her body dissolved. She opened her eyes and looked up at Ymira and Hasani from a thousand different sets of eyes. It should have been overwhelming, the way she could see so much and process it all, but it wasn't. Perhaps that was the way her magic worked.

After a few moments, she returned to human form.

"Good," said Hasani. "I'm curious though. Can you change the size of the spiders?"

She'd never considered that before. She remembered the Paladin Tournament and how she'd managed to change her form to catch up with Jill.

"I think so."

She closed her eyes again. It was easier this time, finding her edges until they dissolved. It felt natural to shift into smaller spiders, but she tried to hold back, to keep from transforming into so many. Her mind twisted and squirmed, shadows melting around her until she opened her eyes again. This time when she looked up at Ymira and Hasani, they were not nearly as tall as they'd been the first time. Instead of a million little spiders, her consciousness was divided into ten large spiders.

She transformed back, her mind and body exhausted from the effort of maintaining a larger form.

Hasani smiled at her, his dark eyes gleaming. "Good. Now let's get to work."

MILLIE's entire body ached as she shuffled back to her room. It was well past midnight, and she needed to be up again at dawn. She held on to the railing as she climbed the stairs, clinging to it like a lifeline. Shifting forms was absolutely exhausting. Hasani had likened the magic within her to a muscle; the more it was used, the stronger she'd get. But until then, she would exist in a perpetual state of exhaustion.

She came to the corridor that led to her room and paused as she saw a familiar figure standing in the center of the hall. The Matron leaned on her cane, staring at her as if she'd been waiting for this very moment for hours.

Millie swallowed. She remembered the fear she'd felt anytime she was around one of the royals, especially the king. That same fear came flooding back anytime she was anywhere near the Matron.

She forced herself to move forward, barely able to feel her legs.

"How was your training, Miss Muffet? Any improvement?"

Millie nodded, her tongue swollen in her mouth.

"Good, good," she said, turning her head to look at a dusty tapestry clinging to the wall. "I came to let you know that three nights from now the Order will be meeting to discuss a few things. We believe the Ohans are planning something. We also believe we may have found another Saint's heir."

At that, Millie perked up. "Really? Another heir?"

"Perhaps, but it is too soon to tell. All I have are reports from one of my spies within the Ohans' household."

Millie's mind swirled with the implications. Some part of her still couldn't believe the Saints' heirs were real, that she was one of them, and that there were more.

"Well, thank you for letting me know," she said, turning to her door. She felt guilty leaving the old woman standing there, but all she could think about was collapsing into bed.

"One more thing, Paladin."

Millie stiffened, her hand on the doorknob. She glanced back at the Matron. "Yes?"

The old woman stared at her. "I understand that your brother was arrested a year ago for murder."

She inhaled sharply. How could this woman know about that? The only person she'd told about the incident was Jack, and she was certain he wasn't about to speak to anyone here.

"I remember hearing about the trial. It was not until the tournament that I made the connection. There was something about the case that bothered me."

"My brother is innocent," she said, a sudden fire in her chest. She would fight with every breath she had to defend her brother's reputation. Her brother was not a murderer.

"Yes, I know that. But I remember thinking, 'Who would kill a king's stable hand? And why?' Nothing was stolen. There was no motive, no disagreement. The boy was of no importance. But someone went out of their way to kill him. Why?" The Matron's eyes bored into her, as if she was trying to communicate something that she could not say aloud.

Millie frowned, shaking her head. "I don't understand. What do you mean?"

"Do you remember anything about the boy who was killed?"

Millie tried to think. There were a hundred stable hands to the king, each more nondescript than the last. She shook her head, an uneasy feeling stirring in her stomach.

"And yet the case was brought before the king and suddenly swept away, the search for the killer put to rest as quickly as possible."

Millie's heart thundered. Why was she so nervous? What was

this woman implying? That the king knew the killer and blamed her brother even though he knew Doon was innocent?

She gripped the doorknob tighter, desperate to hold on to anything that kept her rooted in this moment. She would not let fear overtake her.

"All I wanted to do was warn you, Millie. Be careful. I believe our enemies are far closer than we realize."

39

JILL

An hour later, Jill was packed and ready to go. She hated how slippery her emotions had been over the last few days. Even now, the betrayal on David's face stuck in her head, along with his words. *You give these people hope.*

He didn't understand though. He didn't understand why she needed to save her father, why Jack wasn't ready to be king, or what a regent would mean for her and the kingdom. He didn't understand that she had no desire to let these people down, but that if she stayed, she would. He didn't understand that she needed to become paladin at any cost.

"What are you doing?" a small voice asked, and Jill turned to see Lyra, Asif's sister, standing in the doorway of her tent. She'd made a remarkable recovery, better than anyone else. She stared at Jill, her dark ringlets blowing in the soft breeze outside.

"I'm getting ready," Jill said slowly.

Lyra's expression brightened. "For the celebration?"

"What?" She'd heard nothing of a party. A sinking feeling filled her stomach.

"The celebration for you!" she said, smiling. "And David and Paladin Grimzy! They're having it tonight!"

"Lyra!" Asif came up behind her. "It was supposed to be a surprise!"

The little girl's eyes widened. "I'm sorry!"

Asif shook his head and smiled, looking over at Jill. His eyes landed on her packed things, his expression falling.

"You're leaving?"

Jill swallowed, her gaze landing on the ground. It was one thing to let David down but another to let a child down. They were too young to understand. One day, though, when they were older, they would.

"Yes," she said at last. There was no point in lying. "I have to go."

Lyra looked between them, brow furrowed. "Are you going to hunt more monsters?" she asked.

"No," Asif said bitterly, glaring at her. "She's leaving us to fend for ourselves."

"Asif, it's not that simple," she tried to explain.

He rolled his eyes. "Whatever. You think because I'm young that I'm stupid? You're a coward, and you're leaving us just like everyone else!"

The words cut deeper than she'd expected. Not because they were wrong, but because they were true.

"Asif, I have to do something. I'm not just leaving you. I promise."

But Asif just shook his head. "I thought you were different." He turned and walked away, leaving her feeling worse than ever.

Lyra stayed put, her head tilted, staring at Jill with curiosity. "Where are you going?"

Jill sighed, staring at the girl. "My father is very sick," she said. "I have to find something that will save him."

Lyra looked up at her, bright cat eyes shining through dark lashes. Jill had no doubt that one day her beauty would be overwhelming. "That doesn't seem so bad," she said. "Will you at least stay for the party?"

Jill hesitated. She had already lost nearly two weeks here, and she had no idea how much longer her father would hold out. But as she looked down at Lyra, her big eyes begging Jill not to leave, she couldn't help the small smile that crossed her face.

"Okay, I'll stay for the party. But I must leave first thing tomorrow morning," she said, praying to the Saints she wasn't making a fatal mistake.

"Yay!" Lyra cried, rushing forward to wrap her tiny arms around Jill's waist. Jill started. She couldn't remember the last time someone had embraced her. She wrapped her own arms around the little girl, holding her tightly. At least one person didn't hate her.

Jill spent the rest of her day wandering through the camp. The buzz of excitement in the air was almost contagious. Hunters must have found a nearby herd, as people were roasting large animals on spits. Tents had been cleared away to make space for a dance area. Wood for a bonfire was piled high in the center, and children ran around waving homemade flags.

After days of terror hanging over the camp like storm clouds, the lightness of everyone was a welcome change. Yet Jill still couldn't relax.

They had only killed one monster and were no closer to learning anything about what they were or where they'd come from. There were still more out there, and they could attack at any moment.

Their only hope was that the training they'd given these people would be enough to protect them from attacks in the future. Although Jill would never say so aloud, she doubted it would truly make much of a difference, which was what David had failed to understand. Only trained warriors would be able to withstand such brutal attacks. It was the reason it was so important she find a cure for her father. Why couldn't he see that?

Because he hates my father.

The thought came unbidden and unwelcome, though she could

hardly deny it. From the beginning, David had made his opinion of the king crystal clear. The only thing she couldn't be certain of was whether she agreed with him or not.

Slowly, the day gave way to glittering twilight, the hustle and bustle growing by the hour. Jill was not in the mood for a party. She was not in the mood to be around people, least of all people who seemed to think she was a hero. And she certainly wasn't in the mood to see David when he came walking in, cheers resounding throughout the camp.

Drums started up, and the sound of fiddles tickled her ears. The bonfire was lit and blazed so bright it nearly chased away all the shadows in the camp.

Wine and mead were passed around, though where it came from Jill had no idea. Still, she didn't decline when a drink was passed her way. She took a sip, and the sweet honey mead warmed her from head to toe. She despised being drunk; she hated feeling out of control. But she couldn't deny how the sharpness in her chest numbed to nothing the more she drank.

She stood at the edge of the crowd, watching as a young woman climbed onto a table. Jill recognized her as the young woman who had swept up one of the little boys they'd rescued, a boy who now ran around the fire with the other children, laughing and playing and breathing.

"Quiet, please!" she said, and a hush fell over the crowd.

Jill's palms began to sweat as she took a step back, looking for a quick escape. She didn't like where this was going.

When at last everyone had quieted and the only sound was the crackling fire, the young woman spoke. "As many of you know, my sweet boy, Olly, was taken just mere days ago by those awful creatures." She stopped, her voice cracking. "I thought . . . I thought I'd never see him again. But you—" Her eyes found Jill's in the crowd, and Jill shrank. "You, Jill, and David and Paladin Grimzy, you brought him back to me. You brought our people home."

Cheers rose as people turned to Jill, their faces filled with so much joy, so much hope. Jill could hardly bear it. She pasted on a smile as they began to shove her and David forward. A few people attempted to shove Grimzy, but the mountain man would not be moved, and they quickly gave up.

Jill was jostled and shoved until she and David both stood on the table while the people shouted their names.

If only they knew who I really am. They would not be cheering then.

Beside her, David looked nearly as uncomfortable as she did, doing his best to be polite, the fire glowing against his scars. Even though they stood inches apart, he would not look at her.

When she tried to step down, someone shouted, "Speech!"

Another voice echoed the request. "Speech!"

Soon a chant rose, and with it her anxiety.

"Speech! Speech! Speech! Speech!"

Jill glanced at David, who shook his head. In that moment, she loathed him more than ever before. At last, she cleared her throat, thankful she'd had at least one drink before all this had begun. She'd never been a public speaker. Her brother was the charmer; his words were like weapons. With them, he could engage in a battle of wits, romance a crowd, charm a girl. But the only weapons Jill had were her swords, and those wouldn't help her now.

"Thank you all for throwing this celebration." She paused, staring out at the people. *Her* people. They seemed to cling to her every word, and she hated it. "I don't know many of you, and you don't know me either." She cursed herself for those words. "You think us heroes, but we were only doing what was right. We did what we knew how to do. We fought." She could feel herself rambling, her tongue fumbling for words. "You are the true heroes, surviving day after day, picking up and building a new home. I have no doubt that in time you will slay these monsters your-selves!" She stopped, heart racing. "You give me hope for a better Erinya."

At that, cries rose again. The music started up, and Jill stepped down from the table as quickly as she could, her eyes seeking out another drink.

"Did you mean what you said?"

She spun to see David behind her. She wasn't entirely sure *what* she'd just said. She was just glad it was over.

"What do you mean?" She blinked. In the firelight, his scars seemed paler, and they highlighted his sharp jaw. The air in her chest froze.

" 'I have no doubt in time you will slay these monsters your-selves,' " he quoted, his tone venomous. He leaned in close, his breath warm against her ear. "You may have everyone else fooled, but I can see right through you. You're just as selfish as your father."

Jill shook her head, confused. "David, I just meant—"

"You meant to leave us," he said, cutting her off. "To save your father, who we both know won't send help."

Cold washed over Jill as she looked up at him. She couldn't speak, couldn't utter a single word, because some part of her knew he was right. But he didn't understand what was at stake.

He turned without another word, walking through the crowd. People grabbed at him, dying to touch one of their saviors. It made Jill sick to her stomach. She turned to go. She had no desire to be here any longer than she needed. A small hand grabbed hers.

She turned to see Lyra, whose big cat eyes beamed up at her.

"Thank you." She smiled. "For saving my brother."

Jill's heart twisted. This little girl had gone through a most terri-fying ordeal, yet she was thankful for her brother's safety. Jill thought of her own brother.

Whom you abandoned.

"Come dance with me!" the girl begged, tugging on her arm.

Jill swallowed, looking around. She wanted nothing more than to leave and leave now, but how could she say no? She sighed. "One dance, all right?"

Lyra whooped with delight, dragging her into the crowd of dancers that had formed around the fire. And when the music stopped, Lyra begged for another dance. And another. And with each new song that started, Jill found herself swept into another dance. Someone gave her another drink. And another.

Soon she'd forgotten about leaving altogether. Lyra's joy was infectious. And, if Jill was honest, she wanted for one singular moment to feel something other than guilt.

Lyra twirled and spun, capturing everyone's attention with her graceful moves. Jill thought that same grace would come in handy for fighting one day.

Jill smiled despite herself, letting all the pain, confusion, and hatred that had built up inside over these last few days float away. The fire danced with the people, twisting and rising higher into the sky, smoke swirling into the stars. She looked around and caught a glance of David with an uncharacteristic smile as a young woman pulled him onto the dance floor.

Jill's smile vanished, her chest constricting at the sight of them. The pair laughed as her hands wrapped around his neck. She watched as the girl pulled David's face toward hers, swaying in time with the music.

Jill looked away, anger battling with disgust inside her. She shook her head. He could dance with whomever he liked. And she would be happy for him. Except the tightness in her chest seemed to think otherwise.

She turned to leave, suddenly claustrophobic. What had started as a fun, light feeling now left her head spinning and her breath coming in little gasps. She pinched her eyes shut, pushing through the crowd. Voices swirled together, indistinguishable from one another. Someone grabbed her arm, but she yanked free. Everyone was pressing in, faces staring at her, laughing, cheering. She couldn't think straight.

Suddenly, a hush fell and everyone stilled. Jill looked around and saw a cloaked figure moving through the crowd, striding toward her.

The figure moved slowly, intentionally, and everyone parted to let the figure through. Out of the corner of her eye, she saw David rise to his feet, stepping away from the girl and watching Jill intently.

Jill's heart raced as the shadowed figure gave a deep bow, holding it much longer than Jill thought necessary. Sweat dripped down her neck as she glanced around, sensing everyone's confusion.

"Who are you?" Jill asked at last, breaking the silence.

The figure rose and pulled its hood down to reveal an older woman with frizzy graying hair pulled back in a low bun and piercing eyes as dark as the night sky. She smiled as if she knew some secret Jill did not.

"I could ask the same of you, Your Highness."

Nearby, furious whispers broke out, each one more confused than the last.

Jill's jaw clenched. "I'm sure I don't know what you're talking about. You must be mistaken."

The woman smiled again, toying with her. "I am many things, but I'm rarely mistaken."

"Can I help you?"

"I hope so," she said, staring at her. The fire gleamed off her dark skin, highlighting the fine wrinkles on her face. "May we speak in private?"

Jill stared at her. She had no clue who she was or why she was here, let alone how she knew who Jill was. The last thing she wanted was to be alone with this woman. But she found herself nodding nonetheless, unable to deny her curiosity.

Jill turned back to the people, whose gazes were still drawn to the strange interaction. "I will be back in just a moment. Let the celebrations continue," she said with a tight smile. She hoped it was enough and that no one would ask questions.

They wound through the camp in silence until they reached her tent. Inside, Jill lit a lantern, illuminating the strange woman. In the light the woman looked younger somehow, despite the fine wrinkles and gray hair. It was her eyes that gave Jill pause. They were eyes that had seen too much, had lived more lives than should've been possible.

The tent flap swished open, and David entered. Jill's shoulders tightened as she remembered the way that girl had danced with him only a few minutes ago.

"What do you want?" she asked him, her tone harsh.

"I came to see if you were all right," he said, his voice strained.

"I'm fine. I can handle this."

David stood a moment longer, looking as if he wanted to argue, before he sighed and turned to go.

"Stay, little glass soldier. What I have to say concerns you both."

He froze, turning back to face her. "What did you say?"

The woman smiled again, sadness haunting her expression. "Yes, David. I know all about your curse. I know many things about you." She paused. "I know you think of your mother often and miss the stew she would make for you. I know you hate your father for abandoning you, that you hate the king for tearing you from your mother to fight in a war you don't believe in. I know you blame yourself for her death only a few months later." The woman paused again, her expression changing. "I know who you were really thinking of while you were dancing with that girl."

Jill's blood raced beneath her skin as she watched David, the fear on his face tangible.

"Who are you?" Jill asked again, more forcefully.

The woman turned her attention back to Jill, as if she'd forgotten she was there. "Some call me Mother Goose, Princess Jillianna of Erinya."

"How do you know who we are?"

"I know many things." She raised her head slightly. "Like that the king has fallen ill and you intend to find a cure for him."

"How?" she asked again, both agitated and unnerved.

"Well, if I'm not mistaken, *you* were the ones looking for *me*," she said.

Jill stiffened. "You're the apothecary, the one Millie told me about."

"Ah, yes, Millie Muffet. Poor girl. She hasn't had an easy life, you know." Mother Goose gave her a meaningful look, and unexpected guilt lashed at Jill's chest.

"What do you want?" David cut in, stepping forward. He looked nearly as upset as Jill felt, and she was glad he'd decided to barge into her tent after all.

"I came to warn you." She looked between the two of them. "Your Highness, I fear how you may react to this, but you should know, every day your father weakens. The physicians are doing all they can, but with no success." She took a deep breath. "Your father will not live through the end of the week."

Jill sank onto her cot. She wanted to protest. To yell. To tell this strange, mysterious woman she was wrong, that she couldn't possibly know what was going on in the palace, let alone what the future held. But she couldn't shake the feeling that every word the woman spoke was true.

"Why are you telling me this?" she asked, her voice cracking.

Mother Goose took a deep breath, her eyes straying to the lantern. "I must confess, I have no love for your father, Princess. He has been a ruthless king." She paused, looking back at her. "Your father will die. And because your brother was born only three minutes before you, he will take the throne."

"Yes," Jill said, every muscle within her tightening. "And?" She hated to think where this might've been going.

"Your brother cannot be king."

The statement was so definitive, so precise, that Jill could almost believe what the woman had said was a fact and not a fanciful wish that bordered on treason.

"My brother is the heir," Jill said, annoyed. "There is nothing that can be done."

"Your Highness, you misunderstand me. If your brother takes the throne, he will drive this kingdom into darkness. Chaos and bloodshed will reign. Death will plague this land like never has been seen before."

Dread pooled in her belly as she shook her head. "You can't possibly know that."

"I do," she said, "and I think you do too."

Jill shook her head again, burying her face in her hands, her breathing coming in gasps. It couldn't be true. This woman was lying.

"And what would you have me do? If I cannot prevent my father's death, then there's nothing more I *can* do. A regent would see me married off to a complete stranger."

Silence filled the tent.

"You could take the throne."

Jill looked up at the woman and rose to her feet. "What you speak of is treason. My brother is the rightful heir to the throne."

"And who decided that three minutes determined who would make a good ruler?"

"It's not for you or me to decide!" Jill shouted, her cheeks burning.

"I'm afraid there is no other way."

"There must be. There *has* to be," she said, shaking her head. She didn't want to rule. She didn't want more people depending on her, more people she could let down. All she wanted was to be paladin.

And what if I could make a difference?

The thought was surprising. She had never dared to imagine herself as anything more than a princess or a paladin. She pushed the thought away. To wrest the throne from Jack would mean turning against her own brother. It could mean the start of a war, another war. She could *not* do that to her people. She wouldn't.

"Is that all?" Jill stared the old woman down.

The woman gave a slight nod. "Yes, Your Highness, that is all. Please consider what I've said."

"I have considered it. And you're wrong. I think it's time for you to go."

The woman looked between her and David. "As you wish, Your Highness. But know that I seek only what's best for Erinya."

"As do I. And right now, that means finding a cure for my father."

"You may find the cure you seek will not be of much help to you."

"I don't care. Now leave. I don't think I'm the person you were looking for after all." Jill didn't care how cold she sounded or how sad the woman looked as she left. She didn't care that thinking of her brother's fate made her sick to her stomach or that her father would likely die.

She would not be queen. She refused.

BO

"Your wounds are looking better every day," said Zyla, beaming at Bo.

Bo glanced in the mirror of her room, and her bruised face stared back at her. After her meeting with Ohan-Jin, she had been transferred to a real room on one of the upper levels of the Ohan fortress.

"Thank you for all your help, Zyla," Bo said. "I really appreciate it."

The girl nodded as she started picking up her tools and medicines and packing them back into her satchel. She paused. "Bo, I've been meaning to talk to you. It's about the Order."

Bo's heart skipped. For a week she had been waiting for an opportunity like this, waiting for some way to bring up the convent.

"Yes?"

"We think we may be able to help you escape, that we could hide you in the convent. But first, there's a meeting, and I think you should come to it."

Bo's stomach knotted. She'd been searching for a way into the convent, but it would mean betraying Zyla. Betraying the Order.

The Order means nothing. All that matters is being free of those monsters.

"What kind of meeting?" she asked.

The inkwell girl pursed her lips. "We're discussing something important, but that's all I can say."

Bo frowned. It wasn't much to go on. Actually, it was nothing to go on. "And how exactly am I supposed to go to this meeting? I'm a prisoner here."

Zyla's eyes twinkled. "I know a secret passageway."

Bo stilled. This was what Ohan-Jin was after, a way to get into the convent undetected. Zyla continued to smile at her.

"All right. What do I need to do?"

THE NEXT FEW days passed in a blur as Bo coordinated her plans with Zyla and relayed them back to Ohan-Jin. Any time guilt tried to claw its way into her mind, she told it to leave with a few choice words. She would not let guilt keep her from freedom. If they knew what she'd been through, they would understand. Not that she cared either way.

Now she sat anxiously on her bed, doing her best to steel her nerves. Zyla would arrive just after midnight with a change of clothes for her. Ohan-Jin had instructed his men to turn a blind eye as they escaped and then follow at a distance.

Two short knocks came at the door before it opened.

Zyla was in her blue serving uniform, her satchel no doubt carrying another outfit for Bo. Bo's skin tingled. After tonight there would be no going back.

Zyla shut the door and tossed the uniform at Bo, turning her back to allow her to change.

"We'll need to hurry. The guards are midrotation, and we need to leave before they come back."

Bo nodded. They'd been over the plan a dozen times. But she could not tell Zyla what she already knew. Nobody was going to catch them. Still, her blood thrummed beneath her skin, a beating drum at the base of her skull.

She pulled the clothes on, tripping a little over her leg, but she pushed through. When she was finished, Zyla gave her a head covering, and they slipped out the door.

"Walk slow, head down."

Bo listened and obeyed, a skill that was difficult even at the best of times. She followed Zyla through the long dark halls. Vaguely, she was aware of statues and busts of black marble lining the halls, depicting famous Reptile Clan warriors from ages past.

They turned another corner, and she sensed Zyla falter. The sound of scuffing boots headed their way.

"Keep moving," she whispered. "Give them no reason to be suspicious."

Bo nodded.

Ahead of them, a guard appeared, scaled hands on his cutlass. Bo refused to look up, focusing on the man's boots instead.

The man said nothing, even as his attention followed the pair.

"That was close," Zyla breathed.

"How much farther?" Bo asked. If Zyla sensed this might be a trap, who knew what might happen to Bo.

"Almost there."

Zyla paused in front of a silver tapestry, the threads woven so tightly it looked like a mirror rather than a piece of cloth. She glanced up and down the hallway, making sure it was clear, then pulled it aside.

Black stone greeted them, the same as the rest of the halls. Bo watched her count upward before pressing a stone as high as her head. The stone pushed inward, and a door appeared in front of them, the mouth of a cave looming before them.

Bo's brows shot up, her hand clutching the ring that rested in her pocket, before she touched the stone Zyla had pressed.

"Wow," she breathed.

"I know. The Ohans have many passageways throughout the

fortress, but they've yet to discover this one." Zyla smirked, excitement flashing in her eyes.

Bo quickly stepped inside, closing the door behind her. They were drenched in darkness. For a moment, Bo panicked. And then a small light appeared.

In her hand, Zyla held a glowing bracelet, using it to chase away the shadows. Bo followed in silence as they descended deeper into the passageways. Each time they came to a fork in the halls, Bo would brush her fingers against the stone.

They continued in silence, the only sound that of their muffled slippers against the rock. Sweat rolled down Bo's back even as the chill of the damp cave penetrated her bones.

"Where are you from, Bo?"

Bo jumped, the question taking her by surprise in the quiet. "Uh, I'm from the South. My mother and I lived in Harrow Forest, near the border."

"Really? I've heard rumors about Harrow Forest, about how dangerous it is."

Bo cursed herself inwardly. Why had she told Zyla the truth? She could've said she lived anywhere, yet she'd all but told her that her own mother was responsible for the rumors surrounding those woods.

"They're just rumors," Bo countered. "It's not as bad as everyone says."

"Oh, I guess that makes sense." She was silent a moment. "Why did you leave?"

Images of that night flashed through Bo's head. The explosion. The creatures. "My mother died," she replied, her voice flat. "How much farther?"

"Just around this corner."

Zyla stopped walking, searching for something with the golden bracelet. Bo heard a click and then the grinding lurch of a stone door being shoved open.

A blue-lit arena greeted them, along with a host of the most random assortment of characters Bo had ever seen: humans and inkwells, members of every animal clan except the Reptile Clan, and even a mountain man. The group turned to the newcomers, and Bo refused to meet their eyes.

If treachery was the price of freedom, she would pay it. But that didn't mean she had the guts to watch.

A girl broke from the crowd and ran forward, wrapping Zyla in a hug before pulling away and smiling at her. On the girl's forehead, a flame made of flickering ink burned. Bo looked between the two girls. Their tattoos were different, but the curve of their noses, their bright smiling eyes, the raven hair, all of it was the same.

Zyla turned. "This is my sister, Ymira."

Bo swallowed hard. "Nice to meet you," she mumbled.

Zyla handed the bracelet to Ymira, who slipped it onto her wrist. Bo glanced around the room again, her eyes catching on a woman who stared right at her.

The woman walked forward, leaning on a wooden cane, her gaze hard as stone. Although she was older, the stern look on her face told Bo she wasn't someone to mess with. Her blood pulsed faster.

"I feared it might be you," the woman said.

Bo frowned. "What?"

"I had hoped for your sake that you were not one of the heirs. But I suppose that was wishful thinking."

Everyone was staring at them now, and Bo shifted uncomfortably. She wasn't sure who this woman was or why she spoke to Bo as if they knew each other. It made her feel more on edge than she already was.

"I'm sorry, do I know you?" Bo asked.

The woman looked sad, and Bo hated that. "You do not. But I know you. Tell me, Bo, your mother, how did she die?"

Bo took a step back. "How do you know about my mother?" Her cheeks flamed as she thought of the horrible memory Ohan-Jin had forced her to relive.

"I knew your mother well. She was one of my most promising

students. But then she left, claiming she'd had a vision involving you. I prayed she was wrong."

Bo shook her head. None of this made any sense. In the room, people shuffled, clearly uncomfortable. Bo glanced at Zyla, who looked equally confused.

"What are you talking about? Where are we? Why did Zyla tell me you'd help me escape?" The questions left Bo in a single breath.

"Bo, can you do anything unusual?"

Horror flickered through her. What would they think if they knew what she was, what she could do?

"Maybe. What is to you?"

The old woman sighed. "I am trying to help you. We believe you may be one of the Saints' heirs."

Bo waited for a punch line, for some indication that this was all a sick, elaborate joke. But the silence that followed sent her last ounce of courage fleeing.

A young man walked forward, his dark dreaded hair pulled back to reveal two curved horns sprouting from his head.

"The girl is frightened, confused. Perhaps we'd better get her some real food and continue with the meeting as planned." The man smiled warmly, and Bo's cheeks flushed.

The old woman sighed. "You're right, Hasani. Would you fetch the girl some food?"

He nodded.

A while later, Bo sat on a crate in the corner, picking at a roll and a hot mug of broth. She tried to eat, but her stomach twisted at the sight of food. It wouldn't be much longer now, she was certain.

"Kol, how many blades have you and your smiths been able to make?" the old woman asked.

A young woman looked up, bearing the markings of the Feline Clan. "We're working as fast as we can, but impendium is difficult to work with. At our fastest we can make only six a day."

Bo's ears perked. *Impendium.* That was what the Ohans forced the people of this village to mine, but she hadn't thought anyone else had access to it. Then she remembered that Ohan-Jin had said the Order was stealing from him. Was this what they were stealing? Why would the Order of the Saints need to forge weapons? Weren't they just supposed to pray all day or something?

Unless they were planning something.

"Double that if you can. We have less time than we thought. Every day the monsters grow bolder. With the king sick and the prince and princess—" The old woman paused. "Absent, we'll need to be prepared for anything."

Bo's heart raced faster. They knew about the monsters. And what was that about the king? Movement across the room caught Bo's attention, and she spotted a young girl, not much older than her, clench her fists. The girl's brown face was striking, and she noticed a faint hum emanating from her.

Come to think of it, she could feel that hum from several individuals in the room. She closed her eyes, focusing on that strange thread of connection. She opened her eyes, and they landed on the young man who'd intervened earlier. Hasani, she remembered.

Her eyes found another thread. Ymira, Zyla's sister. And another, an inkwell boy hiding in the corner. Bo's breathing shallowed. What did it all mean? What had that woman called her, a Saints' heir? Like *the* Saints? How was that even possible? How—

An explosion rocked the room.

Stones and bodies were thrown through the air. Smoke and blood flooded Bo's nostrils. Where the hidden door had been just seconds earlier was now a heap of rubble, leaving a black hole in its wake.

And on the other side of the smoke and dust stood Ohan-Jin and his men.

The reptile man smiled, licking his pointed teeth. "Kill them all."

41

JACK

Jack's things had been packed for days. Each morning he woke up determined to leave. And then, for reasons even he couldn't understand, he stayed.

He had been allowed to leave his room and often did, searching high and low for Millie. But he could never find anyone. Still, he didn't leave.

A few times he'd knocked on Millie's door, but she never answered. He wasn't sure if it was because she truly wasn't there or if she refused to answer.

His heart ached either way. He longed for just five minutes to tell her how he really felt, to apologize and explain to her the *thing* inside his head.

I am not a thing. I am far more powerful than you will ever understand, boy.

And you are the reason I can't be with Millie.

Do not blame me for your fear.

Jack wanted to bite back a retort, but he had nothing.

The deep clanging of a bell rang out, echoing through the stone corridors. Jack paused, wondering what it meant.

A surge of panic tore through him.

The convent is under attack. For the first time, the Voice sounded genuinely surprised.

What? How?

It doesn't matter. You must leave.

But—

Now!

Jack grabbed his pack, thankful he'd kept his daggers strapped to his chest. He threw open the door and ran. The bell continued to toll, its haunting echo driving into his bones.

Ahead, he heard shouts and the clashing of blades. Smoke filled the air. He dove into the fray. The flash of steel caught his attention, and he spun to block an oncoming blade before it severed his head from his body.

A scaley face stared back at him, yellow eyes narrowed.

Jack's breath hitched.

"Ohan-Jin, what are you doing here?" he growled, shoving the man back with all his strength.

The reptile man hardly budged. "I could ask the same of you, Your Highness. Aren't you supposed to be searching for a cure for your poor father?"

Jack seethed. How he hated this man.

Around them, the fighting continued, but Jack hardly noticed it. In this moment, only the two of them existed. "As the crown prince of Erinya, I don't have to answer to you. But these people are innocent. This is an act of war!"

The man smiled, and Jack noticed the blood that stained Ohan-Jin's uniform. "I did not start this fight. But I will finish it. You, of all people, should be grateful; they were planning a revolution. They were planning to overthrow *you*."

Jack froze.

No, it can't be true.

"You're lying," Jack ground out, gripping his dagger tighter. His hands were slick with sweat, the clang of metal fading.

"Am I? You know they were stealing impendium, don't you? The impendium needed for the war efforts. They stole it from me and, by extension, you." Ohan-Jin's smile vanished, black scales glittering on his brow. Here was a man who wanted to take Jack's throne from him. Surely he was a liar.

Jack swallowed. Since he'd arrived, no one had told him anything. They had left him out of meetings; they had hardly spoken to him. Even Millie wouldn't tell him anything. And it was clear they were hiding something big.

Millie.

Where was she? Was she safe? Had she been hurt in all this madness?

"So, you see, Your Highness, I am simply serving my future king by bringing these traitors to justice."

Jack considered the man's words, how carefully they'd been chosen. The Ohans had always been the treacherous ones. Even if Ohan-Jin was telling the truth, he had no authority to attack without the king's approval. And the king was dying.

I can give you the power you seek, the freedom to rule however you want.

Jack drew his other dagger. "You know what I think? I think you're the traitor."

Ohan-Jin's lip curled as he clutched his blade. "So be it."

Ohan-Jin lunged with blinding speed, driving his sword at Jack's chest. Jack barely blocked it in time, getting knocked backward several feet.

Anger propelled Jack forward, and he knew the strength he wielded was not his own, but the force lent to him by the Voice. He didn't care. Steel clashed as they struck at each other.

Blood rushed through Jack's muscles as he moved faster than he ever had before. Ohan-Jin was formidable in his own right. The reptile man matched Jack's every move, deflecting his blows like he could read Jack's mind.

A blow landed on Jack's shoulder, slicing the flesh and sending a wave of pain flaming down his body. He collapsed to one knee, looking up at Ohan-Jin, blood pouring down his chest.

Ohan-Jin grinned. "I admit, Your Highness, I do like seeing you this way, kneeling at my feet."

Energy sparked in Jack's chest as he launched forward again, pain splintering his vision as he hacked away at the Ohan man's defenses. Jack swung with vicious strength, pushing the man farther and farther back.

"You royal brat! You will never be strong enough to defeat me!" the man roared, bringing up a boot and smashing his foot into Jack's chest.

The breath left his lungs as he fell onto his back. He was covered in blood, but worse than that was the shame he felt.

If only Jill were here.

If only he had listened to his father.

If only he weren't such a failure.

"You're pathetic. Erinya does not need you as its king. You would lead us to ruin."

Jack tried to stand, to fight. But how could he?

Break him.

Jack rose to his feet, and he knew the Voice controlled him now. It was the Voice who would grant him power, who would fight for him when no one else would. Perhaps the Voice was the only one who truly cared about him after all.

"You don't know what I'm capable of." Jack's mouth moved, but it was the Voice who spoke, a deep and gravelly sound.

Ohan-Jin's eyes widened, and Jack took advantage, rushing forward and slamming him up against the stone wall, his dagger at the man's neck.

"What were you saying?" Jack gritted out, his voice returning to normal.

Blood trickled down Ohan-Jin's neck. "What are you?"

"Jack!"

A voice rang out, and fear clutched at Jack's throat.

No.

But it was too late. Ohan-Jin must have seen the fear that flickered across Jack's face. He smiled. "Ah, little Miss Muffet. I was hoping to see you again."

"Leave her out of this," Jack snarled.

"Jack, what are you doing?" Millie was running toward them, hair falling out of her braid.

The movement was quick. Ohan-Jin drew a knife hidden on his hip and flung it through the air. Jack could only watch in horror as it flew, finding its home in Millie's throat.

Blood burst from her neck as she dropped to the ground, surprise on her face.

Jack screamed, forgetting all about Ohan-Jin, running to catch Millie. He grabbed her, holding her face as blood gushed from the wound.

He heard Ohan-Jin calling for the traitors to be rounded up, to kill any rebels, but none of it mattered anymore.

"Millie, no, Saints!" He pulled her close, desperately wishing he'd said all the things he'd wanted to.

She tried to cough, opening her mouth, but no sound came out, terror scrawled across her features. She clutched Jack's hand, squeezing it.

"Millie, please don't go." Tears rolled down Jack's cheeks now. He couldn't lose her.

She reached up to touch his face, her eyes locking on to his, as if she was trying to communicate something. Then she smiled and exhaled.

And she didn't breathe again.

Jack raged. He screamed and yelled. His vision blurred as he looked down at Millie. *Saints,* she was beautiful. He should have told her how he felt. He shouldn't have pushed her away.

"Help me, please." His voice was weak, broken.

How could I possibly help?

"You can do something! I know you can!" He didn't care that he spoke aloud, that he was yelling at someone nobody else could hear.

Do you truly think so?

"I'll do anything!"

Really? Anything? The Voice smiled in his head. Jack could feel it. He had been waiting for this moment, waiting for a time when Jack was desperate enough to do anything he asked.

Yes. Anything.

I will bring her back, but in return, you must surrender yourself to me.

Jack considered it for only a second. "I'll do it."

Excellent.

The world descended into murky shadow. Jack watched from outside his body as the darkness moved around him, covering Millie like a blanket. A cold wind rushed through him. Someone cried out. And like the first breath of a newborn child, he heard a gasp and then a cry.

The shadows dissipated, and Jack saw Millie lying there, the knife removed. In its place was a scar. A shuddering breath told him that she was alive.

Relief flooded him as he surged forward, back in his body as he wrapped his arms around her, a fresh wave of tears rolling down his face.

Thank you.

Do not thank me yet.

What?

Now you must pay the price. Surrender to me, or I will kill her again.

Fear lanced through Jack. The Voice could kill her again.

As you wish.

A thrumming pulsed at the back of his head, growing louder and louder. His vision went black as pain spliced through his body, darkness pulling at his mind. Images appeared before his eyes faster than he could register them. He sensed his consciousness being pushed back into his mind.

So, this was the price he had paid.

When at last he opened his eyes, he breathed differently. Or the Voice did. He controlled Jack now.

"Ah, it's so good to be in a real body again," the Voice said with Jack's voice.

Jack tried to speak, to open his mouth. But he couldn't. Panic welled inside him. *What have I done?*

"You did the right thing, my prince," he hissed in Jack's voice again.

A tingling buzzed at the back of his neck, growing louder and louder. Jack's heart hammered frantically. *What's happening to me?*

A gasp cut through the silence, and the Voice and Jack looked up to see a young girl standing at the end of the hall. Their eyes locked, and the buzzing intensified.

Jack felt himself smile. "Ah. So, you're the one who has my monsters."

4 2

———

DAVID

*S*leep did not find David that night, and it had nothing to do with the rocky ground beneath him or the howling wind whipping through the camp.

The old apothecary's words echoed through his mind. *I know you think of your mother often and miss the stew she would make for you. I know you hate your father for abandoning you.*

It had been a long time since he'd given any thought to his father, and he tried his best not to think about his mother. But the ache in his heart remained, far more painful than any break he'd suffered.

All of David's life, his father had talked about the Silver Stags, how one day he would find them and he'd be rich. Season after season he went out in search of them, leaving for months at a time. One year, he never came back at all.

David and his mother had assumed the worst.

Then a few years later, after his mother had taken ill, David saw an old man in a musty tavern. The gray man reeked of alcohol as he blabbered away about how he'd seen the stags once. Not a soul listened to a word he said.

When David approached him, he saw a shadow of the man that

had been his father. In his place was a man driven mad by obsession —an obsession so strong it had torn him from the only family he'd had left.

David sat up in his sleeping roll, rubbing his forehead. There was a reason he avoided thinking about his father. It only ever left him bitter and angry, longing for a father he never had.

Instead, his mind turned to other things.

I know who you were really thinking of when you were dancing with that girl.

He sighed, a headache forming behind his eyes. He shouldn't have let that girl drag him onto the dance floor in the first place. But Jill's betrayal had left him wanting to drive out the numbness that had settled in his chest ever since she'd told him she was leaving. It hadn't made anything better though.

If anything, the numbness had only consumed him.

As much as he hated to admit it, the old woman was right. He had been thinking of someone else. As the girl had pressed her soft lips against his, tracing the scars on his face, all he could think about was Jill. Of her eyes, forever melting between a summer day and a stormy sky. Of her fingers, tender despite the callouses from years of fighting.

He shoved those thoughts from his mind. They would lead to nothing good. They would only taunt him with something he could never have. She was a princess, and he was a soldier. She would continue her journey to save her ruthless father and forget all about him.

But he doubted whether he would ever forget her.

A bloodcurdling scream roused him from his thoughts. Instinctively, he reached for his weapon, pausing to listen.

More screams followed, one after another, nearly lost in the wailing of the wind.

Then smoke assaulted him.

He launched forward out of his tent and emerged into chaos.

Plumes of fire raced through the camp, a swarming army of flames leaping from tent to tent.

It was a monster consuming everything in its path.

Jill.

He had to find her. He grabbed his things, already choking and coughing from the smoke.

He ran through the smoke, heading toward her tent. But in the smoke, every burnt tent looked the same.

He ran faster, ash filling his lungs and burning his eyes. Around him, the fire blazed, and he knew soon he would be surrounded, trapped within the flames with no way out.

A low horn blew, deep and wild.

David stopped, his heart melting in his chest. *No.* There was no way. They couldn't be here. They were too far from the border.

The horn sounded again, closer this time, and he knew. He'd know that sound anywhere—a horn made from a bullcat, which could only be found to the far east, over the border in Carthesia.

"David!" a voice cried out through the flames.

David whirled around, searching for her.

"Jillianna!" he yelled, his voice hoarse. He kept moving, running toward where he thought he'd heard her.

Flames lapped at his heels like a biting dog, and he stumbled, the heat growing suffocating.

An arrow zipped through the air, nearly clipping his shoulder.

What the Saints . . .

He scanned the burning tents around him, searching for phantoms in the flickering flames. Another arrow sped toward him, and he barely ducked in time.

This was no ordinary fire. This was a coordinated attack.

A cry tore through the night. Jill's, he was certain. He raced between burning tents, ignoring the flames that licked his skin. He was thankful for his curse for once, for his skin did not burn the way a regular mortal's would. His lungs, however, were another matter.

There. He saw her in the ashes of the camp the fire had already destroyed. She clutched her shoulder as uniformed men surrounded her, four soldiers bearing the Carthesian crest, a ram with three horns.

Behind him, the fire blazed, and ahead, he faced the destruction left behind. Ash fell like flakes of snow.

He approached slowly, watching as they circled Jill. She held her blades together in one hand. But she looked tired, soot covering her from head to toe.

David ducked behind the burnt remains of a tent, pulling his bow free and nocking an arrow.

He released it and watched as it connected with one of the soldier's necks and he toppled to the ground. Quickly, he nocked another arrow and aimed it at the second soldier as heads swiveled in his direction.

The second soldier collapsed.

Jill turned on one of her opponents, drawing a knife hidden at her side and driving it deep into the man's belly. Blood leaked down his front as he crumpled.

The fourth man turned to strike at Jill. But David saw him move and launched himself forward, tackling the man to the ground. David's hands locked around the man's neck, and he began squeezing as hard as he could.

A few seconds more and Jill would've been dead. How many more were dead because of this fire? These men had tried to kill her, had killed so many of his men back on the front lines.

He squeezed harder, the man's face purpling and his eyes bulging.

"David, stop!" Jill's voice broke through the fury that held him captive.

He relaxed his grip, but only a little. He eyed his surroundings. The fire was dying out as quickly as it had started, having burned through everything in its path.

He looked back at Jill, her face filled with fear. A fear of him.

Distantly, he was aware of the screaming and crying, of people searching through the rubble of the flames. It all felt like a feverish nightmare, only he couldn't make himself wake up.

Jill stepped forward, kneeling to look down at the man pinned beneath him.

"Who are you?" she asked, not bothering to hide the tremble in her voice.

The man's gaze slid between them. "Nobody," he sneered. "Unlike you." He gave Jill a knowing smirk.

David tightened his grip. "How do you know who she is?"

The man scowled. "Hired . . . to kill . . . her," he choked out.

David's heart skipped as he looked back at Jill again. Her eyes were wide as she stared down at him.

"By whom?" she asked.

The man clenched his mouth shut, and David knew that was it. If the man wouldn't talk with David's hands clamped around his throat, he wasn't likely to talk given any other threats. He would go to his death with that secret.

"What do we do?" he asked Jill.

She remained silent. He could feel her deliberation and guessed she was thinking the same thing he was: it would be easier to kill the man and move on.

But if someone had hired an assassin to kill the princess, they would only send more. No. They needed him alive.

"Where's Grimzy?" she asked.

"Somewhere in that heaping mess."

"I'll find him. Do something with him."

Kneeling on the man's chest, David pulled some rope out of his pack and tied the man up. The fact that the soldier didn't resist made him uneasy.

Eventually, the sky turned from black to gray to orange as the predawn light began to break through the smoke.

A little later, Jill returned with Grimzy in tow, along with Asif and Lyra. David swallowed hard. In the chaos, he'd completely forgotten about the siblings, but he was grateful Grimzy had taken care of them where he had failed.

Jill bent down to look the soldier in the eyes, his gaze burning with hatred. "I won't bother wasting my time with you. I have far more important things to attend to. But Paladin Grimzy here will make sure you stay on your best behavior as he escorts you back to the palace. And if you feel like talking on your way, you might face an easier trial." She paused, looking thoughtful. "Or a trial at all."

"Your Highness," said Grimzy softly.

Jill turned to him, nodding. "Yes?"

The mountain man bowed his head. "If I may be so bold, let me take him to my people. I fear the palace may be full of spies. I greatly doubt we can trust anyone there."

Jill considered this, arms crossed, her expression lost in thought. At last, she nodded.

"Do what you must. Take the children too, and perhaps any survivors, if your people can take them."

"We will do all that we can to help them."

Jill turned back to the Carthesian soldier. The man stared at her before his eyes slid over to Grimzy, apprehension filling his face.

David nearly laughed. If he'd had to choose between Jill's wrath or Grimzy's, he would have taken Grimzy's any day.

Jill turned to face the rest of them. For the first time, David realized that a crowd had begun to form behind them. And they were looking to Jill.

The shadows in the crowd seemed to deepen as she faced them. Her face was stern, but her eyes were soft. Behind her, the sun rose, bathing her in a light that made her glow. She looked like a warrior, a paladin.

A queen.

He must not have been alone in his thoughts, for people in the crowd gasped, whispers surging forth like a frothing wave.

"People of Erinya," Jill said, her voice giving a slight waver, "I confess I have hidden my identity from you, in part because I was afraid. Afraid of how you would see me. But the time for honesty has come."

Soft murmurs and sideways glances shuffled through the crowd.

"I am Princess Jillianna of Erinya."

The whispers grew louder, some shocked, others angry.

"I did not intend to come here," Jill continued, ignoring the chatter. "I was only hoping to pass through. But when I learned of the monsters, of this place, I knew I could not leave without helping." She stopped for a moment, her eyes locking on David's. "I fear I may have done more harm than good, for the only home you had left has been destroyed." A tear slipped down her cheek, but she quickly brushed it away. "I am truly sorry."

Silence wrapped around the crowd, and the light that shone behind Jill faded.

Grimzy stepped forward, a giant beside Jill.

"For those who would seek refuge, I offer my home in the mountains. My people will do all they can to aid you. We will leave as soon as we have searched for survivors and buried those who did not escape the fire."

The crowd shifted, turning and wandering away in different directions. Whether they were searching for bodies or leaving altogether, David could not be sure. A few people, though, continued to stare, watching the princess carefully.

At last, Jill turned to him. "I need to find that woman again. She knows more than she's letting on. I shouldn't have let her leave last night. It seems she may be the only one who can help us now." Her voice was tired, and he realized then that her shoulder was still bleeding. Dark circles had formed beneath her eyes, and her clothes were burnt and torn.

"I'll go with you." The words were out before he could think them through.

Jill looked at him, giving a faint smile. "Thank you."

His throat tightened. Somehow he knew that she would lead him to his death.

43

MILLIE

When Millie was a girl, she fell out of a tree and broke her arm. For weeks it had ached, throbbing and pulsing. She couldn't remember a time she wasn't in pain.

The pain she felt now was so much worse.

Images flashed behind her eyes, but they were blurry, like she was peering at them through a murky pond. She saw Jack and Ohan-Jin. She saw bodies lying on the floor. A blade flew at her, but she was too slow.

Pain. So much pain. And then darkness.

The darkness wrapped around her like a shawl. Warmth curled in her belly, and for the first time in a long time, she felt herself relax, sinking into the darkness.

A yell shattered the silence, screaming angry words. She couldn't make out what they said, but the scene shifted. Instead of darkness, she seemed to float in a hallway. It took a moment for her to realize that she stood over Jack. Over her own body.

I'm dead.

The thought should have frightened her. It should have angered her. There was still so much left for her to do. But instead, the thought was a relief.

"I'll do anything!" Jacked yelled, holding her body. Tears spilled down his cheeks.

She wished she could reach down and tell him she was all right, that she was at peace. She reached a hand forward, ready to place it on his shoulder, when pain assaulted her once more.

A stabbing sensation pierced her neck, and she gasped, grabbing for her throat. Her breathing was shallow, panic pumping through her veins. What was happening? Wasn't she dead?

The prince does not wish for you to die.

The voice that spoke was like breaking glass, sharp and brittle, but with the deepness of a vast ocean. She shivered, still clutching at her throat. She did not know who was speaking to her or why, but she knew this could not be right.

I will bring you back.

The darkness around her swelled, light pulsing at the edges. She didn't understand. Was she not dead after all? Was someone bringing her back? Was that even possible?

A great snap tore through her body, and when she opened her eyes, she blinked up at Jack. The knife in her throat was gone, but the pain remained. Her eyes rolled back, and she fell into darkness once more.

44

BO

$\mathcal{B}$o stared at the young man before her, her leg wobbling a bit from the effort of standing.

"Ah. So, you're the one who has my monsters," he said, his voice knowing and certain.

Her heart stuttered, her blood heating. How did he know that? And what did he mean *his* monsters?

"Who are you?" she asked, forcing her voice to come out strong. She refused to be bullied into fear. She was tired of all the riddles, the confusion.

The young man smiled, and then something came over his face. His lips twitched, and he shook his head as if there were a bee flying in his face. His eyes cleared for a second, changing from black to green. Fear flooded his expression.

"Help me," he said.

"Wha—"

His face changed again, moving from fear to that knowing smile. His eyes darkened once more.

"It seems the prince is unhappy with our deal. He seeks to take control even though he swore to surrender to me."

Bo stepped back, her bad leg scraping along the floor. An icy hand gripped her heart. She had no idea what this man spoke of, yet it chilled her to the bones.

"Who are you?" she asked again, her voice less certain this time. She knew she should turn and run. The Ohans had all but forgotten her. But she knew the Order likely wouldn't.

The man rushed forward, standing over her. She stumbled back, tripping over her foot and landing on the ground with a bump.

She looked up at the man. He was younger than she'd originally thought, perhaps only a few years older than her, but his eyes were black and ancient—the eyes of a beast that had spotted its prey.

"My name is lost to time," he said at last. "For now, this body I occupy belongs to Prince Jack of Erinya."

Bo swallowed hard. She wasn't sure which sounded more ridiculous, that this man could be the prince or that he claimed to have possessed the prince.

"But the question remains," he continued. "Who are you?"

Bo tried to think. She needed to flee. She didn't like anything about this. Out of the corner of her eyes, she saw the sword of a fallen soldier lying just barely out of reach.

Without giving it another thought, she lunged for it, grabbing the handle of the blade, but a hand reached out and locked her wrist in a grip of iron.

She cried out in pain, feeling her bones grinding together.

Just then, the prince squeezed his eyes shut, shaking his head again and releasing his hold on her.

She inhaled, scooting as far away as she could, unable to tear her gaze from the young man in front of her.

He opened his eyes, and they were green once more. "You," he said, his voice losing its malicious edge. "Where—who are you?" He looked around, dazed.

Bo didn't speak, her blood thrumming. She waited for his eyes to change back to black, for his body to shudder and the cold voice to return. But it did not.

"My name is Bo," she said. "What is going on?"

The young man rubbed his forehead, looking like it had been ages since he'd slept. "I don't know. But I know that you have some power, don't you?"

Bo was tempted to lie, to feign ignorance. But she'd all but confessed with her own lips that she did.

"Yes."

"Those monsters, the ones that have been attacking around the kingdom. They're yours . . . or his. I can feel it, feel them, even as we speak." His eyes didn't meet hers as he spoke, as if he was talking to himself.

Bo's mouth clamped shut. She did not know a single thing she could say to change this. She didn't have any clue what to do next. Should she return to the Ohans? Run while she had the chance and find the monsters?

Some great fear passed through her. She could not run from this. An image took hold in her mind. The monsters would hunt her down, and they would turn on her. She would die.

The prince's eyes flicked back to her. "I need you to come with me."

Bo jumped. "What? No. I'm not going anywhere with you. I don't even know you!" She climbed to her feet, prepared to fight if necessary.

For a second, his eyes flashed black, and his voice lowered. "You will come with me, or I will drag you there."

The prince's eyes flickered back to green, his face impassive. She was beginning to understand, but it couldn't be.

Images of that night flashed before her eyes, of that monstrous form her mother had released. That disturbing presence she'd felt then dwelled within the man before her.

Bo licked her lips. She could try to fight him, try to run. But something told her she would not make it far. And if she did, surely the monsters would obey their true master over her.

"What do you want with me?" she asked.

His face twitched, and he answered with black eyes. "I want to free you."

THEY RODE HARD for two days straight, the prince guided by some voice only he could hear. He had insisted on bringing the other girl along, who had yet to remain conscious for longer than a few minutes at a time.

After they'd fled the Order, they'd stolen a few of the Ohans' horses.

Bo was not nearly the rider the prince was, and he set a brutal pace. Every moment they rode, she felt her uneasiness grow. Was she doing the right thing? Did she even know what the right thing was anymore? Did any of that matter if she could be free?

She squeezed the reins of her horse. She didn't know who to trust anymore. It seemed everyone was against her, everyone offering her promises they couldn't keep.

They rode along the Rose River to the south, back the way to her old home. Something told her she would not be returning there for a very long time. Whatever she'd gotten herself mixed up in, it had no intention of letting her go anytime soon.

After two days, a wood rose to meet them. The trees stood against the river like silent sentinels keeping watchful guard. The prince slowed his horse, and Bo followed suit.

As they entered the forest, a hush fell over them. The only sound that could be heard was the rushing of the river behind them and the wind blowing through the trees.

For the first time in weeks, Bo let herself relax. She had forgotten how exposed leaving the cover of the forest made her feel. Now, under the shade of the trees, she inhaled deeply, clinging to the scent of pine and moss.

Her thoughts turned suddenly to Zyla. Bo had lost her in the attack, and she felt struck with guilt. The Ohans might have killed her, especially since she'd been the one to lead Bo to the Order.

Her heart twisted. Zyla had been nothing but kind to her. She'd saved Bo's life, and yet Bo hadn't even spared a thought for the girl.

And what was that the Matron had been saying, something about the Saints' heirs and forging weapons?

It left her dizzy.

A sudden chill suppressed her, and she glanced up, catching sight of a figure in the distance. Her heart plummeted.

Suddenly, the figure stood in front of them, but Bo swore that she had not seen it move.

The prince let out a curse, then dropped from his horse, approaching her.

"I was told you could help me," he said, his voice terse. So, it was the prince speaking.

Although they had not spoken much over the past few days, Bo had come to realize that there were indeed two people dwelling within a single body. One belonged to the prince, and the other would not give its name. Bo sensed the shift more than observed the changes. A darkness came over her heart as well as a feeling of despair. Fear clutched at her, begging her to flee. But she could not surrender to fear.

"I've waited a long time to see you again, Your Highness," the woman said.

Then, just as the woman had appeared from nowhere, a small house did as well. Covered in vines and ivy, the cottage sat to their right, smoke spiraling out of the stone chimney.

Bo gasped. She'd heard tales of this woman before, and if she'd known this was where the prince had intended to take her, she would never have agreed.

As if sensing her reluctance, the horse backed up, edging away.

"Not so fast, Bolynn," the woman said, and Bo froze. "I've been expecting you as well."

The old woman turned, heading toward her home, waving for them to follow.

Exhaustion lay heavy on Bo. How she yearned to leave this

wretched kingdom and all of its powerful people who sought to use her as a pawn.

Despite all this, however, Bo found herself dismounting, tying her horse, and following the woman inside. The prince helped the girl stand and walk, his gentleness surprising. Who was this girl that mattered so much to the prince?

Bo thought for a moment and then decided she didn't care.

Inside, they were greeted with warmth. A fire blazed in a pit in the center of the small house. On every wall sat shelves of books, potions, and herbs. Skulls and bones sat on one shelf, while strange trinkets and jewelry rested on another. Around the fire were cushions on the floor for sitting, and the girl sat gratefully, looking more alert than she had in days.

A white scar stood out on her neck, stark compared with the rest of her dark skin.

"You bring great evil here," the woman said at last, coming to stand beside the fire with them.

The prince's eyes darkened to black. "I should have suspected a greeting like that coming from you."

The old woman looked vaguely sad. "It is not with hatred I say that, Malum."

The prince's anger flared, his face reddening. "Don't you dare call me that! That's not my name anymore!" His chest heaved, and for a moment Bo thought she was about to witness the prince kill the woman in front of them.

"Jack," came a soft voice.

Immediately, the prince's eyes cleared to green, and he turned to the girl, Millie, the Prince had told her.

"Jack, what's going on? Why are we here?" she asked.

Jack's jaw clenched. "We're here because this woman can tell us where to find the cure we need, the cure that can restore me back to my complete form and return my monsters to me."

Bo stepped back, wondering if anyone would notice if she slipped out. It was clear that this had nothing to do with her. If she could just—

"You will not leave just yet, Bo."

Bo turned her gaze on the woman. "What do you want with me? Why am I even here? Why won't everybody just leave me alone?" she shouted, her heart racing. She was so tired of all of this, of all the lies, the mystery. Everyone just wanted to use her. Was there anybody who actually cared about her?

"I know the hardships you faced, Bo, and the hardships you will continue to face." The old woman paused. "But you are stronger than most."

Bo rolled her eyes. "And just like everyone else, you have said something without really saying anything."

The old woman's glare pierced her, and Bo could sense the power behind the look. "You want the truth then?" she asked, her voice low. "You are a Saint's heir. It is the reason your mother stole you at birth, the reason she attempted dark magic to bring back the Black King. It is the reason that, when he returned only in partial form, the monsters bonded with you. And when the prince went to the Deadwood in an attempt to banish Malum from his mind, he called the monsters to himself instead. It is why they left you."

Bo couldn't breathe. Her chest felt tight and heavy, aching with unwept tears. She wanted to scream at this woman, to cry, to run away from this cursed kingdom and never look back. But she was frozen in this moment of horror.

"You're lying," Bo breathed.

"The truth is cruel, but that does not make it untrue," the old woman said, her eyes softening.

The prince stepped forward his eyes black again, a victorious smirk on his face. "How I have missed you, my sister. You always did know how to break people. Now, tell me, where can I find this cure?"

The woman's eyes flashed, burning with anger. "I will never tell you."

Quicker than should have been possible, the prince drew a knife and shoved the woman up against a wall, pressing the blade to her neck. The two glared at each other.

Bo's heart pounded.

"Jack, stop this," came Millie's voice, strong and clear. "This isn't you. Let her go."

The familiar twitching overtook Jack, and he shook his head. His eyes turned green, and he looked back at Millie. "He will help me overthrow my father. He will help me end this fruitless war. I need him."

"You don't need him," Millie said, tears in her eyes. "Please, Jack, don't do this."

"Listen to her," said the old woman.

Instantly, the blade was back at her neck, pressed harder than before. Tiny droplets of blood dripped down the woman's throat. This time, the prince's eyes remained green. This was his own decision.

Fear clutched at her. She knew she should do something, that she should help. But who should she help? The old woman, who'd told her the truth, or the prince, who'd promised her she could be free of the monsters? Then again, Jack wasn't the first to promise her freedom.

"You don't need him, Jack," Millie pleaded. "Don't you understand what he's doing to you? He's warped your mind."

The prince shook as he stared at the old woman, her face a serene pond. But Bo had no doubt something powerful lurked below. For just a moment, Bo thought he would lower the blade, that he would surrender to reason.

At last, Prince Jack shook his head. "No, he's opened my mind." His eyes blackened.

The old woman smiled even as blood dripped down her neck. "I still won't tell you."

"Fine." Prince Jack spun and rushed at Bo, grabbing her and swinging her around so his knife now rested against her neck. It was so fast that Bo had no time to run or think. She felt the cold steel pressed against her throat, the bite of metal on skin. She struggled against him, but he was too strong. Unnaturally strong.

"Tell me where to find this cure, or I will kill her. I'm sure my children will come back to me then."

Bo's breathing shallowed. She sensed the prince, or Malum, or whoever was in control, would do whatever was necessary. He would not hesitate to kill her.

The woman glanced at Millie, whose eyes were wide with fear. "Jack, please!"

"Can't you see I am not Jack?" he sneered, his voice cold.

The girl swallowed, standing taller. "I know Jack is in there somewhere, and he would never do this."

The blade cut at Bo's skin, and she struggled to breathe without moving too much.

"Sister, tell me where this cure is, or the girl is dead."

The old woman looked at the prince, but instead of anger, there was only sadness. "Do not do this."

"Do you take such pleasure in being an insufferable old woman? Tell me what I want, or I will kill the girl."

The woman's face hardened. "Be warned, Your Highness." She seemed to speak to the prince now. "If you choose this path, darkness will cover the land. Those creatures will devastate everything in their path, turning your kingdom into a desolate graveyard. You will be left with nothing but a ruined reign, and you will die by the hand of the person you trust most."

Silence wrapped around them, her words final and resolute, like the closing of a tomb. Bo was not familiar with prophecies, but she knew good ones from bad ones, and a prophecy like that was definitely a bad one.

"You lie," he said at last. "We have seen the future. We will be the most powerful king who ever lived. We will not cower like my father. All will fear us, respect us. You know nothing, old woman."

She sighed like it was a dying breath, like she could fight no longer.

"There is a well deep in the Enchanted Wood. The water there can heal any ailment or break any curse. It will sever the bond with the girl and restore the monsters to you."

The look was quick, and if Bo had not been watching so intently, she would have missed it. It was a subtle, pointed look from the old apothecary. Her eyes locked with Bo's for a mere second, and Bo knew.

She must drink the water, not the prince. Somehow, she knew it would keep the monsters from returning to Malum.

"Where in the Enchanted Wood is this well?"

"If the well wants to be found, it will be. The wood lives and breathes, but beware, it will twist your mind; it will test you."

The prince let go of Bo, his eyes clear but his face hard.

"Please, Jack," Millie said, "you don't have to do this." She stepped forward to grab his hand, but he shook her off.

"I have to," he said, sounding defeated.

"Your brash words will do you no good here, Your Highness. We both know who has the power."

"This isn't you!" Millie begged.

The prince rounded on her. "You don't know me! You don't know what I've done, what he's made me do!"

The words hung between them, heavy as an anchor. Bo thought Millie might cry; it certainly seemed like something she would do. Instead, she lifted her head, meeting Jack's eyes.

"Perhaps I don't know you. But you once told me that power or no power, I was stronger than I believed. The same could be said of you. Please, Jack, don't make this choice."

"The time for choices is over. I've made my decision." The prince looked resigned.

"There will be no going back," said the old woman.

Jack looked over at her. "Then it's a good thing I never look back."

45

———————

JILL

Jill's and David's horses raced across the plains. It had taken several days before they were able to leave in good conscience, and they'd helped where they could to prepare people to head for the mountains. Silently, Jill prayed it would be safe there.

One of the men who lived in the camp had been able to tell Jill and David where the old woman lived. It was only a day's ride away, but already Jill was tired. A heaviness weighed on her after the events of the last several weeks. It was all too much.

David glanced at her. "We should rest for a bit."

Jill wanted to argue, but they'd already pushed their horses hard, and she knew they needed a break.

She nodded and slowed, dismounting near an outcrop of boulders. Nearby, the Rose River ran, foaming and frothing.

David dismounted silently before grabbing the reins of both horses and leading them to the river. When he returned, he sat down on a boulder beside her.

His quiet presence overwhelmed her, and she inched away from him.

"What are you thinking?" he asked, breaking the silence.

Jill sighed. "I don't even know what to think anymore. Everything about this quest has gone miserably wrong."

"Everything?" David asked, raising an eyebrow. His look was almost playful, but she could not bring herself to smile.

"It should've been so simple. All I had to do was find a cure for my father and bring it back. Then my father would've finally seen how valuable I'd be as one of his paladins. And then I wouldn't have to—" She paused, her throat constricting. "I wouldn't have to marry a stranger from Welynn."

She sensed David stiffen but couldn't bring herself to look at him. Tears threatened to spill over, but she refused to let that happen.

Her thoughts turned to Will. It had been so long since she'd thought of him. His face in her memory seemed to fade more and more every day. She feared the day she would forget it altogether.

"I take you are not the marrying type?" he said.

"I never said that," she said, her heart galloping. She didn't owe him any explanation. "I did once—want to get married, have children even." She had never confessed such things to anyone before, not even Jack.

"Really now?" he said, staring at her. "What changed?"

Jill swallowed, forcing herself to look at him. Although his face was marred, there was something soft and genuine to it.

"The boy I loved was murdered." Her voice sounded hollow. But she felt hollow. She still didn't understand what had happened on that night a year ago now. "The worst part of it all is I know he was killed because of me. He was a stable hand. We could never have been together, but that didn't stop someone from killing him." This time as she spoke, a tear did slide down her face.

A finger brushed it away, and she looked at David, who was suddenly so close. His face hovered near hers, his fingers still lingering on her cheek.

The thought of him kissing another girl entered her head, and she turned away, her face burning.

David cleared his throat. "And what about what that woman said to you? About taking the throne?"

Jill turned sharply. "She has no idea what she's suggesting. It would be mutiny, madness. Treason. I was never born to rule." She shook her head. The mere thought of taking the throne sent panic racing through her. Her brother had been groomed all his life for the throne.

"And when your father dies, what then?"

"That won't happen."

"Eventually, it will. He'll die, and your brother will take the throne, and you heard what that woman said. Something isn't right with him. Would you really let him rule?"

She thought about that. When she'd begun this quest, she'd merely feared her brother wasn't ready to rule, but things had changed. Now there was something darker at work. And judging from the uneasiness she felt, she couldn't simply brush aside the old woman's warning.

The more she thought about it, the stranger Jack's behavior had been in the days and weeks leading up to the tournament. At times he didn't seem like the brother she knew. He spent his days muttering to himself, disappearing for days at a time. Something was very wrong with Jack and she'd been too blind to see it then.

"I won't let him rule. My father—"

"Your father is dying," a voice interrupted.

The two spun to see the old woman approaching. Her face looked severe, but there was something else there as well.

Fear.

Jill stood. "Please, you must help. My father—"

"Your brother," the woman cut her off again, "plans to overthrow the king."

Jill paled, her insides squirming. "What?" she choked out.

"He is headed for the Enchanted Wood to seize the cure you seek."

"Then there *is* a cure," she said, hope rising in her chest. She glanced at David, who only stared at the woman.

The old woman shook her head. "You miss the point, stupid girl! Your brother has no intention of saving your father. He is driven only by that thing inside him."

Jill's face flushed with anger. "What are you talking about? My father needs that cure!"

"Your father will die with or without that cure."

"You don't know that!" she yelled, stepping forward. "If my brother is as bad as you say, then we must do everything to keep him off the throne!"

The woman took a step forward, her eyes piercing Jill with a fury so stormy she was tempted to take a step back. But she would not.

"And what if you get this cure and save your father? Sooner or later, he *will* die, and your brother *will* take the throne. You only delay the inevitable. The people need a leader. The people need *you*."

The words struck Jill like a slap in the face. It was the very thing she feared. David had said nearly the same thing only a moment earlier. It was a matter of *when* her brother became king, not if.

"What do you mean by the thing inside him?" Her voice was low. She was afraid of the answer, but she had to know.

The woman was silent, her eyes traveling between Jill and David. At last, she shook her head. "I knew your mother, Your Highness. You carry her fierce heart."

Jill's heart skipped against her rib cage, all other thoughts flushed from her mind by those few words. "You knew my mother?" she asked, her voice barely above a whisper.

The woman simply stared at Jill, her expression soft until she sighed again. "Yes. That is where this story begins—with her. You must understand, it's not that I didn't pity your mother. After all, I've lost a child too. But she was messing with things she didn't understand, and now the very worst has happened."

Jill's heart slammed within her, blood pumping to every cell in her body as she listened to the woman's words. *What does she mean she lost a child too? Just what was my mother messing with? And what does that have to do with finding a cure for my father?* But as the questions pounded at the back of her mind, she found herself quiet, waiting for the old woman to explain.

"Your mother came to me when she was pregnant with you and your brother. The midwife had given her heartbreaking news. She sensed two babies, but only a single heartbeat."

Jill shook her head. "That's not—"

"Possible?" she interrupted, turning her gaze on Jill. "I assure you, it is more than possible. Babies die in the womb every day."

"Yes, but—"

"But how, then, were you and your brother born alive?"

Jill swallowed hard and nodded, not sure she wanted to know that answer. Her knees already felt weak at the very thought of what her mother must have done.

"I told her there was nothing that could be done. There is no way to bring the dead back to life. She couldn't accept that answer, so she went to someone who wasn't afraid of the consequences."

Silence hung between them, the only sound the rushing of the river at their backs.

"And?" Jill finally asked, her voice barely a whisper.

"And another foolish apothecary performed a ceremony to bring your brother back to life."

Jill's head spun as she tried to understand this woman who claimed so many things. "I don't understand."

"Of course you don't, because you know as well as I do that the dead are supposed to stay dead. When that woman brought your brother back, she tore the veil between life and death, leaving cracks within Jack. When the Black King was freed a year ago, he could not reform completely. With nowhere else to go, his form latched on to Jack. Now, that evil lives inside him."

Jill's knees buckled, and she dropped to the ground. The air was thick around her, sweet, cloudy. Her eyes couldn't focus. David's voice broke through the silence, but she couldn't make out the words.

The Black King.

Jack.

The only person she'd ever cared for, aside from Will. Her only brother. The man she compared all other men too. *It can't be.*

But she knew. Perhaps, somehow, she'd always known. The unexpected anger and cruelty. The sudden violence. And in the last year it had only grown worse. She had chosen ignorance but she could do so no longer.

Jill rose to her feet, her head clearing as she looked at David and the woman. They turned to her expectantly. Jill inhaled. "Help me. Help me keep my brother off the throne. My father may not be the best king, but surely he must be better than Jack will ever be. Please!" She hated the desperation in her voice, but she needed this woman's help. She could not do this on her own.

The woman exhaled deeply. "I knew it would come to this sooner or later. I will help you. But not because I believe in the king." She gave Jill a long hard stare, then sighed again. "At the center of the Enchanted Wood is a well. The water from this well will cure any illness, break any curse, save a man even on the brink of death."

Beside her, David stiffened.

"Thank you—"

"I'm not finished," the woman snapped. Jill swallowed but nodded for her to continue, her heart gathering speed again. She feared what more the woman might have to say. "Your brother is headed there now. I believe the evil inside him wants the water to regain control of the monsters. You must stop him."

Jill's mind whirled. Her brother wanted to control the monsters? No. The Black King wanted control of the monsters.

"He is much changed since last you last saw him, I fear. Every day the darkness within him grows. You must stop him."

Jill nodded solemnly, head pounding, heart aching.

"There is more you should know. The Enchanted Wood will do

everything in its power to keep you from finding the well. But not only that, the forest has been known to show people terrible visions — visions of the future should they succeed or fail in their endeavors." She paused. "Whatever happens, you must not let your brother drink from the well. I fear the cure would only wipe away what little humanity is left in him."

For the first time, the old woman looked at David, her eyes tracing the scars down his face, her gaze sad. "I have seen your face in many visions over the years, David. Your fate is as changing as the wild-winds. May the Saints watch over you."

Jill glanced at David, and his expression was hard as he stared at the old woman. She'd known him only a few weeks now, but already she'd come to understand what that look meant. She hoped what the woman had said was true, that water from the well truly could break any curse.

The old woman looked to the sky, darkness crouching all around them.

"You must go quickly. Head southeast. You shall know the wood when you come to it. And be careful. I suspect the next time I see you, things will be much changed, for if you take this path, there can be no turning back."

Then the old woman turned, leaving them as quickly as she'd appeared. But Jill did not miss the words mumbled beneath the woman's breath.

"Long live the queen."

46

JILL

$\mathcal{I}$t was nearly evening the next day when they arrived at the Enchanted Wood. Despite its name, there did not appear to be anything particularly special about it. But as they ventured closer, Jill sensed the change in the air. Beside her, the horses shifted restlessly, snorting and stomping. David gripped his bow, his eyes flicking at the edge of the woods.

"This is it?" he asked, uncertain.

Jill nodded. Somehow, she knew this was it. She had a similar feeling when they had entered the Deadwood, only then it had felt haunted and cursed. These woods felt full of possibility. Of danger, yes, but the kind of danger that enticed one to walk to the edge of a cliff and peer over. It was the sense of magic.

They tied their horses and walked forward.

The earth rumbled beneath their feet. They were speechless as the trees in front of them pulled their roots from the ground, shifting their massive trunks and limbs. Branches snapped, and wood creaked and groaned until all movement ceased and a path opened before them, leading straight into the darkness.

Jill's hands shook, her heart beating too fast. She knew once she stepped onto this path, there would be no turning back.

"Are you ready?" David asked.

"No," Jill admitted.

"Neither am I." He held his hand out to her, and she grabbed it, squeezing.

Together, they stepped forward onto the path. They had walked only a few steps when the earth rumbled once more. The trees shifted back into place, sealing them in.

At last, the trees settled again, leaving them in an eerie half-light. Specks of sunlight splattered the ground, breaking through the dense foliage high above them. Unlike the Deadwood, animals could be heard here, though it unnerved Jill how few sounds she recognized.

What will we meet in these woods?

They walked in silence. Jill was thankful for David's presence beside her. She wasn't entirely sure she could have braved this alone. A bird swooped across the path in front of them, startling them both before disappearing high into the trees.

Jill let out a nervous laugh. "She did warn this place would play tricks on us."

David looked at her, his scars so pale suddenly that she could hardly see them. In fact, they were fading altogether. Sharp fear rose inside her.

"David, your face," she said, her eyes widening.

He gave her a confused look, reaching up to touch his jaw. The shock was evident to him as well. He pulled up his sleeves, gnarled scars fading to nothing before their eyes.

"I don't understand," he said. "I haven't even drunk from the well yet."

She eyed him nervously. "It could be a trick."

He nodded. "Or a promise."

Their eyes locked, and for the first time, Jill was struck by how handsome he was. Scruff clung to his sharp jaw, and a slightly crooked nose matched his crooked smile. His dark eyes pulled her in with the hint of a secret. Her heart slammed into her rib cage, and she looked away.

"Perhaps. There's only one way to know." She looked to the path ahead of them, winding through the trees like a serpent.

They continued, and Jill's nerves tingled from the strange events. She did not want to think about what might be yet to come.

After just a few more minutes of walking, they came to a fork in the road, a signpost at the center. Her heart froze. The sign that pointed to the left read "Jill," and the sign that pointed to the right read "David."

They looked at each other, then back to the signs.

A bird came flying down in front of them and rested on top of Jill's sign, staring at them. Jill was certain it was the same bird they'd seen earlier, but it was unlike any bird she'd ever seen. It stood half as tall as Jill, its beak the size of her hand and black as oil. Its feathers were white, but when the light hit them just right, they glowed a strange iridescent color. But the strangest thing of all was its eyes, which looked utterly, terrifyingly human.

The bird did not make to move toward them, nor did it make any sound. It only stared, watching them with humanlike intelligence.

Jill glanced at David from the side, unable to peel her gaze away from the strange bird. "Perhaps we should go down one path together."

He nodded. "Yes."

Together, they set down the trail marked with her name, the bird following their movements, its eyes never leaving them as they hurried along the path. Jill's heart raced as she picked up speed, eager to be as far from that bird as possible.

"That was strange," David whispered.

She nodded. There was magic here all right, and every step deeper into this forest they walked, the stronger it became.

Eventually, she lost track of time, focused only on putting one foot in front of the other. Even though they'd entered the forest toward evening, the lighting never seemed to change. Sunshine still cut through, but it never moved. She wondered how much time had passed since they'd entered this place.

Suddenly, they rounded a little bend, and without thinking, she grabbed David's hand to steady herself. Not ten feet away was the same fork in the path they'd come to earlier. The same sign marking their trails stood in the middle.

And that bird was still sitting there, a look in its eye like it had been waiting for this moment, waiting to see them again.

They stepped forward again and without a word nodded to the path marked for David. Again, the bird watched, a gleam in its eye as they vanished down the path, hurrying along.

Jill's face heated as she realized she was still grasping David's hand, and she quickly let go, clenching her fist at her side instead.

When the old woman had told her about the Enchanted Wood, Jill had pictured monsters and mayhem, much like their quest into the Deadwood. So far, aside from the strange bird and the changing paths, they had yet to encounter anything truly hostile. Jill would've rather faced the monsters. Fighting was something she knew how to do, something that ran through her veins.

This place was unlike anything she'd ever experienced. And she didn't like it one bit.

"I have a bad feeling about this," David said.

Jill didn't want to agree. To agree was to confirm her worst fears. "About?"

He stopped, grabbing her hands and looking at her, his scar-free face still foreign to her eyes. "I think we both know what has to happen."

She shook her head, looking to the ground. "No, it's just a trick. She said so."

"It will be okay," he said, and for a moment she could almost believe him.

She looked back up at him. It was strange, but a part of her missed his scars; they gave her something to look at. Now she was forced to meet his eyes, and once she did, she found she could not look away.

"I don't think you're making the right decision, you know. I think you should take the throne."

Her heart turned cold.

She gritted her teeth and yanked her hands from his grasp. "Then why did you come?"

"You know why."

"There was no other reason?" she asked, unable to meet his eyes. She wanted to hear him say that it was because of her, because he wanted to be with her, yet she couldn't shake the sense that to hear him say it aloud would be the greatest betrayal. A betrayal to Will, to his memory. She'd told him everything. And every word poured from her lips had tasted like poison as she'd spoken to him. She knew it was because, as she'd opened up about all that she and Will had been to each other, she had felt herself letting him go.

He fixed her with an unreadable look. "I came for a cure. After that, I think it's best we go our separate ways."

Something in her chest snapped. David was a soldier, a hunter. They'd known each other for only a few weeks. He was not Will, nor would he ever be. And she could not ask that of him. She knew it was better this way.

And yet the sting of his words was worse than the bite of a sword.

She wouldn't let him see that though. Instead, she turned, eyes focused on the path once more. This was why they'd come, to reach the well and stop her brother. They couldn't afford to be distracted now.

"Let's keep moving."

They started again, rounding another bend and coming to the place Jill feared. Once again, they were at the fork in the road. She swallowed hard. David was right. They both knew what needed to happen. But something about this moment, this decision, felt heavy. She could not shake the sense that once they started down separate paths, they would not emerge the same. But it seemed they had no other choice, not if they wanted to succeed.

They stopped at the fork, and her eyes locked on the strange bird. In the stories she'd heard as a child, this was the moment where the bird would speak, would give some strange warning, wisdom, riddle, or insight. They waited, but the bird remained silent.

Perhaps a bird was just a bird.

She looked at David, and his eyes darkened as he started down his own path. When they had ventured down it together, the path had been well lit, albeit quiet. Now as they looked down the path, something had changed. Instead of meandering downhill in the light, the path veered upward, a steep climb as darkness descended on the path before him.

She wished she could go with him. She wished she at least had something to say, some encouragement to offer. But what did one say in an instance like this?

Still, as she watched him begin his ascent, her tongue caught in the back of her throat until she whispered, "Goodbye, David."

She looked back at the bird, its beady eyes fixed on her. An expression not unlike a cruel smile seemed to flick across its beak. She waited once more for the bird to do something, anything. But it did nothing. She swallowed hard. She could prolong her journey no longer.

She turned to her path. Unlike David's, hers remained lit by the sun above. Once again, she wondered if time moved differently here. It seemed everything here behaved differently. What had been a cobblestone path before now took the form of a narrow dirt trail, and she wondered what it all meant.

She stepped forward, plumes of dust rising from the ground. The moisture felt sucked from the air as she took a dry breath in. Despite the shadows of the trees, heat swallowed her as she started down the path. At one point, she looked back, wondering if it was too late. But the fork in the road was gone, as was the bird. And David.

She was all alone now.

·   ·   ·

SHE WASN'T sure how long she'd been walking in the sweltering heat. Sweat dripped down her forehead and the back of her neck, and every few minutes she expected to see the sun set, for the forest around her to darken. But though she'd walked for hours, nothing ever changed.

She pulled her canteen from her hip. She was thirstier than she ever remembered being, and she'd done everything in her power to preserve her water, but she could resist no longer. She held the opening to her lips, waiting for the cool droplets to hit her tongue.

No water came. Not a single drop.

She shook the canteen, desperate for anything, desperate for the tiniest drop to quench her thirst. Still, nothing.

She dropped to the ground, wanting nothing more than to burst into tears. But she couldn't seem to do even that.

Why had she come here? Why was she doing this? What was she trying to prove? Did she even want to save her father?

Or to stop her brother?

Under no circumstances could Jack drink the water from the well, because if he did, all Erinya would be doomed. She still didn't want to believe it. Her mother had died. Her father ignored her. But all her life she'd had Jack. He was her twin, her brother, her closest friend. Now he was slipping through her fingers as well.

She had never felt so alone in all her life. She wished Will were here. But as she closed her eyes, picturing his face, she found it was fuzzy, the memory of him faded with time. She buried her face in her hands, wiping dirt and dust all over herself.

A breeze blew through the trees, a breath of fresh air against her damp skin. She blinked. One moment there was nothing, and the next a bubbling fountain sat in the middle of the path, the sound of flowing water like music to her ears.

In an instant, she was on her feet, rushing toward the fountain, until she stopped short. A warning played at the back of her mind.

What if this was a trick? What if there was no fountain at all? Or perhaps the fountain was poisoned and a single sip would kill her.

She stared at the flowing water, her thirst growing stronger by the moment. Mesmerized, she stepped forward, unable to resist any longer. She dipped her fingers into the basin, the cool water a blessed relief on her dry skin. She dipped her other hand in, cupping the water and splashing it onto her face. Streams of cool water ran down her neck, and for the first time since she'd started down her path, she felt relief.

She cupped her hands in the water once more, this time bringing the water to her lips.

A shock ran through her body like lightning, pain lancing through every muscle. She collapsed to the ground, her body shaking with pain so torturous she could barely breathe.

The temperature dropped. Instead of sweltering heat, she shook with cold. And then darkness shrouded her eyes, the pain fading.

She thought she'd passed out, but it became clear that something else was happening. Distantly, she could feel her body splayed on the ground. But her mind remained alert, surrounded by the darkness.

The black moved like a ghost made of ink, trails of wispy darkness floating around her. This didn't seem like a dream, nor did it feel entirely real.

The darkness pulled away, revealing a gray-colored scene before her.

Her brother and Millie ran through a wood, something chasing them. Alongside them ran another girl Jill had never seen before. Millie's face was twisted in fear as she tripped, stumbling to the ground. Her hands cut open by the rocks, she rose and kept running, unaware of the blood coating her palms.

Jill's heart raced as she watched.

Jack dove behind a large boulder, pulling Millie close and holding her as she shook. "I can't do it!" she cried. "I can't transform!"

"Shh," he whispered, his eyes nearly as wide with fear as hers.

The scene shifted.

An old well sat at the top of a hill, looking broken-down, abandoned, dry. A girl sat on the edge of the well. Her skin was white as bone, her hair black as a raven's quills, but her eyes were hollow pits. She smiled to reveal pointed teeth tinged with black. For some reason, she seemed to be sopping wet, water dripping from her hair, her clothes.

"I can't wait to meet you, Princess," she hissed through her fangs.

Jill stepped back, but there was nothing there. Instead, she was falling, falling through the air.

The next few images came so fast that Jill could barely take in what she was seeing.

She saw Jack drinking from a wooden cup. Saw him collapse. Saw darkness wrap around him like a vise. She heard his scream, her own scream, Millie's scream.

She saw the darkness leach from him. Watched helplessly as a crown was placed on his head. The monsters they'd fought surrounded him like guard dogs. Armies marched across the plains. Screams. Blood. Chaos. Fire. War.

You must not let your brother drink from the well.

The darkness surrounding her dispersed rapidly, a blinding white light flashing in her eyes.

She opened her eyes, her cheek pressed in the dirt, heart racing wildly. She leapt to her feet, all thoughts of thirst gone. She didn't know how long she'd been out; to her it had seemed like only a few minutes, but now the forest was dark, the heat of day giving way to the breath of night.

Gone was the fountain that had bubbled into existence. Gone was the winding dirt path. In its place was solid stone leading straight ahead, out of the forest into a clearing.

She started running, racing toward the light. When she stepped out of the forest into the clearing, the trees shifted behind her, blocking her way back.

But she wasn't concerned with any of that. Before her was a hill she recognized, and at the top was a broken well with the strange girl sitting on the edge, watching her with hollowed-out eyes.

She shivered and stepped forward, beginning the ascent up the hill, dread pooling in her stomach like a coiled snake ready to strike.

The hill was neither high nor steep, and yet every step was a challenge. When at last she reached the top, her blood pounded through her veins, crackling with anticipation.

The girl at the well smiled, looking just as she had in Jill's vision.

"Welcome, Princess. It is such an honor to meet you at last. The savior of us all," she said in mock wonder.

Jill gritted her teeth. "Who are you?"

The girl cocked her head to the side, feigning deep thought, dripping all the while. "I had a name once," she said wistfully, "though I have long since forgotten . . . You may find that life before the well and life after the well look very different."

A nervous shiver raced down her spine at the girl's warning. "But why are you here?" she asked, more forceful this time.

The girl turned back to look at her, her face impossibly young, yet Jill got the impression that she was older than Erinya itself. She forced herself to meet the girl's hollow eyes.

"I am the guardian of the well, the keeper of this forest. Did you like my gift?"

"Your gift?" Jill bristled.

"The water fountain. I do hope it helped." Her voice was like a child's and a snake's, a hissing coo that only served to set Jill on edge.

Jill swallowed, the horrifying images flashing through her mind. "You call that a gift?" she asked, angry now.

The girl cocked her head again. "You were thirsty, were you not?"

Jill gripped her sword. "Yes, and I still am. I need water from this well. And you're going to give it to me." She pulled her sword from its scabbard, pointing it at the girl's chest.

The girl's smile vanished, a snarl curling her lips instead. "Put that away." She raised a hand, and with a simple flourish, the sword was yanked from Jill's grasp and sent flying down the hill. It landed at the bottom, its point driven deep into the earth.

The girl smiled once more. "That's better," she said with a sugary sweetness that turned Jill's stomach. "I will be more than happy to help you, if only you ask nicely." The girl fluttered her eyelashes, a strange sight given she had no eyes.

Jill swallowed. "May I have a cup of water?" she asked, her voice tinged with bitterness. "Please?" She didn't want to be here any longer than she had to. She still had to travel back through the forest and home in time to save her father.

The girl kicked her legs, swinging them back and forth like a small child.

"No." She giggled.

Jill's anger flared. "But you said—"

"Shh!" The girl pressed a finger to her lips. "We're waiting for the others."

"What others?" Jill asked.

At the bottom of the hill, something crashed, twigs and branches snapping. She turned, and her stomach flipped. The girl she'd seen in her vision stood at the base of the hill, and with her were Jack and Millie.

47

DAVID

David hated climbing. He hated this forest. He hated that it had made him split up with Jill. But mostly, he realized, he hated himself. He hated how weak this curse made him, how his father had driven him to hunt the Silver Stags to begin with. It made him hate the last words he'd said to Jill.

But they were words that had needed to be said, if not by her then by him.

She knew how David felt about the king, and still she was going to save him. After all the devastation he'd caused, she was still risking everything to find a cure for him. She could claim it was to keep her brother off the throne all she wanted, but he knew what she was really afraid of.

She was afraid of herself.

He thought it funny how someone could fearlessly stand up to monstrous creatures and angry crowds and yet could not face up to the real issue at hand. She was afraid of taking the throne for herself.

David shook his head and reached a hand up, looking for a hand-hold in the rock. His arms shook; his back and shoulders ached. This entire path had been a steady upward climb in the near darkness.

He pulled himself up, forcing his muscles to move. If he stood still too long, he was bound to freeze up and not be able to move again. He gritted his teeth, sweat beading down his back and forehead. It was strange to see his body without all the scars. He still didn't completely understand what it meant, why his skin looked flawless once more.

He'd been careful as he climbed, like he was still made of glass. The last thing he wanted was to fall and shatter completely, though part of him wondered if he would break at all. Since his skin had smoothed out, he had yet to experience any sort of cracking like he usually did when he exerted himself.

Perhaps it was a trick, a way to lure him into a false sense of security.

He searched for another handhold, pulling himself up a little farther. He was glad the rock face had many little ledges jutting out, giving him a brief respite every once in a while. But the higher he'd climbed, the scarcer they'd become. He could feel his strength waning, his muscles giving in, burning him from the inside out.

He reached up again, his fingers making contact with the cliff edge. *Almost there.* He reached with his other hand, pulling himself up with his last bit of strength.

His hand slipped.

His stomach somersaulted as he felt himself fall. He reached with the other hand, grabbing the edge, fingers digging into the rock. His shoulder wrenched, pain splicing down his body as he scrambled to find a foothold, heart hammering.

He brought his other hand up, arms shaking with fear and adrenaline. He pulled himself up quickly, clambering gracelessly to the top.

For a moment, he sat there, his breath ragged and his body shivering with terror.

He'd almost fallen.

He forced himself to look down over the dizzying edge. It was hard to see in the dark, but he was certain a fall from this high up would have killed any mortal person and, assuming he was still very much cursed, would have shattered him into a million little pieces.

He scooted from the edge, still trying to calm his racing heart and fluttering nerves. He couldn't dwell on what-ifs. He had to keep moving, near-death experience or not.

He forced himself to stand, exhaustion suddenly taking over.

Saints, I hate this place.

A rocky path lay before him, lit only by a silver moon cutting through the trees above. An icy wind blew at his back, and he shivered, a tingle running down his spine. He wanted nothing more than to sit and rest, but he had the strangest sensation he was being watched. He could not have relaxed even if he'd wanted to.

He walked for some time, his only companion the rustling of the breeze, haunting his mind like whispers. Several times he stopped, trying to listen, to see whether there were truly voices or figments of his imagination. But each time he was met only with silence.

When he thought he could walk no longer, something rose in the distance. In the dark, it was hard to distinguish, its shape rather odd. As he approached, his mind turned, his hand clutching his bow. What he'd thought was a strange house was actually a giant shoe, or a boot. It was the largest shoe he had ever seen, as big as a house.

It sat blocking his path, the front door the only way forward.

He stilled, silent as he waited for something to happen. But nothing did. All was quiet but for the pounding of his own heart. Then he noticed smoke rising from the ankle of the boot, a familiar scent filling the air.

My mother's stew.

He inhaled sharply, wondering at the events of the past few days that had led him to this strange place. A few weeks ago, he'd been nothing but a cursed soldier desperately trying to get away from the war. Now he stood on the threshold of what he was sure would change everything. It terrified him more than any fight or battle he'd ever faced.

He took a deep breath and pushed the door open with a trembling hand.

It was small inside, dust covering every surface save for a little fire in the heel of the boot, a cauldron of stew hanging over it. The smoke rose up the ankle and out of the strange little house. A window looked out into a dark forest, the silhouette of a rocking chair beside it.

And someone was in it.

"David, is that you?" a soft voice asked.

He froze.

No. It can't be. She's dead.

But as he approached, he knew it could be no one else. Her tiny, frail form. Her graying hair that had once been a lustrous brown, split and dry as straw. He came around to the front of the rocking chair to look at her, to see for himself.

Her skin was gray and wrinkled, her eyes heavy with unwept tears. She looked so much older than he remembered, so much frailer. She looked on the verge of death.

"Mother?" he whispered, kneeling in front of her.

Her eyes wandered, and that was when he noticed how pale they were, how she could not focus on his face. Was this how she'd looked toward the end? Blind and all alone?

His heart twisted inside his chest. His father had done this. The *king* had done this. He'd taken David away from her. She might have lived longer if he'd been there to care for her.

"David?" she called again, eyes still searching.

"I'm here, Mother," he said, reaching out to grab her hand. "I'm here," he whispered, a single tear sliding down his cheek. He could not bear to see her this way.

"Oh, David!" she cried. "I told them you'd be back! I knew you wouldn't leave me!"

David swallowed. "I'm sorry. I-I had to go somewhere." An uneasiness settled over him as he looked at her. It was his mother all right, down to the small scar on her nose from the day Henrietta the chicken had scratched her with her long claws. David almost smiled at the memory. The next day poor Henrietta had become victim to a chicken stew. "Serves her right," his mother had said.

Still, something wasn't quite right. This wasn't possible. His mother was dead. He'd seen her body with his own two eyes, had helped dig the grave she'd been buried in. Could this forest be home to the afterlife?

Acid burned his throat at the thought. What a cruel afterlife this would be.

"Ma, what are you doing here? How did you get here?"

"Oh, David, don't you remember? Or has it been so long?"

David shook his head. "I don't understand."

She made a tsk-tsk sound in the back of her throat. "We live here, don't you see? This is our home."

"Mother—"

"Shh!" she said, pressing a finger to her lips. Her dim eyes looked past him in a way that set him on edge. "You don't want to wake them."

Them.

David wasn't sure why, but that single word was enough to send his heart spiraling in his chest. "Mother, what do you mean *them*?" He was afraid to ask, but he knew he must.

She smiled, a few teeth missing from her grin. "Why, the children, of course! I told them you were coming; they didn't believe me. Very naughty children indeed. Had to send them outside. They should be back soon."

David looked around the little shoe house. Other than the fire and the rocking chair she sat on, there was nothing there, no evidence of any children, not even a bed or mat to sleep on.

"What children?" he asked. With every passing second, he grew more and more concerned. How could this be his mother? How could any of this be possible? And who were these nonexistent children she spoke of now?

She sighed like she was about to explain a very complex issue to a child. "You know the children, David. There were so many of them. I wanted them all. But the Saints took them from me."

A memory surfaced from the back of David's mind. How his mother had called him her miracle baby, how he was the only one that had lived. He recalled learning she'd been pregnant many times, but she could never carry a child beyond a few months. He had been the only one, and even so, he'd almost died in infancy. His stomach churned.

"I'm so sorry," he whispered, not sure what else he could say.

She reached out and patted his hand. "There, there, you mustn't be sad. The Saints have brought me new children, the children no one wanted."

Slowly, David pulled his hand from her grasp, the feeling of her skin like rotted flesh against his own. He looked around. Something was not right about this place.

"I have to be going," he said, though it pained him to say those words.

"You're leaving me again?" She stopped rocking.

He swallowed hard. Her voice was so betrayed it broke his heart. *This is not real.*

"I'll return, Mother," he said, taking a step back. The lie burned in his throat.

"But the children!" she cried, this time tears leaking from her eyes. "You didn't even meet them!"

"I'll meet them another day," he said, taking another step back.

She shook her head, her blind eyes unable to focus on anything. "No, you can't. They will be gone. Please don't hate me. I tried, but there were too many! And I loved them all . . ." Her words wandered, the phrases disjointed and confused.

His eyes were drawn once again to the window, to the darkness outside. His body shook as he stepped forward, stomach twisting, and forced himself to look outside.

A figure stood at the window, and David jolted. A familiar face stared back at him. Luca. His friend's face was half-rotted.

"Why did you leave me?" Luca asked.

David spun, squeezing his eyes shut, but the image had been burned into the back of his head. *Why?* He wanted to scream. Why had the forest shown him these things?

"Drink some tea, David. It will make you forget." The voice was different now, higher, lighter.

Dazed, he took the cup offered to him, not caring what it was or where it had come from. He drank the tea down, the hot liquid sliding over his tongue without any taste at all. It was gone in seconds.

"Better, David?"

He looked up and stumbled back. His mother was gone. In her place was the most terrifying girl he'd ever seen. Black hair framed her pale face, her eyes hollow as a tomb.

He tried to stand but found himself sluggish and slow. "Who are you? What did you to do me?" His words were slurred, and already the room around him bent and twisted. He could not tell if it was spinning or he was.

"You'll meet me soon, dear David." She giggled, revealing razor-sharp teeth coated in black.

His vision blurred, and he could hear her cooing, a singsong rhyme leaving her lips.

HUMPTY DUMPTY SAT ON A WALL,
   Humpty Dumpty had a great fall;
   All the queen's horses and all the queen's men,
   Couldn't put Humpty together again.

DARKNESS SURROUNDED HIM, her words echoing in the back of his mind.

He stood at the top of a high tower. Jill stood beside him, hair falling loose, blood seeping down her arm. Before them stood a young man David had never met. Shadows clung below his eyes, and dark hair fell around his pale sunken face. Still, there was no denying the resemblance. This must've been Jack.

"How could you, Jill?" he screamed, his eyes wide and wild.

David took a step, hearing himself speak outside his body. "Jack—"

"King Jack!" he bellowed. He turned his attention to Jill. "You would take everything from me? You would betray me like this?"

"Jack," Jill said in a broken voice, clutching her arm. "Please, you're not yourself," she begged.

"No," he said, "I'm not."

Before either could react, Jack marched forward, brought his leg up, and kicked David in the chest so hard he felt it crack. David stumbled back, trying to regain his balance, but it was too late. He toppled over the edge of the tower, gravity pulling at him like a starving peasant.

He heard Jill scream.

He was falling, falling, falling.

And then he landed. To say he was in pain was to describe the ocean as a little wet. Every part of him shattered into a million pieces. He could not breathe. He could not see. He could not even cry out.

At last, it seemed, death had found him.

David woke, trembling and dazed. His heart pounded faster than a galloping horse. Whatever happened, he was certain of only one thing: that would be his future.

Unless I break the curse.

He rose to his feet, gathering his thoughts and taking in his surroundings. The shoe house was gone, along with the terrible memories. There was no trace of either. Up ahead, he saw a light breaking through the edge of the trees. He stumbled forward. He had to get to the well.

He broke through the tree line and into a clearing, a hill in front of him. At the top were several figures and an old broken-down well. He had arrived.

He climbed up the hill, his body numb. Only one thing mattered now.

When he reached the top, he stopped, looking around. Jill stood across from him, her stance tense and her jaw set. To her right stood a young woman with a timid face, and beside her was a face that turned his gut. *Jack.*

Another figure stood to Jill's left, a ruddy-looking girl with a hobbled foot, glaring at Jack with as much venom as David himself felt. And in front of the well stood—

"You," David said, his voice hoarse.

"Welcome, David," said the girl with no eyes. She smiled. "We were waiting just for you."

"How kind of you," he spat. He did not know who this girl was, nor did he care. A hatred unlike anything he'd ever felt burned through his chest as visions of falling assaulted his memory.

She turned back to the others, a look of crazed glee on her haunting face. "I know why each one of you has come here. I'm so delighted to see how this turns out," she hissed.

She waved her hand, and in it appeared a wooden cup, water sliding down the sides. "You've all come for a drink from this magic well." The way she said "magic" made it sound like a child playing a game of make-believe. "But alas, I have some rather unfortunate news." She paused, her smile growing wider as she looked at each of them in turn. "Only one of you may drink from this cup. Only one may break their curse."

48

MILLIE

Only one may break their curse.

Millie's body shook. She could feel the magic of the forest pulling at her, begging her to transform. Bo's forehead was bleeding, and Jack's gaunt face looked gray in the dim light around them. At the bottom of the hill, a young man had stumbled out of the trees looking dazed, his eyes unable to focus on anything until they came to rest on the strange girl sitting on the edge of the well—the girl who had told them she was its guardian.

As the young man had drawn closer, she'd seen pale scars all over his arms and neck and face. The princess's eyes had widened, following him as he made his way toward them. She had no idea who this young man was, but it was clear that Jill did.

For a moment, they were silent, all watching one another, waiting to see who would act first. The girl smiled wider. She would enjoy this, Millie realized.

The scarred man stepped forward. "I'm sorry, Jill, but I need that cure."

Jill's brow furrowed as she cast a glance at Jack. "David, you can't. Think of what will happen."

"I've seen what happens. If I don't get this cure, I'll die."

Jill's expression twisted in pain, a fragile look Millie had never seen on her before. She'd always pictured the princess as unbreakable, but it was clear there was more to her than she'd realized.

Her face shifted, hardening to stone. "You know I can't let you do that."

"And neither can I." Jack stepped forward, his dagger pointed at David's chest. "I'm going to need that."

"Jack, you can't," said Jill, stepping toward him. "Our father needs it."

Rage propelled him forward. "Our father needs nothing from us!" he yelled, inches from her face. "He was a terrible father and a worse king. And you would save him?"

Jill's expression faltered. "You don't know the future I've seen. Jack, I'm begging you. Please do not drink that water."

What he might have said was lost as a force leapt forward and slammed into Jack, sending him to the ground. Bo had knocked him down with surprising force. Bo looked at the princess, and Millie knew she must make a decision.

But she felt frozen with fear. Would she fight with Jack or against him?

At that moment, Jack grabbed Bo and threw her off. She landed in a heap but was up in a second, limping toward him. But now David had joined the fray, drawing his sword. Jack glanced her way, waiting.

Waiting for her, she realized.

David slashed at Jack with incredible speed, but Jack blocked his attack. The two exchanged blows, fierce and deadly. A single mistake would be life ending. They spun, a deadly hurricane, each move calculated and exact.

Behind the duo, Millie caught a glimpse of movement rushing toward the well. *Jill.* While the others were distracted, she hoped to grab the water for herself. Before she could second-guess herself, Millie rushed forward, standing before her former mistress.

"I can't let you take that."

Jill turned, her eyes wide with fear. "Millie, you don't under-stand. If Jack drinks this water, he will tear the world apart. I've seen it."

Millie paused, her stomach churning. There was no denying that Jack was a different person now from when they'd begun their quest. He had changed. He wasn't himself any longer.

Too late, she realized, her hesitation had cost her. The princess rushed forward, bringing a boot to Millie's chest and knocking her to the ground. Pain flared through her, the air swept from her lungs as she struggled to catch her breath. When she finally did, every move-ment felt like torture.

Jill had made her choice. And so had Millie. After all, Jill wasn't the only one with a sick brother.

Before she could let the pain take over, Millie forced herself to transform. Her senses awoke as her mind divided itself into a million different spiders. The pain subsided in this form, but she knew it would be back.

Her swarm charged forward after the princess, and Millie felt a sick sense of glee at seeing the color drain from her face. Jill turned, sprinting down the hill.

Her spiders followed, a landslide of black legs hurtling toward the princess, each of them struggling to go as fast as it could, eager for blood.

At the bottom of the hill, Jill grabbed one of her swords, which had been driven into the ground, while drawing her other sword from her side. Princess Jill was famous for her skill with the butterfly swords. Millie could not hope to fight against her.

With both swords in her hands, Jill turned, her expression fear-less as Millie had ever seen it. Millie continued forward. She had bested her once; she would do it again. And this time she would not feel guilty about it.

"Face me yourself, Millie."

Millie's spiders stopped, an army lined up for battle in front of the princess. Millie's heart, or hearts, raced, adrenaline rushing through her and each of her spiders.

"You can't face me without your power, and we both know it," the princess taunted.

It was a trick, that much she knew. Jill was absolutely right; she could never hope to stand up against the princess in her natural form. The princess was a warrior, a fighter. Millie was a maid. It struck her then how much she wished things had been different between them.

Millie focused inward, calling the spiders back to herself. A shudder rolled through her body as she reformed, facing Jill. She had the knives at her waist, but she didn't draw them, only looked up at the girl who seemed as afraid as she was. All these years she'd thought that she and the princess were different, but maybe they weren't so different after all. Both were trapped in the role they'd been born into, both afraid to be who they were.

"Millie, please," Jill begged. It was such a strange thing coming from the girl who'd once terrified her. "Jack cannot drink from the well! You can't trust anything he says."

Anger flooded her gut. "He trusted you, and you left him."

Pain pulled at Jill's face. "I know, but—"

"Something is wrong with him. There's something evil living inside him."

"I know, which is exactly why he cannot drink from the well."

"The well might cure him."

"It won't."

"How do you know?" Millie asked.

"I've seen the future—"

"You've seen *a* future!"

At that, Jill stilled. "Millie, please don't tell me you've fallen for him."

Millie's heart twisted in denial. She didn't know what she and Jack were, but she wouldn't let his sister see her doubts.

"Despite what you might think, I'm not stupid." The words

lashed out of her like a flaming whip, wild and thoughtless. She didn't care what the princess thought of her.

"Millie," Jill said, speaking like she was talking to a young child, "you are just one more girl in a long line of girls my brother has charmed. I promise it won't last."

The words were ice water in her lungs, not because she was angry, but because she knew Jill was right. But before she could respond, a cry ripped through the air.

They spun toward the top of the hill, where Jack and David continued to fight. Millie struggled to understand what she was seeing as the other man's arm flew through the air and broke on the ground.

"David!" Jill screamed.

David landed on his knees, looking down at his missing arm. Vaguely, Millie was aware that no blood flowed from it, though she wasn't sure how that was possible.

Another cry interrupted her thoughts, and she looked up to see Bo rushing at the prince, more determined than she'd been the first time, but Jack only snarled at her and pushed her to the ground with incredible force.

She watched as Jack walked up to the guardian, who was still sitting at the edge of the well. Glee was written on her face as she handed the wooden cup to Jack.

"Jack, no!" Jill cried again, racing up the hill.

Millie followed close behind. Silence wrapped around her like a shroud of death; the only sound was her beating heart, a funeral drum in her chest.

Halfway up the hill, she realized they wouldn't make it. Jack held the cup to his lips and drank deeply.

Around them, time slowed as they waited. At first, nothing happened. Then the guardian smiled.

Jack turned to face them, his smile mirroring hers. His body shuddered once. Twice. He collapsed to the ground, writhing and seizing.

His body shook as it tumbled down the hill until he lay at the bottom in a heap.

Millie shot down after him, Jill close at her heels.

They dropped on either side of him.

"Jack!" Jill cried. "Wake up!"

Jack's eyes shot open, the irises and whites of his eyes gone. Pure black eyes stared back at them. And then they rolled back into his head, and he passed out. Up the hill, Bo collapsed.

49

DAVID

*P*iece by piece, David put his arm back together. Pain was such a constant friend that he hardly felt anything as his arm healed, mottled scar tissue replacing every crack, every fracture of his skin. He could not let go of the image of himself shattered into a million pieces.

That was what awaited him. It did not matter if the vision he'd seen would come to pass or not; sooner or later, he would break into so many pieces that no one would be able to put him together again.

He'd fought against the prince himself, but in the end he'd lost. Now that the fighting had ended, a solemn silence rolled over them, the quiet before the storm.

At last, he stood, his arm aching, but he ignored the pain. It was nothing compared to what awaited him. He walked down the hill to Jill and the other girl. Millie, he recalled.

Jill looked up at him, tears streaking down her dirty face. The word "princess" conjured up visions of ball gowns and gloves, dances and feasts, quiet and demure. Jill was none of those things. He'd fought alongside her many times now, and with each encounter his respect for her had grown. She was more than a princess. She was a fighter, a leader. More than ever, he wanted to kiss her, to wipe away her tears.

Instead, he clenched his hands at his sides. "I'm leaving."

Jill rose to her feet. "What? Why?"

Fear tangled her features, and for a moment David considered taking the words back. But he knew only death awaited him if he stayed with her. "I'm leaving, just as I said in the forest. There's nothing left for me here."

There is no future for us.

He didn't say the words, but they passed between them, unspoken.

She nodded, glancing away. "Where will you go?"

"I must report to my commander. Erinya is still fighting a war after all."

Jill looked back up at him, her expression neutral. Gone was the fear, the indecision. In that moment, a wall was being built between them, and each silent second that passed, another brick was laid. Soon they would not see each other. Soon they would not confide in one another. The world would be as it was always meant to be.

"I wish you the best of luck. Perhaps our paths will cross again." Her voice was neutral, betraying nothing.

"You as well, Your Highness." He gave a slight bow, a strange and foreign action. In truth, he was not sure he wanted their paths to cross again. It would make his decision to stay away from her that much harder.

At their side, the guardian materialized. They jumped, stepping away from her.

The guardian looked impassive. "A group waits for the girl at the edge of the forest. Perhaps you would take her to them." She looked at David, her meaning clear.

You *will* take the girl to them.

He gritted his teeth but nodded. After all, it wouldn't be right to leave her here all alone.

The guardian turned her attention to Jill and Millie, nodding to

Jack on the ground. "Deep change is happening within him. Perhaps he will be strong enough to battle it and win." She smiled slightly. *Or perhaps not.*

Jill glared at the guardian, turning back to Millie. "We must get him back to the palace. Will you help me?"

Millie nodded, but her eyes were distant and faraway. Jill had told him about the servant girl turned paladin. It was strange knowing this girl had won the Paladin Tournament.

Reluctantly, David helped lift the prince, and when he felt certain the girls had him, he let go. The guardian waved her hand, and a path appeared before them.

"This path will lead you where you want to go."

Without a backward glance, the girls started down the path, and when he could see them no longer, the trees shifted and groaned back into place. And just like that, they were gone.

It was like a punch to the gut. Was he making a mistake? Once, he'd thought he could follow her anywhere, but now he could be certain of nothing. He shook his head. Jill was a princess, maybe even a queen someday. And he was just a cursed soldier. They did not belong in the same world.

David retrieved the girl who'd collapsed. Bo, her name was.

She was heavier than he'd expected. And dirtier. Who was she? Why had she been traveling with the prince only to turn on him? And why had she collapsed when Jack had?

He remembered their fight. The young girl had fought like an animal, doing everything in her power to keep Jack from drinking the water. She lacked the grace and finesse Jill fought with, but her spirit reminded him of Jill.

His stomach curdled. How long would it take before he could think her name without that sick feeling in his stomach?

At the bottom of the hill, the guardian waited for him. She waved a hand, and another path opened, in the opposite direction of Jill's path. It seemed their paths were not ever destined to cross.

You chose this, remember?

Gritting his teeth, he walked forward.

"David," the guardian said.

He stopped but refused to face her. "What?" he snarled.

"Your mother is all right. She feels no pain, no sadness, no weight of this broken world."

His chest tightened. "Why show me those terrible things then?"

"That was not my doing. Those were your own fears being used against you. The wood knows."

"Why are you telling me this?"

"Because I know you have many fears." She stared at him, her empty sockets boring into him, a dagger to his chest. He did not know what she meant, only that he must leave.

"A man and a girl wait for the girl. They will help you on your way," she said as if reading his mind. "Or, if you choose to, you may even join them."

Before David could ask what she meant, the guardian evaporated like a fine mist, there one moment and then gone.

Hesitant, David stepped back into the forest. He wasn't eager for another trip through these haunted trees. Behind him, the path closed.

He thought of what the guardian had said, that his mother no longer felt any pain or sadness. Something broke in him at that moment. A heavy weight lifted from his shoulders, and for the first time in so long, he felt peace.

DAVID DIDN'T KNOW how long he'd been walking through the forest. Every second he waited for something terrible to find him—a beast, a fork in the path, a cliff to climb. But there was nothing. It might have been peaceful if the girl in his arms hadn't been snoring.

Bo showed no signs of stirring, and for the millionth time, David wondered who this girl was and how she'd been mixed up in all this.

Up ahead, light flooded the forest. He was almost out.

He picked up the pace, eager to be out of the wood, to see the sky and feel the breeze. He broke through the tree line and into open space before falling to his knees. At last, the girl in his arms stirred, and her eyes popped open.

She shoved him away, hopping to her feet as a grimace of pain washed over her face. "Who are you? Where have you taken me? Where's my crutch?"

David raised his hands, pulling the crutch off his back to hand to her. He'd expected her to use it to stand on, but instead she pointed it at him like a weapon.

"Whoa! Hold on, I carried you out of that Saints-forsaken forest! My arms are quite sore, by the way. You're heavier than you look." He found it was true; his arms ached from carrying her.

She glared at him. "Sorry I'm not some dainty little princess," she spat.

David shook his head. *Who is this girl?*

"I just mean—"

"Bo?"

The two turned to see two figures riding toward them on gray steeds. The first one pulled up short, a girl leaping down and rushing at Bo.

"Zyla?" Bo's eyes widened, and she gripped her crutch. "What are you—how—"

Zyla, an inkwell girl from what David could tell, threw her arms around Bo, burying her face in Bo's neck.

Bo stiffened, shock passing over her face.

"We were so worried. The Order has been looking all over for you!" Zyla pulled away, holding Bo at arm's length.

David backed away, certain this was a reunion he need not take part in.

"Who are you?" a smooth voice cut in. A man stood behind Zyla. He wore fine riding clothes and carried himself with a confidence that David immediately recognized as power.

"I could ask the same of you," said David, crossing his arms.

The man gave a tight smile before stretching out a hand. "The name's Doyle. Kylian Doyle."

That raised his brows. He knew that name, had heard it from his commander's lips many times, usually followed by a nasty curse.

"You're the king's adviser," he said, ignoring the man's hand.

Kylian frowned, dropping his hand. "I was."

"Was?"

"Yes."

Zyla looked up at Kylian, her gaze suddenly guarded. "Bo, we need your help. After the attack on the convent, Kylian and I and a few others were able to escape, but the rest—" She stopped, swallowing back tears. "The Ohans. They've taken them all captive. We have no idea how many are alive and how many . . ." She didn't finish.

Bo looked between the two, eyes wide.

"What do you have to do with all this?" David asked Kylian. The last thing he wanted was to be dragged into more problems he couldn't solve. But he had to ask what the king's adviser was doing so far from the Citadel and how he'd gotten mixed up with the Order.

"I have been helping the Order for some time. Relaying information. Aiding them against the Ohans. Stealing impendium."

David froze. He knew about impendium, and he knew the Ohans guarded it fiercely. To steal such a thing would have been risky.

"Bo, come with us," Zyla said. "We need your help!"

Bo swallowed. "I don't think you understand—"

"We know you led the Ohans to the convent." Kylian's voice was smooth, calculated.

David turned to look at the girl. She couldn't have been more than fifteen, yet she had somehow become entangled with some of the most powerful people in the kingdom.

Who is this girl?

"It was a risk we took when we brought you to the Order. The Matron knew that," said Zyla. "But we knew we had to help you."

David's mind reeled. There was something strange about all of this, but he couldn't put his finger on it.

"Why is the Order of the Saints stealing impendium?" he asked. "And why is the king's adviser helping them?"

Kylian Doyle gave a sly smile, and David got the sense that this was a man not to be trusted. At last, he said, "We're preparing for war."

"War? But we're already fighting—"

"Not that war. *The* war. The great war that King Jack will bring to us all."

50

JILL

It was a silent trip back to the Citadel. Jill and Millie stopped only at night to rest, plodding forward without so much as a word between them. All the while, Jack never stirred. Every step closer to home felt like a funeral march.

She had failed. Jack had drunk the water. Who knew what he would be when he awoke? If he awoke.

It was a fear that clawed at her heart, love fighting against common sense, and it was tearing her to shreds.

When at last they returned, they were greeted only by Master Ravala and Madame Sorelle. Jill did not know where Doyle had gone, nor did she care. Maybe he'd run away. Maybe he'd poisoned the king.

Days passed, and still the prince did not wake. The physician did all he could, but still her brother slept, his face twitching and forehead sweating. It was not a regular coma, the physician explained. There were forces at work beyond his control.

Jill passed her days on the training grounds, finding solace only in the sound of her swords slashing against the training dummies.

One dark afternoon, she found herself there, wailing on the

dummies. Sweat poured down her back. Every inch of her body ached, but still she continued, slashing away. With every hit, she thought of the people who'd been taken from her. First her mother.

Smash.

Then her father.

Smash.

William.

She whirled.

Jack.

She sliced and jabbed.

David.

She screamed, running forward and battering the dummy with no finesse, no talent, only rage. She wailed on the dummy until the tears forced their way out and she collapsed to the ground, the dummy's head falling next to her.

She heaved, pressing her face into her hands.

"Your Highness?" came a soft voice.

Jill looked up, immediately ashamed of her state. Millie stood in the pillared archway, looking small and concerned.

"Is it Jack?" she asked, rising to her feet. Since they'd returned, Millie had hardly left the prince's side, and Jill suspected it had little to do with her rank as paladin.

Millie shook her head. "It's your father. They sent me to find you."

Jill's stomach churned, but she nodded, wiping her face with a rag before following Millie to the king's chambers.

The walk was both longer and shorter than she remembered, and when she entered her father's chambers, she found only his graying corpse. He was gone. She hadn't even said goodbye, and worse, she didn't care.

THE MONSTERS SHOWED up the next day. Panic and chaos erupted in the town below, but the monsters didn't attack, only stood around the palace like sentries on the lookout, awaiting orders. Jill stood at the window of her brother's room, Millie pacing behind her.

Fear clutched at her heart as those horrible creatures with faces of shadow and teeth surrounded them. It had taken everything in her and David to defeat one. Now there were eleven.

"What do we do?" Millie asked, coming up behind her.

"I don't know."

Behind them, Jack stirred. Another nightmare. Jill hoped it was better than what they were facing now.

"Millie?"

The girls spun to see Jack sitting up, dark hair mussed.

"Jack!" Millie rushed forward, wrapping herself in his arms. His eyes closed, and his fingers tightened in her hair. He clung to her like she was a piece of driftwood in an endless sea. Jill felt the sharp sting of jealousy. In all her life, she had not seen Jack more open with a girl than now. She had thought Millie foolish to fall for her brother's wiles and had even told her so.

Could she have been wrong about Jack's motives after all?

Jill stepped forward. "How are you feeling?"

He glanced up at her, and she froze, heart pounding against her rib cage. There was something wrong with his eyes. Instead of being the sea green she remembered, they were mottled green and black. She did not like to think about what that could mean.

"My pets have arrived," he said, throwing off his blankets and walking to the window.

Jill and Millie exchanged a glance, an unspoken understanding passing between them. This was not the same Jack they had left the Citadel with.

"Your pets?" Millie dared ask.

Jack gave a distant smile. "Yes. They're mine at last. Bring them inside. I would have them for my coronation."

Jill shook her head, confused. "What? Jack, you've only just awoken. You're not strong enough—"

"I'm stronger than ever!" He whirled on her, his teeth bared like a starving wolf. His anger was so unexpected that Jill stepped back. Her brother's gaze was cold and fierce as a north wind.

"How did you know our father is dead?" she asked, her voice a whisper. It was humiliating, to feel so weak in front of her brother.

He turned back to the window. "He was dead long ago. Now I will be king."

The ceremony was rushed. Jack would not be talked into waiting a second longer than he had to. There would be no nobles, no foreign dignitaries, no ambassadors. There would be no feast or ball or a day of rest on the warfront.

Jack dressed in his finest, along with Millie and Jill. Only the palace officials were invited, a mere handful compared with the number of people who'd been there only a few weeks earlier for the ball.

And along the walls stood the terrifying creatures of shadow. They sat beside Jack like personal guards, towering above every nervous person required to attend. The only person who did not show any sign of fear was Master Ravala, who held his head high.

The ancient bishop stood before Jack, looking like he'd seen the founding of Erinya nearly four hundred years ago. His hands shook as he placed the ebony crown over her brother's brow, the look altogether handsome and wicked. Jill's stomach twisted tighter. She thought of the vision she'd seen in the forest. Her brother crowned. And the darkness that would reign alongside him. It was all coming true.

Outside, the wind whipped itself into a frenzy, rain lashing at the tall glass windows of the throne room. Black clouds draped over the land as if it mourned along with them.

"Do you, Prince Jackal, son of King Cole and Queen Elyse, solemnly swear to uphold the laws of Erinya, to put your people and your country above all else, to fight for freedom and justice as long as your life endures?"

Jack smiled. "I do."

"I now pronounce you King Jackal of Erinya. Long live the king!"

"Long live the king," they echoed, a quiet, somber party, much quieter than Jill thought Jack would have liked. But then he turned and smiled at the handful of people awaiting orders.

"I thank each and every one of you for coming." An awkward silence passed over them, but Jack didn't seem to care; in fact, he seemed to relish their uncomfortable looks and stances.

He sat on the throne, looking every bit like the king Jill had always imagined, except she'd never imagined it like this.

"Now, everyone out."

The officials hurried out, eager to be away from their new king. Jill turned to follow.

"Not you, sister. And Millie, you stay too."

Master Ravala's eyes caught Jill's, and she nodded slightly, though she desperately wished he'd stay.

Jill turned to face her brother. She found, after all this time, that she could not look in his eyes. She knew what he would see when he looked at her.

When at last everyone was out, silence descended upon the three of them. Jill glanced over at Millie, who stood by Jack's side, knives strapped to her belt, her dark hair pulled up in an intricate set of braids. She looked beautiful.

She looked like a queen.

Jack broke into a smile. "At last! We are finally here!"

Millie offered a tentative smile, and Jill felt her concern.

"What's the matter, *Jilly*? Aren't you happy for me?" There was a dangerous gleam in Jack's eyes, so foreign from the brother Jill had once had. She felt her heart breaking. It seemed he didn't know the lengths she'd gone to keep him off the throne. Still, she forced a smile and bowed.

"There is another reason I've asked you two to stay behind. You see, our father was obviously poisoned by someone close to us. Because of this, I can only assume someone in our midst is a traitor. And the only people I can trust are standing in this room."

Jill looked up at her brother, sensing the warning in his tone.

He looked between them. "Swear your undying loyalty to me. I *will* be a better king than my father. It's the only way I can be certain one of you isn't the traitor."

The words were an icy dagger plunged into Jill's heart.

Jill locked eyes with Millie. She could see the fear written on her face and knew what her choice would be, just as Jill knew what her own choice would be.

Millie stepped forward and knelt before Jack, head bowed in submission. But Jill didn't miss the slight tremble in the girl's hand.

"I, Millie Muffet," she began, "paladin of Erinya, swear undying loyalty and fealty to King Jackal, high king and ruler of Erinya. Long live the king."

Her voice, though quiet, echoed through the throne room. There was a finality to her tone, like a crypt slamming shut.

Jack bowed his head, an acceptance of her oath. He held his hand out, and Millie stepped forward to kiss it. Bile rose to the back of Jill's throat as she watched the scene unfold.

Jack turned to Jill, the crown hanging crooked over his brow, a challenge in his gaze. She clenched her fists as she stepped forward, her breath catching in her throat.

"*Princess*," Jack drawled, a reminder of her place beneath him.

Her heart beat like a jackrabbit's in her chest, and for a moment she thought she might pass out in the throne room.

"Jack, you know I love you. All my life you've not only been my brother but my closest friend and confidant. You taught me to fight, to hold my ground, to stand up for what I believe in." She paused, gathering her courage. "But you've changed. We both know it. And . . . it's for this reason that I cannot swear fealty to you."

She was met with silence. A shiver raced down her spine, but she stood tall, meeting her brother's eyes.

At last, Jack sighed and gave a humorless laugh. "Jill," he said, a dark smile playing on his face. "My twin. My only *sister*. Tell me you've thought this through. What do you gain by resisting the inevitable? What are you going to do? Where will you go? Will you run away again? You and I both know that didn't work out well the first time." His grin widened, never reaching his eyes.

Everything stopped.

"What?" she asked, breathless. No one knew about her and Will. She'd never told a soul, not even Jack. She'd planned to leave everything behind for him. After all this time, she could still see his lifeless body bleeding out into the hay.

"What was his name again?"

Fear clawed at her throat as she refused to answer. "Jack, tell me you didn't." Her voice betrayed her, breaking on his name. "Tell me you didn't kill him." Blood thundered in her ears, and for a single heartbeat she thought he'd deny it, hoped he would.

And then that moment ended.

His smile faded. "I couldn't let you throw your life away for some penniless stable boy. It was for your own good."

The floor tilted beneath her as she tried to process what he'd said. The room spun as she fought to breathe. Beside him, Millie looked as pale as Jill felt. Jack had killed Will.

"H-how could you?"

Jack scoffed. "Jill, you didn't honestly believe he loved you? That he really wanted to marry you? If so, you truly are more foolish than I thought."

Darkness crowded the edges of her vision, but she fought against it, letting anger flow through her instead. Blind with fury, she surged forward, a tide of uncontrolled rage as she reached both hands for his neck, dragging him to his feet.

He was taller than her, stronger than her, but she was the better warrior, and they both knew it.

He simply smiled as she buried her nails into his skin, drawing blood. "I'll kill you," she vowed.

He snarled, shoving her away easily and slapping her in the face so hard that she fell to the ground, the wind knocked from her. Her face stung, blooming red where he'd struck. Pain turned to wrath as she rose, drawing her twin blades.

Jack's sword was already drawn as she slashed at him. He blocked with unexpected force, sending her weapon flying across the room. Fear gripped her as she brought up her sword to block his strike at the last second. He bore down on her with an effortless, unnatural strength.

"You were right about one thing," he growled. "I have changed. You can't defeat me, can't overpower me. You never will."

Her arms shook as she tried to stand against his weight, but she knew he was right. Sooner or later, she would crumple beneath him. Maybe it was all meant to be that way.

For a moment, she considered taking it all back. Surrendering. Giving in to his will. Swearing her undying loyalty.

But images flashed through her mind. Asif and his sister. The maid from the inn. The people who had looked at her with so much hope in their eyes after she and David had slayed the monster. Her people. The people who deserved a ruler who cared about them, a ruler who would fight for them. And she knew Jack wouldn't. No. That thing inside him wouldn't. That was what controlled him now.

The people need you. The woman's words echoed through her head.

She screamed, shoving him away with all her might. He stumbled back, surprised. But he was faster than she remembered. Striking like a viper, he lunged forward, grabbing her by the neck.

His fingers bruised her throat as he lifted her off the ground. He grinned as the air escaped her lungs. She dropped her sword, clawing at his fist, desperation making her frantic. She kicked and squirmed, but still he held tight, crushing her windpipe.

She looked over Millie, who stood paralyzed next to the throne.

"P-please," she sputtered.

She looked back into Jack's eyes, watched as they turned black. Gone was the boy she knew and loved, the brother she'd grown up with. In his place was only a monster. And he was going to kill her.

Her eyes rolled back in her head, red overtaking her vision. She knew it was only a matter of moments now.

A hiss cut through the air, followed by a sickening thump. Jack cried out as his legs gave way beneath him, and he released his grip on Jill's neck. She dropped to the floor.

She sucked in air, taking in the scene around her. A knife protruded from the back of Jack's knee, pain and anger contorting his features. Millie stared at her own hands as if she couldn't believe what she'd just done. Jack whirled on her, blood dripping down his leg.

Jill looked up at her former maid, the girl she'd been so cruel to, the girl she'd thought a coward, the girl who had just defied the king and saved Jill's life.

Something changed in Millie at that moment. No longer did she cower beneath a stern gaze. Instead, she held her head high, meeting Jack's gaze.

She glanced at Jill and nodded, uttering a single word. "Run."

Jill's legs acted before she could stop them. She grabbed one of her swords, leaving the other.

And she ran.

She heard yelling behind her, Jack's booming voice commanding her to stop. She ripped open the throne room doors, startling the guard before tearing down the hall.

"Seize her!"

The sound of heavy boots and clanking armor echoed up the marble halls as she ran as fast as she could, adrenaline propelling her forward. More guards joined the fray as she passed through each archway into another corridor. Servants scrambled out of the way.

Bitter tears leaked from her eyes, and she could feel the bruises forming on her face and neck. What would she do? Where would she go? Would anyone help her?

"Princess Jillianna, surrender now or risk death," said one of the guards.

Jill swallowed. "Never."

She needed a plan, and fast.

She knew this palace better than anyone. She still remembered the route she'd taken the night she'd planned to run away.

Dashing down a dark hallway, she found what she was looking for: an old statue of some ancient philosopher. Behind it was a tapestry covering a hidden entrance to the servants' quarters. It was an old abandoned tunnel that let out near the river. Her feet still remembered the steps as she ran through the hallway, never once turning to look back, never once considering everything she was leaving behind.

A light shone up ahead, the wind creaking the rusty gate. She raced toward it, and though it was locked, the rusted metal gave way easily as she kicked at the door, heart pounding. Thunder rumbled off in the distance.

Out in the open, she saw the river rushing into the trees, wild and untamed. Rain pounded at her back as she ran alongside it, and soon she was drenched.

She had no supplies, no food, and only one of her swords. She couldn't grab a horse. She would have to travel on foot, but where? Where could she go where Jack's monsters wouldn't find her? Why hadn't they come after her in the throne room? Was there some part of Jack still in there?

At last, she stopped, falling to her knees in the mud, letting the rain drown her tears.

In all her life, she'd never felt so alone. Everyone had left her. She had no one to help her and nowhere to go. She felt like she could outcry the sky. She shuddered with cold.

"Your Highness?" a deep voice said.

Jill turned, drawing her sword and reaching for the other one, but it wasn't there. Without its twin, her sword was not nearly as strong.

In front of her stood the last person she'd expected to see.

"Grimzy!" She rushed forward, surprising even herself as she wrapped the mountain man in a hug. He gave a pat on her shoulders, and she pulled away, wiping her face. "Why are you here? How did you find me?"

"I hear things even in the storms. This storm is the worst Erinya has seen in my lifetime. I knew I should come to you at once."

If Jill had had any tears left, she would've cried with joy. As it was, all she could manage was a weak smile.

"It's Jack. He is king, and something evil lives inside him."

Grimzy nodded as if this didn't surprise him. "The prince has long been haunted by things beyond the borders of our world. Nevertheless, I am sorry, Princess."

She swallowed hard. "Call me Jill. I'm a princess no longer."

"I don't think that is so," he said, his deep voice reassuring.

She looked up at the tall man, water dripping down him. "Why?"

His gaze penetrated her with the knowing glance of an ancient soul—a soul that had seen the passing of time, had seen the rise and fall of kingdoms and empires.

"I think you know."

Her heart pounded as she shook her head. "I can't."

He knelt in front of her, placing a hand on her shoulder. "Your Highness, I have seen the stars, listened to earth, the wind. They all speak of a queen, the greatest queen Erinya has ever seen. I have seen you fight. In Erinya's darkest hour, you fought for your people. Erinya needs you. Your people need you."

It was an echo of what the old woman had told her, what David had confirmed.

Princess. Traitor. Usurper. Queen.

She thought of her people looking up at her with hope. And just as she'd known what would happen to Jack, she knew this also. She would take the throne. She would face her brother.

And then she would become queen.

ABOUT THE AUTHOR

Sabrina Lozier is a Christian and a native Oregonian with an undying love of young adult fantasy. She spends her days chasing her spawn, avoiding laundry, and dreaming of the day her novel gets picked up by for the movies. Broken Crown is her debut novel but she intends to write and publish many more books.

www.ingramcontent.com/pod-product-compliance
Lightning Source LLC
Chambersburg PA
CBHW070602300726
48975CB00006B/1682